AN UNQUIET GHOST

A Mina Scarletti Mystery
Book Three

Linda Stratmann

SAPERE
BOOKS

AN UNQUIET
GHOST

Published by Sapere Books.

11 Bank Chambers, Hornsey, London, N8 7NN,

United Kingdom

saperebooks.com

ISBN: 978-1-912546-07-7

To Peter and Lara

Prologue

Lincoln, 1851

Thomas Fernwood was dying, and it was not the death he had been expecting. A man should die aged, peaceful, content, surrounded by his loving family, his soul slipping away sweetly from the prison of the flesh to join his ancestors in a higher, better place. At fifty-eight he had prided himself on his heartiness and vigour and thought he had many more years to enjoy, but it was not to be. Something deadly was tearing at his insides, eating him away. It was as if hot irons had been thrust down his throat deep into his stomach, and his bowels were molten. For hours he had retched in agony bringing up nothing but searing acid, a river of pain. Now, weak as a child, he was unable even to rise from his bed.

A face hovered above him, grim and anxious, and he recognised with some relief the heavy jowls and grey side whiskers of his physician, Dr Sperley. Thomas struggled through cracked lips to say what he feared might be his final message, but his throat was burned raw, and the words would not come.

'Don't try to speak,' said Sperley, gruffly. 'I know you've taken poison. I've done all I can.'

Only the desperation of the dying could force the mouth to move and what emerged was the merest whisper. 'Mur ... der ...' then Thomas coughed and retched again, a sour dry straining, so fierce he thought his ribs would break. His body had almost nothing left to reject. He felt a cool damp cloth pressed to his forehead, a little water wetting his parched lips. Finally, the spasm passed. Sperley's face loomed closer, furrowed with concern. 'Do you know who has done this? Nod your head if you do.'

The stricken man groaned deeply and nodded. Slowly, a hand that had been clutching the coverlet, opened, and one trembling finger moved on its surface as if he was trying to spell out a word. Sperley understood. 'I'll fetch pencil and paper.' The doctor turned to go, but in that moment Thomas's mouth suddenly bubbled with green bile and he started to choke, his body racked with convulsions so violent that he was almost thrown to the floor, and Sperley had to return and steady him, hold him to the bed by main force. Thomas gasped for air, his chest pumping rapidly, eyes wild with panic, but he gasped in vain. There was anger, frustration, despair, sorrow, acceptance, and finally a blinding light that faded away to nothing.

Chapter One

Brighton, 1871

'The land of the dead' wrote Mina Scarletti, 'is like a mysterious, unknowable sea. It has no horizon; we cannot see where it begins or where it ends, if indeed, it does either. It has no floor, but its shadowy depths go on forever, and sometimes, there arise from the silent deep strange monsters.' She laid the end of her pen against her lips and paused for thought.

Mina's busy imagination was peopled with ghosts and demons. They lived in her dreams and on the pages of her stories, but not in her daily anxieties. Other worlds, she felt, must take care of themselves while she concerned herself with more immediate problems; her mother's changeable moods, her sister Enid's unhappy marriage and her younger brother Richard's inability to find a respectable career. At that very moment, however, Mina was luxuriating in the absence of any demands on her time.

Winter in Brighton was, for those who liked to stay by their own fireside and avoid the centre of town, a season of the most beautiful peace. The oft-deplored Sunday excursion trains, which brought noisy crowds to the streets, had ceased to run at the end of October. November 5th had, as was usual, come and gone without any noticeable disturbances beyond the odd mischievously dropped squib, since the annual drunken dances around roaring bonfires took place several miles away in Lewes.

The professional gentlemen and their families had taken their autumnal holidays and were long gone, and the idle fashionables were arriving. Glittering convocations, balls and suppers that were wont to go on into the small hours of the morning and disturb nearby residents with the rattle of carriages and cabriolets were held far from Mina's home in Montpelier Road, and would not trouble her. More to the point, she had the house almost to herself since her mother was in London trying to soothe Enid, whose twin boys were teething with extraordinary vigour. Richard was also in the capital, lodging with their older brother Edward, after reluctantly, and almost certainly briefly, accepting work as a clerk in the Scarletti publishing company.

Rain pattered on glass like insistently tapping fingers, but Mina had no wish to heed this dangerous call. In the cold street beyond her heavily curtained windows breezes that carried the salt sting of the sea tore mercilessly at the cloaks of passers-by, and a steel sky clouded the sun. Mina's small fragile body did not do well in inclement weather, and she tried not to go out too often in the winter because of the danger of catching a chill in her cramped lungs. The recent charitable bazaar in aid of the children's hospital presided over by illustrious patronesses and held at the Dome had not tempted her, since the crowded conditions were fumed with coughs and agues. She had contented herself with making a personal donation by post. Neither had she gone to see the much talked about panorama of Paris, depicted both in its old grandeur and the conflagrations that had spelled the end of the recent violent disturbances.

Once a week, carefully wrapped against the cold, she took a cab to Dr Daniel Hamid's medicated Indian herbal baths where, enveloped in hot towels, she bathed in scented vapour that opened her airways and eased her chest. Afterwards, the doctor's sister, Anna, a skilled masseuse, used fragrant oils to dispel the strains arising from Mina's twisted spine, and taught her exercises to develop the muscles of her back so as to better support that obstinately distorted column of bones. Mina had last visited the baths only the day before and consequently was almost free from pain.

Mina's bedroom on the first floor of the house was her haven, where she sat at her writing desk, one hip supported by a special wedge shaped cushion that enabled her to sit upright, and created her dark tales. The dumbbells she used for her daily exercises were hidden at the bottom of her wardrobe. Even as she reflected on the quiet she was enjoying she feared that it was only a matter of time before the house was in some kind of ferment not of her making, which she would be obliged to address, and then her back and neck would start to pinch again, but on that blissful evening, with the fire crackling in the grate, her new composition begun, and a nice little fowl roasting for her dinner, all was well.

There was a knock at her door, and Rose, the general servant, appeared holding an envelope. Rose was a sturdy, serious girl who worked hard and uncomplainingly, trudging up and down the flights of stairs that linked the basement kitchen with three upper floors, keeping winter fires burning, running errands in all weathers, and coping with the petulant demands of Mina's mother and the turmoil that usually resulted from Richard's unannounced visits. 'I'm sorry to disturb you, Miss, but it's one of those letters. Shall I put it on the fire?'

Mina hesitated, but she had reached a pause in her work, and a moment more would make no difference. She laid down her pen. 'Thank you, Rose, let me see it first.'

From time to time letters would arrive in a variety of hands that Mina did not recognise, addressed to 'Miss Scarletti, Brighton'. The authors had read in the newspapers of her appearance to give evidence at the recent trial of the mediumistic fraud Miss Eustace and her confederates in crime, which had resulted in those persons being committed to prison for extortion. The unknown correspondents had guessed that due to Mina's unusual surname, letters with such an apparently insufficient address would be safely delivered, and so, all too often, they were. Since the trial had featured prominently in both *The Times* and the *Illustrated Police News*, these letters came from every corner of the kingdom.

Some correspondents believed that they could persuade Mina of the great truth of spiritualism, and wrote earnestly and at great length on the subject, declaring their fervent belief in such miscreants as D. D. Home, the celebrated medium who had tried to cheat an elderly lady out of her fortune, and Mrs Guppy, a lady of substantial dimensions who claimed be able to fly using the power of the spirits, and pass through solid walls without making a hole. Others wanted to engage Mina's services to investigate a fraudulent practitioner, distance of travel not being seen as any obstacle, on the assumption that she would be glad to pay her own way for the fame it would bring. There were also those who declared that she was undoubtedly a medium herself who would or could not acknowledge it, and offered to 'develop' her in that skill. It was with weary trepidation therefore that Mina opened the envelope, with the object of briefly reviewing the contents before they were consigned to the fire.

She found a single sheet of folded notepaper, printed with the name and address of Fernwood Groceries in Haywards Heath, a Sussex village not far from Brighton. 'Quality!

Freshness! Wholesomeness!' she was promised, this notion being enhanced by an engraving of a plump, smiling child clutching a rusk. The letter, however, was not on the subject of foodstuffs.

Dear Miss Scarletti,

Please forgive me, a complete stranger, for writing to you, but I would not presume to do so unless I believed that you are able to assist me in a matter of great importance and delicacy. Please be assured that all I wish to humbly beg of you is your advice on a subject of which, I have been told, you have considerable knowledge.

My name is George Fernwood, and I recently became betrothed to a Miss Mary Clifton. We wish to marry in the spring. There is, however, a matter of grave concern to us, which I will not describe in this letter, but which we both feel should be resolved before we take that joyful step.

I hope you will permit us to call on you at whatever time would be most convenient to yourself.

Assuring you of my sincere and honest intentions,

Yours faithfully,

G. Fernwood.

'Dinner in half an hour, Miss,' said Rose, tonelessly. 'Do you want boiled potatoes or boiled rice?'

Mina had eaten savoury rice when dining with Dr Hamid and his sister and knew how it ought to look and taste. 'Potatoes, please,' she said, absently, staring at the letter. 'And when I have written a reply to this, you must take it to the post box.'

'Yes, Miss.' Rose's face betrayed nothing of her thoughts, but there was something in the tilt of her head and a slight movement of her shoulders that said 'I suppose you know your own business best.'

When the maid had returned downstairs, Mina read the letter again, considering why it was that she had decided to respond to Mr Fernwood's plea. His words were polite and respectful, that much appealed to her, and his object, a warmly anticipated wedding, was commendable. Mina could not see how she might help the couple achieve happiness, but the letter hinted that there might be a mystery to be solved, and she thought that in that quiet November time, such a project might stimulate her mind. As she penned a reply, she did however wonder if she was once more about to explore the dusty veil that lay between the living and the dead.

Chapter Two

Two days later George Fernwood and Mary Clifton were in Mina's parlour. It was a cheery room, warmed by a bright fire, furnished for comfort, and made attractive with framed portraits and ornaments that commemorated family events.

The pleasing cosiness of the room was not, however, something the visitors seemed able to absorb. They were a reserved, polite, diffident pair, and just little nervous. Even though there had been a description of Mina in the newspapers, neither of them could conceal a certain curiosity at her appearance, and gazed at her as if wondering how someone so small and twisted out of the usual shape could actually be alive.

George Fernwood was aged about thirty, with large worried eyes, his dark hair standing up around the perimeter of his scalp in a fluff of short curls which made Mina suspect that he was concealing an incipient bald patch on his crown. He made a stumbling expression of gratitude for being granted the interview, which Miss Clifton echoed, and brought a gift; a package neatly wrapped in clean brown paper and tied about with string. 'Do please accept these, they are the very best currant biscuits,' he assured Mina.

Miss Clifton was perhaps a little younger, her plain square face softened by the affectionate glances she directed at her betrothed. Both, like their offering, were respectably and demurely clad, suggesting that Fernwood Groceries was a thriving business serving the middle classes of Haywards Heath.

Rose brought a laden tray, poured the tea, unwrapped the biscuits and arranged them on a plate. They did look very good, but Mr Fernwood and Miss Clifton could only gaze at the tempting sight with expressions of deep gloom. Rose stared at the couple suspiciously and was more than content to be allowed to leave.

There was a strained silence. Neither of the visitors had an appetite, but held their teacups and sipped carefully as if delaying the dreadful moment when they would be obliged to tell Mina why they had come. Mina decided not to waste time by introducing some subject such as the weather, or the fashionable entertainment of the season, and simply waited for them to speak. At length, Fernwood heaved a deep sigh and placed his cup and saucer carefully on the table.

'I am the grandson of the late Thomas Fernwood, a grocer who conducted the family business in Lincoln. My dear Mary is his great niece, so we are cousins twice removed. We have known each other since we were children.' Miss Clifton said nothing but favoured him with a tender smile. Fernwood suddenly clasped his hands together tightly as if trying to prevent them from shaking, and Miss Clifton, her brow creasing with sympathy, placed a light encouraging touch on his arm.

'Go on, George. We must, really we must, or we will never know the answer.'

He looked at her, patted her fingertips and nodded.

'I know. But it is so hard to actually speak the words, to talk of something that our family has not discussed for many a year, even amongst ourselves.' He braced himself to continue, and faced Mina once more. 'Twenty years ago, my grandfather was murdered.'

Mina hardly knew what to say. She had expected to be told of a death, but not something of that nature. 'That must have been a terribly distressing time,' she said at last.

'I was ten years old then, and Mary just eight, so we children were sheltered from the actuality, we were merely told that he had been taken very ill and passed away. It wasn't until quite some years later that we finally learned the truth.' Fernwood, despite the warmth in the room, shivered. 'He had swallowed poison and died in great agony.'

Mina didn't want to seem to be prying, but since her visitor was having some difficulty in recounting the story he had clearly come expressly to tell her, and she did not wish the interview to last through to dinner, she decided to enquire further. 'I do hope the culprit was caught and punished.'

'No,' said Fernwood, unable to keep the anguish from his voice. 'To this day no-one other than the guilty party knows who was responsible.'

His lips began to tremble, and he pulled a handkerchief from his pocket and pressed it to his eyes, shoulders heaving with emotion. It was some moments before he was able to continue. Miss Clifton held his hand, and Mina politely averted her eyes. At last he calmed himself and went on.

'When my grandfather lay on his deathbed he told his doctor that he was a murdered man and tried to say who it was who had poisoned him, but he died before he could reveal the name. His death has been a dreadful shadow over our family ever since. My grandmother forbade anyone to speak of it and it was only after her death ten years later that my sisters dared to tell me what had really happened.'

Mina refreshed the teacups. 'Someone must have been suspected, surely? Was there a servant who had been scolded for bad behaviour? Or was there a business rival perhaps, who called at the house?'

Fernwood gave a pained smile. 'That is the thing, you see. Every person in the house at the time the poisoning took place, every suspect, was a member of the family, even the servants.'

'Oh?' said Mina, surprised.

'That is unusual, I know, but I am sorry to say that my grandfather was noted for his miserly ways. My mother kept house and cooked; my sisters were given the simplest schooling required by law and were otherwise treated as unpaid servants. After the death of Mary's father, her mother Mrs Dorothy Clifton appealed to my grandfather for assistance. She was especially anxious that Mary's brother, Peter, should be able to complete his education. My grandfather agreed that they could come and live with us — the house was large enough — but only on the condition that Mary's mother should act as cook, housekeeper and nurse to my grandmother. Mary, even though so very young, she was only six years of age at the time, was obliged to help my sisters with domestic duties. There was no respite for my mother. She was sent to work in the grocery shop. All of us in the house were related by blood. And one of us is a murderer.'

'And you want to resolve this question before you marry?'

'We have agreed,' said Miss Clifton, 'that because we are cousins we will not marry until we know the truth.' She lowered her eyes, modestly. 'At least, not for very many years.'

Mina, looking at the stricken faces of the young couple, thought she understood. 'You are concerned that there is a family weakness?'

'Exactly,' said Fernwood, looking relieved that he had not had to explain it.

'But do you have any indication that this is so? Has it shown itself subsequently? Forgive me for asking, but has any member of your family committed a crime or any kind of misdemeanour?'

Fernwood didn't look offended. 'Not to my knowledge, no, and I would not suspect it of any of them. We all live very quietly. But I fear that it is possible that the taint might still lie there, just waiting to appear, if not in this generation, then the next.'

Miss Clifton was close to tears as she pressed her betrothed's hand. 'I have sometimes felt that George's sisters share our concern, although they have never spoken of it. They have never married, or wished to be. My brother Peter, too, is single. George and I have been fond of each other all our lives. We had not spoken of marriage until recently, when we found ourselves unable to deny our true affection for each other. What if there is something in our blood, something that we ourselves are not aware of, but which might be made stronger if the two of us were to marry and pass it to our children?'

Mina sipped her tea thoughtfully. 'What does your family think? Have they offered any opinion on your betrothal?'

There was an exchange of glances. 'To be honest, Miss Scarletti, you are the first person we have told,' Fernwood admitted. 'Mary and I have been brought up so closely and have always been fond of each other. Our family thinks that our affection is more akin to that of brother and sister, and have not remarked on it. In fact, until we can resolve our dilemma we prefer not to make any announcement, and I trust that you will keep our confidence.'

'Of course I will,' said Mina, still not seeing why it was that they had chosen to consult her. 'I think that the question of whether such a trait can be inherited may be one which a medical man might answer. Have you spoken to a doctor?'

Fernwood nodded. 'I have. He said it was impossible for him, or indeed anyone, to predict what might be the outcome if we were to be blessed with a family, and could offer no assurances that our concerns were without foundation. Medical science can give us no answers as yet.'

'That is a very difficult dilemma, I agree,' said Mina, sympathetically; thinking all the while that the Fernwood tragedy would make a wonderful premise for a murder story. 'I suppose after all this time it is very unlikely that the poisoner will confess.'

'If we could only establish that it was some dreadful mistake, and not an act of evil,' exclaimed Fernwood, 'then it would set our minds at rest. But whoever carried out that horrible deed, even if it was in error, has been too afraid all these years to admit to it. After all, how can one prove it was not deliberate and avoid prosecution and scandal? The police might think the years of silence speak for themselves.'

Mina nodded, wondering if the couple had assumed that she was a clairvoyant or a detective. She would have to disabuse them of both notions, but not just yet as she rather wanted to learn more.

'Of course, there was one person who both knew the identity of the culprit and was unafraid to reveal it,' said Miss Clifton. 'That was my great uncle Thomas. But his illness took away his voice. So, when I saw in the newspapers about these spiritualists — well — I began to wonder. What if it was possible to contact my great uncle from beyond the grave, and somehow ask him? George and I have talked about it. I don't think he was happy with the idea at first, but I think I might have convinced him.'

Fernwood looked undeniably awkward. 'I've never been one for mediums and such, and if truth be told, Mary once thought even less of them than I do. What really opened my eyes was reading all about Miss Eustace and her kind. They're just criminals, really, making money from cheating people like us. The trial was most revealing; showing how she went about her work, making enquiries, getting information about folk and then coming up with it at a séance so it looked like she'd heard it from the spirits.'

'But that is only the case when the medium is a charlatan,' said Miss Clifton, gently. 'There has been so much in the newspapers of late about wonders that no-one, even the men of science, can explain. It made me think — yes, there are frauds, but surely there must be genuine people, too, if one can find them? And, of course, anyone residing in Sussex could not play the tricks Miss Eustace did, since they would know nothing of my great uncle's death in Lincoln.'

Fernwood remained sceptical. 'As to genuine, I don't know. But yes, no-one here has ever heard of our family troubles. It was twenty years ago. There was never a trial, and as far as we know, the inquest was only reported in Lincolnshire, and certainly not in Sussex.'

'That is why we wish to consult you, Miss Scarletti,' said Miss Clifton. 'You know so much more than we do about such things. Is there a genuine medium you could recommend to us? I do think that if someone could pass on information that only we knew about then even George would be persuaded.'

Fernwood did not look as easily convinced as Miss Clifton hoped, but he merely gave her a soft smile. 'We have not told any of our family about this quest. I am not sure what they would think. I rather imagine that they would disapprove and try to dissuade us, as it is never talked of or even alluded to. They think the past is best forgotten. But we need to know.'

'Can you help us?' begged Miss Clifton. 'Oh, please say you will!'

Mina chose her words carefully. 'I am sorry to say that so far all the mediums I have encountered personally or read about have been frauds. That is not to say that genuine mediums do not exist, only that I do not know of any. There are several here in Brighton who advertise in the *Gazette*, but I have never visited them, and I don't know anyone who has, so I am unable to offer an opinion. I can, however, give you some advice.'

'We would be most grateful to hear it,' said Miss Clifton, warmly.

Mina glanced at George Fernwood, who looked politely resigned. 'First of all, please avoid mediums who insist they can only work in darkness. Whatever the reason they put forward for this practice, it is really only a cover for cheating.' Mina was better informed than most on this point as she had been advised by her brother Richard's former mistress Nellie, who had once been a conjuror's assistant, and knew some tricks of her own.

'That is good advice,' said Fernwood, gratefully. 'We did go to one such séance, and there was a very unconvincing apparition whose wig fell off. Then we attended a large assembly, where a medium pretended to give messages to people in the audience. We were not granted a message, and I had my doubts about the ones that some of the people received and claimed to be accurate. I think the medium had friends in the room.'

'Now you can't know that for sure,' said Miss Clifton. 'And there was a message from Uncle Thomas, you know.'

Fernwood grunted. 'There was a message from someone who called himself Thomas, which is not an uncommon name, and all it said was that he was happy and living with the spirits. If he had specified brandy as the spirit in question it would have been nearer the mark.'

'As you say, there are many Thomases, and it was most probably a guess,' said Mina. 'Guesses will be right some of the time, and people will remember the things they want to hear and forget what was incorrect. Then they tell all their friends that the medium had wonderful insight.'

'There were three people in the room who thought the message was for them,' said Fernwood. 'We didn't go back. No, I think what Mary is looking for is someone who could give a reading just for the two of us. Do you think that is advisable?'

Mina offered the plate again. This time, Fernwood took a biscuit, and ate it in a distracted manner, while Miss Clifton, who had become more at her ease during the interview, also availed herself of one. 'There are mediums who provide private readings, but they do tend to charge a substantial fee for such a service. Do beware of anyone who makes unusually high demands. I have known people pay sums as large as £30 for a single evening. Worse than that, once the medium knows the client will part with that kind of money they continue to draw on their victim's funds for as long as possible, making ever more extravagant promises, until they have taken all their fortune.'

Fernwood, who had paled visibly at the prospect of his hard-earned profits being drained in that fashion, shook his head. 'I will be sure not to be caught by such a villain.'

Mina smiled. 'There is another test. You could mention my name to those mediums you intend to visit and see how they react. The frauds will not allow me near them for fear that I will expose them. They will tell you that I negate the spiritual energy and claim that their séances will not produce results if I am there.'

'What nonsense!' Fernwood exclaimed.

'Have you heard of a Miss Athene Brendel?' asked Miss Clifton. 'I am told she is very good and sincere. She and her mother have taken a house in Brighton and have invited those who wish to come to her "mystical readings" as she calls them. I am not sure she charges any fee.'

'I have seen something of the sort in the *Gazette*,' Mina admitted, 'but I have not thought to visit her.'

'And then there is a Mr Castlehouse. He is very new and has a slate on which the spirits write messages in chalk while no-one is near. I have heard several good reports, and we are very hopeful of him.'

Mina, who had had quite enough of knockings and rappings and table tiltings and mediums who swathed themselves in phosphorescent draperies and pretended to be ghosts, had to admit that Mr Castlehouse offered something a little different. She recalled reading about the cheating Davenport brothers who had once toured England with their cabinet of wonders. They had pretended to produce a portrait of an angel drawn by spirits on a previously blank sheet of paper. A sceptical visitor had demonstrated that the picture had been drawn before the séance and hidden inside a folded sheet. Such general devices, which were usually pious in nature, meant to reassure sitters that the spirits came from above and not below, could easily be conjured into existence by clever trickery, but the kind of message Mr Fernwood and Miss Clifton hoped for was of quite another order.

'If you do decide to go,' said Mina cautiously, 'I would recommend that you do not give your real names, and neither should you ask questions or say why you have come. One can never know if the medium might have heard of you, or use what you tell them to make a good guess. And I have another warning. If you go for a reading in a small gathering, or more dangerously still, undertake a personal meeting, you will find it extremely hard not to give away your feelings about what you are being told, and provide some valuable clues.'

'We will do our best to heed your advice, and then we can be assured of learning the truth,' said Miss Clifton with approval.

'I hope that I have been able to help you in some measure, and that you will find the answers you seek,' said Mina. 'Would you care for more tea? These are excellent biscuits.'

Fernwood and Miss Clifton glanced at each other once more. 'There is another favour I would like to ask you,' said Fernwood. 'We would be most grateful if you would consent to accompany us when we visit Miss Brendel and Mr Castlehouse. We would arrange for your travel and pay all your expenses, of course. You have seen so much that is fraudulent that I know you would be able to tell us at once if they are genuine or not.'

'Oh, please say you will!' exclaimed Miss Clifton, before Mina could even consider the request. 'For my part I would like to make an appointment to see Miss Brendel first, as she is said to be quite fascinating.'

Mina hesitated, as while she was familiar with many mediumistic tricks she was far from expert on seeing when sleight of hand was being employed. Nevertheless, the conundrum did interest her. 'Very well, but if you make an appointment for any medium on my behalf, make sure to give my real name. If you are refused it will save you a wasted visit.

But I do have one concern. Supposing we attended a séance and you receive messages, how am I to judge whether or not they are true? I know you will say that you would know, but I have seen so many instances of people believing something because it is what they want to believe, that I fear that however much you guard against it, it may still happen.'

'I have thought of that, and I agree,' said Fernwood. He put his hand in his pocket and drew out a small package. 'We found these amongst my grandmother's papers after her death. We didn't even know she had kept them. They are the newspaper reports of the death of my grandfather and the inquest. All are from Lincolnshire newspapers. I have also enclosed some documents I have prepared which will provide you with details of my family. And if there are any further questions you might like to ask before we consult a medium, do write to me and I will answer them all honestly. You will then be armed with as much information as we have. We trust you to keep this confidential, as we do.'

It was irresistible. Mina took the package.

Chapter Three

Once her visitors had departed, their sadness unabated but now coloured with relief and fresh hope, Mina took the package of papers to her room and laid out the contents on her desk. An unsealed envelope contained neatly folded cuttings from several Lincolnshire newspapers, giving full accounts of the inquest on Thomas Fernwood, together with a small clipping of the death announcement, some correspondence from chemists and medical men regarding the risks of using poisons in the home, and a paragraph describing the funeral. No item in the newspapers was subsequent to the date of that event, from which Mina assumed that after Thomas Fernwood's burial his death held no further interest for the press. There were two sheets of notepaper written in George Fernwood's hand, one of which listed the members of the family who had been living in the house at Lincoln at the time of the murder, the other related the history of the family after Thomas Fernwood's death. Mina asked Rose to bring her a light supper and tend the fire, and then she settled down to read.

At the time of his death in 1851, fifty-eight-year-old Thomas Fernwood was master of a large, rambling, dilapidated house in the centre of Lincoln, and owner of a grocery business in a busy double-fronted shop not far from his home. On the death of his father in 1839, Thomas had inherited both house and business. He was a strict master, supervising the family trade with a firm unbending eye, arriving each morning to check that all was in order, and snap out instructions. Twelve years later, however, the main work in the shop and storeroom was carried out by his son, thirty-five-year-old William, with the assistance of his wife Margery. Thomas still liked to think he was the authority, but in recent years his grip had relaxed, and he had taken to arriving later in the morning and leaving before the shop closed.

Thomas's wife, Jane, who was some seven years his senior, was troubled with pains in her legs and back and consequently spent a great deal of her time in bed being looked after by her granddaughters, Ada and Ellen, who, in 1851 were aged fifteen and thirteen. The girls' brother, ten-year-old George, attended a local school. Thomas and Jane Fernwood's only other children had died in infancy; therefore William Fernwood and his mother were Thomas's principal heirs. At the time of Thomas's death his exact worth was unknown, but it was assumed to be a substantial sum, since his chief fault, as agreed by all who knew him, was his extreme parsimony. His only indulgence, one that had, over the years, encroached into a greater proportion of his time, was cheap brandy, of which he sometimes consumed sufficient of an evening to leave him dull and unwell.

Dorothy Clifton was the only daughter of Thomas's late brother. Her marriage to a tea merchant had been happy but short and, on his death in 1849, she had discovered financial irregularities that left her, and her children, Peter and Mary, destitute. When she appealed to Thomas Fernwood for help he had agreed to give them a home and board, and arrange for the education of the son, but only in return for unpaid domestic duties. Dorothy, with the workhouse looming, had been more than grateful to accept. When Thomas Fernwood died, she had been his housekeeper for two years and Peter and Mary were aged ten and eight.

Early on the morning of Friday 5 December 1851 Dorothy had, as she did every day, made a cup of tea for Thomas and brought it up to his bedroom. He and his wife Jane slept in separate rooms, since his movement at night often disturbed her. When Dorothy entered the bedroom, Thomas was still asleep and snoring loudly, having imbibed a substantial amount of brandy the night before. She knew better than to wake him and risk his ill temper, so she placed the cup on the night table beside the bed within easy reach, and slipped away.

It was some half an hour later that the household was disturbed by loud cries of distress coming from Thomas' bedroom. Ada, who had been in the kitchen helping to prepare the breakfasts, rushed upstairs to see what the matter was, then hurried back down to tell Dorothy that her grandfather was very unwell. Dorothy went to help and found Thomas still in his bed, writhing in pain and vomiting a thin, bloodstained liquid. It was naturally assumed that he was suffering the consequences of his over indulgence the evening before, either that or it was a bad consignment of brandy, or some insect had got into the bottle. No-one else had drunk any of the brandy and no other member of the household was affected. As the day wore on, however, Thomas's agonies only increased, and eventually the family physician, Dr Simon Sperley was summoned. He listened carefully to the family's account of Thomas's illness, administered medicines that were rapidly rejected, attempted washings of the stomach with milk and water, and removed the bottle of brandy for examination. Thomas died that evening.

On the following day Dr Sperley visited the house, where the body had been laid out in preparation for burial. He asked the adult members of the family to assemble in Jane Fernwood's bedroom, since she was unable to leave her bed, and informed them that the cause of Thomas's death could not be ascertained, and it would be necessary to order a post mortem examination. He thought, however, that Thomas had not died from a disease such as cholera, but as a result of something he had eaten or drunk, which he had consumed most probably less than half an hour before being taken ill. Sperley asked for a description of what everyone in the house had prepared and eaten for breakfast. Thomas was the only member of the family not to have had breakfast, but it was well known that he expected a cup of tea to be brought to him in bed each morning. Dorothy confirmed that she had carried out this duty, but had not seen him drink it, as he had been asleep when she entered the room. He had not awoken when she placed the cup on the night table, and she had returned to the kitchen immediately. At that time, all the other members of the household were awake and either in the breakfast room or the kitchen, apart from Jane Fernwood, who was in bed, Ada having taken her a tray. Soon afterwards, William and Margery left to open up the shop, Peter and George walked to school and the women and girls of the house went about their domestic duties, until they were alerted by Thomas's cries.

The post mortem examination revealed that Thomas Fernwood had died from the effects of a corrosive poison that had attacked the lining of his stomach. Dr Sperley had been careful to conserve samples of vomit, which on testing revealed what he had suspected all along. Thomas had been poisoned with arsenic. The contents of the brandy bottle were examined and revealed no trace of arsenic, but Dr Sperley had already expected that, since had there been poison in the bottle, it would have taken effect far sooner. It followed that unless Thomas had consumed something that no-one else knew about the poison must have been put in his tea. Thomas would not have noticed any taste but within minutes he would have felt violently sick, with burning pain from the destructive effects of the poison.

All the family had drunk tea at breakfast made from water boiled in the same kettle, and brewed in the same teapot used to make Thomas's tea without any ill-effects, so it followed that the poison must have been introduced directly into his cup. No-one had seen anyone tampering with the cup, but it had been left unattended beside the sleeping man long enough to give everyone in the house the opportunity to slip poison into the tea. Unfortunately, due to the consternation in the house at Thomas's illness and the early assumption that the brandy was to blame, no-one could recall if Thomas had drunk any of his tea, and the cup, one of several similar ones in the house, had been taken away and scoured with the other breakfast things.

The source of the arsenic was not a mystery. In a kitchen drawer was a paper packet labelled 'Mouse powder. POISON' which was used to kill vermin by sprinkling it on bread and butter and distributing fragments in places where mice had been seen about the house. Everyone knew about this practice and had been warned that the little pieces of bread should not be touched. The contents of the packet were pure white arsenic supplied from the stock of the grocery shop. Earlier that year it had been made illegal by Act of Parliament to sell arsenic without some form of colouring matter, in order to avoid the kind of fatal mistakes so often reported in the newspapers, but the packet in the Fernwoods' kitchen pre-dated that requirement. At the inquest Dr Sperley told the coroner's jury that although arsenic did not dissolve well in cold water, it was certainly possible for a fatal dose, perhaps as little as three grains, to dissolve in hot tea if it was stirred well in. Had the cup been available for examination, some undissolved powder would undoubtedly have been visible at the bottom, if one knew what to look for, but this could well have been missed in the usual process of rinsing.

The coroner summed up the evidence. Judging by Thomas's dying statement, it did not appear that he had poisoned himself. There was no suggestion of insanity or thoughts of suicide, no reason for the healthy and successful man to take his own life. Since he took his tea without sugar, and did not use it for the administration of a medicine, it could not have been contaminated with arsenic by mistake. If suicide and accident were ruled out, then it followed that he had been murdered. The one question exercising the coroner's mind was how had Thomas Fernwood known who had poisoned him? One theory was that the deceased must have seen his killer stirring his tea, and assumed that it was done for an innocent purpose, perhaps to cool it. As regards the identity of the killer, it was apparent that during the time between the making of the tea and the deceased drinking it, every member of the family was in the house. None of the witnesses recalled having seen anyone go to Thomas Fernwood's room between his being brought the tea by Mrs Clifton, and being taken ill. During his illness he had been looked after by Dorothy, Ada and Ellen, and visited by his son and daughter-in-law, but none had been able to understand his attempts to speak through an acid-torn throat, and none could offer a clue as to what he had been trying to impart.

The coroner's jury had no difficulty in reaching the verdict that Thomas Fernwood had died from arsenical poisoning, that poison being administered by another person or persons unknown. It was a case of murder, but the culprit was never identified.

Chapter Four

Having learned all she could from the newspapers and George Fernwood's own account, Mina went on to study the history of the family following the murder.

There were no surprises in the will. Thomas's widow, Jane inherited the family home and its contents, and received an annuity, while their son William became sole owner of the grocery business. There were small legacies for Dorothy Clifton, the grandchildren, nephew and niece, which the minors would receive on their majority.

The Fernwoods and the Cliftons continued to live in the old house. It had been much neglected due to Thomas's parsimony, but under its new ownership, it was cleaned, freshened, painted, varnished, better lit and equipped, carpets replaced and the garden made pleasant. Jane Fernwood, who had become very attached to Dorothy, asked her to stay on as her companion, appointing a cook/housekeeper and maidservants to do the domestic work so that Ada, Ellen and Mary could be afforded the education they merited. George had shown an early aptitude for the grocery trade, and on leaving school, became a valued assistant to his father. Peter was less able, but also joined the business in a more junior capacity, and was content with his position.

On the death of Jane Fernwood in 1861, her son William inherited the family home. It soon became apparent that it was only Jane who had kept the family together. Within weeks of her death, the business was sold, and the house converted into apartments and let. All the family wanted to get away from the house of death with its terrible memories. William and Margery

Fernwood retired to a pleasant villa on the coast where they lived comfortably from rents and investments. They were generous to the family with their legacy. Ada and Ellen, neither of whom had married, were able to purchase a small cottage in Dorset where they lived simply and quietly on the proceeds of annuities. George purchased a grocery business in Haywards Heath, which he ran together with his cousins, Peter and Mary, and his aunt Dorothy. The Fernwoods and the Cliftons were as comfortable and content as it was possible to be, but the shadow of suspicion remained.

Now that Mina knew that the murderer could only be a member of the family, there was one question she did not think she could bring herself to ask, and that was, who did George and Mary suspect? They had behaved as if they were mystified by the puzzle, but they would not have been human if they had not had their doubts about at least one person. The most obvious suspect was George's father William, because he had benefitted the most, but that was hardly proof.

Mina returned to the newspaper report of Thomas Fernwood's funeral. There had been a brief ceremony, attended only by his son and daughter-in-law. Friends and business connections were notable by their absence. Mina was struck by what the account did not say, the gaps between sentences, pauses filled by silent insinuation that the dead man was disliked and everyone was relieved to see him dead. In one way or another, and to a varying degree, all the members of the family had improved their situation following the death of Thomas Fernwood, and it would not be pleasant for George and Mary to point an accusing finger.

Mina, having made a name for herself as an enemy of fraudulent mediums, did not anticipate being admitted to the spiritual circle of Miss Athene Brendel, however, curiosity led her to consider the reasons why that lady had attracted such interest in town.

Three months earlier the society page of the *Brighton Gazette* had carried a notice stating that Mrs Hermione Brendel and her daughter Miss Athene Brendel were newly arrived in town, and they and their retinue were to make their home in Brighton for a twelvemonth. Those residents of Brighton who liked to follow the dazzling lives of fashionable visitors were soon deep in discussion about these ladies of fortune and mystery, and rumour spread its tendrils throughout the town like a particularly insistent vine, probing its way into every corner. Mina, while waiting for her appointments with Anna Hamid in the ladies' salon of the vapour baths, did not generally engage in gossip, but it went on all around her, and was hard to ignore.

Mrs Brendel was a handsome and elegantly dressed lady of about forty-five, with a tall figure and an imperious manner. Without giving any warning as to her arrival or her intentions, she had swept up in a carriage in front of a lodging house advertised as available furnished throughout, demanded to see the landlady, and after a brief inspection of the premises declared it to be perfectly suited to her needs, and offered to rent the entire house at a cost of 180 guineas a year, paying a quarter in advance. On the very same day she and her daughter took possession of the property.

Their new home was in Oriental Place, a street lined on both sides with terraces of superior five storey apartment buildings and hotels, which ran north from the seafront close by and parallel to Montpelier Road. Mrs Brendel, it was believed, was something of importance in society and was a well-known and highly respected figure at gatherings in the greater houses in the country. Mr Brendel had not yet been seen but his fortune was said to be in mines and he was therefore obliged to spend much of his time in the north of England where his interests were located.

The daughter, who was twenty, exhibited a delicate and refined beauty, and many rare accomplishments, having been carefully educated in all the necessary arts that would attract a gentleman's interest in such an enchanting maiden. Her most charming skill was said to be her ability to coax delicious music from a piano. An only child, she was the pampered darling of her parents' eyes, and held the promise of a substantial marriage portion, but only if a gentleman could be found to match her in both fortune and temperament.

No sooner had the ladies and their luggage arrived when a visit had been made to Potts and Co, the town's leading musical instrument emporium and soon afterwards a magnificent piano was delivered to Oriental Place. There was, however, so the whispers went, much more to the delightful Miss Brendel than mere music. She was reputed to be a medium of extraordinary sensitivity. While she did not promise to converse with the dead, produce glowing spectres or tell the future, she was able, through an inner eye, to actually see the spirits. not only of deceased persons, but also of those who lived but were far distant. These presences clustered about her, and while others in the same room, but without her gifts, were unable to see them, the psychic energy she gathered to herself enhanced the perceptions of her visitors. Those who consulted her had claimed to receive reassuring news of loved ones whom they feared might be in danger in a foreign land, or messages of comfort from those who had passed over.

If Miss Brendel had hoped to become the sensation of Brighton, she would have been disappointed. That might have been the result had she arrived much earlier in the year, but in recent months, following the downfall of Miss Eustace and her co-conspirators, even the dedicated spiritualists of Brighton had grown wary, and did not make their beliefs public for fear of the inevitable torrent of ridicule that would fall upon their heads. It was with considerable caution, therefore, that only a few adventurous persons approached the shy Miss Athene Brendel and asked to consult her.

Mrs Brendel, however, made bold with any cavillers, and was quick to declare that she and her daughter had nothing to hide. When asked about Miss Brendel's unusual gifts she pointed out that all the séances were conducted in full light, and not cloaked in suspiciously concealing darkness. Miss Brendel did not fly into the air or make flowers appear from nowhere. There were no glowing apparitions, bells or trumpets. Tables did not tip, and there were no knockings on walls. Such cheap, coarse trickery, said Mrs Brendel, was beneath contempt.

Miss Brendel's fame might have flourished as briefly as a late blossoming flower and then faded into the winter of obscurity, but for one remarkable incident. In a sitting attended by several of her most devoted adherents, she had revealed that she saw a man in the room, one who shook his head as if it pained him, and appeared very distraught, wringing his hands and moving about in a distracted manner. She did not know who the man might be, or why he had come, but she felt very strongly that either he had recently passed over, or would very soon do so in highly unpleasant circumstances. It was later learned that a Mr Hay, a Scottish wine merchant who occupied an apartment in Oriental Place, had recently taken his own life by cutting his throat. At the inquest on the unhappy gentleman it was revealed that some years earlier he had suffered a serious injury to his head in a railway accident, and since then had been plagued by pain, despondency and the wholly unwarranted delusion that he was guilty of a terrible crime.

Mina, sitting in the flower-scented salon of Dr Hamid's establishment, had overheard the other ladies discussing Mr Hay's wretched and hideous demise, and the sensational news that the tragedy had been foretold by Miss Athene Brendel. There was even a letter to one of the Sussex county papers to that effect, a piece of information concerning which the editor had declined to comment.

Mina had instructed Mr Fernwood and Miss Clifton that when making their appointment to see Miss Brendel they should not conceal the fact that she was to accompany them; in fact they must make a point of giving her name. She anticipated either that the young couple would be admitted only on the condition that Mina would not be of their party, or all three would be very politely declined with some unconvincing excuse. It was to her considerable surprise, therefore, that she received a letter from George Fernwood advising her that the appointment was made and they would all be very welcome. He and Miss Clifton would arrive in Brighton by train and hire a cab to collect Mina and convey them all to Oriental Place.

Chapter Five

Mina was at her desk considering this news when she heard voices from the hallway below, her brother Richard's strident declamatory tones and, unusually, a titter from Rose. Mina left her papers and proceeded down the stairs as quickly as was safe, carefully clasping the bannister with both hands to avoid a dangerous tumble as her slight form rocked inelegantly from side to side. A stout greatcoat with a heavy shoulder cape was hanging on the hallstand, topped with a tweed travelling cap, its earflaps dangling. Mina had never seen her brother wearing such an ensemble before, but thought it an unusually sensible one. Richard was leaning against the wall, head in the air, gesturing artistically as if reciting a poem, while Rose, her cheeks flushed, was stifling bursts of laughter with her apron.

Richard, with his slender effortless elegance, untidy blond curls and far more charm than was good for him, was a cheerful scamp who could make even carelessness attractive. A constant source of anxiety when Mina was not keeping an eye on him, she realised with a pang how dreadfully she missed him when he was away, and how his unexpected and usually unannounced visits enlivened her days. As ever he had brought only a small and shamefully battered leather bag, since a room and some necessaries were always kept ready for him.

'Darling Mina!' exclaimed Richard, seeing her swaying approach, and Rose looked up, went even redder than before, and scurried away. Richard bounded eagerly up the stairs to his sister, and enveloped her in a warm hug.

'I hope you have not been teasing Rose,' said Mina, trying her best to be severe with him, which was always difficult.

'Not at all. I merely bring a little much needed light into the girl's life, with the occasional quip or *bon mot*. She has just informed me that cook is making a boiled pudding for dinner, which is just the thing in this nasty weather, and if I am very well-behaved there be will jam on it.'

They descended the stairs together arm in arm. 'I hope you are not too dull all alone here, my dear,' said Richard, fondly. 'How terribly you must miss Mother!'

'I keep myself occupied,' she reassured him.

'Ah, those little tales for children that flow so easily from your pen! I am quite envious of your industry. I think, you know, that I do have it in me to be a great author, only whenever I put pen to paper I can't think what to write.' Mina felt somewhat guilty at deceiving her family as to the true nature of her tales, but reflected that if her mother found out she would never hear the end of it, and Richard was as incapable of keeping a secret as he was of doing a day's work. The only person who knew that she was the author under the *nom de plume* Robert Neil of such titles as *The Ghost's Revenge*, *A Tale of Blood* and *The Castle of Grim Horrors*, was Mr Greville, her late father's business partner, who managed the popular fiction department of the Scarletti publishing house.

As they reached the last step, Richard swept Mina off her feet as he would a child, and placed her gently and lovingly on the floor beside him. 'You are in good health? I do hope so! And I swear you may even be a little plumper than you were.'

'Dr Hamid says that I am in the very best of health, and the baths and massages do me good.' Mina was aware that she was a trifle heavier than she had been some months ago, but that was not due to putting on fat. Anna Hamid had been teaching her exercises to help support her spine. Mina's form, while still slender, and far from robust, was developing a protective shell of muscle, which, it was hoped, would prevent any further distortion of her shape and constriction of the lungs. She was becoming like the crab that moved oddly and carried its skeleton on the outside.

Richard rubbed his hands together briskly. 'I know there will be a good fire in the parlour, and Rose will be bringing us hot coffee so let us make ourselves comfortable!' He pushed open the parlour door, sighed with appreciation of the cosy interior, and proceeded to place himself at his ease, slouching in a chair in a manner that his mother would have deplored.

Mina sat by the fireside and gazed at him affectionately. 'Richard dear, I am always pleased to see you, as you know, but I can't help but feel concerned at the reasons for your visit. I hope your employment with Edward is going well?'

Richard pulled a case of small cigars from his pocket, and glanced at Mina in what he hoped was an appealing fashion. She shook her head. 'No, Dr Hamid has expressly forbidden me to go anywhere near tobacco smoke.'

'Ah, yes. Very sensible I suppose.' Richard swallowed his disappointment, returned the case to his pocket and warmed his hands before the fire. 'Edward has not dismissed me, if that is what you are thinking. I thought he might, several times, and I wouldn't have blamed him. Really, the work is so dashed tedious, and if a fellow has been out late in town then where is one to sleep if not at one's desk?'

Mina smiled. 'As I am sure you are aware, sleeping is something you are expected to do in your own time and not the company's.'

'So I was told. But I would never have any time to myself if I had to work all the while. I don't know how Edward manages it. He seems to do little else now that he is betrothed to the bewitching Miss Hooper, his divine Agatha, who promises to be a very expensive wife. Anyhow, I did get most terribly bored by it all. Do you know, Edward insisted that I learned how to spell! What use is spelling to anyone? Then he told me to cut pieces out of newspapers; I have no idea why. So I used my idle moments to amuse myself by drawing little sketches. Just faces, mainly. Well, would you believe it, when Edward saw them, he said how good they were, and next thing, he asked me to do more.'

'For publication in the paper, you mean?'

'I think so, yes. He showed me some photographs of public figures — ugly fellows with big moustaches and little eyes — and asked me if I could copy them and I did.'

'So you may have found your *métier* at last! I am very pleased for you!' Mina tried to sound encouraging, even optimistic. Richard was forever looking for some method of becoming rich without the necessity of working, and had launched and abandoned several hopeless schemes, usually on funds borrowed from his doting mother. Honest work was a new adventure for him, and Mina hoped that this time he would succeed.

Richard did not share Mina's enthusiasm. 'A low paid one, I am afraid. But then, I thought, why should I not find a wealthy patron, someone who will pay well for a flattering portrait? Edward said that newspapers want pictures to be as close to the original as possible, so people who can't see the real thing can at least know what they look like. But those ugly gents and old ladies like to think they are handsomer than they really are, so that is what I will draw. I did try my hand at oil painting, but the wretched stuff takes an age to dry. I managed a halfway decent self-portrait but I don't think I mixed the paint right; the colours ran and it looked hideous. I put it in the attic — I might come back to it later.'

'You will not do any painting here, I hope,' said Mina, knowing that it would be impossible for Richard to confine the inevitable mess to one room.

'No, drawings are far quicker. I can finish one almost before I am bored with it.'

'Does Edward know you are here?' It was a natural question, given Richard's usual habit of acting on a whim.

'Of course he does. I borrowed his hat and coat after all. I suggested that I should come to Brighton for the season, and draw ladies in the high life and write about how they spend their husbands' money. He's about to start a ladies' newspaper, and they like that kind of thing. *The Society Journal*. It will be like *The Queen*, only different. He has even appointed a lady editor, a Mrs Caldecott, who, I understand, knows everyone and everything — if they are worth knowing, that is. She used to write society gossip for one of the London papers.'

'Do you know anyone in Brighton who might effect introductions in the right circles?'

'That's a bit of a poser, because I don't yet. Although Nellie might have moved up in the world by now.' He sighed. 'How is dear Nellie? I do miss her, you know. None of the London girls are half as much fun.'

Richard and Nellie had parted as lovers, although they still retained a warm regard for each other. She had married a Mr Jordan, a partner in Jordan and Conroy, dealers in high-class ladies and gentlemen's clothing and accessories. She was now a walking advertisement for the business, lavished with all her husband could afford and Richard could not.

'Nellie is as lovely as ever. I see her often and she assures me that her life is all she would wish it to be. She and her husband have just taken possession of a new home, where they mean to entertain prodigiously. Their drawing room will be a sea of French fashion.'

'Then I shall go there and bathe in silk. The ladies will clamour for my sketches, and if I am in luck I will meet a rich widow who will fall madly in love with me.'

Mina could only feel grateful that her value in the marriage market was so low. She did not broadcast her monetary worth, the comfortable annuity she had inherited from her father nicely augmented by the income from her stories, and since no man looked past her appearance she had never had the occasion to disappoint a suitor. Many years ago, as she was emerging into womanhood, and the twist in her spine had first become noticeable, a doctor had told her that she ought never to marry and she had learned to be content with that. The more she saw bargains being made based on money and breeding the more she prized her friendships.

Rose arrived with a tray. Either it was warm in the kitchen or she was still blushing after Richard's jokes. She set a large pot of hot coffee on the table, with cups, milk, sugar and a dish of little cakes.

'Oh, my favourites!' exclaimed Richard.

'Were those not for teatime?' asked Mina.

'I'll ask cook to make some more, Miss,' said Rose, and almost ran back to the kitchen.

Mina poured the coffee. 'Have you seen Enid recently? I do worry about her.'

Richard took a large bite of cake. 'Not as much as Mother does, I can assure you.'

Their sister Enid's troubled married life had been far happier in the summer due to the extended absence of her husband, solicitor Mr Inskip, who was abroad conducting property business with a foreign Count. She had been still more cheerful when visiting Brighton that autumn, after plunging into a highly indiscreet flirtation. The object of her admiration was Mr Arthur Wallace Hope; Viscount, war hero, explorer, lecturer, author and passionate advocate of spiritualism. Mina had no idea how far the indiscretion had gone, but it was clear to her why it had occurred. Mr Inskip was a dull fellow, with a slinking gait, wan complexion and eyes like a dead newt. By contrast, Mr Hope's robust masculine physique and impressive history of narrow escapes from death made Inskip seem to be merely a pale shadow of a man. That unwise affair, if affair it had been, had ended abruptly when Hope had left Brighton to avoid exposure in a scandal involving another lady, and Enid's health had been poor ever since. Her condition had worsened substantially on receiving a letter advising her that Mr Inskip was planning to be home before the winter set in.

'I hope she is no thinner,' said Mina anxiously, since it was Enid's habit to eat almost nothing and lace tightly.

Richard looked gloomy. 'Mother says there is no danger of that. She is being dosed on pennyroyal and Widow Welch's Pills which claim to be able to remove obstructions from the female system. But the obstruction is still there, it seems, and may be so for some time. Mother thinks it will not be relieved for six months at least.'

'Oh,' said Mina, understanding his meaning. 'I hope when Mr Inskip returns he will not be dismayed by her condition. He is an educated man and can do arithmetic.'

'I am told that no further correspondence has been received from Mr Inskip. In fact, no-one quite knows where he is. Perhaps he is lost like Dr Livingstone, or he may suddenly appear on Enid's doorstep, groaning and rattling his chains. Enid hopes he has been killed in an avalanche while traversing the Carpathians. He might be more entertaining as a ghost than he ever was as a living man.'

'When did he set out for home?'

'I'm really not sure.'

'I had assumed he was simply delayed by business. Well, I shall write to Mother and Edward to let them know that you have arrived safely. Maybe they will have more news. And I will make sure to tell Edward that you have his coat and hat, just in case you forgot to mention that you were borrowing them, and he has had someone arrested for their disappearance.'

'And write to Nellie, for me, won't you?'

'I will.'

Richard washed down his third cake with a gulp of coffee. 'We had such fun last summer, didn't we? Nellie pretending to be a medium, and you showing up Miss Eustace and her tricks! And then all that business at the Pavilion. That was a bit near the mark, wasn't it? I suppose Brighton is free of hauntings nowadays?'

'So I understand. But there are still mediums plying their trade. A Miss Brendel who has visions and a Mr Castlehouse with a slate that writes by itself. I have decided to visit them both.'

Richard laughed. 'Goodness! They must be shaking in their shoes! I rather thought you had determined not to visit mediums again. Unless these be the most abominable villains, and you must have them put in prison for the public safety.'

'That remains to be seen. But they do have the attraction of novelty.'

'If you should need any assistance I am your man!' He ate the last cake. 'When is luncheon?'

'In half an hour as I am sure you know.'

'Splendid! And afterwards, while I am waiting for an invitation to Nellie's fashionable *salon*, I will go about Brighton looking for pretty ladies to draw. One must suffer for one's art, you know.'

Mina wondered how much, if anything, Mr Jordan knew about her brother's former association with his wife, and what kind of reception Richard might receive if he decided to call on her. In the past Richard's visits to his former *inamorata* had tended to coincide with those times when her husband was not at home, and preferably abroad on business.

Soon after luncheon, and newly spruced, Richard donned his coat and hat, borrowed a guinea from Mina, and went out. Despite the promise of boiled pudding, he did not return until well after Mina had gone to bed.

Chapter Six

Dear Nellie,

I trust that this finds you in the very best of health and Mr Jordan likewise. I do hope that the removal to your new home proceeded as well as these things possibly can. As I write this I am recalling my family's move to Brighton, which was not achieved without a certain amount of quarrelling, hysteria and broken china. I am sure you have managed it more successfully. I know you have great plans and I look forward to hearing all about them.

I do not go out a great deal in the present season as I am under strict orders from Dr Hamid to spend the entire winter closely blanketed like a baby and existing on a diet of nothing but beef tea, coddled eggs and sherry. But I do go to the baths, of course, where the herbal vapour affords me great relief, and Miss Hamid's ministrations drive any discomfort from my shoulders.

My brother Edward has sent Richard to Brighton on business. He is to make sketches of fashionable visitors and residents for a new society journal. If you could think of some way to obtain commissions for him to advance his career without his actually getting into any trouble, I would be eternally grateful.

Kindest wishes,
Mina

Dear Mina,

I know how trying the winter must be for you, so I am delighted to hear that you are well and taking great care of yourself.

My new home will, once properly furnished, be a wonder to behold, and I look forward to you seeing it in all its glory. Yes, there will be gatherings and entertainments galore! I have such plans!

So Richard is to be an artist? How exciting! I promise to devise something very special in his honour, and I know he will be greatly in demand.

Kindest wishes,
Nellie

Dear Mother,

I hope this finds you well. The weather here is cold but I am pleased to see from the newspapers that you are enjoying better conditions in London.

Richard has just arrived. At Edward's suggestion he is developing his talent as an artist, and will be preparing some sketches for a fashionable society journal. He has every confidence that one day he will be a great name, and much in demand in the very highest circles.

Do send me news of Enid. I trust that her health is improving. Has anything more been heard from Mr Inskip? I do hope his business abroad has prospered and he will be safely by his own fireside very soon.

Please kiss the twins for me.
Fondest love,
Mina

Dear Mina,

It is impossible to describe the dreadful situation here, which has made me as miserable as I have ever been in my life. There is a terrible epidemic of bronchitis and other even more horrid things in town, and I hardly dare stir from the house, so there is no entertainment to be had even if I felt strong enough to endure it, which I do not. You must not come to London at any cost; it would be the death of you.

Enid is in a state of distraction. The twins are strong and well grown, but their gums are so red and swollen that I fear for their very lives. Their cries are piteous and give me the most terrible pain in my poor head so I can hardly think. I try to comfort Enid as best I can but there is no helping her. She is not permitted to go out, and exists in the very depths of melancholy. I fear it will be many months before there is any prospect of recovery.

There is no news of Mr Inskip. We cannot discover if he is alive or dead, and in view of his long silence must fear that he is no more. Enid is so distressed that she cannot even bear to hear his name spoken, the very thought of his fate sends her into paroxysms, so we do not speak of him at all now. Edward came to see us, saying he wanted to help, but as soon as he started explaining things to me, I knew it was useless to listen to him. There are some papers in the house but I can do nothing with them, I am far too ill. Perhaps he can make sense of them.

Richard is my only comfort. He is a dear good boy and will make something very fine of himself one day.

Your unhappy
Mama

Dear Edward,

I trust that you and Miss Hooper are both well, and that the business flourishes.

First of all, the news here. Richard, you will be pleased to know, has arrived safely, thanks to your kindness in lending him your warmest coat and hat. He is very eager to start making sketches of the fashionables in town, of whom there will shortly be very many as they are even now arriving for the season. He has already been busy seeking admission to the best houses and gatherings. He is working so hard that I have scarcely seen him since he arrived.

Please let me know the news concerning the whereabouts of Mr Inskip. Richard tells me there have been no letters from him for some time. I hope Enid is not suffering too much anxiety on that account. How is Mother bearing up under the strain of caring for Enid and the twins?

Fondest love,
Mina

Dear Mina,

The good news is that I am pleased that scallywag Richard is actually consenting to do some work and I hope something will come of it, but you will understand that I have my doubts. Tell him not to damage or lose my best warm coat and hat, or I will have to take the cost from his wages.

I suppose Richard has told you about Enid's indisposition. It is very irritating but there is nothing I can do, the foolish girl must take the consequences. It is pointless to remonstrate with her. I tried to question her about Mr Inskip, to discover whether he left any instructions before he went away but she laughed so hard she became hysterical and had to be given a soporific to calm her. She really tries my patience.

Mother is Mother as always. I now find myself obliged to spend some considerable time going through Mr Inskip's papers, as Mother, despite having so much time on her hands refuses to take any practical action, so it has all been left to me. It is very hard when I have the business to attend to as well. To be blunt, it was a relief to dispatch Richard to Brighton as he takes up more time in the office than he saves. Fortunately my dearest Agatha has been very patient and understanding. I have made sure not to trouble her with our family woes.

I will write again if I learn anything,

In haste,

Affect'ly,

Edward

Chapter Seven

'We have given our names as Mr Wood and Miss Clive,' said George Fernwood, as he and Miss Clifton arrived by cab to convey Mina to Oriental Place for the séance with Miss Brendel. 'As you asked, I gave your full name to Mrs Brendel when securing our places, and she raised no objections.'

'Perhaps, as she is only recently arrived in Brighton she knows nothing of me?' suggested Mina. She knew she should not have felt a little disappointment at this, but could not avoid it.

Fernwood smiled. 'She knows you very well by name, since others who have consulted Miss Brendel have mentioned you and your history. You are seen by some as a violent opponent of all things psychic. They have even recommended that she invite you to meet her daughter as they feel that such an encounter would change your views on spiritualism.'

'I have no views on spiritualism, so it would be hard to change them,' said Mina. 'I have very strong views on people who extort money from the bereaved under false pretences.'

'I understand,' said Miss Clifton, warmly, 'and believe me, we are of a like mind on that subject. These false practitioners should be rooted out and punished. How else can we reach the great truth?'

The wind was brisk, with a hint of approaching frost. Mina, who had no wish to encounter the great truth any sooner than was necessary, was grateful that the journey would be a short one, grateful too that she had spent more money than her mother would have approved of on a deeply lined cloak. Rose had made sure she was carefully wrapped with a heavy veil and a thick muffler to protect her face, so that she should not draw the cold air directly into her lungs. There was a small flask of hot water for her to clasp in her hands, and Dr Hamid had provided some herbal sachets that gave out a scent that was very comforting to inhale. It was a great deal of trouble for a ride lasting just a few minutes, but it was time well spent. Fernwood opened the cab door and entered first, then reaching out, he took both Mina's hands and drew her inside, ensuring that she moved at her own pace, and had all the support she needed. The driver, one whom Mina recognised, as he liked to wear a tartan muffler in the winter, watched the process, and she knew that had she required it, he would have jumped down and lent a hand as he had often done in the past.

At last they were all comfortably settled, and the cab moved off. On the way, Mina faced her companions and found herself considering them as a stranger might on a first meeting. What, if anything, could Miss Brendel deduce from their appearance? Their good state of health and robust serviceable clothing suggested a comfortable life in the middle portion of society, but not the more elevated echelons of the gilded idle, where garments were as much a matter of displaying position as practicality. There was no hint of mourning about either, not so much as a ribbon, locket or edge of a handkerchief, which at once told any onlooker that neither had been recently bereaved. If Miss Athene Brendel was to offer this information and tried to suggest that it came from the spirits, Mina would be less than impressed. She also had to consider their voices, touched with a gentle accent that might well suggest they were born and bred north of Sussex, but not so distinctive that their origins could be traced to Lincoln.

The cab drew to a halt outside their destination, a double-fronted house, rising to a full five storeys above ground, its exterior painted cream and garnished by carved scallop shells, with spider-black railings around the basement area and first floor balconies. Mina wondered how many occupied the residence, as it seemed large for a family of two, and the landladies of these superior properties did not take kindly to unauthorised subletting. Perhaps Mrs Brendel meant to entertain. Perhaps she just wanted to inform the town of her correct place in society.

Mr Fernwood assisted Mina down the steps of the carriage as if she was a piece of bone china that might break if dropped. The muffler slipped down from her face, and she quickly pulled it back into position. The air was as cold as a knife blade, as the wind, travelling from the surface of the chilly sea, swept up the narrow channel of the street to disperse itself in the alleys and byways of the middle of town.

The street was almost deserted apart from a youth clad too thinly for the weather, who was walking past rather more slowly than was advisable if he wished his movement to keep him warm. To Mina's surprise, as they advanced towards the house, he suddenly changed direction and darted around the carriage as if intending to cross to the other side of the street. This, however, he did not do, neither did he enter the carriage. She gained the impression that he was lurking behind the vehicle to hide from view. She glanced at her companions but neither appeared to recognise him or consider his strange behaviour to be of any note. Was he hiding from the new arrivals, or the house they were visiting? There were only two shallow steps up from the pavement and Mina and Miss Clifton mounted them arm in arm, while George Fernwood hurried ahead up the pathway to ring the doorbell. As Mina heard the cab draw away she looked back and saw the lone young man move quickly to cower behind a nearby gatepost.

They were met at the door by a maid, who, Mina thought, must have come with the house like the hall furniture, as she was not in her first decades of her life, and rather wooden but well-polished. 'Party for Miss Brendel?' asked the maid.

'Yes, Mr Wood, Miss Clive and Miss Scarletti,' said Fernwood.

The maid glanced up the street, from right to left, then looked the visitors over, her eyes lingering on Mina for a moment, before she nodded. 'This way.'

Once cloaks and bonnets and mufflers had been dealt with they were led along the hall. It was a little cooler than Mina liked her home to be, and she was pleased to have brought a warm shawl. The maid knocked on a door and opened it to announce the arrivals, then stood back for them to enter.

'How delightful!' exclaimed the lady who rose from her chair and came to greet them. 'I am always so happy to make new acquaintances in town. I am Hermione Brendel. Do please come in and make yourselves at home.'

Mrs Brendel, while no longer young was nevertheless both elegant of figure and quick of movement, giving the impression of an almost girlish vivacity, although Mina sensed that her air of good cheer rested lightly and transparently on a steely determination. The drawing room was of a good size for entertaining, well-lit and with a bright fire burning in the grate. Mina, expecting a séance, made a careful study of her surroundings, but saw none of the usual arrangements. There was no curtained recess, no rows of seating for the faithful, no table surrounded by a close circle of chairs, for the practice of tipping for messages. Since the house was let furnished it was not possible to come to any conclusion about the family from its interior, which was nicely appointed although not brand new. One item did stand out, however, a pianoforte in figured walnut with fretwork ornamentation. Potts and Co had been advertising them in the *Gazette* as the very latest thing.

'Allow me to introduce my daughter, Miss Athene Brendel. Athene, we have new members for our little gatherings, Mr Wood, Miss Clive and Miss Scarletti.'

The young woman who was the only other occupant of the room had been seated with her head slightly bowed, but on the arrival of the visitors she slowly looked up and gazed on them evenly and without emotion. She was as light and frail as a fairy with large, bright, pale violet eyes. Her skin was almost white, her hair, like that of her mother was dark and abundant, further accentuating her almost unnatural ghost-like pallor.

While neither she nor her mother could be described as beautiful there was something very striking about the appearance of both that demanded attention. In the mother it was her energy, and the searching expression in her eyes, and in the daughter the transparency of her form, like a fading picture. Mina, recalling her father and sister Marianne, both of whom had died far too young, was obliged to wonder if Miss Brendel carried within her the seeds of consumption that would shorten her life.

'I am so very pleased to meet you,' said the young woman, softly, moving one hand in a welcoming gesture. Her wrist bones stood out as bony knobs beneath lace cuffs, and her fingernails were like cloudy pearls.

Mrs Brendel motioned the visitors to sit down. 'We are expecting some more to our little gathering, who I am sure will be here directly. Mr Wood and Miss Clive, are you newly arrived in Brighton?'

'Ah, we are here just for a brief visit,' said Fernwood.

'And Miss Scarletti — your fame precedes you,' the lady beamed. 'So much so that I am given to understand you have quite frightened away those practitioners of deceit who have plagued Brighton of late.'

'So I am told,' said Mina, 'I can't say how true that might be.'

'Oh, I do so hope it is. You cannot imagine how mortifying it is for those who are genuine mediums to see charlatans using their tricks and wiles, and demanding payment, which we never do, and giving the art a bad name.'

'I hope you don't mind my commenting,' said Mina, 'but I have been to a number of séances, and your room is not prepared in the way I had expected. Can you advise me how the evening is to be conducted? How do you expect the spirits to address us?'

'Oh, there will be no scratchings or knockings, you may be quite sure of that. It is simplicity itself. Think of tonight only as a gathering of acquaintances. There may be spirit visitors, and there may not. If there are, Athene, with her special gifts, will be able to see them. Most people, I have found, are not so gifted. We cannot be sure that Athene will see anything of note, but should she do so, then she will describe her visions to us. We will then concentrate on what she imparts and her insights will in many cases open up our minds so we will achieve clarity.'

Mina thought this very clever. Miss Athene promised nothing, and asked for nothing. If she received any impressions, since no-one else could see them, she could not be contradicted or exposed. Anything the guests might gain from the exercise was solely due to their own efforts. Under the circumstances it could prove impossible to determine if the medium was genuine or a cheat, and as Mina waited for the séance to begin, she feared that she was due to have a very dull time.

Chapter Eight

A gentleman arrived dressed in mourning clothes, and was introduced to the company as Mr Harold Conroy. Mina had never met him, but she knew his name, since he was the younger brother of Frank Conroy, the business partner of Nellie's husband. He was aged about thirty-five, and, like his brother, was very portly with every sign that this robust demonstration of prosperity would increase over the years. His face was florid, and his extravagant auburn side-whiskers failed to conceal the sagging throat or the neck that had begun to bulge over his collar. Mina recalled that he conducted a successful business manufacturing uniforms for the army and navy. He had been widowed in the previous year, and was the father of four children all less than ten years of age.

The next arrivals were an elderly couple, both clad in deepest black, who were introduced as Mr and Mrs Myles. They walked together arm in arm for mutual comfort, creeping along with small shuffling steps. Conducted by their hostess to a sofa, they sat together like a dark mound of misery. Everything about them announced a recent bereavement, but Mina found herself wondering if this was true. The Queen herself, after all, had been in mourning for ten years with no sign of it abating. This couple wore their grief like a mantle that they were unable to remove, and who could tell how long ago they had put it on?

A gentleman of about sixty was next to appear, tall and spare of figure, very upright in his posture, and faultlessly dressed, with white hair expertly coiffed, and a smartly pointed beard. He was introduced as Mr Honeyacre. He was not clad in black, but wore both a wedding ring and a small mourning ring, which suggested that he had been widowed some years before.

The next visitors were a Mrs Tasker, a lady of mature years and figure, with her son, a youth in his twenties, who showed by his sulky expression that there were very many other places he would rather be, and was accompanying his mother under sufferance. Neither was in mourning, but a locket worn by the lady suggested that she was there in remembrance of a close family member. Young Mr Tasker both walked and sat with a miserable slouch, which his mother repeatedly corrected by tapping his arm with an insistent finger. Each time this happened, he scowled, and straightened his shoulders unwillingly, then let them slump again almost at once. Mrs Tasker gave elaborate greetings to both Mrs and Miss Brendel, and pushed her son into doing the same. He barely recognised the presence of other persons in the room, but the one thing that did attract his interest was the piano, and as they took their seats he fastened his attention on it to the exclusion of all else.

The gathering was completed by a Mr Quinley a man in his middle years, who said nothing about himself, but greeted everyone briefly with an ingratiating smile, sat down, and remained determinedly silent.

A tray was brought with a large pot of tea, and all the company was served with the exception of Miss Brendel. There was a delicate china cup on the same tray, one with pretty flowers painted around the rim. It was filled from a smaller pot and handed to Miss Brendel by her mother without the addition of either sugar or milk. Mina was too far away to see what was in the cup, but wondered if it was something medicinal in nature.

Slowly, gasping with the strain, Mina rose to her feet and rubbed her shoulder. 'I hope you don't mind, Mrs Brendel, but my poor back aches so when I remain idle. Might I take a brief turn about the room? If I do, I will be well again directly.'

'Oh, please do,' said Mrs Brendel.

'May I assist you?' asked Fernwood, leaping to his feet.

'Yes, thank you,' said Mina, gratefully, 'if you could just let me lean on your arm.'

They made slow progress about the room, watched with anxiety by the other occupants, and Mina made sure that her path took her close enough to Miss Brendel to see the contents of her teacup, a brew so pale that it could hardly be flavoured at all, and had no very strong aroma.

Once all were back in their places, and it was established that Mina was quite restored by her walk, Mrs Brendel gazed happily about her. 'How pleasant it is to see so many familiar faces, and also some new ones. Some of you may already know Miss Scarletti, by reputation at least. She is held in great regard here in Brighton.' Those who had thus far been too polite to stare at Mina now took the opportunity to do so.

George Fernwood coughed gently. 'As this is the first time we have come here, I would be very obliged if we could be told when the proceedings are about to start.'

'Oh, there is no start,' said Mrs Brendel, with a smile. 'Neither is there any end. Athene's gifts cannot come and go as a candle is lit or extinguished. Athene sees what she sees at any moment. She may see something tonight or she may not.'

Athene's large brilliant eyes turned about the room. 'I do see,' she said. 'I see the figure of a man. His eyes are open, as one who lives, he gazes far away, but he does not move.'

Mrs Myles uttered a loud sob. Her husband patted her arm. 'Can you describe him?'

'He is young. His face is much sunken, the expression melancholy.'

'Where is he?'

'He is standing behind your chair.'

Inevitably the other occupants of the room, apart from the surly Mr Tasker, looked to where Miss Brendel indicated. There was nothing to be seen.

'Please! Address him! Does he have a message for us?' begged Mr Myles.

Miss Athene smiled indulgently, from which Mina supposed that it was an entreaty she had heard before. 'Sir,' she said, to the vacant air beside Mr Myles, 'if you are able to speak, please do so. Say whatever you will.'

There was a long pause, silent except for the sound of breathing, which as far as Mina could make out was produced only by the living occupants of the room. 'Oh, do tell me what he says!' asked Mr Myles at last. 'That may be our dear boy, our darling Jack, who we laid to rest ten years ago.'

Miss Brendel shook her head. 'I cannot tell. He is gone. But I have seen him before. I think he will come again. Perhaps next time, he will have a message for you. Be patient.'

Mrs Myles choked back a paroxysm that threatened to close her throat.

'Oh, that is our poor son, I know it!' exclaimed Mr Myles. 'Come to bear witness to his place in Heaven!' He pulled a large handkerchief from his pocket; white with the broadest edge of black Mina had ever seen, pressed it to his face and sighed into its depths.

'Do you see anyone by me?' asked Mrs Tasker, impatiently.

Athene sighed and shook her head. 'No, but my art is not certain. I do see a gentleman standing by Miss Scarletti. I have not seen him before. He is neither young nor very old. He seems troubled. That is all I can say.'

George Fernwood and Miss Clifton glanced at each other.

'How is he troubled?' asked Mina. 'It is an affliction of the mind or the body?' Despite herself she could only think of her father, and realised how easily one could be drawn into hope and belief.

'It is hard to tell. He is walking about the room. He does not see any of us.'

'I hear no footfall.'

'Nor do I,' said Miss Brendel. 'That is one way I know that the people I see are apparitions. I see them walk, they seem to be present, but their feet make no sound.'

'Do you know if this is someone living or one who has passed?' asked Mr Honeyacre. He spoke not as someone who thought he might know the apparition, but from simple curiosity.

'I cannot say. Both the living and the dead appear before me, but I can only distinguish between them if they are known to me. The gentleman is gone now. But there are several more persons, who have appeared, some close, some distant. Both ladies and gentlemen. I can't see their faces. They move back and forth as if passing each other in the street. They stop, and greet each other, then walk on. Some have bright clothes, others are dull as if the colours have faded.' Athene closed her eyes, and raised a skeletal hand to her forehead. 'I must rest for a while.'

Mrs Brendel fetched a carafe of water from a side table and poured a small glassful, which she pressed into her daughter's hands. Athene looked weary, and sipped very carefully.

'Are you quite well?' asked Mr Honeyacre, gently.

Athene favoured him with a kind smile. 'I am, only so many visions are an unusual exertion and I must rest from time to time. I will be recovered in a moment.'

'Can you tell me if the figures you see appear to be as real and solid as actual persons or if they are more like shadows or mist,' asked Mina.

'For the most part when they first appear they are like actual persons. If you were to see one, you would assume it was a living being and address it as such. I can see the colour of the skin and hair and clothing quite distinctly, and they move and walk like real persons in every way. But they are not aware of me, or at least they do not seem to be, and after a while they start to fade and become transparent, like a painting on glass. I can see the room through them. And then they vanish.'

'Do they make any sound at all? Do they speak?'

'There is no sound. Sometimes I can see their lips moving, some of them even converse with each other, but I cannot always distinguish what they say.'

'Have you ever approached one to touch it?'

'I have. I once saw my father at a time when I knew he was far from home. He walked about the room and smoked his pipe, but I could not smell the tobacco. Then he sat in his favourite armchair, and I went to touch him, indeed I made to sit in his lap. But there was nothing there and he vanished immediately.' She set her glass down, and her eyes took on that dreamy look, a distant gaze that suggested that a vision had appeared.

'What do you see?' asked Mr Conroy, hopefully. 'Is it a lady?'

'Yes, I see a lady; she is very aged, dressed all in black. She has white hair.'

Mr Conroy looked disappointed.

'My grandmother, perhaps?' said Mrs Tasker, hopefully. 'She passed away seven years ago. Perhaps she has a message for me? Or for Geoffrey? He was always her favourite. How might I receive a message?'

'Close your eyes and think of her. If it is she, it may be that her words will come to you.'

Mrs Tasker obediently closed her eyes and smiled. 'Ah, yes, I think I can hear her now. Her voice was so — distinctive. She has a message about Geoffrey.' She patted her son's arm, reassuringly. 'All will be well.' Geoffrey shrugged off his mother's touch.

Mina wondered if like she, he was unconvinced that the message came from anywhere other than his mother's wishes. Mrs Tasker had some very definite motives for bringing her son to the séance. Whatever the underlying intention, and that was not clear to Mina, she obviously wanted her own wishes to be amplified by sage advice from one who had passed and therefore could be said to have divine understanding.

Miss Brendel was obliged to rest once more, and after a whispered conversation with her mother, it was announced that the sitting was over, although the guests might remain for light refreshments if they so wished. Miss Brendel rose and guided by her mother's hand, left the room. Mina wondered if her ghosts accompanied her or remained. There was no way of knowing.

Mr and Mrs Myles decided to take their leave, as did the Taskers. Mr Quinley stayed and said nothing, but watched the company as if they were simply visions of his own, and therefore not to be disturbed.

Mr Honeyacre rose and went to speak quietly to Mrs Brendel. Mina observed the conversation though it was conducted in tones too low for her to hear. Mrs Brendel listened, and nodded and he seemed pleased with that response.

Mr Conroy, deep in thought, approached Mina, and sat by her. 'Miss Scarletti, we have not met before, but your name is known to me; you are a great friend of Mrs Jordan.'

'Yes, we often take tea or, in clement weather, we like to drive about the town.'

'You are new to this circle. But I think I can guess your mission. You hope to find some fault with Miss Brendel, uncover plots to show her to the world as a fraud. But I can tell you now that you will fail.'

'Oh? How interesting! Please tell me how you have come to that conclusion.'

'I have attended four meetings, and the lady is undoubtedly sincere. She does not, as the cheats do, ask for payment or gifts. She has a rare ability and she uses it selflessly to bring comfort to others who are in sore need of it.'

'Have you ever seen the visions she describes?'

'No, and I would not expect to. I do not have her gifts.'

'Has she ever seen a vision which, from her description, is of someone known to you?'

Conroy paused. 'The first time I was here, I thought, yes. I expect you know I have been widowed for almost a year. All my tender thoughts since then have been of the fine wife I have lost. Otherwise I have distracted myself with my family and business matters. But —' There was a long silence, and he puffed out his cheeks like a man who dared not say more. He pulled his watch from his pocket. 'I'm sorry. I have an appointment and must go at once. I can see you are a sceptic, but in my estimation, Miss Brendel will confound all criticism.' He rose to his feet and bowed. 'Good evening.' After briefly taking his leave of the hostess who was still conversing quietly with Mr Honeyacre, he hurried away.

'I wonder what that was about?' said Fernwood.

'Oh, but can't you see?' said Miss Clifton with a knowing smile. 'He was distracting himself from his grief, but then he comes here and finds Miss Brendel more of a distraction. In six months we may hear of an engagement.'

Fernwood raised his eyebrows. 'Is it the lady or her fortune that tempts him, I wonder? Probably the latter.'

'And what do you think of Miss Brendel?' asked Miss Clifton turning to Mina. 'Is she true or false? We both thought the vision of the gentleman might have been my great uncle Thomas.'

'There was little enough description,' said Mina. 'How many families have a gentleman of that age, or an old lady with white hair? But I saw no sign of conjuring, and there could have been none. She merely states what she sees and cannot be contradicted. She does not even pass on messages but leaves it to us to gather what we wish for.'

'But does she believe in it herself?' asked Fernwood. 'She could be a deliberate deceiver, or subject to delusions, or genuine. She may have some fault with her eyes. How can we know which one she is?'

'As to her eyesight, there is a doctor who might be able to advise me on that point.'

'That is very kind of you,' said Miss Clifton. 'Once we know more we can decide if we should pay her another visit. For myself, I feel that she shows great promise, and I would very much like to see her again.' Fernwood said nothing but Mina saw from his expression that he did not share Miss Clifton's optimism.

Moments later, Mr Honeyacre also made to leave, but as he departed, there was a small careful movement, in which he produced an envelope from his pocket and slipped it into his hostess's hands. Mina glanced about but her companions were gazing at each other and had not noticed, and Mr Quinley if he had noticed was not about to reveal that he had.

'I do have one question,' said Mina quietly to George Fernwood. 'As we walked about the room, did you happen to see what it was in Miss Brendel's teacup?'

'Some variety of tisane, but without being able to smell it, I could not say which one.'

'We must find out what it is. It could be innocent, or it could just be the key to what we need to know.'

Chapter Nine

Mina made sure to be warmly wrapped against the sharp weather before she emerged with her companions onto Oriental Place. As they descended the steps she was surprised to see, cowering in the shadows thrown by the yellow glow of the gas lamps, the same youth who had been outside the house before they went in. He looked chilled, and she realised that he might well have been lurking there the whole time.

'Ladies,' said Fernwood, 'please remain here by the gate where there is some shelter from the wind, and I am sure there will be a cab in moments.' He strode purposefully up the street. Before long a vehicle approached and he quickly hailed it.

To Mina's surprise, once the maid had withdrawn into the house and the front door was closed, the youth emerged from his hiding place and crept shyly forward to speak to her and Miss Clifton. He was clad in a greatcoat too thin and mean to be adequate for the cold weather, and he was clutching his arms about his chest in the vain hope that they might lend him some warmth. His face, which bore an expression of extreme meekness, was stark white, pinched with blue. There was nothing threatening in his manner, neither did he look like someone about to beg alms, nevertheless it was an unusual thing to do. Mina glanced anxiously at Mr Fernwood, who having seen what was occurring, was hurrying back to their side.

'Please excuse me, ladies,' began the youth, 'I don't mean to alarm you, and I know I should not address you in this way, but I beg you to hear me out. I assume you have been to one of Miss Brendel's séances?'

Fernwood reached them. 'We have,' he said suspiciously. 'What is it to you?'

'I was wondering if you could tell me if the lady is in good health? I am concerned that she is in some dreadful decline.'

'I am afraid that none of us have met the lady previously and so cannot judge if her health is any better or worse than previously,' said Mina.

'But did she look well? Was she weary?'

'I am sorry,' said Fernwood, brusquely, 'but we cannot have this conversation in the open street. The ladies may catch a chill.' The cab had drawn up and he went to open the door.

'I agree,' said Mina, but her curiosity had been piqued. 'Let us all enter the cab and talk there.'

Fernwood looked surprised, but reluctantly agreed, and before long they were all four settled and comfortable.

'My name is Ernest Dawson,' said the youth. 'I am twenty-one and I live with my mother and two sisters on Upper North Street. I am employed by Potts and Co, the music emporium on King's Road, and work on the counter selling sheet music. Some three months ago Mrs and Miss Brendel came to the shop and purchased a piano, which was delivered to their lodgings in Oriental Place. Miss Brendel is very adept at the piano — I heard her play and it was delightful — and she also purchased some music. I — I must confess,' he added bashfully, 'that I found her extremely interesting. On a later occasion when she came to purchase more music, we conversed for some while, and I think — in fact I am sure — that she returned my regard. I did go to the house to attend one of the séances, but really my true reason in doing so was to see Miss Brendel again. When I went a second time I enquired of Mrs Brendel whether her daughter had a sweetheart, and if she did not, I asked if I might be permitted to call upon her. This Mrs Brendel absolutely refused. She was not unkind at first, but became harsher as I continued to entreat her. It was made very clear to me that my fortunes were insufficient, and I must not entertain any tender feelings for Miss Brendel. I do, of course, I cannot repress my feelings, but now I know I must be content only to be the lady's sincere and concerned friend. It is in that capacity that I ask for your assistance.'

'What do you expect us to do?' asked Mina.

'I am very worried indeed about Miss Brendel's state of health. Even in the few times I have seen her I have noticed a decline. I cannot discover if she is being attended by a medical man — I have never seen one enter the house. Neither Mrs Brendel nor the maid will speak to me. The maid, Jessie, I think is not unsympathetic but she is governed by her mistress. Miss Brendel rarely goes out nowadays, so I cannot think that she is consulting anyone. I fear for her, I really do! I wonder — would you be so kind as to deliver a message to her from me the next time you visit? Her mother has forbidden me to call again, and I am sure she would intercept any letters.'

Mr Fernwood and Miss Clifton looked at each other, but Mina spoke sternly before they could respond. 'Mr Dawson, if you have any sense at all, you will know we cannot do this. The mother's word, whether or not you agree with it, is law. If she has forbidden you the house and ordered you not to pay court to her daughter I cannot intervene in this underhand fashion.'

'Even at the cost of a life?' he pleaded.

'Is she really in such danger? How can you know for sure? You are not a medical man.' Even as she spoke, Mina had to admit that she too, had concerns for Miss Brendel's health, but at the same time, was hardly in a position to advise.

'I know what I see, and,' he shivered, 'I have still graver suspicions.'

'Go on, do.'

'I think that Miss Brendel's visions may well be produced either by her declining health, or something she consumes — a herb or medicine. Mrs Brendel is using her daughter's special gifts to achieve fame and position, but in doing so I very much fear that she is administering some poisonous substance, which may if she is incautious, kill her.'

'Do you have any proof of this?' asked Fernwood. 'It is a serious allegation.'

Dawson shook his head. 'No, or I would have told the police.'

'Then I doubt that there is anything you could do.'

'I have no funds to engage a professional man to see her, and even if I did her mother would not allow it. I thought, if I could get a message to her, and find out if she is well and happy ...' His shoulders slumped miserably. 'In the meantime, all I can do is watch the house whenever I can.'

'Miss Scarletti is right,' said Fernwood. 'We cannot interfere between mother and daughter without good reason.'

Mina suddenly recalled a remark that Dr Hamid had made to her some months ago. Some of his patients at the baths had reported seeing the ghosts of the recently departed. He had been mystified as to the reasons for this, but perhaps he might now have further observations to share as to the likely causes of this phenomenon. He might even be tempted to go and see Miss Brendel out of curiosity. 'Mr Dawson, do you have a card?'

All the other occupants of the cab looked startled by the question. 'Er — no, but I have a card of Potts and Co.'

'Then let me have it and write your address on it. I have a card of my family publishing company and you may have it with my address. I will make some enquiries. I have a medical friend who might be able to advise me. But I make no promises.'

'Oh, I am so very grateful!' he exclaimed. 'Any hope at all is better than none! Tell me, was there a fellow there by the name of Quinley?'

'Yes, there was.'

'I thought so. He is not a guest but a solicitor, he manages all Mr Brendel's affairs.'

'How do you know this? He gave no clue when I saw him. In fact, he said nothing at all.'

'I know because of the purchase of the piano. Mrs Brendel's bills are paid by the husband through Mr Quinley. In Brighton he is the wife's watchdog. He chases away impecunious suitors, even the noble ones. No lordling need think he can trade his title for settlement of his gambling debts.'

The cards were exchanged, and after Mina was taken home, it was agreed that young Mr Dawson could be taken to his apartments before George Fernwood and Miss Clifton travelled on to the railway station. As Mina turned the key in her front door a thought struck her. All the arrivals at the Brendel séance had been preceded by the doorbell. All but one, Mr Quinley. Which suggested that he was already in the house.

Chapter Ten

Before she retired for the night, Mina started to plan another tale. In this story there was a witch who only used her powers for evil. She was jealous of a much younger witch who only used her powers for good. The wicked witch kidnapped the good witch and cast a spell on her, so that the good witch believed she was the wicked witch's daughter. Out of daughterly duty the good witch did everything her supposed mother told her. Thus, the wicked witch made use of the good witch's powers for her own purposes.

Mina thought this was a promising start, but wasn't sure how to end the story. It was too easy to have a handsome prince arrive unexpectedly and fall in love with the good witch and set her free. Far better for the good witch to fight her way out of her predicament using her own resources. But how? A magical amulet she just happened to have forgotten she had, or even discovered by chance? No. Mina did not like to bring more coincidence into a tale than was necessary. What if the good witch had a dream about her real mother and realised she had been practised upon, and that broke the spell? Better. That at least had the attraction of greater possibility.

Or maybe, thought Mina, the good witch just wasn't the docile creature the wicked witch had taken her to be, and every so often she wanted to be very naughty and disobey her mother? Yes.

Mina scribbled happily for so long that she even heard Richard creeping in late.

Young Mr Dawson's distress had given Mina substantial cause

for thought, and the following morning she considered the mysterious Brendels, and what action she might reasonably take. Mrs Brendel, who had arrived in Brighton in the autumn season knowing no-one of any position, was, she felt sure, trying to attract the kind of attention that would provide her with an invitation to fashionable circles, not merely for herself but for her pretty, accomplished, unusual and oh-so-eligible daughter. Miss Athene Brendel was undoubtedly a little strange and a trifle delicate-looking for many men's tastes, but a large marriage portion would soon overcome any hesitation.

It occurred to Mina that apart from watchful Mr Quinley, the deeply mourning Mr and Mrs Myles, and her own party, those present at the séance — she could hardly think of it as anything else — were widowed Mr Conroy, an unmarried youth and his mother, and a veteran who was almost certainly a widower, too, Mr Honeyacre. All these gentlemen were therefore potential suitors for Miss Brendel. Mina was consumed with curiosity as to what was in the envelope Mr Honeyacre had passed to Mrs Brendel. Money? An invitation? A letter? A proposal of marriage? It was obvious that whatever the nature of Miss Brendel's peculiar ability, she was, in the best of traditions in moneyed families, being displayed as a valuable commodity by her mother. The presence of a solicitor, as advisor and protector, was understandable.

Mina was obliged to remind herself that there was no reason for her to interfere in Mrs Brendel's plans, apart from the mischievous pleasure it would bring her, as well as providing fuel for her stories. Had the séance been the kind of performance she was accustomed to seeing, with glowing apparitions and trumpets that played by themselves and similar chicanery, she would have had no difficulty in telling her companions that Miss Brendel was a fraud to be avoided, but this was altogether different and she didn't know what to make of it. She needed sensible expert advice, and there was no-one she could rely upon more than Dr Hamid.

The truly important issue in Mina's mind, and the one that might require some action by an outside party, was the state of Miss Brendel's health. Was she, as Mr Dawson suspected, being poisoned by her mother, either deliberately or unintentionally, and was this the source of her visions — or was she subject to a wasting illness, one, perhaps, that had gone unnoticed by her family and for which she was receiving no treatment? Or was Mr Dawson simply a susceptible young man, being led astray by his anxiety and Miss Brendel's undoubted attractions? Mina recognised that she was not equipped to answer these questions, but she knew a man who was.

It did occur to her, however, that as Dr Hamid was a widower with a thriving business, a circumstance that could well earn him a warm welcome from Mrs Brendel, she ought to issue a gentle warning to him. Once his period of mourning was over, society would consider him highly eligible and ripe for remarriage. The doctor was undoubtedly a fine-looking gentleman, his interesting complexion a tribute to his Bengali father, a well-respected man of medicine in his own right, who had married a Scottish lady and settled in Brighton. He was also clever, well-mannered, and anxious to do good in the world. A friend of Mina's mother, Mrs Mowbray, an ample and mature widow, had long admired Dr Hamid in a manner wholly obvious to everyone, with the exception of the doctor himself, who was oblivious to the passion he had inspired. His loving devotion, with which he was well supplied, was not addressed to any ladies other than his sister Anna, his daughter, and the memory of those who had passed from the world.

When Mina wished to consult Dr Hamid in fine weather she simply took a pleasant ride to the baths, but on this occasion she sent him a note, in which, so as not to cause alarm, she reassured him that she was in good health, but wished to speak to him on another matter involving the health of another individual. He quickly replied saying that he would be able to call on her after his last appointment of the day, and Mina instructed Rose to arrange suitable refreshment. She might have included Richard in the interview, but she discovered that he had gone out, having failed to inform anyone of where he was going or when he was to be expected back.

There had been no mention in Mina's letter that she was once again delving into the world of the psychic, but when Dr Hamid arrived, his expression told her that his suspicions had already been aroused.

'How is your sister?' he asked, as they made themselves comfortable in the parlour before a roaring fire with a jug of hot cocoa and toasted and buttered currant cakes.

'She is in delicate health, but my mother is attending to her, and is confident that all will be well in time.'

'And your mother?'

'She will outlive Methuselah I am sure, for all her protestations. Edward's business thrives, and he is looking forward to his wedding to Miss Hooper next year. Richard is back in Brighton, and he is the same as ever.'

He nodded. 'So it is not a family member you are concerned about?'

'No,' said Mina cautiously. He gave her a wary look. 'Have you heard of a Miss Athene Brendel? Is she perhaps a patient of yours?'

'She is not, but the name is familiar.' It took a moment's thought for him to recall it. 'The lady claiming to see ghosts? I have read about her in the newspaper, and some of my patients have mentioned her. She is in Brighton with her mother. How have you come to know her?'

Mina chose her words carefully. 'I was asked to attend a séance on behalf of an acquaintance who wanted my opinion as to whether or not she is genuine. On the basis of what occurred I was unable to form any opinion.' Mina described her evening at Oriental Place, with particular reference to Miss Brendel's appearance and manner. Dr Hamid listened to the story with mounting disquiet.

'You believe that Miss Brendel is in poor health?'

'Yes, she seems very delicate. Of course, I have only seen her once, so I have no means of knowing if this is her usual appearance. As my friends and I were leaving the house, however, we were accosted by a young man, a Mr Dawson who works at Potts and Co, the music emporium. He was very anxious about Miss Brendel, and undoubtedly has tender feelings for her, but her mother has refused to allow him to pay court to her daughter, as he has no fortune. He told me that he thought Miss Brendel's health was in danger, possibly even her life, and that her mother was not making the efforts to care for her that she ought. In fact, he even suggested that Mrs Brendel was quite unintentionally giving her daughter something that was harming her. Of course, he may be wrong, but everything I have seen suggests to me that there might well be cause for concern. I noticed especially that Mrs Brendel gives her daughter a drink, some kind of tisane, which she does not serve to others. Who knows what it is?'

'I am not sure what you wish me to say,' said Dr Hamid, cautiously. 'I can understand the reasons for your disquiet, but you do appreciate that if Miss Brendel is already being attended by a doctor then, leaving aside a sudden emergency, there is nothing another man can do unless he is consulted?'

Dr Hamid had often given in to Mina's requests for help, even when he had felt them to be somewhat beneath the dignity of a practitioner of medicine, but this time his tone and expression told her that here was a path he would not cross.

'There would be no harm in an informal enquiry, surely? I seem to recall our first meeting when you asked if I would be willing to consult you.'

'But on that occasion you had already advised me, quite forcibly as I remember, that you distrusted doctors, so I felt safe in assuming that you were not already under treatment. I am glad that you have spoken to me about Miss Brendel, as the information could well be of value if I am ever asked to attend her, but I am not sure what you wish me to do at present.'

'I only seek an opinion. But there are two issues here. I feel they may be connected but I am not qualified to determine if they are, I can only observe. Yes, I know that strictly speaking none of it is any of my business, since neither I nor a member of my family is involved.'

'Why do I think that will not stop you?' said Dr Hamid, dryly.

Mina waited for him to raise an objection, but as he made no protest she continued. 'The most important thing is Miss Brendel's safety. If she is in danger and I know about it, I can hardly stay silent. Then there are the visions. She may be merely playing a role, but I felt, and, of course, I could be mistaken, that she genuinely saw something, although the nature of what she saw no-one can tell. I think you know more about these things than most men, in fact more than most doctors. I remember you once told me that some of your patients had reported seeing ghosts. You said that these patients appeared to be sincere and not delusional. So you have encountered others who have made similar claims to Miss Brendel. You would know if there was some reason relating to their state of health that might produce such visions. And I feel certain that you have some curiosity about this condition.'

He smiled. 'As to the explanation for the visions, I am not sure if I have one, but you are right about the curiosity.'

Mina did not mention it, but in one of his more confiding moments he had confessed to her how he wished he possessed the ability to see images of those who had passed; not simply as a picture in his mind, but something outside himself, so he could sit at home and look on the faces of his late and much-loved wife, Jane, who was ever in his thoughts, and his dear sister Eliza, both of whom who had died that year.

'Can you tell me more about your patients? What did they see? How did they explain it?'

There was a long pause for thought, partly occasioned by the buttering of a teacake, partly, Mina felt sure, by Dr Hamid considering what, without betraying the confidence of his patients, he could safely say. 'There were two. I cannot name them, of course. One was a gentleman, who was suffering from anxiety, mainly concerning his business. He was in constant discomfort from indigestion. He told me, not without some hesitation, that he had begun to see the figures of men and women in his house, people he knew were not actually there. Of those he recognised, some were deceased and some living, others he did not know. He attributed the visions to a disturbance of the brain, and was afraid that he was losing his mind. His own doctor advised sea bathing and also recommended that he consult me.'

'The gentleman did not think he saw the spirits of the dead, or living phantoms?'

'No, not at any point. Once he had established that the figures were not actually present, he was quite sure that the visions emanated from his mind and were not real.'

'Did he speak to the figures or try to touch them?'

'He did at first, but they took no notice of him, and if he attempted to approach them either they vanished altogether before he reached them, or his hand passed through them and then they faded away.'

'Does he still see them?'

'No. His health improved with a regimen of vapour baths and massage. His digestion returned to its normal robust condition. Also, he very sensibly retired from business and decided to go and live abroad. Just before he left he told me that the visions had decreased as his circumstances improved and he had not seen one in some time.'

'And what of your other patient?'

'A lady of advanced years who was much afflicted with a cancer in her intestines. Her illness was progressing rapidly and she knew there was no hope, but she came to me for an easing of her pain. She told me that she saw animals and birds in her house, which no-one else could see. She received only two treatments and passed away not long afterwards.'

'Did she believe she saw ghosts?'

'She liked to think so, and never attempted to question the reality of what she saw. She was very fond of animals, and the visions comforted her.' He looked wistful.

'Miss Brendel and your patients cannot be the only people in the world who have seen such apparitions. Can you explain how these visions occur? Where do they originate? How are they formed?'

'I am not convinced that the visions had any origin other than in the mind of the person seeing them. But I find it hard to conceive how a thought can become so real that one actually sees it outside oneself as a solid person. Neither of my patients was insane. Anxious, yes, unwell, yes, but both were in full possession of their senses.'

Mina refilled his cocoa cup. 'I have a favour to ask you.'

'I had feared as much. As long as I am not expected to creep about spying on people. I am no detective.'

Mina had once asked him to do this for her when there had been no alternative. He had found it highly embarrassing and she had promised never to ask him to do so again.

'No, I wish to draw on your special knowledge. Would you be prepared to visit the Brendels for one of their evening gatherings? It occurred to me that Mrs Brendel might not have seen or recognised the signs of illness in her daughter. Since she sees her daughter every day she might not have noticed any slow changes. After all, my mother never noticed the trouble with my spine until the dressmaker pointed it out. Might there be something very specific to which you could draw her attention?'

He considered this. 'It is certainly possible, but if Mrs Brendel does not choose to consult me there is nothing practical I can do.'

'A gentle hint might be all that is required. Enough to make her think of what she might not have seen, that a trained eye has noticed. Enough to suggest that she consults a doctor. Otherwise I am afraid that Mr Dawson will try and effect a cure by taking Miss Brendel away from her mother and removing her to Gretna Green.'

'Would he do so?'

'He seems very devoted. But you will go?' She offered another currant cake, which he took.

'If only to prevent a misguided elopement, yes. But I am no great expert on the eye and its connection with the brain. I have had another thought, however. There are a number of oculists in Brighton with whom I have a slight acquaintance. They have made the special studies I have not and might be able to offer some insights into the nature of illusions. Would you like me to make enquiries? I am happy to do so as it would help me if I was to encounter any further cases in my practice.'

'Please do. If you find an oculist who can enlighten me I should like to meet him. Perhaps he might be willing to call on Miss Brendel? But before we make such an arrangement I would first need to know if he is a married man.'

Dr Hamid looked a little shocked at the question. 'Why is that of importance?'

'I do not ask on my own account. I ask because Mrs Brendel seems to be favouring eligible gentlemen for her guests. I think she is hoping to marry her daughter into the moneyed classes, someone who will match the father's fortune and not squander it. A professional man, perhaps, one with a thriving business.' She allowed a meaningful pause to follow.

Dr Hamid nodded and it was only gradually that realisation dawned and he looked alarmed. 'Oh! No! I have no intention of marrying again. Not now, or ever.'

'Then you should be immune to Mrs Brendel's wiles. But you can be assured of a warm welcome in her house.'

Dr Hamid did not meet this information with any pleasure.

'On that subject, are you acquainted with an elderly couple, a Mr and Mrs Myles? They were there that night. Also a Mrs Tasker and her son, and a Mr Honeyacre.'

'Well, none of them are patients of mine. Honeyacre, hmm, that name does sound familiar. I'll give it some thought.'

Mina very much wanted to ask Dr Hamid about the prospect of criminal tendencies being inherited; whether they lay dormant only to emerge several generations later, and if they could be multiplied by the marriage of cousins, but she decided to remain silent. George Fernwood and Mary Clifton had already consulted a medical man, without result. It seemed unlikely that Dr Hamid would have a better answer and all she would have done was arouse his suspicions and betray the confidence with which she had been entrusted.

'If you can let me know what days are convenient for you I will write to Mrs Brendel and arrange a visit for us both.'

'I knew you would have your way. And let me consider what I might reasonably do concerning Miss Brendel. If I do not overstep the accepted bounds I might venture some simple questions, but I will take no action which would be unprofessional.'

Mina nodded. Dr Hamid's firm and careful manner was a steadying influence. He was a source of calm and thoughtful advice, which was always welcome. If, on the other hand, action needed to be taken that was both foolhardy and dangerous, and which no man in his right mind ought to attempt, she knew that Richard would do it without being asked.

Chapter Eleven

Once Dr Hamid had departed Mina quickly made notes of a new idea for a story that had just occurred to her.

An impoverished but noble-minded young man was in love with a beautiful maiden who possessed a fortune. Mina hesitated over the word 'beautiful'. This would imply that the young man was shallow enough to admire the maiden only for her outward appearance. It was, however, an inevitable part of popular stories that a heroine who was much loved and sought after should always be beautiful. Surely, Mina thought, those who were not so favoured could be loved as well? And could only beautiful women have adventures in storybooks? It seemed so. Mina gave the question further thought and crossed out the word 'beautiful.' No doubt her readers would simply assume it was there in any case. This, however, presented a new difficulty since it now appeared that the youth was not in love with the maiden at all, but only wooed her for her fortune, which was not at all the idea that Mina wished to convey. She began again.

An impoverished but noble-minded young man was in love with a virtuous maiden, who although not rich, was in herself a priceless jewel and deserving of his devotion. She loved the youth in return, and they had promised each other that one day they would marry. There was, unfortunately, an obstacle to their happiness. The honest maiden of indeterminate appearance and meagre dowry was being pursued in marriage by an elderly rich gentleman, and although she did not care for him, her avaricious mother had agreed to the match. The interest of the old gentleman in a bride who was one third of his age, even if she was neither beautiful nor rich, did not, Mina thought, need to be explained. The wedding to the aged suitor took place much against the daughter's will and she was immediately carried off to her new husband's castle. Meanwhile the youthful admirer had discovered that the elderly gentleman had been married many times before, always to very young wives who died soon afterwards, sometimes on the wedding night. He hurried to the castle, arriving just in time to rescue his beloved from a grisly fate. The elderly husband, seeing that he was about to suffer for his catalogue of dreadful crimes, threw himself from the battlements and perished. The tale ended with the wedding of the maiden to her deserving swain.

There were a few details to be smoothed out. Since the youth was poor he would not own a horse, and therefore could not pursue the newly married couple in their wedding coach and arrive in time to avert disaster. A youth of such impeccable character would, however, be bound to have a loyal friend who would happily lend him a steed. Mina would also have to insert a scene in which the hero braved death to save his love — always popular with the reader. Once the wicked husband had plunged to his death, the maiden bride, now a widow, was wonderfully wealthy, thus satisfying her mother's avarice. After the wedding, the dutiful daughter rewarded her mother with the gift of a fine house with servants — at some considerable distance from the castle.

Richard was not yet home when Mina retired to bed, but next morning he arrived at the breakfast table, late, dishevelled, dull of eye and thirsty for strong coffee. She knew better than to question him about where he had been and with whom. Rose brought him a dish of bacon and kidneys, which he smothered in Brighton sauce and fell to as if he had not eaten in a week, while Mina, studying the morning post, contented herself with a boiled egg and a toasted muffin. 'It is a good thing Mother is not here to see you with your collar in that state,' she observed.

'Oh, Mother has more things to worry about than my collars,' said Richard, pouring his third cup of coffee. 'But you are doing duty for her, I see.'

'Someone has to. I have received a letter this morning from Edward. He says I must make sure you don't misbehave yourself and you are to work hard. I would like you to manage at least one of those, but preferably both. He wants you to post back a sketch to him every day.'

Richard looked appalled, and almost choked on his coffee. 'Every day? Surely not!' he spluttered.

'That is what he has asked for. Well, you did say you could complete them quickly, and I am sure he knows it, so the request is not unreasonable. How many sketches have you completed since you arrived?'

He wiped his mouth with a napkin and shrugged. 'Not many. These things take time. I have to settle myself to it properly before I can begin. Get my surroundings just so; be in the right artistic frame of mind. You understand, don't you? It must be like that when you do your writing.'

'No. So I assume you have done nothing, which means you had better make a start. And Edward says that each sketch must have a story attached to it.'

Richard groaned and knuckled his eyes. 'But where am I supposed to find these stories? They don't just lie in the street to be picked up.'

Mina took pity on him, and opened the newspaper. 'Look here. The papers are full of them. Town gossip is awash with stories, and some of them are even true. The *Gazette* has a whole page, sometimes more, about the society events taking place in the season. You've missed the panorama of Paris in flames, I'm afraid, which was a very popular attraction, but the County Hospital Ball is tonight. There will be carriages all around the Pavilion and the Dome. Everyone will be there. And Mr Burrows was elected Mayor last week, for the third time. That is a very notable event. You could offer to sketch him. Oh, and look here — Dickinson's Gallery on King's Road is displaying a new portrait of the Queen. Every fashionable person in town is sure to be there to see it.'

Richard picked up the paper and stared at it, but the prospects of work it offered did not cheer him.

'And this is only the beginning. Next week the whole town will be preparing for Christmas.'

'Already? But it's not even December yet.'

'No, but people like to start early.' She reached out and squeezed his hand. 'Richard, let me help you. If you can do the sketches, and tell me who they portray I will write a few words to accompany them. Is that not a reasonable offer?'

Richard's despondent moods never lasted long. A smile brushed his face like sunshine, and he patted her hand, so tiny that it vanished beneath his like a child's. 'You are the very best sister a man could have. Dearest Mina — I don't suppose —?'

'But I won't lend you any more money.'

Dear Mr Fernwood,

I have recently consulted a medical man of my acquaintance who has some experience of patients who see apparitions. In his opinion the question of what such visions mean and how they come about is one that should be addressed to someone who has made a special study of the eye and its connection to the brain. He may well know of a suitable individual to approach, and I hope to be able to advise you further in due course.

87

In the meantime, I am pleased to say that he has consented to pay a call on Miss Brendel and consider if there is any foundation to the unusual anxieties of Mr Dawson.

Yours,

Mina Scarletti

Dear Miss Scarletti

Mary and I are most grateful for all you have done on our behalf and your continued interest in our difficult position. We anticipate your next communication with interest. As soon as time permits we will return to Brighton and see Miss Brendel again, as we feel there may be more to learn there.

We have decided to pay a brief visit to Lincoln, in the hope of reviving old memories of the place. We intend to look once again on the house where we lived as children and also ensure that my grandfather's grave has been properly tended. Who knows but that his shade might rise up and tell us what we wish to know and then he will confer his blessing on our union? At least that is what Mary hopes, and for her sake I would like to think so, too.

I will write again on our return,

Yours,

George Fernwood

Chapter Twelve

As Mina had anticipated when she applied for two invitations to the next séance, there was no difficulty in Dr Hamid being welcomed to the Brendels' home. He hired a cab and called for her, taking great care before he would even allow her to leave the house, to satisfy himself that her health would stand the exertion. The weather, he warned, had taken another wintry turn, and he supervised Rose as she prepared Mina for the outdoors, instructing her to use every means possible to protect her mistress against the cold air.

While this was in progress, Mina, as she had done with George Fernwood and Miss Clifton, studied Dr Hamid's appearance for clues that he would provide to a medium. He wore the usual signs of mourning; the black gloves and the band around his hat and sleeve. His wife had died the previous March and it would therefore be several months before it would be acceptable to make some variation to this attire; indeed, he might, as the Queen seemed to be doing, decide to make it a permanent state. This was valuable information to a fraudster, but since Hamid's vapour baths were well known in the town, Mina thought it was very likely that the Brendels already knew something of Dr Hamid or had found out his history in anticipation of his visit. Like Mina, he could hardly disguise his appearance since he was quite probably the only gentleman of Anglo-Indian descent in Brighton. Apart from those obvious considerations, there was, she thought, nothing else that could be learned.

By the time Mina had been enveloped in shawls, cloak, hood, veil, mittens and a muff, she felt ready, with the addition of a good ship, some dogs, a sled, and a team of native guides, to undertake a mission to find the North Pole, where, so a recent expedition had informed the press, there was thought to be a sea swarming with whales. Horrible as the North Pole must surely be, she thought she could understand its allure for the adventurous. Not only was it a challenge to both body and spirit, offering the thrill of discovery, and the opportunity of claiming new territory for one's nation, even if it should only prove to be a useless drift of ice, but it was also an escape from what might be the even greater cares of civilisation. No-one at the North Pole had to organise Christmas for a family whose members had scattered itself to the four winds in upset and disarray.

It occurred to Mina that one never saw a whale in the sea at Brighton. She supposed that the climate did not suit them. Of course, anything might happen in a story. She made a quick jotting in the little book she always carried with her to record ideas.

The transfer from doorstep to cab was done as quickly as possible. The driver was so heavily wrapped in multiple shawls that only his eyes were visible through the narrow slit between the folds of material and his hat. The interior of the cab was chill, but at least they were sheltered from the cutting wind, and Mina, clasping her flask of hot water, held it up before her face to warm the air.

Dr Hamid turned up the heavy collar of his greatcoat, and thrust gloved hands into his pockets. 'Of course, moments after we last spoke I recalled where I had heard the name Honeyacre. I found it in our record books. The gentleman was not a patient of mine, but his late wife suffered from an affliction that all the skills of medicine could not cure. They lived in the country, quite close to Brighton, and from time to time she was brought here to the baths, where her visits afforded her great relief. I later learned that she had passed away peacefully and without pain, which was the best outcome that could have been hoped for.'

'How long has Mr Honeyacre been widowed?'

'About five years. After that I think he went travelling abroad for a while. I don't know when he returned. I mentioned his name to Anna, and she informed me that he is now resident in Brighton where he has recently been paying court to a spinster of his own age, a Miss Macready. An engagement has yet to be announced, but is believed to be imminent.' He smiled. 'I am sure you know that Anna is not one for gossip of that sort, but ladies like to talk about the news of the town while she is treating them.'

'So, from what you say, he is neither a recent widower nor a suitor for Miss Brendel's hand?'

'That would appear to be the case.'

'You surprise me. Those are the very two reasons for which I would expect him to have attended the séance. Is he wealthy?'

'I believe so. He owns a number of estates in the county and amuses himself by collecting art and antiquities.'

'Perhaps the Brendels hope he can introduce them to the cream of Brighton society?'

'He is more likely to introduce them to the Brighton Antiquarian Society.'

Mina was mystified. What was the reason for Mr Honeyacre's visit to the Brendels, and what was in the envelope he had passed to his hostess? If it had been any other medium Mina would have assumed that the envelope contained money, but Mrs Brendel had been adamant that she did not require payment for the evening, neither had there been the slightest hint that a little gift would be appreciated.

The answers to those questions might well provide some insight into Miss Athene's vaunted abilities, and deliver a firm answer as to whether she was genuine, a fraud or a victim of her own illusions.

On their arrival at Oriental Place it was no great surprise to find young Mr Dawson pacing back and forth outside the house, stamping his feet, blowing on his fingers, and making the most out of a thin muffler. 'Miss Scarletti!' he exclaimed, advancing towards her as she descended from the cab, then broke into a fit of coughing.

'Young man!' said Dr Hamid, severely, placing himself between Mina and Dawson. 'Keep your distance! You are a danger to the lady's health and a danger to your own if you persist in this behaviour! I know who you are, Miss Scarletti has told me all about you. You cannot help Miss Brendel by making yourself ill. Go home and warm yourself by the fire. If there is anything you can usefully do, we will inform you.'

Mr Dawson had the good grace to look ashamed. 'I meant no harm,' he wheezed.

Dr Hamid might have pointed out that the man who had carried an infection into his home that had killed his sister Eliza had also meant no harm, but the words lay unspoken on his lips. He could not, thought Mina, be so unkind. 'I know,' he said, more gently. Then he took a card from his pocket and handed it to the youth. 'You need a herbal bath to ease your lungs. Have one, gratis, if you present this. Then you will be of some use.'

Dawson took the card, croaked his thanks, and with a polite nod to Mina, began to walk away, coughing.

'Oh, please take the cab!' said Mina, signalling the driver to remain.

Dawson hesitated, and she realised that he did not have the fare and was unwilling to accept money. 'I'll walk home,' he said. 'The fresh air will do me good.' He stifled a cough as he hurried away.

'Come, let us go indoors quickly,' said Dr Hamid, offering Mina his arm.

'Poor young man!' Mina exclaimed. 'I hope he takes your advice.'

Chapter Thirteen

They were not the first to arrive. Mina was especially delighted to see her friend Nellie Jordan, who greeted them both with her usual sparkling good humour. Nellie was resplendent in the newest winter ensemble, her shapely form coddled in dark blue velvet with deep sleeves heavily trimmed in fur and all accessories to match, a costume she carried off in perfect style, and which probably weighed as much as Mina did.

Although Mina had not seen any hints of conjuring or sleight of hand in Miss Brendel's performance, she thought that Nellie's expert eye on the evening's events could prove invaluable. She suspected, however, that Nellie's presence in Oriental Place was more to display the latest Paris fashion acquired by her husband's business than any interest in the proceedings. It was very noticeable that Mrs Brendel eyed Nellie's gown and its trimmings very closely, as if calculating their cost and how they might enhance her own standing.

The other persons who assembled around the fireside were young Mr Conroy, Mr and Mrs Myles, the Taskers, Mr Quinley, as watchful as ever, and Mr Ronald Phipps, a junior partner in one of Brighton's most prestigious firms of solicitors, together with his elderly spinster aunt. Miss Phipps' presence was not altogether surprising, as she liked to be taken to every new entertainment in town, where she would drink a cup of tea and then fall contentedly asleep. She relied on her youthful relative to squire her safely there and back, and he managed this very well, hardly ever appearing to be either bored or discomfited by the arrangements. Mina wondered if Mrs Brendel knew that Mr Phipps had been of assistance to her before, providing the information and advice that had enabled her to unmask the frauds that had tried to cheat her mother and friends. Perhaps Mrs Brendel, confident in her daughter's abilities, did not see Mr Phipps as a threat, in the same way that she had welcomed Mina's visits. There was also the fact that Mr Phipps, a young professional and single gentleman, with a sound future, must in the mother's eyes, be a possible match for Miss Athene. Whether or not Mr Phipps was aware of this, only time would tell.

On being introduced, Mr Phipps acknowledged Mina with a polite inclination of the head, but took care not to reveal that they were already well acquainted. Given her previous activities in investigating tricksters and cheats, Mina surmised that he was thinking that she was present for the same purpose, and was therefore wary of revealing more than he thought she wanted Mrs Brendel to know. Miss Phipps was less reliable in the area of confidentiality, but since she gave every impression of being asleep almost as soon as she sat down, this was not a great worry. After seeing that his aunt was comfortable, Mr Phipps looked about him very carefully, trying not to make his inspection of the room appear to be any more than polite interest. He was probably, thought Mina, searching for the paraphernalia of the dark séance, as she too had done on her fist visit, but as she already knew, there was none, neither was there an obvious start or end to the sitting.

Mina had hoped that Mr Honeyacre would be present, as Dr Hamid would then be able to converse with him, and she might learn something useful, but disappointingly, he did not appear.

Mrs Brendel greeted Dr Hamid with an acquisitive gleam in her eye and extravagantly welcoming gestures, commenting that she knew him both by name and reputation. It was only now that Mina noticed that Mrs Brendel had a peculiar way of addressing her gentleman guests. She had been misled on her first visit by her hostess's undisguised interest in herself, but now saw that her manner to the gentlemen was different in quality. It was as if she was weighing them, like a commodity, viewing them as one might a row of plump fishes lying on a slab in the market. One could almost imagine her saying 'yes, he will do, I will have that one.' Was there a scale, Mina wondered, a balance in which the ambitious Mrs Brendel set one man against another? And what was she using for weights? Dr Hamid, having been forewarned as to how he might be regarded, was cool courtesy personified.

Miss Athene, her dress a drift of light grey silk, her complexion little better, was no thinner or paler than she had been before. Young Mr Tasker, who remained impervious to the lady's personal charms, was instead irresistibly drawn to the piano and asked Mrs Brendel, almost in a whisper, if he might hear Miss Brendel play. The mother agreed at once, and taking her daughter's hand, spoke briefly to her, then led her to the piano. She sat before it like a ghostly presence, her slender fingers seeming barely strong enough to turn back the lid and expose the keys. She laid a light touch on the music sheet, then began to play. The sound flowed like the gentlest of wavelets, very soft and sweet. Mrs Tasker, seeing her son stand by Miss Brendel so devotedly, made no secret of the pleasure this sight afforded her.

'I want to play as well,' said Mr Tasker, and although his manner was abrupt, no sooner had the words left his mouth than another seat was brought and he and Miss Brendel sat side by side and caressed the keys. Both mothers looked on appreciatively at this development, and exchanged meaningful glances.

When the tune was done, everyone settled comfortably for the séance, and the maidservant brought a tray with tea, once again serving Miss Brendel with a different brew.

'I hope you don't mind,' said Dr Hamid, 'but I do not customarily drink tea at so late an hour. Perhaps some of that delicious smelling tisane if there is enough for another person?'

'Of course, I quite understand,' said Mrs Brendel, nodding to the maid, who poured some of the contents of the smaller pot into Dr Hamid's cup. Mina was near enough to appreciate a delicate flowery scent rising from the golden fluid.

'Do you find it pleasant living in Brighton?' she asked, sociably.

'We do indeed,' said Mrs Brendel. 'Our home in Yorkshire is not nearly as comfortable in the winter, and Athene far prefers the climate in the southern regions.'

'What part of Yorkshire do you hail from?'

'We live in the environs of Wakefield.'

'I have never travelled so far north. Will we see Mr Brendel here in Brighton for the season?'

'I think not. Aloysius dislikes society, in fact it would be true to say he detests it; not only that but he fears to be away from his business concerns for too long. But he is happy for me to travel with Athene and make new friends.'

Mrs Myles sniffled into a black lace bordered kerchief but it was not clear why. The noise did have the effect of drawing attention away from Mina, which might have been the desired result. 'Are you quite comfortable, my dear Mrs Myles?' asked Mrs Brendel, kindly.

Mrs Myles nodded wordlessly.

'Miss Brendel, if I might be permitted to ask you a question?' began Dr Hamid, who had been sipping his golden tea with every sign of enjoyment.

'Of course,' whispered Miss Brendel with a shy smile that spread over her face like a dream.

'How long have you been able to see things that others around you cannot?'

It was not a contentious question since Miss Brendel did not even glance at her mother before she replied. 'I think the first occasion was about six or seven months ago.'

'That must have been very frightening for you.'

'It was unsettling, certainly.' She stroked her thin teacup and its painted flowers with the tips of her fingers. 'I was sitting in the library, and my father came into the room. I was surprised to see him, as I knew he was away on business, and was not due to return until the next day. I made some comment to him to the effect that he had come home early, but it was obvious that he had not heard me. He walked about the room, and even stood by the fire as he usually did. I questioned him again, still without receiving any response, but then I saw that his clothes were more faded than usual, as if some of the colour had been washed from them. As I looked on, the colour became still fainter, until it was gone, and all I could see was his form like a cloud tinted in grey and white. Then he vanished altogether. My chief fear at the time was that I had seen some premonition of an accident befalling him. I told Mother about it, of course, and I am sure that she did not believe me.' Athene cast a glance at Mrs Brendel, who acknowledged that this had been the case. 'The next day my father returned home in good health, and indeed he remains so to this day.'

'Were you especially anxious about him before he went away?'

'No more than usual. I had no reason to be. I missed him, of course.'

'But you also see forms of the deceased,' interrupted Mr Conroy, his heavy face flushed and furrowed with thought.

'I do. There was poor Mr Hay, the gentleman who made away with himself recently. I had sometimes seen him walking about the street holding his head as if it pained him. He appeared before me in this very room, making the same gesture. I have also seen others whom I do not know, but who are recognised by my visitors as relatives they have lost. There is a lady sitting in that chair now.' Athene indicted a small armchair, which to the eyes of everyone in the room was empty. 'She is very distinct but I can tell, since she was not there a moment ago, that she is a spirit. She is reading a book.'

'Can you describe her?' asked Dr Hamid, unable despite himself to disguise a slight catch in his voice. His late sister Eliza had been an avid reader.

Miss Brendel turned her large bright eyes towards him. 'I can only say what I see. She wears spectacles. Her hair is grey and her features are regular, her expression is content.'

Mina saw Dr Hamid struggling with himself. He wanted to ask if the lady was of a complexion similar to his own, he wanted to ask if she was misshapen due to scoliosis even more advanced than Mina's, but he knew that such questions would be a mistake. Charlatans, as he had already learned to his sorrow, could take those hints and use them to convince the sceptical. They could bend facts to their own uses — suggest for example that if the ghost had a straight spine then although twisted in life it had been healed in the spirit world.

'My late sister was a great reader,' said Mr Myles, eagerly. 'It must be she. What book does she hold? Is it a work by Mr Dickens?' He turned to the empty chair. 'Amelia? Is that you?'

'She turns the pages,' said Athene. 'It makes no sound. Her lips are moving, but I cannot hear her voice.'

'Can she hear me?' asked Mr Myles, becoming increasingly agitated. All eyes were now on the chair, and it seemed that everyone was straining to see, but only Miss Brendel was calm and serene.

'She fades — she is gone.'

Mr Myles groaned. 'If I could be granted just one word! It is Amelia, I know it!' His wife sobbed noisily, and he patted her hands.

'Miss Brendel,' said Dr Hamid. 'Is it possible for you to teach another person your skill?'

'I have never tried to,' she said. 'But I doubt that I could since I don't know myself how it comes about.'

'But when it first started, was there any special circumstance you can recall? Was the weather warm or cold, for example? Had you just dined or were you about to?'

Mina could see what Dr Hamid was attempting to do. While carefully moving about the margins of the subject, he was trying to discover without direct questioning if the visions had their origins in an illness suffered by Miss Brendel.

Miss Brendel opened her mouth to reply, but was prevented by the interruption of her mother, which was a little too sharp for courtesy. 'There was nothing of any significance as I recall.'

'Forgive my questions which come naturally from scientific curiosity,' said Dr Hamid. 'If we can rule out circumstances such as the weather or a disturbance in the balance of the constitution, it may simply be, although I am not an expert in this area, that Miss Brendel has better than usual eyesight and can see what most others cannot. Has any examination taken place?'

'Athene places her gifts before society to do with them what it wills,' said Mrs Brendel, firmly. 'We do not question, or examine; we do not attempt to explain. I will not under any circumstances allow my daughter to be treated as a medical curiosity.'

'Certainly not!' said Mr Conroy, glancing harshly at Dr Hamid for his temerity.

Mrs Tasker looked thoughtful. 'Your daughter does seem very delicate,' she observed. 'Is she quite well?' She leaned forward and stared at Miss Brendel. 'You are not about to faint, are you my dear?'

'Athene is in excellent health,' said Mrs Brendel, although this time the chilly severity of her tone was directed at Mrs Tasker. 'The ladies of our family always appear frail but we often live to be a hundred. Appearances can be most deceptive.'

'Then I am reassured,' said Dr Hamid, quickly. 'I am sorry if I gave any offence, and in recompense I would like to invite you both to partake of the facilities of the steam baths, which are most refreshing and without the dangers that may attend sea bathing in the winter months.' He handed Mrs Brendel a card. 'The ladies' salon is very select and patronised by the best of Brighton society.'

Mrs Brendel looked willing to forgive, although Mina wondered if she would take up the invitation and risk submitting her daughter to the doctor's closer scrutiny.

The evening was completed with less controversial conversation, music, and some more gossamer visions, which from Miss Brendel's description might have been anyone, but which Mr and Mrs Myles were convinced were departed relatives.

'What is that strange tea?' asked Mina, in the cab home. 'It is not China.'

'Camomile,' said Dr Hamid. 'It has many benefits, and is more soothing to the system in the evenings than the usual teas. I often have it myself.'

'Then it is not responsible for Miss Brendel's visions?'

'I very much doubt it.'

'What was your impression of Miss Brendel?'

'She certainly appears frail, but it is hard to say more without an examination. I could not take her pulse or listen to her heart, or look into her throat. But I did not see any of the obvious signs of poison as insinuated by Mr Dawson. She has a youthful constitution, but I do feel that there is something that is holding her back, not allowing her to achieve her best. I don't know what it is, and I would very much like to. However, we must thank Mrs Tasker for alerting Mrs Brendel to the fact that some of her visitors have doubts about the daughter's health and this may make her send for a doctor. I have done all I can.'

'Have you heard from the oculists you have consulted?'

He took a deep breath before replying. 'Some, yes, and their general opinion is that what ails Miss Brendel is not a disease of the eyes but the brain, and her mother ought to send her to an insane asylum for her own safety.'

Mina was shocked, though not entirely surprised. 'Surely that is not what you believe? I seem to recall when I was first examined for scoliosis several doctors told me it was all my own fault, and accused me of standing on one leg or carrying heavy weights on one side, and when I denied it they refused to believe me. Is everyone mad or harming themselves when they have a disease that doctors cannot explain?' Mina found it hard to keep the anger out of her voice.

'Now I hope you exclude me from that accusation,' said Dr Hamid, mildly.

'I do, of course I do, or I would not be attending the baths.' Mina had avoided doctors as soon as she was old enough to follow her own inclinations, and had often been urged by friends to take the vapour bath 'cure' long before she ever met Dr Hamid and finally found in him a man she could trust.

'There might, however, be some hope. I have been told of a Mr Marriott, an oculist who has made a special study of patients who report visions. I will find out where he practises and write to him. But what do *you* think of Miss Brendel?'

'I don't know what to think of her. There is no pattern to her visions. She does not pander to the wishes of her visitors, as she would do if she was simply a deceiver. But that may just be her subtle ways. I do not rule out deliberate deception as an explanation. However, I have only seen her when presented on a stage for admiration, as it were. I am sure the maidservant sees and knows more than any of us will ever know.'

'I doubt that the maid would consent to be interviewed, and Mrs Brendel would never allow it, if that is what you are planning,' said Dr Hamid.

'Oh, I had a quite different plan,' said Mina.

Chapter Fourteen

'This is proving harder than I had imagined,' said Richard at the breakfast table next morning. 'I called on Mr Burrows as you suggested, but while he was very polite he said he has no need for a sketch as there is a very fine portrait in oils of him already which is on display in a gallery, and he is thinking of commissioning an engraving of it. I have seen engravers at work in London and how they do it I really don't know. But while I was speaking to him I was able to note his appearance. I did a drawing of him from memory afterwards, and must hope he will not sue.' He showed Mina a pencil sketch and while she was obliged to admit that it was not of the first quality it did capture quite recognisably the intelligent and dignified features of the new Lord Mayor.

'I think Edward would welcome this for his new journal, and I promise to append some words to explain its significance. And if Mr Burrows has not yet commissioned his engraving you will have the advantage of showing your picture to the public first. Priority is very important, and not everyone will have seen the painting.'

'That is something I suppose,' admitted Richard reluctantly, 'but I receive nothing for it. I was thinking of presenting it to him, but I have been told that he does not have a daughter so there is no advantage in that. So I might as well send it to Edward. That will content him for a day at least, and maybe he will send me a few pennies out of charity.' Richard, digging into a large platter of eggs and bacon, gave Mina a piteous look, but if he was trying to resemble a needy orphan he failed.

'I may have good news for you,' said Mina, briskly, 'I have found a marvellous subject for a sketch, and the work would be both profitable and a diversion, as well as useful to me.'

Richard was alerted at once. 'Oh, Mina my dear, you are up to something, I can tell!'

'I won't deny it,' she said, and described her visit to the Brendels, emphasising the fact that the mother was ambitious for a place in society. 'Miss Brendel has very unusual gifts, but I cannot establish how they have come about; whether she is genuine or feigning or if they are caused by some disturbance in her system. There is something very strange about that household and I would like to know what it is, but it is something I would never, as a guest, be permitted to see. If, however, you were to gain a commission to sketch Miss Brendel, offering to publish her portrait in a fashionable magazine, you would be very well placed to observe her.'

'Is she young, pretty and rich?' demanded Richard.

'She is all three.'

'Then I will call on her immediately!' He began disposing of the bacon and eggs at speed.

Mina held up a warning hand. 'It might be as well to wait a short while. If you were to reveal that you are as yet a humble clerk, even one connected to the Scarletti family, you might be suspected of being a fortune hunter and be shown the door by the Brendels' solicitor Mr Quinley, who acts as their protector. There is a poor young gentleman, a Mr Dawson, who admires the lady and wishes to court her, and he has been refused admission to the house for precisely that reason. What you need is proper business credentials. Leave that to me. I will write to request a letter of introduction.'

Richard, never cheered by the prospect of having to wait for anything, grunted with disappointment and helped himself to toast and coffee. 'If I must. Of course, if this Quinley is a suspicious type who thinks the worst of everyone, he will think I am your spy. Which, of course, I am.'

'That is a good point. It would not do to call yourself Richard Scarletti, or you would be most unlikely to learn any secrets. Very well, I will ask for the letter in the name of Richard Henry,' said Mina, Henry being the name of their late father as well as Richard's middle name. 'And it had best not be on Scarletti company notepaper.'

Mina found that her brother had finished the coffee and rang for more. 'It might take a while,' said Richard. 'Rose is cleaning a wine stain out of my coat. She's a good girl.'

'Edward's coat,' Mina reminded him.

Richard shrugged. 'He'll get it back. So, what am I expected to do apart from sketching the lady? Do I have to marry her? I am sure I could win her over. What of the mother? Married or widow?'

'Married,' said Mina, unsure how much of a difference that made to Richard. 'But you are not required to woo anyone. In fact, I absolutely forbid it.'

'Not even a little?' he pleaded.

'Not at all. You are going there to get information. I have a feeling that the Brendels' maid, Jessie, might know something, but I have not had the opportunity of speaking to her alone. You might do better. In fact, I would like to discover a great deal more about the Brendels. If they are as rich as they claim, then surely your editor, the lady who knows everybody of note, might be able to tell us all about them.'

'Yes, Mrs Caldecott, the fount of all society wisdom,' said Richard. 'After all, we know almost nothing of Mr Brendel, in fact, since no-one in Brighton has ever seen him, we do not know for certain if there *is* a Mr Brendel, or even if there ever was a Mr Brendel. We only know that there is a Miss Brendel, and that could mean anything at all.'

Mina duly wrote to her late father's former business partner, Mr Greville, who managed all her publications at the Scarletti publishing house, asking him to supply the required letter for Richard, mentioning that a Mrs and Miss Brendel had created a stir in Brighton society and might well consent to him drawing the eligible maiden for the company's new journal. She added that any information that Mrs Caldecott could provide about the Brendel family might well prove to be the deciding factor in her brother gaining this important commission.

For Mina, the warmest and most deliciously comfortable place in Brighton was Dr Hamid's baths, where she could exist for a blissful hour enveloped in scented vapour, with fragrant herbs easing her lungs. When this was done, hot towels continued to soothe her aches, as she lay on a softly draped table, while Anna Hamid applied the Indian medicated 'shampoo' or 'massage' as it was also called. In the months that Mina had been attending the baths, Anna's skilled hands had learned every twist and knot of strained muscle, as it fought against Mina's distorted spine, which tilted her ribs and hip. Anna also noticed changes from week to week, and it was always apparent to her when Mina's mind was troubled.

'I see your brother is visiting again,' she commented.

Mina smiled. 'Is it so obvious?'

'There is a kind of strain that crosses your shoulders when he is about. He is a good soul, but with an instinct that leads him astray.'

'At least his current activities seem not to have involved him in impropriety or crime. As far as I know, that is. It's the part I don't know about that worries me.'

'I understand from my brother that you have been dabbling in the spirits again,' Anna continued, her skilled fingers giving the impression that she was endowed with more than the usual number of hands. Her quiet almost unemotional tone was nevertheless insufficient to conceal her disapproval.

'I am not seeking to expose a fraud, since the lady concerned asks for no payment. I am making enquiries simply to satisfy the curiosity of some acquaintances. I didn't mean to draw Dr Hamid into that aspect of the Brendels' séances, but there are medical concerns, one of which I know he finds especially pertinent, since it relates to symptoms reported by some of his patients. But, I have to admit it, Miss Brendel is very interesting and I am not at all sure what she might do next. Have Mrs Brendel and her daughter attended the baths? Your brother gave them his card, but I rather think they will not come.'

'He has described them to me, and I can only agree.'

'Do you happen to recall a Mrs Honeyacre? Her husband has visited the Brendels. The lady passed away some five years ago, but she was a patient here for a while.'

Anna anointed her hands with fresh, warm oil and her fingers explored the hollow under Mina's shoulder blades, working on the protesting muscles there. 'I do recall her. She was suffering from a painful illness, which could not be cured, only relieved. I did what I could for her. She was very courageous; she knew what the future held. I remember her husband, too, he was very kind and attentive. Nothing was too much trouble for him. Her only fear was that he would be lonely once she was gone.'

'They had no family?'

'I believe not.'

'A Mrs Myles is not a patient of yours, is she?'

'I don't know the name. Is she another of Miss Brendel's adherents?'

'She is, and her husband, too. Then there is a Mrs Tasker and her son.'

'Ah, yes. Mrs Tasker comes here often and speaks of nothing but her son to all who will listen and many who prefer not to. He is her only child and she says he is a great trial to her, although her devotion to him is absolute.'

'He is a skilled pianist, that much I know.'

'Mrs Tasker acknowledges this, and says it is a worthy accomplishment, but she feels a man of twenty-five should have another interest in life and he does not. He prefers objects to people and music to everything else. His one desire is to learn by heart every piece of piano music ever written and he is apparently a fair way to achieving this.' Anna transferred her attention to the long muscles on either side of Mina's suffering spine, curved and stretched and pulled out of all reasonable shape.

'I think Mrs Tasker may be hoping her son will marry Miss Brendel, as they have a fondness for music in common, but having observed him, I think all his desires are directed towards the piano.'

Anna gave the smallest sigh of regret. 'One cannot command inclination in another, or even in oneself. But that will not stop mothers from trying to do so in their children.'

Mina did not think she had any inclinations, or if she had, she had so stifled them that they never troubled her. Were these feelings really so hard to control? She thought of Enid and her unwisely precipitate marriage and the illicit passion that had been aroused by Mr Arthur Wallace Hope, and wondered just how much her sister really was to blame.

Later that day, seated at her writing desk, Mina tried to write a sympathetic letter to Enid, but no matter how hard she tried, she could not find any words which her beleaguered sister would not interpret as a cruel reminder of her own unhappiness.

Dear Edward,

I hope this finds you in good health. Poor Mother, she must be sorely tried. I would come to offer some assistance but Mother believes that the London air would do me no good and I think she may be right. Please let Enid know that I wish her well and think of her and her dear boys every day.

I believe I may have found some suitable subjects for Richard to draw, and you may expect some sketches from him soon.

I send my regards to Miss Hooper, and look forward to knowing her better.

Fondest love,
Mina

Chapter Fifteen

Mina was eager to discuss her recent visit to Miss Brendel with Nellie and a note soon brought that lady to Montpelier Road, riding up in her smart little carriage that was hardly large enough to contain both her and her new winter ensemble.

Had Mina been anticipating a visit from any of her mother's friends, there would have been a thick sponge cake and custard tarts to eat. Dr Hamid and Anna preferred sandwiches, buns and almond biscuits. Mina had nothing to tempt Nellie's appetite that she herself could not obtain at home or in the gilded teashops she frequented, and cook, while a capable hand with short paste and pound cake, would have been highly surprised to be asked to bake French fancies. Mina therefore ordered only tea, and sent Rose to the best pastry-cook's to purchase a tray of those delicate little sweetmeats that Nellie loved so much.

What Mina always had in store, which she knew would draw Nellie to her fireside, was the promise of interesting conversation, and the ladies settled down in the warm bright parlour to a fragrant brew, tempting confectionary and appetising gossip.

'I am fascinated to know the reason for your visit to Miss Brendel,' said Nellie. 'Mine must have been very clear to you, but I am sure you did not wish to consult the lady and her imaginary ghosts. Is this another of your adventures? I do hope so! You know I will assist if I can.' She bit into a crisp iced biscuit the size of a penny, topped with a sugared violet.

Mina did habitually take Nellie into her confidence as to her activities, however on this occasion she felt obliged to adhere to the promise she had made to George Fernwood and Miss Clifton. She sipped her tea and chose her words carefully. 'Miss Brendel has been described in the newspapers as a gifted spiritualist, and friends have also mentioned her to me. I went there to observe her and judge for myself if her claims are genuine. Dr Hamid attended out of professional curiosity. But given what took place, it was beyond both our abilities to come to any definite conclusion. I was very pleased to see you there as I always value your opinions on these subjects.'

Nellie smiled and pressed a napkin to her lips. 'I observed her most carefully, too. I may be a respectable wife nowadays, but the theatre is in my blood and always will be. My opinion is that if Miss Brendel hopes to commence a career as a stage illusionist she would be best advised not to think of it. She has nothing to offer beyond her face, figure and manners, and that is not sufficient. She has no skills that I could detect. There was nothing to draw the eye; nothing to deceive the eye. We are simply asked to believe that she sees the visions she describes. The entire performance is dependent on an atmosphere of expectation in which the guests are receptive to anything she says, interpreting her visions as best suits them. Of course, with many people, that will be highly effective. But it is a parlour game, not a profession.'

'I was surprised that they seemed perfectly happy enough to admit me, despite knowing that I have exposed frauds in the past. In fact, they welcomed me, and decried the cheats and charlatans.'

'That was most probably because they knew that there was nothing for you to question, no conjuring, no trickery. And since they make no charge, they can never be accused of taking money under false pretences, so they cannot be prosecuted. And there is more, perhaps,' Nellie added thoughtfully. 'Your very presence there, the fact that you have exposed others but cannot expose them is something that they can make use of. They gain from it; it is a mark of approval which will weigh with the public they hope to attract.' Nellie's tone suggested that for her, that was the final word required on the matter. She selected a glazed almond and nibbled at it, her white teeth crunching through the coating.

Mina considered these comments, especially the uncomfortable conclusion that her interest had only enhanced the fame of the medium. 'You are right. Miss Brendel is safe from criticism because she does not employ illusions or sleight of hand. But what I cannot determine on the basis of my visits, because I have been to see her on a previous occasion, too, is whether she genuinely sees apparitions, is a deliberate deceiver, or is simply deluded.'

Nellie paused in surprise, her teacup halfway to her lips. 'Is that of importance to you? In the past you have only concerned yourself with dissemblers who extorted money. Miss Brendel provides an unusual evening's diversion at no charge. Yet you have made two visits to her. Why so?'

Mina could see how strange that must look and thought quickly. 'It is true that she may ask for nothing now, but she might do so in future, once she has a great assembly of the faithful.'

Nellie did not appear convinced by that argument. 'Yet the family is reputed to be wealthy. Surely she has no need? Unless the father is mean with his allowance.'

Mina decided not to comment on that point, as it would show she knew more than she might be expected to.

'As to whether or not she is a cheat,' Nellie continued, 'she might not know it herself. Even those who start out as blatant deceivers can come in time to believe their own lies.' Nellie's fingers hovered over the tray of delicacies once more, but withdrew without making a selection. 'They are so tempting, but I must be prudent. Have you considered that Miss Brendel might do more good than harm? She gives comfort to the bereaved.'

'But no real answers to those who seek them. There are a Mr and Mrs Myles, for example, they are hoping for something, but I don't know precisely what it is. They seem to grasp at anything that might have some meaning for them, but they take no comfort from it. And when I was there before, a Mr Honeyacre received nothing of any note and did not call again.'

'The mind is a strange thing. It denies the truth, deceives the eyes. If it did not, there would be no magicians. Perhaps Mr Honeyacre did receive something but you were unaware of it. Something that only he could recognise, because it was already there, waiting for him.'

Mina was thoughtful. 'Are you saying that people look for answers when they already know them? But the answers are hidden from them in some way, and just need to emerge?'

'Possibly. If people receive answers to their questions after consulting with Miss Brendel, and if her visions have no existence in reality, then there is only one place those answers could be. They lie within the questioner, and are brought out when Miss Brendel quite unwittingly helps her visitors to concentrate their minds. A magician often asks his audience to direct their thoughts and attention in a particular way. Of course, it is the way that suits the illusion. But people can deceive themselves quite well without the need for a conjuror, and all it needs is for them to engage their minds in the right way to reveal the truth.'

'So, even if Miss Brendel is deluding herself, she can still help people, but not in the way she imagines.' Mina finished her tea and poured another cup for them both. 'Do you know anything of a Mr Castlehouse? He too has been mentioned in the newspapers, and I am thinking of visiting him. He persuades the spirits to write on slates for him.'

'What, with ghostly glowing hands?' said Nellie with a teasing laugh.

'I'm not sure. It would be a sight to see, even if he did charge a shilling for it.'

'You must watch him carefully and then tell me everything about him.'

'Have you ever seen a slate-writer at work?'

'No, but I have heard about them. Their tricks are not very mysterious to those who know what to look for. In fact, many conjurors do something very similar, as part of a performance in which they ask someone to think of an object and the words appear on a slate. They do not, however, pretend to be receiving messages from the deceased.'

'Then these slate-writing mediums are all charlatans?'

'So I have been told. Even the most famous of them have been caught cheating.'

Mina had no great objection to someone providing an evening's diversion for a shilling, and would not on that account have devoted herself to the exposure of Mr Castlehouse, but she had agreed to see him and provide her opinion to Mr Fernwood and Miss Clifton. There was always, she reminded herself, the possibility that the slate-writer was secretly demanding much larger sums from the vulnerable for private sittings, and if he was, then the young couple might well be in a position to advise her if this was taking place.

'If you like we can go to see him together, you and I,' said Nellie. 'But not quite yet as I have a scheme in mind to help

Richard's new career, and that is engaging all my energies.' She succumbed to another glazed almond.

'I hope you succeed. He talks incessantly about drawing and how it will gain him fame and fortune, but so far he has done very little actual work. That is always the way with him, as you know. At least this scheme will not place him in the bankruptcy court, or prison, or even worse — disappoint Mother.'

'I will tell you my grand plan. I will host a *salon*, to which I will invite Richard, and yourself, of course, and as many people as I can muster to view his work. He did a sketch of me recently and while I am no great expert on art, I did think that he has ability.'

'I would like to see that.'

Nellie's smile told Mina that the drawing in question was not for public display. 'I have been buying paintings for my new home from Mr Dorry's gallery in town, so I am hoping that he will come to my *salon* and bring some of his customers, too. If he likes Richard's work he might even purchase a sketch or two. He is known for encouraging young talented artists. I am sure that I can persuade him at the very least to exhibit some of Richard's drawings at the gallery, where they may well attract attention. Also, an old friend of mine is coming to stay in Brighton soon, Miss Kitty Betts. She has a season at the music hall in New Road where she will perform as Princess Kirabampu, the only lady contortionist in the world.'

Mina knew better than to ask if this claim was true.

'She would be a wonderful subject for a portrait,' Nellie continued. 'Kitty's performance, I promise you, is the height of elegance, grace and good taste, delighting the gentlemen without shocking the ladies. What is not permissible in an Englishwoman may be tolerated and even admired in a foreigner, especially if she is from the Far East and knows no better. I have thought it would be an interesting novelty if I were to place an easel in the drawing room and have Richard sketch Kitty as we watch. She would be fully dressed, of course, and I would make her promise not to place her feet behind her ears, as the company might find it alarming. Oh, do say you will come.'

'I would be delighted. I ought to mention that Richard now draws under the name Richard Henry, not Scarletti.'

'So he has informed me.' Nellie leaned forward and pressed Mina's hand, confidingly. 'Mina, my dear, I can guess that there is something you cannot tell me, and I am sure that you must have the best of reasons for it. I am not offended. We all have our secrets, and many of them should remain so.'

While accepting that Miss Brendel and her mysterious visions could benefit those visitors who were looking for general comfort or whose answers were locked within, Mina wondered if was possible for her to help in the very peculiar circumstances of Mr Fernwood and Miss Clifton. At first glance it seemed she could not, which meant that Mina should advise them not to continue their visits. But, she reminded herself, both those individuals had been in the house at the time of Thomas Fernwood's murder. As children they had naturally been shielded from sights of suffering and death, but it was possible that either or both held a memory of some apparently trivial incident that seemed to have no bearing on the tragedy and was therefore long forgotten, but which was in actuality, the vital clue needed to reveal what had occurred.

Mina reflected that chance comments or circumstances could sometimes bring to the forefront of her mind events from long ago, that she had not thought of since they happened. There was no reason to suppose that she was unique in that respect. Perhaps further visits to Miss Brendel by Mr Fernwood and Miss Clifton might lead them to the truth.

Mina decided to write to George Fernwood, and to word her letter very carefully. She wanted to encourage him to continue visiting Miss Brendel, but without putting into his mind any expectation of what might be achieved by it that might add false colour to any recollection.

Dear Mr Fernwood,

I do hope your visit to Lincoln is productive, and look forward to hearing from you further.

I have paid a second visit to Miss Brendel, which was conducted in the same way as the one you attended. In view of the fact that Miss Brendel does not produce any apparitions or sounds that her visitors can detect, it is not possible for me to determine whether or not she has genuine abilities. On the other hand, I cannot, on the evidence of what I have seen, declare her to be a fraud. I therefore suggest that you continue to attend her demonstrations as long as you feel there is the possibility of some benefit.

Yours faithfully,
M. Scarletti

Chapter Sixteen

Dear Mina,

Thank you for your recent letter. As you requested I assured Enid of your concern for her welfare. She received this information entirely in the manner that you might imagine, and she and Mother quarrelled over it. I am not sure which one of us was deemed to be more to blame.

I have now completed my examination of Mr Inskip's papers; several days of painstaking work for which I cannot expect to be thanked. Mother and Enid are impossible to talk to on the subject, so I must address my findings to you, as you appear to be the only other sensible person in this family. What Agatha must think of us! My darling girl is a saint!

I have very little to report for my efforts. I have found notes of Inskip's travel plans, although whether he actually followed those plans or was diverted from them by circumstances is, of course, unknown. My only useful discovery is that since travel in that dreadful part of the world is so primitive, there are not multitudes of different routes or means of conveyance for me to investigate.

If Inskip's last letter from Carpathia is anything to go by he had intended to depart for home in the first week of October, the weather in the mountain regions being so very inclement in the winter months, something he wished to avoid. His journey home would undoubtedly have commenced by coach, obliging him to follow some very indifferent roads. He would have been entirely at the mercy of the climate, the horses, the drivers, the vehicle and the terrain, none of which inspire me with any confidence. I have no means of knowing the prevalence of accidents in that region, but I would not be surprised if they were frequent. Gangs of robbers composed of desperate cutthroats are far from unknown. If all these dangers can be avoided, it would take the coach two days to traverse the mountain pass, and reach a civilised town from where it would be possible to catch a train.

Even the worst locomotive would reach the coast of France in four days from where he would have boarded the next steamer. He should, therefore, have been home in little more than a week. Inskip was usually meticulous about advising family and colleagues of the progress of his journeys, and would surely have sent a telegram on the way. The fact that none has been received is a great cause for concern.

I have written to the telegraph, railway and steamer companies to discover if there is any news. I have also written to the Carpathian count, but even if my letter were to reach him I would not expect a reply for at least two weeks.

On other matters, I have received a sketch from Richard, which might well do for the Journal. The accompanying notes, I judge from the spelling, must have been written by you. Please don't indulge him too much. He has not returned my coat and hat, and I dread to think what state they will be in when I next see them.

Affect'ly,
Edward

In the same post was an invitation to Nellie's select *salon* for lovers of fine art.

Richard, finding himself obliged to produce some work to display at that occasion, had retired to his room with a plateful of boiled eggs and buttered muffins, and a pot of coffee. Mina found him sitting at his desk, hunched over a sketchbook with a pencil grasped in his fist, his face contorted in an expression of agony. As she entered he quickly flipped the cover of the book to close it so she could not see what he was drawing.

'It isn't finished yet,' he said. 'And I don't know if it ever will be. It's not just about eyes and nose and mouth and the shape of the head, it's about — oh, I don't know — something else. Whatever it is, I don't think I can do it.' He clutched distractedly at his hair until uncombed curls threatened to stand up straight from his scalp.

'Perhaps all you need is practice,' said Mina. 'I am sure the best artists doubted themselves from time to time.' She showed him the invitation, and he looked at it despondently. 'It is very kind of Nellie to host a *salon* to show off your work.'

'Yes, and she is a darling girl, but I am to have at least six pictures done beforehand. Why has it all become so dashed hard? It was jolly fun when I used to do little drawings in the office.'

'That was because you were drawing instead of working. Now the drawing *is* work. But do your best and you may find a patron yet.'

Richard did not look hopeful, and Mina, although offering words of encouragement, did not anticipate any great success from this new venture. She saw Edward's coat and hat draped across the bed, liberally spattered with mud. Leaving Richard to his labours she told Rose to send up another pot of coffee and rescue the garments from disaster.

Chapter Seventeen

Mina was looking forward to seeing Nellie's new home, a townhouse not far from the Marine Parade, which must have cost her husband a small fortune to purchase and another one to furnish. Mr Jordan, when a single man, had been content to conserve his pennies by residing in an apartment above the fashionable emporium he commanded, attended by just one servant, but soon after the wedding he was informed by his lovely bride that this would no longer do. His married life, in which he was able to display Nellie as a great prize to the envy of half of Brighton, also involved acceding to her every wish, and he seemed to be content with that arrangement.

Mina's home was run by Rose and the cook, with regular visits from a charlady, all supervised by Mina, and this was sufficient for their needs. Since her marriage, Nellie had found that it was impossible to do without a general maid, a lady's maid, a scullery maid, a charlady, a washerwoman, and a cook/housekeeper. Additional servants were to be brought in for the evening *salon* to ensure that her guests were comfortable and had every article of food and drink they required. Mina wondered how many servants Nellie had had to wait on her when, in her former life as assistant to Monsieur Baptiste the conjuror, she had existed in a series of theatrical lodgings, and rather suspected that there had been none.

The pride of Nellie's home, and the space to which all the guests were ushered, was the drawing room in which, at her insistence, every item was brand new. The seating had been carefully selected to ensure that the ladies dresses were not crushed but could be displayed to their full advantage, and while the ornamentation was expensive, there was a quality of restrained luxury, so that the surroundings could not outshine the occupants. It was like a stage, where the curtain, scenery and furniture should never appear more important or eye-catching than the performers.

The paintings that Nellie had chosen to decorate the walls with were bucolic scenes in which hearty sons of the soil gathered harvests while buxom wives stirred puddings for a feast and trees waved in the distance across a vista of golden cornfields. Several of Richard's sketches were on display, and these were exclusively pencil portraits of ladies. One, Mina realised, with some surprise, was of herself. She rarely gave much thought to whether her appearance would please anyone or not, since so few troubled to look beyond her twisted back to appreciate her face, but Richard had brought out the expression in her watchful eyes, the shape of her pretty chin and sweet smile. Had her spine been straight she might have attracted some attention. She realised that it must have been this picture he had hidden so quickly when she had walked into his room. Mina tried to look at her brother's work in an unbiased fashion, and concluded that the portrait of herself was the most successful of his drawings, most probably because he knew the subject and could convey character as well as outward appearance.

The one thing Mina was unable to judge was whether Richard had talent enough to make an appreciable living from his work. As the guests strolled about the room, sipping wine from chilled glasses and nibbling warm savoury tartlets brought to them by footmen bearing silver trays, she noticed a tall and extremely broad gentleman staring at the sketches though an eyeglass with more than the usual degree of curiosity.

'Who is that gentleman?' she asked Nellie, hoping that his interest might result in a sale.

'Ah, that is the famous Mr Dorry, who owns the art gallery in St James's Street where we purchased our paintings. Come, I shall introduce you.'

'Do remember it is a great secret that Richard Henry the artist is really Richard Scarletti. Can Mr Jordan be trusted not to reveal it?'

Mina glanced across to where Nellie's husband stood at the edge of the room, neither mingling nor circulating, but in close conversation with his business partner, the elder Mr Conroy, and casting the occasional hard glance at Richard. For all that they took any notice of the art it might not have been in the room.

'He would not have agreed for Richard's sake but he would never risk offending you,' said Nellie with a smile. She took Mina's arm and led her to where Mr Dorry was still examining one of Richard's sketches. 'Mr Dorry, I would like you to meet Miss Mina Scarletti, my very particular friend.'

The gentleman turned to face them, revealing a physique of substantial dimensions, and a magnificent expanse of floral brocade waistcoat. Such was the volume of his figure that it was hard to determine whether his tailor was more troubled by his height, his width or the extent to which his abdomen preceded the rest of him. His complexion was as florid and pitted as a blood orange, his hair and whiskers abundant, and of a reddish shade like a sunset worked in paint. There was a moment or two before he realised he had to adjust his gaze downwards to take in Mina's tiny form. She recognised the look of uncertainty that appeared on the faces of so many persons on first meeting her, while they decided on the best manner of address. 'It is a great pleasure to make the acquaintance of any friend of Mrs Jordan,' he said at last, in a voice that purred resonantly from his throat.

'I am delighted to meet you,' said Mina. 'I have heard your name mentioned as a great expert in the art world.'

'Oh, what flattery!' he laughed, with a toss of his leonine head. 'But I do have some experience in these things, having bought and sold art for many years.'

'I would be interested to know your opinion of these sketches. I believe they represent friends of Mrs Jordan's.'

'Yes, and Mrs Jordan has directed me to look at them most particularly.' Dorry pursed his lips, his expression less than enthusiastic. 'They are quite good, the artist has some skill, but I am afraid they are not very much out of the common way.'

Nellie had left them, crossing the room to find Richard, and Mina felt pleased that neither had been near enough to hear this less than glowing appreciation. When Nellie returned to Mina, she was leading Richard by the arm. Mr Jordan's eyes flashed darts from the other side of the room at the sight of that touch.

'Mr Dorry,' announced Nellie, 'allow me to introduce Richard Henry, who is the talented hand behind the sketches.'

'I do hope you like my little pictures,' said Richard, with his most engaging smile.

Mr Dorry gazed at Richard. He studied him as he might have done a portrait, and seemed to like what he saw. 'Indeed. Very attractive; very desirable. My compliments to you, sir.'

'Thank you. It is so hard to judge one's own work, but I believe I have some talent in drawing beautiful ladies in a way that will delight them.'

'Ah, yes, beautiful ladies, what gentleman of taste does not admire them!' Dorry took a glass from the tray of a passing footman, raised it in a toast and drained it at a gulp.

'Mrs Jordan has asked me to sketch a friend of hers tonight, so you will be able to see me at work,' Richard continued.

'Oh, that will be a fine treat. I should like to see that very much. But what we have here,' said Dorry, with a sweep of his plump hand to indicate all of Richard's work, 'is the art of the pencil. Oh, don't mistake me, delicacy has its place, but I also like something deeper, more robust. Have you ever worked in oils, Mr Henry?'

'Very little, I'm afraid, I think that sketches are my forte. Would that prevent me advancing in my career?' Richard added anxiously.

Dorry waved aside the slight inconvenience. 'Not necessarily; some of my customers do prefer the refinement of a drawing to the richness of oil. Are you a married man?'

Richard blinked in surprise. 'Um — no, I am not.'

'Betrothed?'

'No. Does that matter?'

Dorry smiled and patted Richard's cheek playfully. 'Oh, it is good. Very good indeed. All the young gentlemen I promote are of the single persuasion. No artist should ever be married; it is too much of a distraction. And then there is the expense!'

'Are artists not very rich men?' asked Richard, innocently.

Mr Dorry permitted himself another laugh. 'Not as a rule. For the most part they suffer the most terrible privations, driven by their art, and expire tragically young in a cold cheerless attic in which there is no food, since they have spent their last shilling in the world on paint.'

'Oh dear!' said Richard, since this was clearly not the future he had in mind.

'But you, sir,' said Dorry, taking Richard warmly by the shoulder and speaking to him as if he was imparting a confidence, 'you may be the exception, if you are able to work quickly, and allow yourself to be guided by me.'

'We are ready for you now,' said Nellie, indicating the easel, sketchbook and pencils that had been brought by a servant. 'And here is your model. I would like to introduce Miss Kitty Betts. Kitty this is Mr Henry, the artist, Mr Dorry who is a great expert in all matters artistic, and my dear friend Miss Scarletti.'

Kitty Betts, also known as Princess Kirabampu, the exotic contortionist, was a lady of about thirty in a scarlet gown. She was not beautiful in any meaning of the term, but possessed a fine figure, and a lively manner that only just stopped short of being dangerously enticing. She greeted all her new acquaintances with friendly eyes and a smile that indicated she could derive excitement and pleasure from almost anything.

'My dearest Nellie, I am overwhelmed with delight! Such surroundings! Such company! And your husband is so handsome and charming! Oh, do show me where I must sit. I can hardly wait!' She approached Richard, tilting her face up to him. 'Mr Henry, may I take your arm? You must advise me how I might best display myself to your eye.'

Richard complied all too willingly and offered his arm, which Kitty, unblushingly, took. A velvet-upholstered armchair had been placed ready, and Kitty settled herself into it like syrup that had just been poured into a sauceboat and was reaching its natural level. She released Richard's arm with a noticeable sigh of reluctance. Mina might have felt a little concerned at this had she not received the impression that Kitty had the ability to make any man feel he was the object of her undivided attention, and Richard was not of any special regard to her other than as an artist. As she might have predicted, once Richard had moved behind the easel, he no longer interested

Kitty, who, now he was not in view, behaved as if he had ceased to exist, and passed her gaze about the room to see what other gentlemen she could charm.

'Miss Scarletti, what a pleasure it is to meet you again so soon,' said a voice beside Mina, as the assembled company gathered in a circle about the artist and his model to watch the process of sketching.

Mina looked around and recognised Mr Honeyacre, who, she quickly recalled, was a collector of art and antiquities. 'Do you have a special interest in art?' he went on.

'I am interested in many things, although on this occasion I have been invited here by Mrs Jordan who is a friend of mine.'

'I am here at the suggestion of Mr Dorry, whose gallery I frequent. He has been offered a display by a new artist, whose work is said to be very interesting.' Mr Honeyacre shook his head in a manner that did not promise well for Richard's future. 'I am sorry to say that the sketches I have seen do not encourage me. But allow me to introduce Miss Macready who is a dear friend.'

Miss Macready was a stern-faced lady in her late fifties, very plainly dressed in a gown of dark green. The plainness was not, Mina thought, a matter of expense, since the material was thick and luxurious, and she concluded that it must be in accordance with the wearer's taste. Miss Macready greeted Mina very formally, with no change in expression.

'Miss Scarletti and I met recently when attending the sitting given by Miss Brendel,' Mr Honeyacre explained.

'But of course,' said Miss Macready, 'your name is known to me from that dreadful affair over Miss Eustace. If ever a woman deserved to be in prison it is that one. You have done a good service to all right-thinking persons.'

'Thank you,' said Mina.

'But what do you think of Miss Brendel? Is she, too, a dreadful fraud? I suspect she is, but Mr Honeyacre thinks she may not be.'

Mina chose her words carefully as this was not the occasion to offend either the gentleman or the lady. 'It is hard for me to tell since she does not produce apparitions or claim to fly through walls. Had she done either I would have had no hesitation in agreeing with you. In fact, she seems to do very little, so little that I am unable to make any judgment. Do you intend to go and see her for yourself?'

'Oh no,' said Miss Macready in a tone of fierce determination. 'I do not wish to attend any occasion in which spirits are invited. The very idea makes me shudder. Either Miss Brendel is a fraud and should be stopped, or she is genuine, and may therefore by chance or ineptitude call up something that should have been left where it was. The dangers cannot be calculated.'

'So, you do believe that the living can communicate with spirits?' asked Mina.

'I am sure we can, but I do not think it is always advisable. I certainly do not approve of tempting fate by meddling with things we do not understand. My mother was a great believer. She was especially devoted to table tipping, which she indulged in whenever she could. It became her passion and made her quite deranged. No table in our house was safe from her. Unfortunately, she believed everything she was told, so was often gravely misled. She gave a great deal of money to people who were later found out to be scoundrels. I would not be at all surprised if the spirits stay away from such people out of sheer disgust. Once all the conjurors have gone then we will look to find a higher, purer art, but not before. My belief is that if the spirits wish to speak to the living then they will do so of their own accord, through dreams and visitations. They do not need to be called up or made to appear.'

'Is it not possible,' said Mr Honeyacre gently, 'that some spirits are not able to reach the living without some assistance, however much they might wish to? Surely that is the task of the medium, to be the channel through which the spirits can convey their messages.'

Miss Macready's attitude failed to soften. 'I cannot say that I am convinced of that.'

'Will you be visiting Miss Brendel again?' Mina asked Mr Honeyacre.

'I rather think that one visit was enough,' snapped Miss Macready, before Honeyacre could reply.

The gentleman looked pained. 'I will not attend another séance, although I would very much like to invite Mrs and Miss Brendel to a supper with myself and Miss Macready at my lodgings.' He glanced at Miss Macready with an expression of earnest appeal, tinged with apprehension. She remained unmoved. 'Miss Brendel is a modest and refined young lady, with the most beautiful manners and there is nothing at all to be afraid of.'

'Is there not?' queried Miss Macready. 'You have told me that the lady is frail, and it may be that the visions are consuming what little strength she has. If that is the case, even if she has so far been a channel for benevolent spirits, her weakness might open the way for a different kind of spirit from another place entirely. If that should occur I wish to be nowhere near it.'

'She does look frail,' agreed Honeyacre, 'and I think her mother may protect her a little too much. She needs to move in society, make new acquaintances, marry.'

'When she is a respectable wife and no longer concerning herself with things she can neither understand nor control, I will sup with her, but not before,' said Miss Macready.

Mr Honeyacre wisely declined to debate the matter with her further, and made an effort to change the subject. 'But look, we have a sketch nearing completion,' he commented brightly, nodding towards the easel.

While they had been talking, Richard's pencil had been at work, and something was taking shape on the paper that might have been a face. It was not promising to be his best work, and he was looking a little flustered at being stared at by so many people. 'How long can it take to draw a picture?' said Miss Macready, severely. 'That young man is far too slow. Can there be anything duller than watching a man draw?' She moved away to where a fresh tray of savouries was awaiting attention and attacked it with relish.

Mina felt more emboldened in her questioning of Mr Honeyacre. 'Do you really believe that Miss Brendel is genuine? Only, you can probably guess why I was there but I was not sure about your reasons. Of course, if it is a matter you find too painful to discuss, you must tell me to mind my own business and you will hear no more of it.'

He smiled. 'Miss Brendel has an unusual gift, and there is no doubt in my mind that she is sincere. As you have observed, Miss Macready is somewhat scathing of the spiritualists who have been working in Brighton of late, and in many cases, with good reason. But she is so blinded by prejudice that she cannot see that lying amongst the dross there is much that is good and pure and holy. Spiritualism is something that I have never previously explored, but in recent years it has come to interest me deeply, and I want to know more. In fact, I mean to make a study of it; a serious study. I want to discuss it with men of learning and assist them in experiments to reach the truth of the matter. Have you read *The Brighton Hauntings* by Mr Arthur Wallace Hope? It is a recent publication. I have just procured a copy and it promises to be very interesting.'

Mina was disturbed by the fact that the noted explorer and seducer of her own sister had sought to record the spiritualistic scandal of the previous autumn in a book that elevated the work of charlatans into a supernatural mystery. Her last meeting with Mr Hope had been a tempestuous one, and he had not come out of it well. 'I will make sure to obtain a copy,' she said.

'I would not take my interest any further, however, without the approval of Miss Macready. I therefore wish to introduce Miss Macready to Miss Brendel so she can see for herself that a medium may be a virtuous individual, and the spirits that appear through her are benevolent.'

'I can see that Miss Macready's opinion is of great importance to you.'

'It is.'

Mina did not say it, but if the rumours were true and Mr Honeyacre wished to marry Miss Macready, then their differences of opinion on spiritualism would be a major obstacle to her accepting his proposal. The supper he planned was of mutual benefit. If Miss Brendel could reassure Miss Macready of the purity of spiritualism, then Mr Honeyacre would achieve his bride and there would be harmony in the marital home. Miss Brendel and her mother would gain Mr Honeyacre's approval, which for them could be a further step into the more elevated areas of Brighton society. However much money the Brendels might have, it would always be tarnished by the dark dirty whiff of the coalmine.

'Until a few years ago,' Mr Honeyacre continued, 'I lived with my dear late wife Eleanor on an estate just outside Brighton, but our home was too small to accommodate my growing art collection, so I purchased a manor house in Ditchling Hollow, meaning to restore it to its former elegance. Eleanor fell in love with the old house, and we looked forward to making it our home. The work had hardly begun when Eleanor fell very ill and despite all the care I could give there was no hope. She suffered very much at the end. She was a good, brave, generous, kind-hearted lady and I will never meet her like again. After she passed away I closed up the house and travelled a great deal. It was only last year that I returned to Sussex. I now live in apartments in Brighton. It was here some months ago that I first met Miss Macready. It is now my intention to complete the work on the manor house and make it my home. My servants are delighted, as they also loved the old house. The cleaning and restoration has already commenced. But I am sorry to say that when I told Miss Macready my intentions she declared very firmly that she will not set foot in it.'

The statement was left hanging in the air for Mina to make of it what she would.

'I think I understand. The purpose of your visit to Miss Brendel was not to consult her as a medium, but to assure yourself that she is a suitable person to convince Miss Macready of your point of view?'

'How perceptive. Yes, it was.'

'You were not anticipating that Miss Brendel would enable you to converse with the spirit of your late wife?'

'No, and she did not.'

'Does Miss Macready fear encountering your wife's spirit at the manor house?'

'If she does, she has not said so. But that can hardly be. A spirit that haunts a house is a troubled soul. Eleanor is at rest and content to await me in heaven, of that I am quite sure.'

'Have you asked Mrs Brendel if she and her daughter will take supper with you?'

'I have and they were delighted to accept. But thus far, Miss Macready has refused to meet them.' A sudden thought struck him. 'But I think I know how I might persuade her. It is clear that she holds you in some esteem. You have exposed the frauds she so despises. If you would be kind enough to join us she might yet agree. Would you be willing to attend?'

'If my evening is free, which it almost certainly will be, and the winter holds off a little more, yes, I would.'

'Then I will make the arrangements.' Mr Honeyacre provided his card and Mina responded with hers.

'There!' announced Richard, standing back from the easel. 'It is complete!'

'Oh bravo!' said Nellie. 'Well done! It is an excellent likeness.'

'Please may I see?' enquired Kitty, although she did not wait for permission but bounced from the chair as if ejected by a spring, and twirled around like a dancer to see the drawing.

Just for one heartfelt moment Mina knew that she would have given up all the little beauty of face she possessed to Kitty just to have her supple spine. She saw at once that this was a foolish and unworthy thought and pushed it away, hoping that it would never emerge to trouble her again.

'It is very fine, I agree,' said Kitty. 'What lady would not wish Mr Henry to draw her so elegantly!' She smiled up at Richard admiringly.

Mr Dorry examined the picture through his glass, but looked less enthusiastic.

Mr Jordan had sidled up, still directing a hard look at Richard. 'What do you think of it?' he asked Dorry. 'I am no judge of art. I leave all that to my wife.'

'Hmm,' said Dorry, thoughtfully. 'It is well enough, but I do not think the artist has fully developed his talent, which may lie in quite another direction.'

'Well, I'm glad I have talent, at least,' said Richard.

'A word in your ear.' Dorry linked his arm comfortably through Richard's and drew him away from the other guests, who crowded around the portrait while Kitty uttered bursts of laughter like the chirping of tiny birds. Mina slipped away after her brother, and was able to lurk nearby unnoticed. 'Tell me,' said Dorry, 'have you ever tried the art of the landscape?'

'What trees and that kind of thing? Well, no, I haven't. I'm not sure I could draw a tree. All those leaves and branches. I don't know why they're so complicated. And grass. That's even worse. Grass must be impossible.'

'What about the sea? It is a very sought after subject in my gallery.'

'Is it? I can't imagine why. I'd much rather look at a pretty lady.'

Mr Dorry handed Richard a business card. 'Why don't you try your hand at it? Just a simple sketch. Put in a ship if you like, and then show it to me.'

Richard took the card but looked dubious.

'Make it a stormy sea so it will be more interesting. Big waves, cloudy sky. A steamer in danger of sinking. Can you do that?'

'I can try, yes.'

Mr Dorry leaned closer to Richard, and spoke so confidingly that Mina was hard put to make out his words. 'I make no bones about it, sir, I am interested in buying sketches of that nature and I think you can draw them. When you have completed your sketch, come and see me at the gallery, and I will show you a book with illustrations of the kind of thing I am looking for. If you can achieve something in a similar style it would be to your advantage.'

'What about my own work? My portraits?'

Mr Dorry chuckled and patted Richard's arm. 'Take it from me, sir, there is no originality in your work; no individual style at all. It is empty. You are a blank paper, which, in the world of art that I inhabit, can be a much better thing.'

Chapter Eighteen

Mina had received a letter from George Fernwood to say that he and Miss Clifton had returned from their brief stay in Lincoln, and an arrangement was soon made for them to visit.

Mina wished she could have discussed Mr Fernwood and Miss Clifton's difficulty with another individual. Had she been allowed to speak freely she would have placed the position before Dr Hamid who could be relied upon for common sense and caution. As she awaited the couple's arrival she was therefore obliged to delve into her own thoughts to consider how best they might solve their dilemma.

There was no doubt that they were an affectionate pair who very much wished to marry, and hoped to welcome children. If they did not succeed in resolving their question, she feared that they might well feel doomed to remain single until such a time as it was impossible for their union to produce offspring. Both were young and the wait would be a long one; a severe test of their devotion. Were they equal to it? Mina thought they were, but it was hardly the preferred solution, and what an unhappy marriage that barren partnership would be.

What were their prospects of success in their quest? Mina examined the possibilities. What if they were unable to find a genuine medium who might help them discover the truth? Mina, though she had never met such a person, would not go so far as to say that this rarity did not exist, but since she had encountered or read about so many frauds, she felt it was far more likely that they would unwittingly fall into the hands of a charlatan who would be able to convince them of his or her genuineness. Here at least, she might be able to assist them.

The next question, however, was whether or not being duped by a skilled fraud was a bad thing. Could such a person, even though unacquainted with their question, provide quite by chance, an answer that might satisfy them? In Mina's experience, spirit messages passed on by charlatans were always soothing and reassuring since this was what their clients wanted to hear. They were especially anxious to reinforce the notion constantly promulgated by adherents of spiritualism that mediums always acted in a pure and devout manner. It was further asserted that anything indelicate or irreligious in a message should be attributed to malevolent spirits masquerading as the deceased. Mina concluded that there was little likelihood of a charlatan providing a message containing an accusation of murder, especially against a named living person who might reasonably object.

Given the ages of Mr Fernwood and Miss Clifton, it would require no great skill for a medium to guess that there was a deceased grandparent. In the absence of any clues, the most probable kind of communication they were likely to receive was something suggesting that their ancestor was content in his life in the spirit. If they could be led to believe that the message was from Thomas Fernwood, it might be all they needed to put an end to their quest and marry with confidence. Under such circumstances, Mina would have no hesitation in advising them to marry. If the spirit was content, she would argue, then it must feel that all its troubles were over and they should likewise be content. She would not say this to them, but she thought that their mutual affection and determination to raise happy carefree children would be sufficient to overcome any unwelcome family tendencies.

Mina found herself obliged to consider next what might occur if they actually succeeded in contacting the unquiet ghost of the murdered man. Supposing the spirit named the person who had killed him; the answer could be either satisfying or devastating. But what if Thomas Fernwood, lying on his bed of pain, had been mistaken? What if he had simply seen someone stirring his tea for some innocent purpose? Had his mind and eyesight been fuddled by the brandy he had consumed, and the pain of his final agonies? One granddaughter, seen through clouded vision might well resemble the other. This raised another question. Did the dead have all the truth revealed to them after they had passed, or were they as ignorant as they had been on earth?

Mina realised that beyond the facts that Thomas Fernwood was authoritative, careful with his money, and over-fond of the brandy bottle, she knew almost nothing about him. Was he a truthful person? Was he motivated by prudence, honour, or malice? And did people, whether good or bad, undergo a change of character after death? Could spirits lie? Might Thomas Fernwood accuse an innocent person from beyond the grave, simply to get some revenge he had long harboured when alive? This quest for the truth was, now she had given it so much thought, a highly dangerous business.

Before the comforting crackle of the parlour fire, Mina once again entertained the young couple to tea. It was very apparent from their demeanour that the journey to their old home had brought them no comfort, no resolution.

'I am sorry to say that our visit was a great disappointment,' said Miss Clifton, sadly. 'I had hoped so much that going to the place where my uncle was born and raised and lived all of his life we might get closer to him. But I felt — nothing. I am certain that if Uncle Thomas was able to speak he would tell us at once what he had tried so hard to impart on his deathbed. I can only conclude that there is some special gift in speaking to those who have passed which neither George nor I possess. How must my poor uncle feel, to be unheard all this time with never the chance to accuse the person responsible for his death, or to absolve us all from blame by admitting that there had been a mistake. If he can look down and see us now, and how the uncertainty mars our chances of happiness, I know he would want to help us if he could. It would be a mercy to him, too, to let him say what he holds hidden, and bring his spirit peace.'

'He cannot be the only person in spirit who is afflicted in such a way,' said Mina. 'We often hear stories of apparitions who cannot rest easy but must haunt the living with unfinished business on earth that must be completed before they can find contentment.'

She decided not to mention that she herself had written several stories with that theme. It was an old device but one that readers never seemed to tire of.

'We visited his grave; we even stood by it and called upon him, but he did not appear to us there,' said Fernwood. 'We went to the house where our family had once lived, and asked the present occupants if they had seen him, or had any communication from a spirit but they said they had not.'

'They may do so in future, of course,' said Mina, feeling only pity for the current tenants, who might not previously have been aware that a murder had been committed in their home. 'What I cannot understand is why, if he is so restless as you believe, he has not spoken before? There have been twenty years of silence on the subject. There is no lack of mediums. Any one might do. Why has he not haunted the perpetrator of the crime to force an admission, either as a spirit or in dreams? In fact, what prevents his spirit from acting as he might have done had he survived the poison? Rather than make his complaint through a medium he could take it to a justice, who would be the proper person to deal with it.'

Fernwood shook his head. 'I cannot fathom how those in spirit can act. They may have ways mysterious to us, their own rules of what they can and cannot do.'

'Perhaps he has left messages with mediums who could not interpret them,' said Miss Clifton. 'And he might well be haunting his murderer. If that person has any conscience at all they will be unable to rest easy at night, but will not dare to reveal what ails them.'

'Can you tell me more about Thomas Fernwood?' Mina asked. 'I have gathered that he had a firm manner, was careful with money, and enjoyed his brandy, but I know very little more about him. Was he loved by his family? Did he treat them well? His son? His daughter in law, his other grandchildren? What about in business? Was he honest? Did he have rivals? Friends?'

George Fernwood and Miss Clifton glanced at each other. 'Most of what we know we learned after he died,' said Fernwood. 'But he and my grandmother spent very little time in each other's company, especially as she was an invalid, and she would not speak against him. Yes, he was strict. He had always been so, even with himself, which was why he owned a successful business. In recent years, however, he had left most of the labour to my parents, and indulged himself more with the brandy bottle. He expected all the family to do his bidding without question and work hard, whether at school, in the house or the shop. He chastised us when he felt it necessary, and I never knew him to be kind. But there are many men like that, and it is hardly a reason to commit murder.'

'He took almost no notice of the girls,' said Miss Clifton. 'We were his blood relations but he regarded us only as servants. I don't think he ever spoke to me other than to give orders. But had he not taken in my mother and brother and myself I don't know what would have happened to us. We were grateful to have somewhere respectable to live and food to eat.'

'Was there no-one he disliked or quarrelled with?'

'Not especially,' said Fernwood. 'Why do you ask?'

'I just feel that I need to know as much as I can so I can judge whatever messages you might receive in a séance. I was wondering about asking another member of your family for any details that could provide enlightenment, but if as you say, everyone is a suspect, that would not be for the best. Have you still not told them of your betrothal?'

'We have not. My grandfather's death is a subject we avoid discussing at all times. Mary and I have explained our absences from the business by saying that we are visiting old friends or finding new suppliers for the shop.'

'Was your grandfather a truthful man? If you do receive messages that you feel confident are from him, how can you be sure that he is telling the truth?'

'Can a spirit lie?' asked Fernwood.

'We don't know. Or he could simply have been mistaken in whatever he saw.'

'Even if he was mistaken in life he would surely know the truth of it now,' said Miss Clifton, confidently.

'And there is another question,' Mina went on. 'We only have one witness, Dr Sperley, to say that your grandfather even suspected that he had been deliberately poisoned, and knew the identity of the culprit. He might have been unable or unwilling to tell anyone else earlier, or perhaps he only realised the truth as he lay dying. But I need to consider if Dr Sperley was telling the truth. Is he trustworthy?'

'Eminently so, I would say,' replied Fernwood, obviously shocked by the question. 'He continued to attend my grandmother up to her death, and I had the opportunity of getting to know him well. I would respect and believe anything he had to say.'

'Oh, but Miss Scarletti is right to question everything,' said Miss Clifton. 'What if Dr Sperley gave my uncle the wrong medicine by mistake after he became ill from the brandy and then invented this story to conceal his error? Even the best of doctors can make mistakes sometimes.'

'I refuse to believe that of him,' said Fernwood, resolutely, 'convenient as it would be to do so. He was an honourable man. Surely he would have admitted a mistake. To invent a story that threw suspicion on the family he had attended for over twenty years! He would not have made us suffer so. No, I am convinced that he spoke the truth.'

Mina knew too well that doctors prized their professional reputations above all else, and it was almost impossible to get them to admit to an error, especially one that had proved fatal to a patient. If Dr Sperley had indeed made a mistake that had killed Thomas Fernwood, and wanted to avoid blame, then the most likely person he would have pointed to was the dead man himself, suggesting perhaps that he had taken something in error that had been left in the sick room to kill vermin.

'I suppose you have had no correspondence with Dr Sperley recently?' said Mina. 'Would you object if I wrote to him?'

'I'm sad to say he passed away six months ago or we would have paid him a visit when we were in Lincoln,' said Fernwood. 'Poor man, he was in decline and his wife nursed him as if he had been a child.' There was a long pause during which a thought hovered in the air that a deceased Dr Sperley might still be capable of providing some information.

'What will you do next?' asked Mina.

'George wishes to continue to visit Miss Brendel in the hope that she can help,' said Miss Clifton, 'but I would like to go and see what Mr Castlehouse can do. Have you been to see him?'

'I have not.'

'He actually receives proper messages written on slates, and that sounds very interesting.'

'I agree. We should arrange to go very soon.'

Mina's study of the newspapers had told her that Mr Castlehouse was a recent arrival in Brighton, where he had taken lodgings. His first advertisements in the *Gazette* were to the effect that he would be holding slate-writing demonstrations at his address once a week. Admission was one shilling per person, payment to be made at the door. There followed another advertisement only two weeks later to the effect that due to the popularity of the demonstrations and the demand for admissions, they would now be held twice a week. Soon afterwards this was increased to five times and to avoid disappointment tickets, which were now priced at two shillings, should be purchased in advance from the larger bookshops. Mina showed a recent advertisement to Miss Clifton who said that she would buy the tickets and call to collect Mina on the following Wednesday.

By this arrangement, none of the attendees would have to give a name, which was all very well for Miss Clifton, however Mina could hardly disguise herself. She would have to take the chance that Mr Castlehouse had not been warned to avoid a lady who was four feet eight inches tall with a twisted spine, who had a reputation for disrupting séances and sending mediums to prison. Even if he had been so warned he might believe himself immune to Mina's observation, either because he thought his art to be true or he had some means of avoiding being detected in fraud. Mina had to remind herself that there was always a chance that Mr Castlehouse might prove to be the genuine article. Nellie had decried all slate-writers as frauds, but she did not know them all.

Chapter Nineteen

Later that day, Richard returned home, shaking rain from the thick tweed of his coat. Rose ran up quickly and took the rumpled garment from him to be brushed, together with the travelling cap that had water dripping from its peak.

'Have you been to see Mr Dorry?' asked Mina, as Richard slumped before the parlour fire, dragging his fingers through the wet curls on his forehead.

'I have, and showed him my drawing of the sea, which he thought promising. He does not intend to buy any of my pictures of ladies, which is a great shame, because I think they are the best of my work, but he showed me some books with pictures in by famous men and asked me to try and copy one. I did, there and then, and he seemed pleased with it, so he has sent me away to do some of my own. They need to be very like, but not exactly like, the ones in the book.'

'How unusual. I always thought artists drew their own favourite subjects unless commissioned for a portrait. Is there much demand for these kinds of pictures?'

'Yes, well, he explained it all to me. There are some artists who are very popular indeed, whatever they draw or paint, and their pictures sell for high prices, only they are dead so there is no more work to come from them, but people still want their work or something as like as makes almost no difference. So, if I can make copies that are "in the style of" as Dorry put it, people will buy them and hang them up and their visitors will be very impressed, and only the buyer will know they are not the real thing.'

'I hope you are not going to make a great mess with paint. Or is it just drawings he wants?'

'Just the drawings for now. Paint is such a bore. But I shall still want to draw pretty ladies — for my own amusement, you understand. I — er — I don't suppose I could borrow a little something from you? Just until I sell a picture or two.'

Mina looked stern. 'I have lent you money before. I am not a bank. In fact, no bank would lend to you on the same principle, that you never pay it back. Doesn't Edward pay you a salary?'

'It's a pittance!' Richard protested. 'No-one could live decently on a clerk's wages! And have you seen the price of pencils? We artists can't use just any kind of pencil, you know.'

'Then I shall buy you a big box of them as a Christmas present.'

Richard took no cheer from the promise, although he brightened when Rose brought hot cocoa and biscuits. She also had a letter for Mina.

Mr Greville was manager of the Scarletti Library of Romance, the division of the publishing house that produced the horror tales written by Mina under the *nom de plume* Robert Neil. He had received far stranger requests from Mina than her recent one for a letter of introduction for Richard under a *nom de crayon*. It was therefore no surprise when she opened the envelope to find that he had readily obliged with a formally composed letter, recommending artist Richard Henry, on notepaper printed with the name of the *Society Journal*. In the covering letter to Mina he did not trouble to ask why the name Scarletti was not to be mentioned. Given her previous activities in investigating psychics, he no doubt thought this to be a superfluous enquiry.

'This is the letter of introduction which we hope will admit you to the presence of the fair Miss Brendel,' said Mina, handing the document to Richard. 'And I have a note here from Mr Greville. He has discussed the Brendels with Mrs Caldecott but all she could tell him is that Mr Aloysius Brendel hails from Yorkshire, and is something in mining. He is of common stock, and chooses not to mix in society, but devotes all his energy to making money, of which he is said to have a great pile. I suggest,' she continued, seeing Richard's eyes light up at the prospect of piles of money, 'that you exercise considerable caution. Start by sending a note to Mrs Brendel, asking her permission to call. If she is the woman I think she is, there should be no difficulty. After that, I leave it to your charm to gain an entry to the house and will pray for some good sense to ensure that you are not ejected. Be polite and respectful, and find out what you can without exciting suspicion as to your real motives.'

'That should be no trouble at all, and with the added pleasure of spending time in the company of a pretty young heiress. To add to my fame I can show them Mr Dorry's business card.'

Richard was looking more cheerful, and hurried away to write the note to the Brendels, and make a start on new drawings for Mr Dorry. It was an unusual level of industry for him, but in both cases there was the prospect of glittering rewards.

The following morning, Richard received a reply from Mrs Brendel, saying how delighted she would be to see a portrait of her daughter gracing the pages of the *Society Journal*, and an appointment was made for him to call. Richard had completed the drawings requested by Mr Dorry, and took them to the gallery. He returned in time for luncheon with more good news.

'He was very pleased indeed with what I have done and has engaged me to draw pictures of the sea at Brighton, which he says is an especially popular subject. In the current climate I shall not have to use my imagination for the storm, and there is an old toy ship of mine that will be shown battling the waves in fine style.'

'What will he pay you for the work?'

'That is to be determined when I deliver the drawings. He has every confidence that they will sell, if not in Brighton, then in London, where he also has a gallery. And would you believe, Edward was delighted with my sketch of Miss Kitty Betts, and has actually sent me some wages. After luncheon I shall go to Jordan and Conroy's and purchase a new cravat the better to impress the Brendels.'

Chapter Twenty

When Mina waited in the ladies' salon at Dr Hamid's baths for her weekly appointment with Anna, she often saw groups of gossips who dropped their voices and spoke very quietly from behind lace-clad fingers, after first glancing in her direction to ensure that she was far enough away not to hear them. Mina had learned to ignore this, as there was hardly anything they might be saying which she had not heard before, often far more offensively worded, and shouted at her in the street by children. She was used to pity and rudeness, and they rolled from her like drops of winter rain leaving no trace.

Recently, however, she had overheard the start of a lively conversation on the subject of Mr Castlehouse, who was thought to be very mysterious, and this was far too interesting to be ignored. One lady had remarked that he was such a funny little man that she could hardly look at him without laughing. She was quickly hushed by her companions who indicated with glances and flickering eyebrows that Mina was in the room. That aspect of the conversation was quickly dropped, but it went on to the effect that the gentleman did produce very convincing spirit messages, and had become all the rage. There followed another glance at Mina and rapid whispers punctuated by giggles, from which she could only gather that the gossips had concluded that she and Mr Castlehouse were deemed by their strangeness to be an ideal match for each other.

There was one lady amongst them, young, with a nervous look like a startled fawn, who, while listening but not contributing to the unkind chatter, had the good grace to feel ashamed of her companions' sly remarks about Mina. Once or twice she glanced at Mina, with an expression of regret, and when their eyes met, her lips moved to say 'I am sorry' and Mina smiled to show that she was not offended.

When Miss Clifton next called on Mina, having purchased the tickets for Mr Castlehouse's séance, it was detectable that the visitor was in a state of breathless anticipation. 'I know that Miss Brendel has achieved great things,' she said, 'and George will continue to see her and be a witness in case she has anything of value to say to us, but since we last spoke I have been making some enquiries about Mr Castlehouse, and all those who have seen him have been *so* impressed.' She gave a little gasp of excitement that was almost a squeal and looked ready to bounce out of her chair like a balloon inflated with the heady gas of optimism. 'I am really very hopeful indeed.'

Mina saw danger signs in the lady's manner and spoke to her calmly and evenly. 'Miss Clifton, might I make an observation?'

'Yes, yes, of course. Please do. You know how much we value your experience in these matters.'

'I recall that at our first meeting Mr Fernwood mentioned that you were once a non-believer in the work of sprit mediums.'

Miss Clifton dismissed the comment with a laugh and a little shrug. 'I know, but that was before I began to look into it properly. I have learned so much more about it and I am sure that if we consult the right person we will have our answer. I have been trying to convince George, but he is too inclined only to believe in what he can actually see.'

Mina was not reassured. 'Then I beg you most earnestly to beware.'

'Oh? Of what must I beware?' said Miss Clifton, startled. 'If you mean false spirits and demons, of course I know they might come, but I am armed by my faith, and will resist them.'

'That is not what I meant. A convert to a cause can be as ardent in its favour as he or she was once against it. Do not allow your natural enthusiasm to mislead you; do not be too willing to believe. We need calm heads and common sense.'

Miss Clifton looked at Mina with reproachful eyes, her antipathy slowly melting into acceptance, her tightly tensed posture settling.

'You are right, of course. But I so much want to believe that either Mr Castlehouse or Miss Brendel, or some other medium who we have not yet seen, will have the answer that we are hoping for. That is why George and I have been so careful to say nothing about our purpose, to say not one word about our dreadful past or even give our real names. But even if Mr Castlehouse can tell us nothing, perhaps he can at least demonstrate that it is possible to communicate with the spirit world. That would be some comfort.'

'Be cautious, that is all I ask. And if Mr Castlehouse should ever approach you privately suggesting a special reading at a high price, you must let me know at once.'

Miss Clifton promised, although it was all too obvious that the prospect of a special private reading interested her, and was not in her estimation the warning sign that it was in Mina's.

It was time to depart and there was a cab ready waiting. There were the usual wrappings to see to, and Rose fussed over Mina like a nursemaid with a delicate child in her care. Both ladies were thankful for a pleasant turn in the weather that had lessened the ferocity of the sea breezes.

Mr Castlehouse's lodgings were in a well-kept family house, near Queens Park, respectable, but too plain and too far from the sea to be fashionable. They approached the door, tickets in hand, and were met by the maid, a tall woman of advanced age and gaunt features who seemed better suited to managing a house of mourning. She studied the tickets, looked piercingly at Mina as if she was a performing animal that ought to be on a chain, and finally ushered them in, with every appearance of reluctance.

They were shown to a spacious and well-lit apartment on the first floor, where rows of chairs had been assembled to seat about twenty persons in close proximity. Many of the chairs were already occupied, and the majority of those in attendance were ladies. Mina was relieved to note that none of her mother's friends were there, having already been alerted to the deceiving ways of mediums by the example of Miss Eustace. One of those present, she noticed was the timid individual she had seen in the ladies' salon at the baths, sitting very quietly alone. Others were more communicative, and a hush of whispered conversation told Mina that many of them had attended these demonstrations before and were anticipating this one with barely repressed eagerness.

At one end of the room and facing the seated gathering, was a sideboard, on which lay a pile of slates of the kind typical of the schoolroom, a dish of coloured chalks, several dusters, a length of cord, a bowl of water and a sponge. In front of it was a table with two side flaps, both down, and three dining chairs of the usual kind.

'Shall we take a look at the slates?' asked Miss Clifton. 'Are we supposed to? Do you think it is allowed?'

'If we were not meant to examine them then they would not have been left out unguarded,' said Mina. 'Let us do so by all means.'

'I feel quite nervous,' Miss Clifton confided. She took Mina's arm. 'Do come with me.' She and Mina went to the sideboard and together they examined the slates, dusters, chalks and sponge, finding nothing unusual. Most of the slates were single sheets in wooden frames, but there were also some of the double folding type, which hinged in the middle and closed like a book. Mina could not be sure if the items were as innocent as they seemed or if there was something she should have noticed but had not. On reflection, however, and recalling what Nellie had said about the conjuror's art, she decided that anything on open display must be innocuous and if there was deception it must lie elsewhere.

The door opened again and admitted the deeply mourning couple who had attended Miss Brendel's séance, Mr and Mrs Myles. As before, they appeared enclosed within themselves, and hardly looked about them as they crept to two empty seats, but in doing so, Mr Myles chanced to notice Mina and nodded in recognition. Mina wondered if the couple, swaddled in grief, had been going to every medium in Brighton, looking for a solace that they had not yet received. Moving as quickly as she could, Mina was able to take the seat by Mrs Myles, and Miss Clifton trotted after her.

'Good evening,' said Mina.

'Oh!' said Mrs Myles, gloomily. 'Yes, yes indeed, I trust it will be.' She crushed a black-edged handkerchief in her hand, and Mina saw she wore a mourning ring, an onyx dome with a lonely seed pearl at its centre like a teardrop.

'Have you attended a sitting with Mr Castlehouse before? This is my first visit.'

'Yes, we have seen him several times.'

'Has he provided messages for you?' asked Miss Clifton, hopefully.

'There have been communications,' said Mrs Myles, although this circumstance seemed not to have brought her any joy. 'Many of them highly evidential.'

'The sittings are not always successful, so you must persevere,' said Mr Myles. 'Sometimes the spirits do not come. The atmosphere can impede them. You might need several visits before you achieve success.'

'Atmosphere?' queried Mina. 'Please do explain.'

'I refer to the weather. It may be cloudy or stormy, and then, I am not sure why, they find it hard to come through. But today has been a little milder and I feel we will be fortunate.'

Miss Clifton opened her mouth to speak again, but Mina quickly shook her head, as a signal to be silent in case she revealed too much. Miss Clifton realised her potential error, nodded and said nothing.

Mr Conroy the younger was next to arrive, and seeing so many places taken, looked about him with a worried expression on his heavy features, and finally secured a seat at the edge of the company.

After a few more minutes during which further visitors filled the room to capacity, the maid entered, looked about to see that all was ready, and withdrew. At last, the door opened to admit Mr Castlehouse. He was a short man, barely five feet in height, which was mainly due to greatly bowed legs that gave him a waddling gait. He was aged about forty, with piercing dark eyes, a full head of glossy black hair, worn rather long, and a luxuriant moustache, very full in the middle and coming to fine waxed points at either end. To compensate for the reduced size of his legs, his arms looked too large for his body, the hands highly expressive with long slender fingers.

He smiled at the assembly, as well he might as they were paying two shillings apiece, and bowed. 'My dear friends,' he announced, in a voice that sang from his chest, 'I am very happy to see that so many of you have returned to me again, and happy too, to greet newcomers. All are welcome. I cannot, of course, promise you what will transpire this evening. That much is in the hands of the almighty —' He made a dramatic gesture to the ceiling — 'and to the spirits he commands. But let us begin.'

Mr Castlehouse now made himself busy, lifting up one of the end flaps of the table, and securing it in place, then drawing up three of the dining chairs. He next picked up a slate from the pile on the sideboard, in a casual manner that suggested it was a chance selection, held it up so all could see it was clean, and turned it about to display the other side. Despite his curious gait there was something tidy, deft and practised in every movement.

'As you see, nothing is written on the slate, but to make quite certain of it, I will ask any person here present to pass a wetted sponge over its surface to ensure that nothing at all is there, no hidden marks, no paint, no pencil. Quite clean. Would anyone like to do so?'

Miss Clifton rose immediately and came forward. Mina was anxious at first in case she gave anything away but reflected that it would be useful to learn her impressions later on. Mr Castlehouse bowed respectfully, and handed over the slate and sponge. Miss Clifton carefully applied the sponge to both sides of the slate, showing by the energy in her shoulder and dexterity of her action that she was no stranger to scouring surfaces, then took it to one of the gas lamps to examine it more closely. 'It is perfectly clean,' she announced, and handed it back to Mr Castlehouse.

'Excellent. You may now return to your seat.' She looked disappointed but complied.

He placed the slate on the edge of the raised flap of the table, then selected a white chalk, broke a small piece from the end of it and dropped it on the surface of the slate. Mina watched, unsure if she was about to see the fragment of chalk move by itself, propelled by a ghostly hand, but was not so rewarded. 'I would like to ask two members of the company to come forward and sit at the table.'

Miss Clifton glanced at Mina as if to suggest that she might like to go, but Mina suspected that if there was any trickery about to take place it was those closest to Mr Castlehouse who might be the most deceived. Mr Myles and another gentleman came forward and, at the medium's invitation, sat facing each other across the table, the seat by the raised flap remaining unoccupied. Both the sitters glanced at the slate but neither appeared to notice anything unusual. Mr Castlehouse now took the third seat nearest to the slate, and requested the gentleman on his left to take hold of his hand. With his right hand, he lifted the slate, and proceeded to slide it carefully under the table as if it was a drawer, keeping it perfectly flat and in contact with the underside as he did so. His thumb remained on the tabletop, although his fingers were now out of sight. 'Gentlemen, I would be obliged if you would both hold the slate with one hand as I am doing, keeping it pressed firmly against the table. There must be no gap between the edges of the slate and the table.' Mr Myles and the other sitter complied, Myles resting his free hand on the tabletop where it could be clearly seen by everyone. 'I am sure we are all agreed that in its current position no human agency can write on the upper surface of the slate.'

Mr Myles nodded emphatically. 'Oh yes, I can attest to that.'

Mr Castlehouse inclined his head with a smile. 'I thank you, sir. If you have a question to ask the spirits, please do so.'

Mr Myles directed an anxious glance at his wife, who was sitting with her head bowed, then turned back to address not Mr Castlehouse, but some more lofty place, his face tilted upwards as if hoping his words would fly through the ceiling and the rooftop, and find the heavenly regions. 'I would like to ask if Jack is happy.'

'That is a good question,' said Mr Castlehouse, approvingly. 'Ladies and gentlemen, you may speak amongst yourselves if you so desire, and we will wait to see what transpires.'

There was a clock on the mantelpiece, a heavy dark timepiece with a loud deep tick like a wooden hammer striking something hollow. Mina knew that in séances things usually did not occur immediately in order to build anticipation amongst the sitters and make them more receptive. She glanced at the clock, which showed some fifteen minutes past the hour and resolved to memorise how long it took before Mr Myles received his answer. As they sat, Mr Castlehouse appeared to tremble a little, and breathe more rapidly, then he grew calm. Time passed, and the sitters began conversing in whispers.

'Is it usual to wait so long?' Mina asked Mrs Myles.

'It is, yes. The spirits must pass through the ether to reach us.'

'I suppose it must be a long way,' said Mina. 'I did not know they were subject to such requirements.'

'There is so much we do not know about the spirit world,' said Mrs Myles, and it was hard to tell from her voice whether she was unhappy at the general state of ignorance or hopeful of finding out more in the near future.

'Why does the slate need to be under the table?'

'The spirits require darkness to perform.'

'Ah. I understand.' Mina was familiar with séances that were conducted in almost complete darkness, affording maximum chances for trickery. Here, where the séance was performed in the light, only the slate was hidden from view. The wooden frame of the slate meant that a space a small fraction of an inch in depth existed between the underside of the table and the writing surface, and that crucial space was in darkness.

Mina glanced at the clock. Ten minutes had passed.

'Shall we see if there is any message?' asked Mr Castlehouse, and with the agreement of Mr Myles and the other gentleman the slate was carefully withdrawn from under the table for inspection. All three gentlemen seated at the table gazed at it, but it was clear from their expressions that it remained clean. Mr Castlehouse asked the second gentleman to fetch the cloth and then employed it to rub the surface.

'Let us try once again,' he said, replacing the tiny chip of chalk, and the process of sliding the slate under the table was repeated with Mr Myles being particularly exhorted to hold it securely against the underside of the table, and think deeply of his question. 'And if there are other questions, from anyone here present, please state them now, speak them aloud, it will encourage the spirits to come.'

'I would like to know if the spirit of my late wife is here,' said the second gentleman, and other voices chimed in.

'Can the spirits advise if I should sell my house?'

'What are you called?'

'Write the name of my mother.'

'Does the sun shine in heaven?'

'What is the name of the last book I read?'

'Is there a message for me?' asked Miss Clifton.

'Let us all think of the spirits of our departed loved ones, that they can be strengthened on their path to us,' said Mr Castlehouse.

The clock ticked, Mr Castlehouse trembled again, and the sitters were now quiet in thought. Everyone was listening. At last, a tiny noise, high and clear, brought gasps of appreciation. It was the sound of scratching, the noise made by chalk moving on a slate. Mrs Myles uttered a sob.

'I swear,' gulped Mr Myles, 'the slate is being held against the wood as firm as firm can be! No human hand can write on it!'

The scratching noise lasted for only a minute then ceased. Everyone waited in case it should come again, but after a few moments, there were three loud taps that made several people start in surprise.

'That is a sign that the message is complete,' said Mr Castlehouse. 'Let us see.'

Once again, the slate was slid out from beneath the table. On its upper surface were two lines of writing. 'Can you read what it says?' he asked, handing the slate to Mr Myles.

'Oh yes, yes I can!' exclaimed Myles, with some emotion. 'It says — "I am in heaven with the angels. I am happy. Jack."' His shoulders shook, and he pressed a handkerchief to his eyes.

Mr Castlehouse, after permitting the other gentleman to see what was there, held up the slate for all the sitters to see, and Mina noticed something surprising. Had the writing been made by a spirit or prepared by the medium in advance, she might have expected it to start either near the top of the slate, or in the middle. If Mr Castlehouse had been able by some manipulation to slide his fingers between the slate and the table and write the words himself with that tiny fragment of chalk, then the lines of writing would have been placed at the edge of the slate nearest his hand, the tops of the letters furthest from him. When Mr Myles was handed the slate by Mr Castlehouse, he would therefore have been obliged to turn it around to read from it. Instead, the writing was at the edge furthest from the medium's hand, with the tops of the letters towards Mr Castlehouse, and Mr Myles had not needed to turn the slate about. Castlehouse, with his thumb in clear sight on the tabletop, could not have stretched even his long slim fingers to reach the far edge of the slate. Had he been able to do so, he would have then been obliged to write upside down, not a simple skill. Either way, any secret writing carried out by Mr Castlehouse would have had to be performed without the other two gentlemen holding the slate noticing that it had been tilted away from the underside of the table to enable the medium to introduce his fingers, or with both of them being in collusion with him. The only other possibility that occurred to Mina was that either Mr Myles or the other gentleman had written on the slate, but to do so they would still have needed to tilt the slate without losing the little crumb of chalk, and write in a sideways style. The only interesting thing about the writing itself, as far as she could observe, was that it was uneven in size, and not keeping to a straight line, as if it had been produced by someone unable to see what he was doing.

'Tell me,' whispered Mina to Mrs Myles, 'is it always the same two gentlemen Mr Castlehouse selects to sit with him?'

'Oh no, it is different persons on each occasion. This is the first time Mr Myles has been chosen.' Mina glanced about the room, but could not imagine that everyone there was a confederate of Mr Castlehouse.

'Thank you, gentlemen,' said Mr Castlehouse. Mr Myles and the second gentleman returned to their seats. Mina thought that if more persons were wanted she would try next, but on

Mr Castlehouse asking for two more, in the time it took her to rise from her seat she was forestalled by Mr Conroy and a stout lady who was so determined that she might have elbowed her aside had she made the attempt.

Mr Castlehouse returned the slate to the table and rubbed it well with a cloth, and then Mr Conroy inspected the surface minutely before it was once again slid underneath. Ten minutes elapsed before the scratching sound made itself known. Mina watched carefully, slipping down in her seat as far as she dared, trying not to make it too obvious that she was attempting to peer underneath the table, but she was not able to deduce anything. After the three taps were heard, Mr Castlehouse withdrew the slate. This time the message for their consideration was 'Heaven is a beautiful place.'

Other messages followed and Mina tried to memorise as many as she could. They were in the nature of 'I cannot advise you now' — 'all good souls go to heaven' — 'be comforted, the future will become clear' — 'there will be a wedding soon' — 'you are looked upon with love' — 'you will know great happiness' — 'I am here,' and finally 'you are blessed by the spirits.'

Mr Conroy and the stout lady returned to their places, and Mr Castlehouse laid aside the slate and took up a set of hinged slates from the sideboard. He placed it on the table, then with a smile, beckoned forward a lady from the company. It was the timid lady, who, after looking about her, and making sure that it was indeed she whom he had chosen, rose and came forward very slowly. She was asked to clean the slates thoroughly with the sponge and dry them with a duster. Mr Castlehouse showed the company that the slates were clean and unmarked, then placed a fragment of chalk on one slate, closed the pair, took a length of cord from the sideboard and tied the closed slates shut. The slates were then placed on the table.

'Please be seated at the table,' he said, ushering the lady to a chair. 'Now, I would like you to place your hand on the slates. Do not remove your hand at any time. There is nothing to be frightened of.' She complied, and he too, laid a hand on the slates. 'I now call upon any spirit here present to write a message if the conditions are favourable.'

There was a pause, but soon the familiar scratching sounded again. The lady jumped with fright, and almost withdrew her hand from the slates, but Mr Castlehouse smiled and encouraged her to keep her hand in place and lean forward to press her ear against the top slate so she could confirm that writing was taking place. As she did so, her eyes opened wide in amazement. 'I feel the movements most distinctly,' she said.

At length the scratching noise stopped and the three taps sounded. Mr Castlehouse withdrew his hand from the slates and asked the lady to untie the cords and open them up for everyone to see. It was a long message this time, not in the untidy scrawl of the previous ones, but neatly written in a bold flowing easily legible hand. 'Please read it aloud,' said Mr Castlehouse.

The lady took the slates. 'The conditions are favourable. I will do my best for you, although at the cost of great effort. There are many persons here present who are mediums but are not aware of it. They have the power within if they could develop it. My advice is take the trouble to sit often and it will come. You must be patient. The result will be great happiness. The power is fading. Good-night.'

Mr Castlehouse rose and faced his audience. 'Ladies and gentlemen, I fear that the spirits have become exhausted by so many communications. That is all we will have tonight, but once their powers have been restored, we shall hear from them again.'

Chapter Twenty-One

A cab was ordered to take Mina home before going on to convey Miss Clifton to the railway station. Miss Clifton, who had been required to keep firm control of her excitement and very nearly succeeded, was now visibly trembling as her emotions threatened to overflow. 'Well? What do you think? Was it not marvellous?'

'I have never seen anything like it,' said Mina, truthfully.

'I am as certain as it is possible to be that no human agency can write on a slate when it is pressed against the underside of the table. I tried very hard to see how it was being done, but all the time the chalk was writing the slate didn't move at all. And Mr Castlehouse didn't move, either. And the double slate tied with a cord was actually lying on the table in plain sight when the spirit wrote on it. If anything had been done by trickery the other ladies and gentlemen who were holding the slates would have noticed.'

'Not necessarily,' said Mina. 'I have seen conjuring performed in front of my eyes which I knew to be conjuring, but I still could not see how it was done.'

'But we were both looking to see if there was any trickery,' said Miss Clifton. 'And from some of the questions that were asked I think we were not the only ones. Yet not one person stood up and accused Mr Castlehouse of cheating. If the slate had been moved or tilted so someone could write on it, would people not have seen?'

'I am not sure,' said Mina. 'But I know I cannot explain what I saw.'

'And I received a very clear message, which gave me great hope for the future!'

'You did?' queried Mina.

'Oh yes, didn't you hear?'

'I — don't know — there were so many. Was there something you might have recognised which I did not perhaps?'

'I was very careful as you advised — I gave no clues. The message said, "there will be a wedding soon," you must recall it.'

'Oh, yes, I think I do. And you are quite sure it was for you?'

'I am sure — I hope it was. Oh dear! Do you think it was for someone else?'

'I too hope that it was for you,' said Mina soothingly. 'Who else could have received the answer with such pleasure? The question we must ask is who wrote it?'

Once she was home, Mina went straight to her writing desk and recorded to the best of her memory, a full account of the events of that evening. When she tried to remember all the questions and answers she realised that it was not possible after the first question to be sure whether the subsequent ones had actually been answered, since the replies were very general and could have applied to more than one question or even to some that had not been asked. It was also apparent that while some of the questions were seriously meant, since they were directed at the spirits of the departed, others seemed to be aimed at no more than testing whether or not an answer could be given on the slate.

Eager to discuss her visit to Mr Castlehouse, Mina wrote to Nellie asking if she could call, and sent Rose out to obtain *macarons* and wafers, offering her the loan of her warm cloak.

Richard, looking handsomer than ever in his new cravat, was abundantly cheerful at supper. 'I have just spent a delightful hour drawing the beauteous maiden, looked upon very sternly all the while by the maid, Jessie, in case an improper syllable should leave my lips. But I shall win her over, have no fear. I think I have half done so already. The girl, however, says almost nothing. She sits staring into a far distant place where saner people cannot, and most probably should not go. The man who wins her hand will live forever on the edge of damnation, and will have to weigh up whether or not the reward is worth it. The mother, who is a far handsomer creature, and has an unforgiving spirit that I can only admire, comes in from time to time, to measure with her eyes the distance that lies between me and her precious jewel of a daughter. At least five feet is the minimum. We must not be able to touch fingertips. If anything is required in the matter of arrangement of the charming model, then Jessie is to carry it out at my direction. There were no refreshments offered, apart from a curious smelling tea which Miss Brendel sipped and the maid declined.'

'Camomile, I believe,' said Mina. 'Dr Hamid has told me it is beneficial. Did you learn anything else?'

'The mother seems very anxious to know about the new *Journal.* She asked me how many society people read it and when her daughter's portrait would appear. I didn't know the answers so I made them up. And she questioned me very closely about Mr Dorry. She wanted to know if he was a wealthy and prominent man in town, and whether he was married. I had to say that he was rich, and very prominent indeed, and almost certainly a bachelor, but my feeling was that he was not the marrying kind of gentleman. But I have not disgraced myself, and I am to call again.'

'Was Mr Quinley there?'

'Yes, he looked in once, and gave me a very hard stare. I think it was a warning. Then he left the room and I heard some discussion in the hallway with Mrs Brendel about some papers that needed to be examined, and they moved away. It was all business and no endearments, but —' he shrugged — 'who can tell?'

Chapter Twenty-Two

Mr Honeyacre had finally prevailed upon Miss Macready to attend a supper with the Brendels, as evidenced by the charming little printed invitation Mina received to join them, accompanied by a notelet expressing his gratitude. After enjoying her weekly steam bath and massage she decided to discuss the forthcoming gathering with Dr Hamid, and found him in his office where he was grateful to find an excuse to put aside his paperwork.

'You are looking very well,' he observed.

'I feel very well,' said Mina. 'Miss Hamid knows how to frighten away the demons that tug at my back.'

He brought two glasses and poured out drinks of the herb and fruit mineral water produced especially for customers of the baths. 'I have not reached any further conclusions concerning Miss Brendel, I am afraid.'

'Ah, but I am hoping to have some new information for you soon.'

As Mina mentioned the supper invitation, which would afford her the opportunity to make a further study of the young medium, Dr Hamid bent his head in concern and folded his arms across his body. 'You are venturing out quite frequently and you know how cold and wet it has been of late. The newspapers have just reported a substantial increase in cases of bronchitis, many of which have proved fatal. See how unwell the Price of Wales has been, and still is.'

Mina nodded meekly. The Prince, a robust man of thirty was dangerously ill with typhoid, a condition that Mina knew she would be unlikely to survive. She could only hope that the sanitary arrangements of Brighton would prevent an outbreak closer to home.

'I must be very firm with you about this,' Dr Hamid continued. 'Take no unnecessary risks. In the daytime, if the weather is mild, a little excursion for fresh air may be beneficial. After sunset, or in inclement weather you must take great care. If you suspect for a moment that anyone at an event you are attending is suffering from a cough or fever or shortness of breath, you must leave at once. Do not breathe in cold air. Do not breathe in infected exhalations.'

Mina could not resist a smile. 'I am permitted to breathe?'

'Please do, for as long as possible.'

He fetched a stethoscope and listened carefully to her lungs, an expression of intense concentration gradually mellowing to relief. 'Well, it all seems sound. Had it not been I would have forbidden you to go out for at least a week. But remember my instructions.'

'I will do my best,' said Mina.

'This gathering at Mr Honeyacre's, what is its purpose? The guest list suggests to me that he has some scheme in mind. A séance, perhaps?'

'Mr Honeyacre has recently taken a keen interest in spiritualism and wishes to pursue a study of it. He is, so I have been led to believe, intending to offer marriage to a Miss Macready, who has grave doubts as to the safety of conjuring spirits. He has been anxious to convince his intended bride of the purity of spiritualism, but the lady has so far been resistant to the idea. So, as you have detected, there is a scheme. He will introduce her to Miss Brendel at a convivial supper, in the hope that this will have the desired effect. But Miss Macready was loath to break bread with Miss Brendel and would not have consented to attend the supper unless I was present.'

'Miss Macready must be a sensible woman. If Mr Honeyacre is fortunate he will be the one persuaded of his foolishness. Very well, I will allow you to go. Write to me afterwards describing the event and also the appearance of Miss Brendel, whose health is, I agree, a matter of concern. And if you feel unwell, send for me at once.'

'Did young Mr Dawson attend the baths?'

'He did, as it was gratis, and I doubt that he will return, but I can report that his lungs have cleared, and he is well again. He is young but does not look after himself properly. He tried to extract information from me concerning Miss Brendel, but I could tell him no more than I told you. Then he begged me to intervene but I said I had done all I could. And finally, would you believe, he asked me to go and see her again and carry a message from him, to be delivered secretly and out of sight of the mother. Of course, I said I would do nothing of the sort. He departed in a very bad state of mind.'

'I hope he will not do anything unwise.'

'He has been unwise enough already. There are no medicines to cure that, I am afraid. I wish there were. I tried to talk sense into him, but I doubt that he listened.'

'Poor young man,' said Mina. 'After the supper I will write to him and reassure him that Miss Brendel is well, but that is all I can do.'

'I do have some good news for you, however. I have today received a letter from Mr Marriott, the oculist, who has confirmed that he has a special interest in the phenomenon of apparitions, and has himself been consulted by several people who have been afflicted in that way. He would be very happy to meet us both and share his knowledge. If you agree I will arrange a meeting at your home.' He wagged a warning finger. 'No more of this unnecessary travelling about!'

Nellie, sipping her preferred China tea in Mina's parlour was eagerly anticipating her account of the visit to Mr Castlehouse. 'Tell me all,' she said. 'Was it a success? Did you receive a visit from chalk-writing spirits?'

Mina described, as well as she could, everything that had occurred, using the notes she had made on the same evening. As she did so she saw how valuable it had been to write everything down so soon afterwards. She did not think she could have recalled as much or so well, without having done so.

'What interested me particularly was that the séance was conducted in the light. However, where the actual effect was taking place, the space between the surface of the slate and the table, or between two slates, was in the dark. I was told, as one so often is, that the spirits needed darkness in order to work, but why that should be was not explained. I was simply expected to accept it, as many do, but, of course, I do not. After all, if the spirits descend from the heavenly regions to write on Mr Castlehouse's slates they must pass through areas of light in order to do so. But I decided not to mention this to Mr Castlehouse, as I don't know how he deals with criticism. If badly, that would have been an end of the demonstration which would have been considered a failure, and then the fault would have been laid at my door.'

'From what you tell me the messages were of a very general nature, and given that there were so many people present each reply could have satisfied more than one of the sitters.'

'I agree,' said Mina. 'The only reply that actually supplied a name was the one given to Mr Myles, and he had already spoken the name aloud, so that was not a great surprise. He received words of comfort, but there was nothing to prove that the reply came from a spirit. But there remains the question of how the writing was done on a slate that was pressed against the table.'

Nellie bit thoughtfully into the crisp edge of a wafer. 'I recall some years ago, when the interest in slate-writing first began, there was a man in London who made a great deal of money from it. Some of his dupes were simply gullible people hoping to find hidden knowledge about the world. Others, I am sorry to say, were grieving for lost relations, and willing to pay him any amount for a message from beyond. Ellison, I believe his name was, and he became very rich. Stage magicians, who never pretend to provide anything other than entertainment, regarded him with distaste. Then a conjuror by the name of Angelo decided to expose Ellison's tricks, and went to a number of his séances incognito. He later wrote an account of his campaign and it was very instructive. The first time he went, he was quite mystified as to how the effect had been brought about, and, as he freely admitted, was very nearly convinced that he had actually seen something marvellous. But he went again, and the second time he began to see just a little of how it was done. He continued his visits, so often that Ellison must have hoped he had a new devotee he could draw into his net, little thinking that he had met more than his match. Each time Angelo went, he was able to observe more, and, finally, not only could he conclude how the illusion was done, but he then taught himself how to reproduce it. He went on to demonstrate the trick to a number of people in a mock séance, and fooled them all, before he revealed to them how it had been achieved. The result was that Ellison fell out of favour and there was even a suggestion that he should be arrested. I think he went abroad; at least he has not been heard of since.'

'I suppose,' said Mina, 'that the difference between a conjuror and a false medium is that a conjuror's audience knows they are being misled and enjoys the spectacle. The medium's audience wants to believe that what they see is real. But what of those people who go to mediums in order to study them to see if they are genuine? There are a few such, and I wish there were more. Some are convinced, others are not, but they all see the same thing.'

'They do see the same thing, but they may not recall the same thing. Some may miss details that others see. Some might even recall seeing something that did not in fact occur.'

Mina refilled the teacups. 'I shall be speaking to an oculist soon and will ask him about that. The eye is such a miraculous thing, how can it be so deceived?'

'Our eyes play tricks on us all the time. We are confident that our eyes tell us the truth, but they are the most easily deceived of all the organs of sensation. Every conjuror knows that. It is how he makes his living.'

'But it is not only the eye, itself. What of the mind that interprets what the eye sees? Can that be fooled?'

'Oh, indeed. Have you never seen a shadow and thought it was the figure of a person?'

Mina nodded. 'Yes, fears and fancy can delude us.'

Nellie selected a *macaron*, tasted it, and smiled. 'The art of the conjuror is to ensure that the audience sees what he wants them to see and does not see what must remain hidden if the illusion is to work. This does not always mean that things are concealed; it may only require that they are misinterpreted. To achieve this, he must lead the onlookers' attention away from what is important and direct it to matters that are not. Events that are seen but appear to be trivial and may even be forgotten by observers may be crucial to the entire proceeding. Now, you told me that you were watching very carefully when you heard the sound of the pencil on the slate.'

'Yes, I think everyone was. Mr Castlehouse's thumb was on the table, and did not move, and Mr Myles and the other gentleman who held the slate seemed quite unable to detect what was happening.'

'That is because nothing *was* happening. I suspect that the sound was produced not by chalk on a slate, but by Mr Castlehouse scratching a fingernail on the table.'

'So, when were the messages written?'

'Angelo, when he exposed Mr Ellison, stated that it was quite possible for messages to be written on a slate without making any sound at all, and without the other man holding it to be aware of it. All it needed was for the medium to make some trembling movements to suggest that some great power was passing through his body, and that would be enough to conceal what he was doing.'

Mina cast her mind back to the event. 'I think Mr Castlehouse did do something of the sort. But not when we heard the sound of writing. Well — the sound we all took to be writing. So, the message was written — when — before the sound?'

'You said that the slate was held under the table for ten minutes without result.'

'Yes, and then he brought it out and showed it to us. It was blank.'

'On both sides?'

Mina paused for thought. 'I assumed so. But now you ask, I am not sure.'

'Half the people there will swear on the bible that they saw both sides blank. Some will say they were only shown the side that was against the table, the side where the piece of chalk was laid, while others remain unsure. I would be willing to wager that you were only shown the side that was uppermost.'

'Are you saying he wrote on the underside? But there was no chalk there. The chalk was between the slate and the table.'

'That was not the chalk he used to write. It is easy enough to conceal a piece of chalk in the fingernail. He might even have a tailor's thimble with a piece of chalk glued to it in his pocket, that he slips on his finger before he places the slate under the table.'

'So,' said Mina, thinking it through. 'He places the slate under the table and writes on the underside. Then, he draws out the slate for the first inspection, and shows us only the blank side?'

'Yes.'

'But when he next withdrew it, the writing was on the upper side. So — he must have turned it over before he replaced it?'

'Yes.'

'Can he do that without anyone noticing?'

'Oh yes, it is easily done if he is dexterous enough.'

'But the writing — and I am sure of this, because I paid particular attention to it — was at the far end of the slate from his hand, a place he could not have reached while his thumb was on the table.'

'Did he perform any action as he took the slate out to look at it the first time?'

'I don't think so. No. Well, he rubbed it with a cloth. Oh! Oh I see. Or at least I didn't see. The cloth was a cover for some action he performed. Now I understand! The use of the cloth seemed to have one purpose but actually it had another. He used it as a cover so he could turn the slate around before he replaced it.'

'Now, I can't prove that is how it was done, but that is my guess. I would not expose the methods of a conjuror, but Mr Ellison denied conjuring and said he received messages from the spirits. What we have discussed is what Angelo said was the method by which Mr Ellison worked his frauds, and he made his conclusions public.'

Mina sipped her tea, thoughtfully. 'I can see now that Mr Castlehouse could have written the short messages himself, but what about the message on the hinged slate? That was a long piece, covering most of the slate. It must have been prepared before, but I examined all the slates very carefully.'

'If you were free to examine them that was quite deliberate. And there would have been nothing unusual about them. Were they all of the same type?'

'Yes, I think so.'

'I am sure they were. He would have had an identical set of slates already prepared, kept hidden, perhaps under his coat, and there are a multitude of ways he could have distracted his audience so as to make the substitution. A skilled man could do it in moments and never be suspected.'

'The other people who attended were convinced he was genuine. Even those who were not sure of him at the start were won over by the end. How could I convince someone that he is a mere conjuror? I am not a magician, or ever likely to be. And if someone receives a message that comforts them, they will be most unwilling to doubt it.'

'Is he demanding large sums, like Ellison?'

'Not as far as I know. Not yet. Two shillings a performance, and he gets as many as he can crowd into his rooms.'

'Would you like to test him?' Nellie smiled mischievously.

'How might I do that?'

'You could try taking along your own slate for him to use. A double slate hinged in the middle is best, as you can then tie it closed with a cord. It must be a type different to the ones Castlehouse uses. It is unlikely that he will have something identical that he can substitute for yours. But all the same, do take the precaution of marking it in some secret way so there is no doubt that it is yours. Place the piece of chalk there yourself, then close and tie it securely. You must do your best to observe it constantly, in fact try not to let go of it even for a moment.'

'Do you think he would agree to this?'

'I think he would. After all, it would not reflect well on him if he refused in front of so many people. He might even see it as an advantage to have you test him in that way, as your attention would then be fastened on your own slates and not on his. If he is the trickster we suspect him to be, then he will obtain results from his own slates, but not with yours, and he will then make some excuse, perhaps claim that the spirits are not active.'

Mina nodded. 'That is a good test, but a believer would accept his explanation.'

'Oh, do not think you can expose him in a single visit. Tell him that you would like to return and bring your own slates once more. He may then decide to trick you. If he asks you to make a second trial, do so. He will in the meantime try to obtain a set of slates that could pass for yours, and if he succeeds, then he will prepare them before the demonstration with a message, and using some means of distracting your attention, substitute his own. But his slates will not have your secret mark, and you can then point this out.' Nellie took another *macaron*. 'Are you prepared to do this?'

178

'I have done far worse. Will you be able to come with me? It would be so much better to have your eye on the proceedings.'

'I should like nothing better, but Mr Jordan and I are going to London for a fortnight where he means to display me to a host of dull men who speak only of profit, and their duller wives who speak of nothing at all, often at great length. I shall miss our conversations.'

'I expect you will miss Richard also,' said Mina with just a hint of potential mischief in her voice.

'He is such delightful company, but I am sorry to say that Mr Jordan cannot abide him, and only permits him in the house when part of a large company so he may safely ignore him without appearing to be openly impolite.'

Mina wondered if Mr Jordan's decision to remove his wife from Brighton and introduce her to London's commercial society had anything to do with Richard's recent appearance. 'I feel you are not happy,' she ventured.

'One does not marry for happiness in this world,' said Nellie. 'And certainly not for love, not of the romantic kind at any rate. Love may grow, even on barren ground, but once it has bloomed it can only fade, and lead to disappointment. Marriage is woman's only real business and she must make a profit from it. I will not always look as I do now, but I must make sure to do so for as long as possible.' She stretched out her hand for another *macaron*, but thought better of it.

Chapter Twenty-Three

That evening Mr Honeyacre had been kind enough to engage a cab and send it to collect Mina so she could be conveyed to his home with the minimum of trouble. He currently lodged in a superior apartment far from the low-lying centre of Brighton and the damp collections of mists that settled there. He favoured the elevated eastern part with its bracing air, although sufficiently distant from the sea to avoid the glare of the winter sun from the steel grey water.

The visitors were entertained in a large drawing room, furnished for peaceful repose, with a substantial fire blazing in a brass-fronted grate that amplified the golden flames. There were armchairs and sofas replete with deep comfortable cushions, and thick-fringed draperies everywhere to prevent draughts. Gas lamps glowed from cut-glass lanterns like so many full moons, and paintings in elaborate frames hung from panelled walls. On the sideboard was a large tureen from which a delicious savoury scent emanated, and there were soup cups and plates piled with thin slices of bread and butter, as well as pies, tarts, salads, roast meats and relishes. A tower of small plates accompanied by dessert forks held the promise of another course.

Mr Honeyacre, with a hopeful smile fastened to his face, greeted his guests as they arrived, while Miss Macready, standing by his side like a monolith, looked on with features of stone.

Mrs Brendel, proudly displaying a new winter ensemble in dark red, remarkably like the blue one that Nellie had worn to the séance, swept into the room like a fighting ship, with her daughter, a reluctant ghost dressed in pale violet, trailing after her. Mina, while not warming to Mrs Brendel's company, could quite see why Richard admired the older woman's energy more than the insipid attractions of Miss Athene.

'Mrs Brendel, Miss Brendel, it is my great honour to introduce you to my dear friend, Miss Macready,' said Mr Honeyacre in a voice that shook just a little.

'Delighted to make your acquaintance!' gushed Mrs Brendel.

'Likewise,' said Miss Macready, but her eyes said something else.

Mr Honeyacre's manservant, Gillespie, a tall fellow, dignified and impeccable, ushered the visitors to seats and placed side tables within convenient reach. 'What a charming apartment!' exclaimed Mrs Brendel, carefully ensuring that her daughter took the place closest to herself. 'How lovely this must be in the summer!'

'Brighton has its charms at any time of the year,' said Mr Honeyacre, 'although I shall not make it my home for much longer, as I plan to live in the country.'

'But I can hardly believe you mean to remove from such a delightful location.'

'Oh, I shall still frequent the coast and enjoy the sea air, the galleries, museums and concerts, that is for certain, but I am determined to open up my manor house in Ditchling Hollow, which is not far from town, and entertain there. It has lain empty for too long.'

'A manor house?' Mrs Brendel could hardly have appeared more pleased if it had been hers. 'But is it entirely closed up at present?'

'No, my housekeeper and her husband live in the servants' quarters and look after the house and grounds for me, or it would undoubtedly have fallen into dangerous disrepair. When

I told them of my intention to return they were delighted. The entire property is now being cleaned and restored. I even mean to engage my former cook who has not been entirely happy in her new situation since I went abroad and would be very pleased to come and manage my kitchen again.'

'Is it not a very ancient property?' said Miss Macready. 'I am not sure that such a house can be made entirely comfortable. Are there no horrid draughts, and what of the noise of the wind in chimneys and creaking boards keeping everyone awake at night?'

'I do not recall it being so inhospitable before,' said Mr Honeyacre. 'And I am sure that any defects, if there be such, can be corrected. If you would only agree to view the house I am sure you would see how it can be made very comfortable indeed.'

Miss Macready did not look convinced.

'Perhaps it is haunted?' ventured Mrs Brendel. 'I believe so many of these old houses are.'

'I have never experienced anything to suggest it, and neither have my servants,' said Mr Honeyacre. 'I wonder if Miss Scarletti might venture an opinion. Have you ever seen a ghost?'

'I have not,' said Mina. 'I do not say that I will never see one, only that I have not yet done so.'

'Neither have I,' said Miss Macready, in a voice that would have dismissed a dozen inquisitive ghosts, 'and I have no wish to. I am sorry to say it in this company, but I feel that no good can come of calling up spirits.'

'Ah, but I hope you do not think that my daughter does so?' said Mrs Brendel. 'The spirits come to her, she does not call them and has no means of dismissing them.'

Miss Brendel had been sitting silently in her drift of violet silk, like a drowning woman in a river waiting for her skirts to drag her down. 'I do not call them, I assure you,' she said softly. 'I have often wished them not to come, and when they do, I have asked them to leave me, but they do not, they will go only in their own good time.'

'Well, let us have some delicious soup before it cools,' said Mr Honeyacre, cheerily. 'Gillespie, please serve our guests.'

The manservant ladled the soup deftly into cups and brought it to the guests with a serving of bread and butter. It was a concoction of boiled fowl and leeks, a very grateful drink on a winter's day. Athene took a cup, but her mother, while accepting bread and butter for herself, declined it on her daughter's behalf. There was much appreciative sipping and complimentary comments.

Miss Macready drained her cup, and beckoned Gillespie to serve her a second portion. 'Miss Brendel, I do not mean to insult you, or call into question what you claim, but I must ask you this; how can you be certain that the spirits you see are really who they purport to be?'

Athene allowed the tip of her tongue to savour the last drop of soup on her lips, and put the cup down. 'All I can tell you is that I have never seen anything that has frightened me, and no-one who has attended the evenings has ever felt alarmed or upset.'

'Only benevolent spirits reach out to my dear daughter,' said Mrs Brendel. 'She has been most carefully brought up, and properly instructed in the scriptures. Her likeness will shortly grace the pages of a society journal of the most elevated character!' Mrs Brendel glanced about her as if to imply that neither of the other ladies present had any chance of being so honoured.

'But what I don't understand,' persisted Miss Macready, 'is that some of the spirits are of those who have not yet passed?'

'Yes, sometimes they are,' said Miss Brendel.

'There was that business with poor Mr Hay that was in the newspapers.' Miss Macready turned to Mina. 'He was the unfortunate Scotch gentleman who made away with himself. Now that was a troubled spirit.' She put two thin slices of bread and butter together and ate them as one.

'Did he appear to you before or after he passed away?' asked Mina.

'I — I don't really know,' said Miss Brendel. 'I only know that I saw him.'

Mrs Brendel interrupted in a very determined manner. 'I believe you will find that he appeared before Athene at the very second he passed.' She seemed so confident in this assertion that no-one sought to contradict her, although Mina thought there were any number of reasons to question this statement.

'Well, I only hope we shall have no such things as that tonight!' said Miss Macready.

Once the soup cups were cleared the guests were invited to help themselves from the plates on the sideboard with the deferential assistance of Mr Gillespie. Mina selected a slice of savoury pie and salad, Mrs Brendel served herself with pie, tart and relishes, and placed some slices of lean meat on another dish which she brought to her daughter, and Miss Macready piled a plate high with some of everything. Gillespie, who clearly knew what his master liked, brought him a slice of tart, although he looked too distracted to eat it.

Miss Brendel picked listlessly at the meat with her fork. Her mother spoke to her quietly and gently, but Mina was unable to hear the words, and the room then fell into the soft sounds that people made when trying to eat politely.

Miss Brendel had been staring at her plate, but daring to glance up while lifting some shreds of meat to her mouth, looked sorrowful, paused, and slowly put the fork down, the food untasted. 'I see a lady,' she said faintly.

'You mean — a lady in spirit?' asked Mr Honeyacre, hopefully.

Miss Macready made a sharp intake of breath and placed a hand over her face as if shielding herself from contamination.

'Yes, I am sure she is. She sits peacefully, but she does not move. I'm not sure why that is. I cannot say whether or not she has passed.'

'Where is she?' asked Mina.

Miss Brendel hesitated, and appeared for once curiously unwilling to reveal this information. At last she said, 'She is there, sitting on the sofa beside Mr Honeyacre.'

'Oh!' exclaimed Honeyacre glancing at the empty place at his side. 'Does she speak?'

'No. Her lips do not move, her eyes do not blink, but her form is very clear.'

'Describe her, please, I beg you!'

Miss Brendel laid her plate aside, and studied what no-one else could see. 'The lady has a round face, her hair is grey, and there are little curls at her temples. Still she says nothing, does nothing. There is a cameo brooch at her throat and on her lap a puppy dog. Her hand rests on its back, like so...' Miss Brendel gestured with her fingers, held as if curling affectionately around the cherished animal. 'There is a portrait behind her, not one in this room, but somewhere else. An old portrait, the man wears a ruff and has a pointed beard.'

During this speech Miss Macready's protective hand had gradually dropped to her side, and she stared at Miss Brendel with an expression that combined astonishment with outrage.

'Why, you describe my dear Eleanor and her favourite pet, also a portrait she much admired,' said Mr Honeyacre, joyfully. 'That is marvellous, all the more so because I know you can never have met her, but your description — it can be none other! Are you sure she does not speak?' he continued. 'Is she happy? Is she at peace? Does she smile? What message does she have for me?'

Miss Brendel looked blank, then alarmed. She shook her head as if trying to dislodge an unwelcome thought.

'Oh, but I think I can guess what she is saying,' cried Mr Honeyacre enthusiastically. 'She wishes me well in all my future endeavours, does she not?'

Miss Brendel appeared to be struggling with a conflict between her ideas and what she could see. She looked away from the vision. 'I — don't know. I am not sure.'

'But you must be!' he insisted.

'Mr Honeyacre,' said Mrs Brendel firmly, 'if my daughter cannot hear the message then she cannot hear it.'

'She smiles, though, does she not? Eleanor smiles? Please say she does!'

Mrs Brendel took her daughter's hand and patted it. 'There, my dear. Don't strain yourself. Just rest and take a deep breath and open your eyes so you can see properly. It's a simple question. Does the lady smile, or does she frown?' Was it imagination or did Mina see Mrs Brendel give her daughter's hand a squeeze on the final word.

Miss Brendel stared at her mother. 'She frowns. Yes. She frowns.'

'No! Surely not!' exclaimed Mr Honeyacre. 'It can't be! Eleanor would be happy for me, I know it.'

'Oh, I have heard enough of this!' said Miss Macready, putting aside her plate with a loud bang on the table that made everyone start, and rising to her feet in a fury. 'What is happening here? Is it a play? Is it a pantomime? Perhaps a comedy to be given at the music hall. Will the lady float up into the air? Will the puppy dog do tricks?'

Mr Honeyacre rose quickly from his chair. 'Miss Macready, I am sure nothing is wrong. Miss Brendel, as you see, is sincere.'

'A sincere fraud!' bellowed Miss Macready. 'It is outrageous; I will not be played upon in this way! There has been some confederacy between you, I know it!'

Athene started to weep. 'Please! I don't know anything about it, I only say what I see!'

'Miss Macready, I merely want you to understand that there is no danger in communicating with the world of the spirit,' pleaded Mr Honeyacre.

The lady uttered a derisive laugh. 'If that is indeed what is happening, which I somehow doubt.' She turned to Mina. 'And what of you, Miss Scarletti? What part did you play in all this?'

'None at all,' said Mina, bemused at being suddenly taken to task in that way.

'I am not so sure of that,' Miss Macready hissed with a curl of her lip.

'But my dear —' protested Mr Honeyacre.

Miss Macready rounded on him. 'Enough! I forbid you to address me so! I am appalled and insulted at being treated in this fashion. Do you think I am so foolish as to be taken in by such a sham? I am leaving this house now, and I have no intention of returning. Have your man call me a cab.'

'But —'

'Not another word! Now do as I say, or you will regret it! I am something in Brighton society, as you well know. If I have my way your reputation will not survive this!'

Mr Honeyacre looked defeated. He nodded and signalled to Gillespie, who, without a change in expression, went to fetch Miss Macready's cloak. The lady was gone within minutes, declining to take her leave of the company either by word or gesture.

Mr Honeyacre sat down heavily, silent and shocked, unable even to glance at his other guests. Mrs Brendel stayed beside her distressed daughter, stroking her hands. Miss Brendel turned to her with a tearful face. 'Did I say something wrong?'

'No, my dear, of course not. You cannot help what you see. You are not to blame if the truth is rejected or ill understood.'

Mina was not sure what to do. It was an embarrassing situation but she felt that if she was to learn anything she ought to remain at least until it was suggested the guests should go. Nothing more was said for a time, but whether that was because there was nothing that could properly be said, or Mr Honeyacre and the Brendels did not wish to discuss what had occurred with someone else present, Mina could not decide.

Gillespie returned. 'I secured a cab, and have seen Miss Macready safely on her way. Will there be anything more, sir?'

'It is time we were going,' said Mrs Brendel. 'Athene needs her rest. These events always take so much out of her.'

Mr Honeyacre sighed. 'I am so sorry it has come to this. Of course, Miss Brendel must be our first concern, and I will see that you are both conveyed home at once. Miss Scarletti — I cannot say how upsetting this has been and I am deeply ashamed that you have been obliged to witness it.'

Mina decided not to say that it had been a more than usually interesting evening. 'One can never predict how these things will turn out,' she said.

He gestured to the laden sideboard. 'Please, everyone, select anything you wish to complete your supper. Gillespie will make up a parcel.'

This was soon done, and before long the Brendels and Mina had both departed, sharing a cab since their homes were so close.

Miss Brendel was a mere wraith of herself. She didn't speak, but sat beside her mother, who held her in her arms and rested the girl's head on her shoulder. 'My poor dear,' she said soothingly, 'we will go home and you will have some of your lovely tisane, and then you will rest and you will be as good as new in the morning. That dreadful woman was quite deranged. It wouldn't surprise me if Mr Honeyacre never spoke to her again. And to think it was rumoured that he was intending to marry her. If you ask me, he has had a lucky escape. He is such a very good man, and deserves far better.'

Mina said nothing, but thought back to what Mr Honeyacre had said when he had invited her to supper. His declared intention in introducing Miss Macready to the Brendels was to allay her doubts about spiritualism by showing that a medium could be respectable. Mina was now beginning to think that he had only told her half the story, and had been planning far more than just a sociable encounter. What could not be in doubt was that the evening had, from his point of view, been a disaster. Far from strengthening the attachment to Miss Macready, the debacle had parted him from her, perhaps forever. The question arose whether the turn of fate had occurred by chance, or if, unknown to Mr Honeyacre, it had been engineered by Mrs Brendel.

The motive was all too clear. Although Mr Honeyacre was the oldest of Miss Brendel's single male visitors, he was also the most promising. Young Mr Tasker, for all his interest in music, did not warm to the lady. Mr Conroy had four small children who needed mothering, a task for which Miss Brendel was ill suited. Mr Phipps was not yet something in the world. Dr Hamid was too recently widowed to be seriously thought of. Mr Dawson was ardent but had no fortune. Mr Fernwood's dress marked him indelibly as trade. Mr Honeyacre, however, was wealthy, eager to marry and had no dependents.

There was nothing Mina could do in the face of these frauds and delusions. She could voice her ideas, but there was no proof. She thought it unlikely, when Mr Honeyacre had made his arrangement with Mrs Brendel, that any money had changed hands. The only thing that had changed hands was an envelope, and Mina was beginning to suspect what had been in it.

Chapter Twenty-Four

Next morning, with the breakfast table groaning with Mr Honeyacre's discarded pies and tarts, Mina was surprised to receive a note from Miss Macready asking if she might call. Since Mina's last conversation with this lady had ended with an accusation of deceit, she was not sure what to make of the request except that the interview promised to be more interesting than most. The note revealed that Miss Macready lived in a highly desirable apartment building in Kemp Town, which confirmed Mina's opinion that she was not without means. Mina said nothing about the proposed call to Richard, and decided also not to describe the turbulent end to the supper, saying only that the previous evening had been one of good food and conversation. He was due to sketch Miss Brendel again, and she did not want him to accidentally reveal that he had learned about Mr Honeyacre's private gathering and its outcome, or the Brendels might suspect a connection. Instead she wrote to Dr Hamid saying that she had had a very instructive evening which she would describe when they next met, and replied to Miss Macready saying that she would be delighted to receive her.

After a hearty luncheon in which Richard was able to demolish much of the excess foodstuffs, he departed with the intention of drawing the chain pier and then proceeding to Mr Dorry's gallery.

Miss Macready arrived soon afterwards. She was conducted into the parlour, where Mina greeted her politely, offered her a comfortable chair, faced her with equanimity, and waited to hear what she had to say. It was clear from her expression that

Miss Macready's anger of the previous evening had evaporated very little considering that many hours, a night's sleep and two meals had intervened. Nevertheless, she was calmer and did not look at Mina with the same ferocity.

'I have given a great deal of thought to the events of last night. I recall that in my annoyance, which I am sure you will agree was perfectly natural under the circumstances, I suggested that you might have had a hand in the atrocious deception that was practised on me. You denied it, and I can now inform you that on further consideration, I accept that denial.'

'Thank you,' said Mina, realising that this was the nearest thing to an apology she was likely to hear.

'Of course, your reputation in this town is one of uncovering fraud and deception, not of promoting it. Therefore, it is most improbable that you conspired against me. In fact, your part in the affair has now become clear. You could not have known it, but you were invited there as one who inspires trust, to be a witness to a deception, and to be deceived yourself.'

'I was invited because Mr Honeyacre hoped that you would consent to meet Miss Brendel and he thought you would not do so unless I was present.'

'In that he was correct.'

'He places considerable value on your good opinion. I believe that he hoped to allay your concerns about spiritualism, and so smooth the way to a closer association. What transpired was as much a surprise to him and to me as it was to you.'

'That much was apparent. Well, at least you have not disappointed me. But you have seen this young person's performances before. What do you think of them?'

'I have doubts about Miss Brendel's claims to be a medium, but thus far I have not been able to explain her visions. She may be feigning, of course, but somehow I don't think she is, or her descriptions would have more purpose, and appear to be designed. I think she really is seeing what she says she does, but how that comes about, I can't tell. Perhaps she has some disease of the eye. Usually she sees very clear images of people she knows, such as her father, but there are also vaguer descriptions of others, perhaps people she has just seen in passing. But last night was different. She saw a lady who she was able to describe in considerable detail, such that Mr Honeyacre was able to identify her as his late wife, yet Miss Brendel cannot have met her.'

Miss Macready laughed. It was a grating noise at the back of her throat, with no hint of humour. 'As to that, there is no mystery to me, and I am sure you will be interested to have an explanation. You cannot have failed to notice that the image Miss Brendel claimed to see was of a lady seated in front of a portrait, and not moving or speaking, a lady with a puppy dog in her lap.'

'Yes, and again that was different to her previous visions. She usually sees people walking about, or even if seated they are moving in some way. This was more like —'

'Like she was describing a painting, or a photograph?'

Mina was pleased that the suggestion came from another. She was feeling surer of her conclusion. 'Yes.'

'I do not know whether to be angry with her or offer my sympathy. Personally, I think the mother is the one to blame. What Miss Brendel saw, or claimed to see was not the late Mrs Honeyacre at all, but a portrait of her. It was a *carte de visite* made about two years before her death. I know because I have seen it. She is seated with her pet dog on her lap, in front of a painting. There are a number of these cards in an album. She liked to collect them. I expect Mr Honeyacre forgot that I had looked through the album or did not realise how well I had noted the portrait. Either that or he was not aware that Miss Brendel would describe it in such detail.'

'Then Miss Brendel must have seen the portrait in question.'

'She must, and there is only one reasonable way she could have done so, if Mr Honeyacre himself provided her with a copy.'

'I am sure you are right.'

Miss Macready shook her head with an expression of grim distaste. 'What a dreadful business this is! Not only does he have no understanding of what he is meddling with, but he hopes to draw me into it with fraud and trickery. Outrageous!'

'He may not have seen it as defrauding you, since he sincerely wants you to believe what he himself believes.'

Mina's attempt to soothe the bad feelings between Mr Honeyacre and his intended fell on unsympathetic ears. 'Do not speak for him; he is a scoundrel, a deceiver! He tried to manoeuvre me in a most underhand way. That is an action I shall never forgive. He wants me to condone his dangerous and foolhardy pursuit of spiritualism, something he knows full well I will have no truck with.'

She made a dismissive gesture. 'But let him do as he wants. I care nothing about him anymore. He has been hinting for some while that he will offer me marriage and I had thought I might accept him, but that will not happen now. I am done with Mr Honeyacre. I have more than enough money of my own, and I have no wish to see my fortune turned over to him so he can spend it on mediums conjuring who knows what, and restoring that horrid old ruin of a house in the middle of nowhere. I much prefer to live in Brighton as he is well aware.'

'Have you spoken to him since yesterday evening?'

'No. He has sent me several notes and I have returned them all unopened.'

'Would you like me to speak to him?'

'On my behalf? That is quite unnecessary. I have nothing more to I wish to communicate, and there is nothing I wish to hear from him.'

Mina could see that Miss Macready was the kind of lady who once her mind was thoroughly made up, would not relent, and there was little point in her pleading Mr Honeyacre's case any further.

Her visitor rose to depart. 'I wish you well Miss Scarletti. I shall seek contentment in my own way and not depend on another for it. We may meet again; I would not object to that.'

Soon after Miss Macready's departure a note arrived from Mr Honeyacre requesting Mina's permission to call, to which she replied in the affirmative. He arrived soon afterwards, bearing a posy of hothouse flowers, which he proffered as one might a hopeful addition to an altar. He was miserable and desperately apologetic, with the strained look of a man who had been without sleep. It was probably only the ministrations of his manservant that had sent him out in his customary state of good grooming.

'I am so terribly sorry for what occurred last night,' he said, rubbing chilled hands before the parlour fire. 'I know you will have concluded that the upset was all my fault, which indeed it was, and I have suffered mightily for my dreadful mistake. But you must believe me, I never intended that it should happen in that way, which only shows the unpredictable nature of spirits, I suppose. One may not command them to do one's bidding as one might a servant. I called on Mrs Brendel this morning and spoke to her at some length. She was very kind, far kinder than I deserved, and has explained everything to me.'

'And now I hope you will explain it to me,' said Mina.

'Yes, yes of course. You merit no less.' He took a deep breath of preparation. 'You may have heard, because I know it is gossiped about in Brighton, that it is my hope to one day make Miss Macready my wife. That is true, but unfortunately there are certain obstacles in the way, such that I have not yet dared to ask the question. The chief of those is my close interest in spiritualism, which she perceives as dangerous, and, of course, in the wrong hands it might be. But I cannot persuade her that it is entirely safe provided one only uses the most devout and respectable practitioners. I also believe that she might be afraid that Eleanor's presence is still influencing my life and that she would disapprove of a successor. That may well be at the root of her concerns about living in the manor house, which Eleanor had so loved and wanted to make our home. I had hoped that Miss Brendel with her gentleness and modesty would easily overcome the first of those objections. There was also, to my mind, a very strong possibility that she might be able to pass on a message from Eleanor to the effect that she was content with my choice. I asked Mrs Brendel if that could be achieved and she said she thought it could. But somehow, it all went counter to the way I had anticipated. I really don't understand it,' he concluded sadly.

'You gave Mrs Brendel a copy of a photograph of your late wife,' said Mina.

He had been staring into the fire, but looked up, startled. 'How do you know that?'

'It was obvious. Both to me and to Miss Macready.'

'But is that not a commonly done thing — to supply a picture of the subject one wishes to contact? The medium uses it as a focus for her energy.'

'Is that what Mrs Brendel said?'

'Yes. I have consulted other mediums and many of them ask for something similar.'

'And do they then produce apparitions of the deceased?'

'Indeed they do,' said Honeyacre, missing the implications of Mina's comment. 'But I can see that you are not willing to be convinced of this,' he added, regretfully.

'My mind remains open, but it has not yet been satisfied.'

'I am always disappointed when a person of keen perception cannot see the truth. One day, I am sure you will. But that is not the reason I am here — I was hoping that you might agree to intercede with Miss Macready on my behalf. She is angry with me and has returned all my messages, but I am sure that if she would just allow me to see her and explain my intentions, I could make amends. I know she said some hard words to you, but that is just her way. She undoubtedly respects your opinion.'

'It so happens that I spoke to her earlier today.'

'You have? How come?'

'She called on me. I did attempt to calm the troubled waters that lie between you, but I am sorry to say that she was adamant that she no longer wishes to be friends with you. If you are looking for a wife then I suggest you abandon all thoughts of Miss Macready and make an offer to Miss Brendel.'

His eyes opened wide in astonishment. 'But I have no interest in Miss Brendel! None whatsoever! Whatever gave you that idea?'

'Oh dear. Mrs Brendel will be very upset to know that, as she went to such great pains to chase away Miss Macready.'

Honeyacre struggled to understand. 'Chase away? Whatever do you mean?'

'Mrs Brendel wishes to marry her daughter to a gentleman of fortune. You are a gentleman of fortune. The only obstacle to the match, as far as she was aware, was Miss Macready. You must have suggested to Mrs Brendel that you hoped to receive a message that would encourage Miss Macready to believe that your late wife approved of your intentions. What she actually and quite deliberately arranged was the exact opposite. She must have shown her daughter the portrait you provided and asked her to describe it as if it was a vision. She also prompted her daughter to suggest that your late wife disapproved of your intentions. But Miss Macready had already seen the portrait in an album and recognised Miss Brendel's detailed description of it, so exposing the deception.'

Mr Honeyacre gasped and ground the heels of his hands into his eyes. It was some moments before he could speak. 'That dreadful conniving woman! Have I been taken for such a fool?'

'It seems so,' said Mina, softly.

'But Miss Brendel's powers are genuine, I am sure of it!'

'I cannot say if she simply memorised the picture or if studying it actually produced a vision. That is a matter for a doctor or an oculist to advise on.'

Mr Honeyacre sat in a welter of unhappiness. 'Well, you will think me such a silly old man.'

'Not at all. Please, may I offer you some refreshment?'

'No, thank you, I have no appetite.' He stared into the fire again, and there was a long reflective silence. 'The truth is,' he said at last, 'I lead such a solitary existence. I have wealth, I have comfort, I have friends, I have all the beautiful things I have collected over the years, but no companionship. What I seek is a respectable, sensible, intelligent lady to share my life, one with whom I can converse on subjects such as art and literature.' A thought struck him, and he turned to Mina. 'Miss Scarletti, I don't suppose you might do me the honour of considering —?'

'No.'

'But if you would just take a little time and give it some thought —'

Mina was about to refuse him a second time, when the parlour door burst open, admitting Richard, impetuously tousled. 'Mina, my darling, I have just come from Mr Dorry's and he has actually advanced me some funds on the drawings!'

Mr Honeyacre sprang to his feet in a state of confusion. 'I am so sorry!' he gasped. 'My apologies for anything I might have said. I have taken up too much of your time already. Please don't trouble the maid, I will see myself out.'

He dashed past Richard without even a glance at him, and moments later there was the sound of the front door opening and closing.

'Well, how very peculiar!' exclaimed Richard. 'What was that all about?'

Mina smiled. 'Mr Honeyacre has just proposed marriage to me, and I refused him, but since he is now under the impression that I am your mistress, I will not need to refuse him again.'

Richard laughed. 'So, he's seen off the old dragon, has he? Well done! He's not a bad sort, and pretty well heeled. You might do a lot worse. I'll go after him and explain, shall I?'

'Please don't. I doubt that he will be spreading my shame all over Brighton, and if he did, no-one would believe it. In any case, I have no wish to marry Mr Honeyacre or anyone else.

Wait until you are done pretending to be Mr Henry and then you may set the record straight.'

Richard seemed happy with that arrangement, and flung himself into a chair. 'Is there any tea on its way?'

Mina rang to summon Rose. 'When are you due to visit Miss Brendel again?'

'This very evening.'

'Has anything been said about payment for your sketch?'

'Not yet, but I have promised them the original when it is done. That ought to be worth something, surely.'

'I am pleased you have some payment from Mr Dorry.'

'Yes, two guineas. He wants six more pictures, though.' Richard looked unenthusiastic at the prospect.

'I assume you are signing them as Richard Henry?'

'No, I'm not signing them at all.'

'Oh? But why? I thought pictures ought to be signed.'

'Mr Dorry has explained to me that at present it is better not to. A picture that is not signed attracts more interest because there is a mystery about it.'

Mina thought this a little strange, but as she was not well versed in the art world, was unable to question it. The one person who might have been able to advise her, Mr Honeyacre, was unlikely to welcome her company.

Chapter Twenty-Five

Mina peered out of her window at passers-by battling through showers of needle-like rain, driven by eddying gales, and saw the baleful threat of approaching December. She thought of Richard spending his days trying to draw the sea and was thankful he had a warm coat and hat. Mina loved looking at the sea, but in winter she dared not venture to the promenade on foot. One thunderous wave, one blast of wind, could sweep her to that eternity where all her questions would be answered. She could be patient. There were too many challenges, too many concerns in her earthly life to give her time to think about the one to come.

Dr Hamid arrived, eager to hear about the supper with Mr Honeyacre and to reassure himself that Mina had come to no harm from her risky expedition. On learning about the debacle and subsequent visits of Miss Macready and Mr Honeyacre, he became concerned. 'We now have a strong indication of the ways in which the mother is both controlling and exploiting her daughter, who is in fragile health. I am sorry to say that I fear this will not end well.'

'Is there really nothing you can do?'

'There is no proof that she is actually ill-treating the girl. You said that she was all tenderness and care towards her. The tea is a calming and beneficial brew. I could see no obvious symptoms of disease, but concerns about Miss Brendel's health have already been expressed and dismissed. If you should learn anything that suggests Mrs Brendel is harming her daughter, let me know and I will act at once. But we may have answers to some of our questions when we see Mr Marriott. He will be here tomorrow afternoon at three.'

Dear Edward,

I trust that everyone is as well as can be expected. I wait anxiously for news of Mr Inskip. This uncertainty as to his whereabouts must be extremely distressing.

There is good news about Richard, who now has a patron for his artwork, a Mr Dorry who has a gallery in Brighton, and is reputedly very important.

Fondest love,
Mina

Dear Mina,

I am no further forward, and I feel we must consider Mr Inskip lost, although I dare not say so to Mother or Enid. Agatha's father is pressing me to name a day for the wedding, but I feel it will be hard to do so if this matter is not resolved one way or another. Indeed Mother has hinted in the most obvious manner that she would be quite unable to think of attending a happy occasion while her thoughts are with Enid's plight. My wishes are not to be considered, of course, and I must be patient until June at least.

I have now heard from the various railway, telegraph and steamer companies, and can confirm that Mr Inskip has not dispatched a telegram for several weeks, neither has he travelled by train or steamer in the last two months, or even so much as purchased a ticket. I then thought to make enquiries about the weather in that ungodly part of the world, and it was as I feared. Winter arrived early this year with unusual severity and there were heavy snows and avalanches on the Borgo Pass, wherever that is. The area was blocked, and no coaches have been able to get through in either direction. Anyone trapped there and unable to reach shelter would be unlikely to be found alive. There are two possible hopes, one is that the snow descended before Mr Inskip's coach entered the pass, in which case he might have been able to return to the castle of his client, and is safe, but unable to travel or send messages. The other is that although trapped, he might have been able to reach an inn. The men of that harsh region seem to subsist on the vilest of foodstuffs, but at least they know how to survive the winter. In either case he will be obliged to remain where he is until the weather clears and we will hear nothing from him until next spring.

I decided to inform Enid of this, as she has a right to know, but took care to tell her in the gentlest possible way that she must prepare herself for bad news. Her distress was so profound that, at first, she seemed unable to react at all. She did ask me how long it would be before Mr Inskip could be presumed dead, and I was obliged to inform her that the law requires seven years since he was last heard from. At this she flew into a tirade in which she was almost incoherent. I know she suffers but I wonder why she is obliged to do so at such great volume.

So, Richard has a patron? How extraordinary! I have heard of Mr Dorry who has a gallery in London, too. Perhaps there is more to my brother than I thought. Please make sure he continues to send sketches for the Journal. One a day ought not to tax his energies, surely.

The weather continues cold here. If Richard can send me back my coat and hat that would be appreciated.

Affct'ly,
Edward

Dear Mina,

The news that Richard has a rich patron for his art has brought a little light into my unhappy existence here. I always knew I could rely upon him. Please make sure he has everything he requires in the way of nourishment, a warm and pleasant place in which he can draw, and peace and quiet. I am sending him a few guineas so he cannot want for paint or whatever it is he uses. Really Edward is so mean with his wages, and I cannot persuade him even to indulge his own brother, it is positively cruel. He has complained so much about Richard borrowing his coat and hat

that it has made my head spin. It would be very nice if Richard could write
to me and say how he progresses, but I suppose he must be very busy, and
perhaps I oughtn't to trouble him.

Enid and I are not to stir from the house or it might kill us both.
London is awash with the most terrible diseases, and everyone thinks the
Prince of Wales will die. The poor Queen, I know how she suffers!

There is no news of Mr Inskip. I don't know what Edward is doing, if
anything, he tells me nothing at all. If he was interested in soothing my
anguish he would go out there and look for himself, but he makes no
attempt to do so, pleading business duties, which may just be an excuse.
All he seems to talk about is Miss Hooper, or Agatha as I am expected
to call her now, as we are almost related. I cannot see what he finds
attractive in her, she is so very quiet and reserved, and says so little, but I
suppose I must make the best of it. She has no interests at all apart from
making pressed flowers, and that is of limited usefulness to a wife. At least
there is money in the family.

Your beleaguered,
Mama

Mr Marriott was an oculist with a practice on the Old Steine.
In addition to attending to his patients, he had made a great
study of unusual conditions of the eye, and was consequently
in demand for lectures on the subject. It was with keen
anticipation, therefore, that Mina awaited his arrival together
with Dr Hamid. Rose had been ordered to provide generous
refreshments, and Richard was strictly enjoined not to
interrupt their conference. He looked sulky for a moment
when she told him this, but when she explained that it was a
discussion on scientific matters, declared that it would
probably have sent him to sleep in any case. He donned his
coat and hat, which were looking in need of a good brushing,
and took up his sketchbook and pencils. 'Now for something

to draw! I still have to send sketches to Edward, more's the pity. What a slave driver he is! What do you suggest? Is the aquarium completed yet?'

'There is no hope of that until the contractor and the company have settled their differences in court. We are promised grand archways and gothic structures as well as gigantic fish, but all we have so far is a new sea wall and promenade by the East Cliff. You could try sketching fashionable persons visiting the Pavilion or the Dome.'

'Mr Dorry wants me to draw waves breaking against the end of the chain pier with a view of the Pavilion behind it.'

'Really?' Mina tried to imagine this. 'Can one see the Pavilion from the pier?'

'Not very well, but he said that didn't matter. Artists are allowed to move entire buildings if it makes for a better picture. Dashed cold work, though. I'm glad of this good coat!'

Mina didn't have the heart to ask him to return it.

Chapter Twenty-Six

Dr Hamid arrived promptly at 3pm, together with the distinguished oculist. The gentlemen were ushered into Mina's parlour, which had been made warm and welcoming. All three gathered about the table and Rose brought a tray of refreshments.

Mr Marriott was a tidy-looking individual, aged about fifty, his face adorned with neat gold-rimmed spectacles. He carried a little leather case, which he placed carefully on the floor beside him, and smiled as Mina gazed at it with interest. 'I like to make visual demonstrations to illustrate my words,' he said. 'All will be revealed.'

'I have already advised Mr Marriott of the reasons for this discussion,' said Dr Hamid. 'We are principally concerned with the phenomenon whereby a man or woman, who is apparently quite sane, sees apparitions. There are many questions to consider. Is this a natural process relating to the power of eyesight? Are such people sensitives who can see the souls of both the living and dead? Or is it the result of disease?'

Marriott nodded at each point as Dr Hamid spoke. 'These are not new questions; they have occupied the minds of men of science for almost a hundred years. In earlier times, it was rarely doubted that apparitions were due to some supernatural agency, especially if the person who saw them did not seem to be disordered in the mind. Have you by chance read the works of Sir David Brewster? His *Letters on Natural Magic*, especially.'

'I regret that I have not, but I will amend that fault,' said Dr Hamid, and Mina wrote the information in her notebook.

Marriott leaned back in his chair with a smile and laced his fingers. 'Brewster once wrote, "The human mind is at all times fond of the marvellous". He knew all too well that where a phenomenon may be explained either by a mundane truth or a more fantastical supposition, many persons would far prefer the latter; more than that, they will be irresistibly drawn to it, so it will be their very first conclusion. Now then —' he went on, raising a warning eyebrow — 'before I say any more, I have a word of caution. I speak only of our modern world, in which we may explain certain occurrences by means of scientific principles, which show that they do not bear the supernatural character often ascribed to them. I make no such claims for what is recorded in the Holy Scriptures and believed to be attributable to divine agency. That is something which I am sure we can agree is a quite different matter.'

'Leaving that aside, of course,' said Dr Hamid. 'Now, I appreciate that there are many instances where the organs of perception do not perform their proper function and mistakes will occur, but two of my patients who had otherwise good eyesight nevertheless reported phenomena which I found quite mystifying. They told me that they had seen ghosts of both the living and the dead; men, women and even animals. If this is due to a disease, is it the eye or the mind that is affected, or both? Or must we suppose that ghosts are real and some persons have unusually acute perception?'

'We must accept, however,' said Mina, 'that some people who claim to see ghosts are simply practising a deception. Both Dr Hamid and I have recently observed a Miss Brendel who claims to be a spirit medium and says she has visions of people both living and dead. I really don't know what to make of her.'

'Not all persons who claim to see visions are practising fraud,' said Marriott. 'There are many things to consider, not only the eye and the mind, but the feelings and beliefs and the state of health of the individual.'

'Ah, yes,' said Dr Hamid, thoughtfully.

'You have said that you believe your patients to have been of sound mind?'

'I do, and having observed Miss Brendel, I saw about her nothing to suggest mania or hysteria. I think she may have a weak constitution, but she seemed perfectly composed and sane. Neither was there anything to suggest feverishness. I am sure she was not under the influence of a drug. Since I am not her doctor and cannot examine her, I am unable to say more. Even my most sensitive questioning was greatly resented by her mother, who declared her daughter to be in good health, and said that every appearance to the contrary was misleading. I did wonder if Miss Brendel has a disease of the eye, which can so easily be missed.'

Marriott nodded sagely. 'Perhaps, but not necessarily. Even where there is no detectable fault, either in the eye or the brain, it can happen in certain states of bodily disturbance that are not located in either organ, that impressions which have their origins in the mind will determine what the eye sees. There are, of course, many instances which are well known to oculists where even in a person who enjoys perfect health, the eye can play tricks on the mind.'

Mina recalled how not long ago she had witnessed a conjuror's illusion in which it appeared that a disembodied hand was able to write, a trick created by the use of mirrors, and Nellie had once demonstrated that she was an adept at sleight of hand, making a card seem to disappear and reappear.

'The human eye is a truly marvellous thing,' enthused Mr Marriott, 'so singular, so exquisite, capable of such power and variety of movement. Compare sight with all the other senses

— touch and taste may be exercised only by contact with our bodies, smell in close proximity, hearing at a further but measurable distance. The eye, however, can look to the heavens and see the stars. It is like a small *camera obscura*.'

He opened his leather case, selected a booklet entitled 'The Anatomy of the Eye' and opened it. 'Here you see a diagram of a section through the eye. It shows how light from external objects passes through the front of the eye and falls on the retina, this surface here at the back of the eye, and the impression is then conveyed via the optic nerve, which travels from the retina to the brain. Only then do we truly see.'

'But as you say, our eyes may be deceived,' said Mina. 'Conjurors do it all the time, they rely on it.'

'Indeed they can and most profoundly,' said Marriott. 'Either from the inner working of the mind, or from the dexterity and artistry of others, which persuade us that we have seen something impossible, '

'But the eye, even in full health, is not a perfect organ,' said Dr Hamid. 'Is it not true that in the place where the optic nerve leaves the eye, no image can be detected?'

'That is true,' said Marriott 'and it can be demonstrated very simply.' He removed a piece of card from his case. It was black apart from two white circles side by side and a few inches apart. 'Now then, if Miss Scarletti would be so kind, I will hold this card before her eyes.'

'Oh, please do,' said Mina eagerly.

He held up the card. 'Do you see the two white circles?'

'Yes, very clearly.'

'Now, if you would be so good, place your hand over your right eye, and direct your gaze to the circle on the left.'

Mina did so, and to her surprise the right hand circle had disappeared.

'Is the circle on the right visible?' asked Marriott.

'No. I can see only the one on the left.'

'Please don't be concerned, that is quite usual. Now, if you would cover your left eye and gaze on the right hand circle.'

Mina complied. 'The one on the left is not visible now.'

'Exactly. That is no trick; I do not have the skill of a conjuror. It merely shows that a small part of your retina, where the optic nerve leaves the eye, is insensible to light. When one has two eyes working together, this slight inconvenience is not noticeable. Another curious illusion is that when the eyes stare fixedly at an object, other objects which are seen indirectly nearby may seem to disappear and then reappear. It is a phenomenon which is especially powerful in semi-darkness.'

'And that is the condition under which most séances are conducted,' said Mina. 'In fact, I believe that people are far more likely to report seeing ghosts in the dark than the light.'

Marriott smiled. 'They are, and I believe the phenomenon may account for many tales of apparitions, and also for the fact that spectres are usually white. They are white because in near darkness, no colours can be seen. Inanimate objects when seen by moonlight or the glow of a candle, especially ones of irregular shape, may have different parts that reflect light differently and might appear to change in form and even move. A figure might seem to vanish altogether.'

'Yet people commonly say that "seeing is believing",' Mina observed.

'They do, and often cannot or even refuse to accept how easily they can be deceived. If they see something they are unable to explain, and believe in ghosts and apparitions then their imaginations will do the rest. And remember, I speak only of the eye in full health.'

Mina pondered this statement. 'I have watched Miss Brendel very carefully, and listened to how she described her visions. At no time did she see something the rest of us saw and place a different interpretation on it. She claimed to see persons in the room that no-one else present could see. She said that they appeared to her to be quite real and moved as real people do. The only exception was when she claimed to see a vision of a lady who did not move, but she had previously only ever seen that lady in a portrait. My question is, were these pictures produced by the eye or the mind?'

'I have never met Miss Brendel, so it would be hard to say,' observed Marriott, cautiously. 'There are people who see visions produced by an overheated mind, and they often believe that demons are tormenting them. But what you describe as the very particular case of Miss Brendel does not smack of such disturbed behaviour. You think she is quite comfortable with her visions?'

'She is, yes, at least she has no fear of them.'

'Many doctors believe that seeing an object which is not present is evidence of a weak or troubled mind, or a disease of the eye, and that may sometimes be the case, but not, I think, always. You know, of course, that if you stare at a bright object then turn your eyes to look at something dark, the shape of that object will appear before you still, and will take some time to fade. It has long been known that the eye will retain the impression of an object for a time even after it is gone from view. That is a normal effect in the healthy eye.'

He took something new from his bag, a disc of painted card. The disc had two perforations on opposite edges, and a cord had been threaded through each hole. 'This delightful toy is the thaumatrope. There are two images, the one on this side,' he held it up, 'is a beautiful bird. But the bird alas, is not in its cage. The cage —' he reversed the card to reveal a drawing of a birdcage — 'is on the other side. The puzzle is, how can we put the bird in the cage so it will not fly away? I can do so by using the ability of your eyes to retain a picture.' He wound the strings on either side so that they were twisted. 'Now, when I pull the strings, the card will rotate, and it will be made to appear that the two scenes have become one.' He did as promised and while the images were not as clear as before, they had become combined, so the bird seemed to be in the cage. When the movement stopped, Marriott once again showed that the two pictures were on opposite sides of the disc. 'Now this retention of the image lasts a very short time indeed, but many people believe that in some cases images may be remembered and appear a long time after they were initially seen. Sir Isaac Newton that great man of science, experimented on himself, by staring at the sun, and he found that the effect lasted for some months, if indeed it ever disappeared.'

'I know that the mind can retain pictures,' said Mina. 'If I think about someone, my dear late father, for example, I can see him in my mind. But that is not the same thing as seeing his ghost standing in the room.'

'Quite,' said Marriott. 'So, before we consider what it is that Miss Brendel and Dr Hamid's patients were actually experiencing, let us define what it is we are talking about. We all know that there are those who practise deception, or mistake something natural for a ghostly apparition, and then, of course, there are ghost stories told purely to entertain, such as Mr Dickens's *A Christmas Carol*. But think of this — if no-one had ever seen a ghost, would there be ghost stories? Would people imagine that a curtain flapping in the breeze was a ghost, and run away in terror? I don't think so.

'Tales have been told of people confronting the spirits of the dead since antiquity. I find it impossible, therefore, to believe that these reports have no foundation in actual experience. So, the question we need to resolve first, before we even consider how people see apparitions is, what is a ghost? I will not consider here those situations where someone has seen a patch of mist or a shadow and persuaded themselves that they are in the presence of spirits. Only those cases where a human or animal form has been clearly observed deserve our attention.'

Mina and Dr Hamid glanced at each other. Both were concerned but also stimulated by the turn of the conversation, which had veered away from mere consideration of eyesight.

'Nowadays,' said Mina, 'people generally suppose that a ghost is the spirit of a deceased person. That is why in séances the mediums strive to demonstrate that there is some intelligence behind the communication.'

Marriott nodded agreement. 'That belief has its roots in ancient times. The Egyptians, the Romans, the Greeks, all believed that ghosts were spirits returned from the mansions of the dead to impart important information and issue dire warnings, even prophesy doom. They were rarely a sight to be welcomed, and I do not think they were often encouraged to appear. But that is only one hypothesis; there have been many others. Some philosophers suggested that ghosts were composed of thin films of ash and salts sloughed off from bodies, fermenting in the earth and rising up to form the shape of the deceased, but I think that idea has been long abandoned. Others believe they are what is called the astral body, something said to lie between the physical body and the soul, a part of the individual quite separate from the gross form which is laid in the ground. None of these theories, however, explain why apparitions are normally seen clothed, as they would have been in life, although we must be grateful that this is the case. Another explanation is that ghosts are created by the imagination, and given colour by fear and superstition. Still another, is that there is a derangement of the mind which renders it incapable of differentiating between ideas and reality. Demonologists naturally suggest that ghosts are actually agents of Satan sent to torment the minds of men.'

Marriott looked at the rapt faces of Mina and Dr Hamid and smiled. 'But there is another view and it is the one preferred by men of science. This is not a new thing; there have been papers on this subject going back many years. It is the idea to which I personally subscribe. Ghosts are simply true images preserved in and recollected by the mind, which for some reason have become as vivid as reality.'

'So, they are memories made flesh, as it were?' asked Mina.

'Appearing to be flesh, yes.'

'Which would mean that a ghost could only ever be of an individual that the person who sees it has previously seen?'

'Yes, although the acquaintance might be very brief. The clearest visions are of persons well known. As you observed earlier,' said Mr Marriott, 'when you think of your father, you can easily recall his picture to your mind, yet you are well aware that this is an image only in the mind and not before you. Supposing, however, there is some way in which that image can appear to be real, corporeal, and seem to lie outside yourself? Then you might be persuaded that you have seen a ghost.'

'Is that possible in a sane person?' asked Dr Hamid, wonderingly.

'It is, and there are many cases on record. The mechanism is far from being understood. It was Sir David Brewster's belief that in certain states of health, the mind, which has retained a memory of what the eye has seen, can produce those images again, but in the form of spectral illusions. In many cases, the person subject to these illusions simply assumes that they are of supernatural origin and does not question them. I am sure that there are many who choose not to speak of them in case they are considered insane. In a few cases, however, they have been studied scientifically. There was a German gentleman called Nicolai whose case is well known. He was a bookseller and writer, a thinking man, who had strained his resources due to overwork. Startled on seeing a vision of a deceased person, which others present could not see, he soon realised that the image was not of external origin. He recorded his experiences, and gave a paper to a learned society on the subject. Sir David Brewster studied the case of a lady who suffered from a disorder of the digestion, and experienced both visual and auditory illusions.

'A Dr Hibbert made an extensive study of the phenomenon. He was convinced that these spectral images are ideas or memories produced by the mind when the individual is indisposed. They may be extremely vivid and convincing. Indeed, the mind's eye may produce a greater impression than the eye of the body. His work and that of Brewster have had a powerful influence on scientific thought.'

'That is most encouraging,' said Mina, writing down the name 'Dr Hibbert'. 'One does need a healthy antidote to the claims of the spiritualists who try to delude the public into parting with their fortunes.'

'Oh, I doubt that the charlatans will take any note of men of science,' said Dr Hamid. 'They prefer the unscientific, the mysterious, the unprovable.'

'Might it be possible to meet Sir David Brewster and Dr Hibbert?' asked Mina. 'I should like to speak to them, or correspond at the very least.'

Mr Marriott paused. 'Not unless the mediums are correct after all. The gentlemen are both deceased.'

Mina frowned. 'When did they publish their theories on illusions? And what of Mr Nicolai?'

'Oh, Nicolai's paper was some seventy years ago. Hibbert, if my memory serves me correctly, wrote on the subject in the 1820s, and Brewster not long afterwards.'

Mina was astounded. 'I had not realised that illusions had been studied and explained before the advent of spirit mediums.' She fell silent in thought.

'But if someone was to see what they believed to be a spectre,' asked Dr Hamid, 'how would they know if it was a genuine ghost with an existence external to themselves, or simply an illusion created by the mind?'

'An excellent question. You know that you can strain the eyes in such a way as to make objects appear double? In doing so, any external object would be doubled, but one produced by the mind would not be. Also, many persons who have experienced these illusions soon learn to notice the difference; they report that they are paler, fainter than real persons, move soundlessly, and will often simply vanish.'

'Like ghosts.'

'Yes. Although sometimes they will still be seen when the eyes are shut.'

'You have mentioned the state of health of the individual as a factor,' said Dr Hamid. 'Is this something that only occurs to a person who is unwell?'

'In the examples that have been studied the bodily health of the individual was disordered. Many diseases will create conditions in the body that can affect vision; the pressure in the blood vessels, for example, with which the eye is provided, may be affected by an affliction in another part of the body such as the stomach. In a balanced system if these illusions do occur they are weak and will never appear more prominent than genuine objects. I also believe that grief, such as follows the loss of a loved one can bring about something very similar.'

'Miss Scarletti has been very thoughtful,' commented Dr Hamid. 'In fact, there was a point in the conversation when she became quite lost in her own thoughts. I should inform you, Mr Marriott, that that is the moment when men of good sense should be on their guard.'

'Would you be willing to share your thoughts?' asked Mr Marriott.

Mina roused herself to speak. 'I was thinking about how long ago Dr Hibbert and Sir David Brewster did their work. And then there was Mr Nicolai before them. So, scientists believed they knew the cause of spectral apparitions long ago, yet now, it is as if their work had never taken place. All about us are stories of ghosts, and charlatans taking people's money to practise deceptions on them. People want to believe they can speak to the dead, and receive messages from them. They want to be reassured of the existence of the immortal soul. I really think that no amount of scientific endeavour will ever shake the belief in psychics. Yet the bible teaches us that after we die we sleep to awaken only at the Day of Judgment. Our spirits do not wander about waiting to be called up so our relatives can ask us if we are happy or where we buried our treasure.'

'For that belief we must thank the writers of ghost tales,' said Mr Marriott.

'But the stories are only meant to amuse and they often have a moral,' Mina protested. 'They are not meant to be received as truth.'

The idea troubled her, however. Would she one day hear someone relate one of her own tales back to her as if it had really occurred? Would a believer in the work of mediums choose to deny that her work was fiction at all? Mina glanced at Dr Hamid but he said nothing. Mina had given copies of some of her tales to his sister Eliza, although she had been careful to select only the lighter ones, and spared her the more blood-curdling efforts, which, now she thought about it, were the ones that sold the best. Dr Hamid and his sister Anna, to whom Eliza had enthused about the stories, were the only persons apart from Mina's publishers who were aware that she did not exclusively write for children.

'They have another purpose,' said Marriott. 'They keep superstition alive as the counterbalance to science. For some they are a more acceptable truth. To my mind it is possible for science and religion to co-exist, but many church leaders have felt concerned at the rise of materialism, and have striven to maintain belief in the wonderful, something beyond what is found in the bible. Witches, prophecies, demons, ghosts. Stories not of ancient times, but in this modern age.'

'But this opens the door for criminals to practise on people's credulity,' said Mina. 'The church is welcoming and offers comfort, but it should not tolerate false mediums making a fortune by cheating the bereaved.'

'I am sure that sensible persons will be able to tell the difference between the words of the bible and stories of haunted houses,' said Dr Hamid. 'And as for charlatans it is for science to show them up for what they are.'

Mr Marriott was due for another appointment, and took his leave, but Dr Hamid, seeing that Mina was anxious to speak further, remained, especially as cook had made some of her excellent sandwiches.

'That was a most enlightening interview,' said Dr Hamid. 'The most important thing I have learned is that the individuals who experience these illusions all appear to have one thing in common, a failing in their health, either through disordered digestion, or the stress brought about by overwork or grief. Since the latter does not appear to apply to Miss Brendel the answer to her situation might well lie in her stomach.'

'Is it possible,' Mina wondered, 'that Mrs Brendel is more aware of the situation than we have supposed? She wants her daughter to make an advantageous marriage and may be deliberately concealing any weakness from potential suitors. Could the camomile tea be of importance here?'

'I have read further on the properties of camomile tea, and there is nothing that causes me any concern.'

'Perhaps Miss Brendel has an unusual sensitivity to it. She drinks it during the day as well as in the evening.'

'She does? How do you know?'

'Richard has been going there to sketch her for a society journal. He has observed the arrangements in her house, and is trying to win the confidence of the maid.'

'Is that wise? I mean your brother going there?'

'The visits are carefully chaperoned. All he has told me so far is that Mrs Brendel places a careful guard on her daughter.'

'A precaution of which I strongly approve. This was your idea, I suppose?'

'It was, yes, and I hope we will learn something by it.' Mina was thoughtful. 'Do you think ghost stories by their nature lead people into the clutches of frauds? Have I been guilty of the very thing I despise?'

'Your stories are designed to entertain, not mislead. They deal with the battle between the forces of good and evil; they have a moral. If someone is not wise enough to tell the difference between a fiction and what is real, then they will be at the mercy of every kind of fraud and not just the false mediums.'

Despite this reassurance, Mina remained concerned.

Chapter Twenty-Seven

Richard returned late, and a heavy gloom had descended on him. It was a state that he rarely remained in for long, but this time there was a cloud of unhappiness in his eyes, and Mina was obliged to hug him.

'Would you believe, Mr Jordan has gone and taken Nellie to London?' he complained. 'If I didn't think better I would imagine he was deliberately stopping me from seeing her. She is a good friend, and I ought to be able to see her whenever I please. I know she likes my company.'

'Mr Jordan might think she prefers your company to his,' hinted Mina.

'Oh, he doesn't think so, he *knows* so. After all, who would not?'

'She'll be back in Brighton soon enough. In the meantime, now that you have less to distract you, you will be able to concentrate your mind on your drawings.'

'All I can think about drawing is Nellie, not the sea and ships and rusty old piers. She would inspire anyone. Is that bad of me? If I was rich I would have married her in an instant. And now that I am to be a great artist and make a lot of money it is too late.'

'Are you continuing your visits to Miss Brendel?'

'Yes, I have been a second time, but I'm not sure if I can make many more excuses to call again, or the mother might suspect me of wooing her daughter.'

'Does she still drink the camomile tea?'

'Yes, I can't think why. I wouldn't touch it. Smells like some nasty medicine.'

'Medicine?' said Mina, in surprise. 'But camomile has a light flowery scent. It's quite pleasant.'

He pulled a face. 'Not this kind.'

'Richard — did you get a glimpse of it? Was it pale yellow?'

'No, it was more of a green colour, and I can promise you there was nothing flowery about it. Nothing of the sort.'

'How interesting! Of course, it might be nothing, it might be another harmless beverage or some beneficial infusion Mrs Brendel is giving her daughter, but it just might be the cause of what ails her. Richard, I know this might be difficult without arousing suspicion, but do you think you could obtain some of it next time you visit? If you could, I will send some to Dr Hamid. He knows so much about herbs and is bound to be able to say what it is.'

'Hmm, well, I might be able to help you there. I was trying to ingratiate myself with the charming Jessie by helping her with the teacups and I think I got some of the blessed stuff on my shirt cuff. If Rose hasn't sent the laundry out yet, you might just rescue it.'

By the time Rose had retrieved Richard's shirt from the laundry basket, he had gone out. Mina examined the cuff with its pale green stain, and had to admit it was like no tea she had ever known. On the question of scent she could only agree with Richard. It was certainly not camomile. She wrapped the shirt in brown paper, wrote a note to Dr Hamid, and told Rose to ensure that it was delivered without delay.

She was gratified when later that day she received a note from the doctor thanking her, with the comment that some investigation would be needed to determine the composition of the strange brew.

When Miss Clifton next called on Mina, she reported that there had been an unexpected incident at one of Miss Brendel's séances that Mr Fernwood had attended. Once again, the séance had not produced anything he regarded as being of significance to their concerns, although events had taken a remarkable turn.

'You recall a Mrs Tasker and her son who were there before?' said Miss Clifton, full of amusement at her story.

'I do, and the son looked most unwilling to attend at first, but then he saw the piano and seemed more content. He plays very well. I believe music is his chief passion in life.'

'George said that he and his mother looked to be on the verge of a falling out almost from the moment they arrived, and it became still worse when Mr Tasker determined that he would do nothing but play all evening. He went straight to the piano, and sat there and opened it without even asking permission. It was terribly impolite, and you could see that his mother was mortified by his behaviour. And then he started to play so loudly that no-one could hold a conversation. Both Mrs Brendel and Mrs Tasker told him to desist, and he became very angry, almost violent, so much so that he alarmed all the ladies. Mr Quinley and Mr Conroy were obliged to intervene, and George had to go and help them, because it really looked like Mr Tasker would overthrow them both. There was a horrid struggle and a great deal of noise before his mother managed to calm him.

'Of course, Mrs Brendel told the Taskers she could not tolerate such a dreadful display of bad manners and they were not to come again. There were high words spoken on both sides before they left. Then Mr Conroy said that he was most unhappy with the proceedings and he would go too. A Miss Landwick was there and she was so upset by the scene that she also decided to leave.'

'Was that the end of the séance?' asked Mina, regretting that she had not been there.

'No, George still remained, and Mr and Mrs Myles were there, and they all wanted to continue if Miss Brendel felt able. So, Mrs Brendel sent for some tea to bring a little calm, and when everyone was more composed, Mrs Myles was told of a vision which she felt sure was that of a deceased relative and took great comfort from it.'

'Does Mr Fernwood intend to go again?'

'He says he will. He has not learned anything so far, but while the visions continue and other sitters do receive good evidence there is still hope that we might. Also, he feels great sympathy for Miss Brendel, who is hardly more than a child. Her mother imposes on her too much and is in danger of draining her of any little strength she may still possess. That young fellow who accosted us in the street, Mr Dawson; I fear he was right about one thing. George went to see him at Potts Music Emporium, and under the pretence of an interest in purchasing an instrument, they conversed privately. They both agreed that Miss Brendel was being paraded before some unworthy suitors, and might be forced into marriage, but there was nothing they could do about that. George does not, however, believe that the young lady is being poisoned.'

'No. Her mother gives her herbal tisanes, camomile, which is soothing to the mind and one other, I believe. She may benefit from them. I hope Mr Dawson did not try and persuade Mr Fernwood to pass Miss Brendel a note?'

Miss Clifton gave a little sigh of regret. 'I am sorry to say he did, and begged most piteously, but, of course, George refused. Since Mr Dawson is still barred from the house he implored George to go again, and come back to tell him how Miss Brendel does, and he has agreed to do that much.'

'I do have some further information which may affect your confidence in Miss Brendel. I have consulted an expert gentleman, an oculist, who told me of other people who have had similar visions to Miss Brendel's when their constitutions were disturbed. He felt that something similar might lie behind her situation. One can only hope that she will recover her health, and then she may be cured of these apparitions, which she does not especially welcome.'

Miss Clifton seemed reluctant to accept this explanation. 'But, whatever the cause, her visions can still be real. They can still be messages from those who have passed. Mr and Mrs Myles are quite convinced of it.'

'If I have the chance, I will speak to them and discover more about why they are so sure that they have been in touch with the spirits. But I also have something to say about Mr Castlehouse. An acquaintance of mine knows about the art of slate-writing, and told me that many of the tricks done by Mr Castlehouse have been performed by other mediums, all of whom have later been exposed as frauds.'

'That does not mean that Mr Castlehouse is a fraud,' said Miss Clifton, a trifle petulantly.

'Of course not, only that it is possible to do all the things he does by means of conjuring. He might be writing on a slate himself, or he could, by distracting the attention of his audience, be substituting a slate he has already written upon for one that is blank.'

'I don't see how that can be. I was watching him very carefully. We both were. We didn't see anything of that sort.'

'Neither of us is expert enough to see through a conjuror's skills. Just consider — if a conjuror stood on a stage and did exactly the same as Mr Castlehouse does, you would not for a moment entertain the idea that he was summoning spirits.

However, we do have a way of determining whether he is genuine or cheating. If he is a cheat it will be harder for him to produce his results if he is not able to use his own slates, especially if they are sealed. So, this is my suggestion. We purchase a set of folding slates, of a type sufficiently different from the ones he uses that no substitution is possible. We then place a secret mark on them so there can be no mistake, and ask him to use them.'

Miss Clifton considered this. 'I don't know. We shall look as if we do not trust him.'

'I am sure we will, but I doubt that it will be the first time he has been asked such a thing. The worst that can happen is that there will be no result.'

'But that will prove nothing,' objected Miss Clifton. 'There are many reasons why there might not be a result. Sometimes the spirits just don't have enough power, or the conditions may not be right.'

The visitor was hard to convince, but Mina persisted. 'That is one explanation, but if we see that Mr Castlehouse consistently only achieves results when he is in full control of the circumstances, which means using his own slates, and never when we test him, that will be a very good reason to suspect him of deceit. After all, if the writings are genuinely produced by the spirits then what does it matter to them whose slate they write upon?'

'I suppose you are right, as ever,' said Miss Clifton with noticeable reluctance. 'But I do want to believe so very much! And he may pass our test, which would be a wonderful thing. If he does not, and proves to be a cheat, then there must be others we can test until we find one who will prove true.'

Mina fixed her visitor with an intense and determined stare. 'We must be strong; we cannot allow ourselves to be led astray.

In a matter of such importance it is essential that we are sure of our ground. Remember, the answer could mean life or death to someone.'

Miss Clifton wavered, then acknowledged the force of Mina's statement. 'You put it so well, Miss Scarletti. I will take your advice, and we will do as you suggest. I will buy tickets for us both to see Mr Castlehouse next Wednesday and call for you with a cab. And I will purchase a set of slates as well, as different as possible from the ones Mr Castlehouse uses, and mark them secretly. If he is a scamp, which I hope he is not, then at least we will know the worst.'

Chapter Twenty-Eight

Later that day, Mina received a much-anticipated visit from Dr Hamid. He brought a neatly-wrapped parcel which contained Richard's shirt, nicely laundered.

'Now tell me,' said Mina, eagerly, 'is Mrs Brendel poisoning her daughter?'

He smiled. 'Not at all. The infusion, judging by its scent is composed of a number of commonly used medicinal herbs. None of them is poisonous in the quantities used in that way, and none are known to produce illusions. Many ladies like to rely on regular doses of their preferred medication, not always wisely, but if this is the worst thing Mrs Brendel gives her daughter I would not interfere.'

Mina, while relieved that Mrs Brendel was not, after all, doing harm to her daughter, was disappointed that she was still no nearer an answer. 'But what is the purpose of her giving it?'

'I really can't say. Half the persons who take medicines that are not prescribed by their doctor could not tell you why, or even what ailment they think they are treating. They might have read in the newspapers that it is good, or seen an advertisement, or a neighbour recommended it, or it helped their aunt and they think it might help them too.'

'Well, if it is harmless as you say, then Mrs Brendel should be asked what it is and why she gives it, and should not object to replying.'

'That is true. Are you still going there?'

'No, but an acquaintance of mine is. Perhaps a general enquiry on the benefits of herbal tisanes might stimulate a conversation on the subject without arousing suspicion.'

'Let me know if you should learn anything more. And now it is I who have a favour to ask you.'

'Please do.'

'I am thinking of writing a little memoir. An account of the medicated vapour baths and the other treatments provided. There are very few establishments of this nature in England, and I think it would be of some interest.'

'I am sure it would. Do you want me to recommend it to Edward? The Scarletti publishing house does issue works which are not children's stories or sensational fiction.'

'Oh, that would be so much appreciated. But,' he hesitated and Mina detected a slight embarrassment, 'the work is not yet written. It is barely started. In fact, every time I attempt it, I find that writing is not my forte. I know what I wish to convey but perhaps my sentences are not very elegantly formed. And to be truthful my spelling is a little weak. I hoped, if I could write a chapter or two, would you look at it and advise me? I am sure any publisher would regard the work more kindly if it was readable.'

'I would be delighted to help,' said Mina. A sudden thought struck her. 'Tell me, is it very common for doctors to write a memoir of this kind?'

'Not all do so by any means. A doctor might have a specialist practice, or work in a location that is of interest, or have observations on unusual cases. Then he might well believe that he has something to impart to his fellow doctors or to the public, and publish a memoir.'

Mina thought carefully before asking her next question. 'Supposing a doctor was called to a case in which murder was suspected, a poisoning, perhaps? Might he write about it?'

Dr Hamid smiled knowingly. 'I can see that you are planning another of your stories.'

Mina saw her opportunity and seized it. 'I am. How did you guess? I was thinking of writing a tale in which it is believed that a man has been murdered, but there is a great mystery attached to it. No-one knows who the culprit is. It is easy enough to think up a mystery, of course. The hard part is how to solve it. The detective who is examining the case can't simply dream the answer, there have to be clues for him to find, or the story would not be interesting. You have just suggested how he might proceed. Perhaps the doctor who attended the man suspected a certain individual but did not have enough proof to make an accusation. He might have written a memoir and the detective finds it. The doctor would not have openly denounced someone, but perhaps, hidden in his words — there might be a clue. Does a doctor who writes his memoirs ever mention his patients by name?'

'I certainly don't plan to. I suppose it might just be permissible if the patient is deceased but one has to consider the feelings of the family. In the circumstances you describe I very much doubt that the writer would actually name his suspect, or he would risk prosecution for libel. But someone who knew the family might be able to guess to whom he was alluding. It sounds like an interesting story; I look forward to reading it. If you need any medical advice, you have only to ask.'

'And this time, I promise, there will be no ghosts,' said Mina. 'I do have another question for you. I don't suppose you know anything about art?'

'I'm afraid not. Is this for another story?'

'No. It is just that Richard has been engaged by Mr Dorry of the new gallery in town to do some drawings for him. I am very pleased about it, as it seems a respectable enough career, but Richard tells me that Mr Dorry has asked him not to sign them. I always thought pictures were more valuable when signed, but Mr Dorry has said not.'

'I would have thought the same, but, of course, Mr Dorry is the expert on such things.'

Mina rose and peered out of the window. 'I think, if the weather permits, I would like to visit the gallery and see for myself how Mr Dorry is displaying Richard's work. Is that permitted?'

'I'm not sure. You really ought not to go alone. Perhaps you might consult a doctor on that point.'

'Would you take me there? Rose can call a cab and the gallery is still open.'

'Not tonight. It is late, and there is a threat of frost. Tomorrow morning, if the wind drops, I will call for you at ten o' clock. Can you still your impatience until then?'

Dear Edward,

I trust that the situation in London is not too trying for you, and hope that everyone is as well as possible.

I am writing on another matter. I know that the company has recently been publishing some historical and biographical works. Would you be interested in a medical memoir? Dr Hamid, who is very famous here in Brighton and owns a fashionable establishment that provides an Indian herbal vapour bath and medicated 'shampoo', is composing an account of his work, which should prove very interesting. I hope you will consider it when it is complete.

Dr Hamid informs me that many medical men publish memoirs that can be very useful to their fellow practitioners. I was wondering how one might discover whether or not a leading medical man has ever published? The gentleman in question is a Dr Simon Sperley of Lincoln.

Fondest love,
Mina

Mina hoped that her careful wording had made it appear that the enquiry regarding Dr Sperley's possible memoir was not on her own behalf, but that of Dr Hamid. It was as Mina put the finishing touches to the letter that she realised that something had been at the back of her mind, troubling her like a slight itch. She had tried to ignore it as something trivial, but now she understood what it was. It was probably meaningless but she needed to resolve it.

Chapter Twenty-Nine

Next morning, Mina looked out of her bedroom window with some anxiety, since she knew that severe weather would inevitably result in the arrival of a short note from Dr Hamid postponing their excursion, and she was not sure she wanted to wait to see Mr Dorry's gallery until the following spring. Fortunately, there was no more than the usual sea breeze, and a heavy layer of grey cloud even suggested a slight rise in the thermometer. The note did not arrive, but at 10 am a cab drew up bringing Dr Hamid.

With an engaging diffidence he proffered a small package of papers, which he said comprised the introduction and commencement of the first chapter of his volume. 'If you would be so kind...'

'I will study it with interest.'

'Richard is not accompanying us?'

Earlier that morning Mina had gone to find Richard when he had not appeared at breakfast and found him slumped across his writing desk, pencil in hand, snoring loudly. A drawing of doubtful delicacy portraying Nellie was lying before him. Mina had decided not to disturb him.

'No, he is hard at work on a new commission. And, in any case, I would like to speak to Mr Dorry without my brother being present. He is drawing under the *nom de crayon* of Richard Henry, and I don't think Mr Dorry knows he is my brother. He will be more open with me if he does not.'

Dr Hamid smiled, appreciatively. 'I think your idea of writing about a detective is a good one. You have the mind for it.'

Mr Dorry's gallery was on St James's Street, just north of Old Steine. Their ride took them past the entrance to the new West Pier, which was crowded with visitors during the warmer months, but now afforded a walk and a view of the surging waves only for those very determined to brave the winter weather. Ahead, she caught a glimpse of the old chain pier, which was falling out of fashion as it had fewer attractions than its more modern rival. The sea was whipping it without mercy, as if determined to erase it altogether. Part of what had once been a handsome frontage including an esplanade and a tollhouse had been taken over by the new sea wall and promenade necessitated by the proposed aquarium, leaving the old pier with a narrower and less inviting entrance. Mina was sorry to see the chain pier being squeezed out of existence, as she liked its calmer atmosphere, and feared that it was only a matter of time before it was dismantled and forgotten.

St James's Street had long been a centre of fashion in Brighton. Its residents had money to spend and this was reflected in the jewellers, hatters, furniture dealers, confectioners, hairdressers and purveyors of fancy goods who thrived there. Mr Dorry's gallery was a recent arrival and occupied a single-fronted premises. The window display was a marvel of taste and restraint, since it was composed of two easels, on each of which rested a landscape painting. A sign at the very front of the window proclaimed in bold lettering that that Mr E Dorry, who was connected with several of the great art houses of London, was interested in buying collections or single items of merit. He would also, for a fee, examine works of art, offer his expert opinion of authenticity and provide a certificate of valuation. Mention was made that a larger selection of highly sought-after pieces was held at his London gallery.

'This is very impressive,' said Dr Hamid, with some surprise. 'If your brother has attracted Mr Dorry as a patron he has done well.'

'Yes, I must admit, this was not quite what I had been expecting,' Mina confessed. 'In fact, I am not at all sure what I was expecting.' She didn't say it, but she had feared that Mr Dorry might be one of those cheats who made money from the labour of others and failed to pay their bills when due. Of course, that could still be the case.

Dr Hamid pushed open the glassed and gilded door, which was very heavy, and they entered. They were met by a subtle aroma of old paper, wood and varnish, with a hint of something floral. Although the premises were not large and the items on display were few they were presented with great care, offering the promise that further treasures could well be available.

In the centre of the gallery was a marble statue on a plinth of a handsome youth in classical Greek style, since he was in a state of undress that might have been quite disturbing had his loins not been draped with a silken scarf. A card read 'Adonis. Not For Sale.'

At the back of the gallery was a separate display counter for artists' materials, and a schedule of costs for framing works of art, which to Mina's scant knowledge seemed extraordinarily expensive. A svelte young man stood behind the counter, showing boxes of paints to a man whose entire wardrobe was probably worth less than a single tube of colour.

Most of the pictures that hung about the walls were oils, with a few watercolours, but there was a small section of pencil and ink drawings, and Mina noticed that one of Richard's works was included, enclosed in a very simple wooden frame. She went to examine it. It was a view of the chain pier being inundated with ferocious waves, and threatened by lowering clouds. Far out to sea, she recognised Richard's favourite penny toy ship, struggling manfully to stay afloat, while on the shoreline the Royal Pavilion had managed to creep forward from its usual position until it occupied a prominent position on the Marine Parade. The drawing was labelled 'The Chain Pier, Brighton. Unknown artist, in the style of J. M. W. Turner.'

'Is this your brother's work?' asked Dr Hamid.

'Yes, and unsigned as he said.'

'I am no judge of art, but it does have its merits.' He peered more closely and pointed. 'Should the Pavilion be there?'

'Richard said that didn't matter.'

'Really? If I was a stranger to Brighton and saw this picture I would be quite mystified when I paid a visit and found the Pavilion not where I thought it ought to be.'

'So, if you had studied the picture it would have become more real to you than the actuality?'

'It might have, at that.'

Mina glanced about but there was no sign of Mr Dorry.

The customer left the shop, a small paper bag clutched in his hand indicating a humble purchase. Almost instantly the svelte young man appeared by their side, as if conjured into existence by a spell. 'Good morning, Sir, Madam,' he said, with a polite inclination of his sleek head and an ingratiating smile. 'Does this picture interest you?'

'It might do,' said Dr Hamid, cautiously.

'Perhaps you could tell us something about it?' asked Mina.

'But, of course.' The young man made a graceful gesture towards the work. 'It has been recently acquired, but is already attracting considerable interest from collectors. Notice the charming, almost primitive style, the deceptively careless way in which the pencil has been used. The pier has been well rendered, the little storm-tossed ship is quite delightful, evoking the vulnerability of life when man is at the mercy of the sea, while the texture of the waves shows a young artist still exploring his skills.'

'I don't think the position of the Pavilion can be quite right,' said Dr Hamid.

'Ah, but that is where the eye of the artist places it,' said the young man with an indulgent smile. 'In his mind it achieves such a measure of importance that he perceives it as larger and closer than it really is in that view, and so gives it the same prominence in his work that it has in his imagination.'

Dr Hamid did not look convinced by that argument.

'The drawing does not appear to be signed,' said Mina. 'What is the name of the artist?'

'I regret that I am unable to say. But it is very common with works such as this one for there to be no signature. It was probably never intended for sale at the time it was composed, perhaps merely as a study for a major work in oil. But these sketches are now becoming very sought after in their own right. If you are interested you could see Mr Dorry and discuss a price. But I cannot see him letting it go for under ten guineas, and it could well fetch much more at auction. We have only a few examples of the artist's work, which are quite rare.'

'Might we have a moment to consider?' asked Dr Hamid.

'Of course, Sir, Madam.' The young man bowed and withdrew.

'I suspect,' said Dr Hamid, 'that Mr Dorry is hoping to make a very large profit from your brother's work, by paying him a pittance. I fear, however, that he is in no position to bargain at present, but if the drawings do sell, then he should ask for an account of what they fetch and in future demand a fair portion of the sale price.'

'I will make sure to advise him.'

'Have you seen all you need? I have an appointment with a patient soon. I can take you home and then I must return to the baths.'

Mina was about to assent to this, when Mr Dorry hove into view, like a leviathan risen from the deep.

'Why, good afternoon Miss Scarletti. What brings you here?'

'I had never visited your gallery and was curious to see the display. Mr Dorry, allow me to introduce Dr Hamid.'

Dr Hamid proffered his card.

'Ah, a steam bath! Just the thing.' Mr Dorry pressed a hand to the small of his back, which was doing extremely well to support such a very large front. 'I might well avail myself of your services. Do you collect art, Dr Hamid?'

'Not at present.'

'Well, if you see anything that attracts you, just let me know.'

'In fact, I must depart now, as my work calls.'

'I think I would like to remain a little longer,' said Mina.

Her companion gave her a look that told her he knew she had some plan in mind, but he could not very well discuss it with Mr Dorry present. 'Very well, I will send the cab back here to bring you home. And do take care.' Dr Hamid took his leave.

'So, he is your personal physician?' asked Mr Dorry.

'Yes, the treatments I have received at Dr Hamid's baths have been very beneficial. But do tell me something about this drawing. I see it is unsigned and described as being by an unknown artist.'

'It is.'

'And yet, as I look at it, it is plain to me who the artist is, and I am sure it is plain to you, too.'

Dorry looked down at her, and one enormous eyebrow rose until it resembled an arched rustic bower. 'Oh?'

'Yes. I recognise the style of Mr Richard Henry, the young man who was sketching Miss Kitty Betts at Mrs Jordan's salon. Please don't deny it, it is very plain. The manner of rendering the sea is so like the lady's coiffure.'

Mina could see he was debating whether or not to contradict her; finally he conceded with a little smile. 'How very acute of you, Miss Scarletti. What an eye you have!'

'Then perhaps you could explain to me why the drawing is described as being by an unknown artist?'

Mr Dorry chuckled, a noise that thundered deep in his throat to which the rest of his vast form vibrated in sympathy. 'Ah, now I understand your query. Allow me to explain. When we in the art business say "unknown artist" it does not mean that we do not know the identity of the artist only that he is not a known name in the world of art.'

Mina wasn't sure if this was true but she could hardly dispute it without more information. 'He might gain a name if he signed his work.'

'Be assured by me, at this early stage in his career it is better if he does not. It lends an air of mystery and is more likely to stimulate discussion and attract interest.'

'The picture has similarities to the work of another artist.'

'Exactly. As it says on the card, in the style of Mr J. M. W. Turner. Very highly regarded.'

'Forgive my ignorance, but when copying a style is it necessary to consult the artist one is copying?'

'Not at all, as long as one labels the work correctly. And in any case Mr Turner is deceased.'

'I hope your customers don't imagine this drawing is by Mr Turner?'

'If they do, they do not say so. Also, the drawing is not priced as a Turner. It has a low price, a humble price. Not the price a Turner would command.'

'But is there not a danger, since the work is unsigned, that the buyer might delude himself into believing that he has seen a bargain.'

Mr Dorry was disconcerted for a moment. He glanced about, but there was no other customer in sight, and he took on a more confiding tone. 'He might, but what he believes is his own business, surely? Suppose he sees what he thinks, or suspects might just be an undiscovered Turner, not one of his finest, of course, an early work, perhaps a study for a future painting, something he himself discarded as unworthy and therefore quite deliberately did not sign. Is the customer going to reveal his suspicions, and say to me, "Oh, Mr Dorry, you have found a rare thing here and are offering it so cheaply!" No, of course not. He hopes that he has seen what I have not. He hopes to secure something valuable at a low price. He knows that if he alerted me to his suspicions, then I would put up the price and that would never do. So, he stays silent, and buys the drawing for more than he would pay for an unknown artist. Part of the price is the picture, and the rest is for that hope, the chance of a bigger prize, a hope I never gave him.'

'What you are saying is that you are not cheating them, they are in effect cheating themselves.'

'Precisely. I cannot know what the man is thinking. I do not tell him it is Turner. If he was to ask me outright is it Turner I would say no, it is not, it is in that style. You see the card; all it attests to is the style. Everything else is in the eye and the mind. If the customer flatters himself that he is cleverer and more observant than I am, if he hopes for a handsome profit, then he might see what he wishes to see. But I do not put the thought there.'

Mina could only wonder at how vulnerable people were to their own deeply held desires. Mr Dorry pandered to greed, while Mr Castlehouse, who performed the same feats as a conjuror, promised more than just diversion. The slate-writer's sitters felt they had been gifted with an insight into the greatest mystery that life had to offer, received a special, deeply personal and secret knowledge, an advantage over others not so blessed. The svelte assistant saw artistic merit in a deliberate artifice, and persuaded not only collectors, but himself, also, that it was the expression of a unique imagination. Both Mr Dorry's and Mr Castlehouse's customers accepted all that their deceived eyes told them, all that they profoundly wished to believe.

'Oh, Mr Dorry!' said the young man, moving lithely towards them like an eel slipping through greasy water. 'There is a cab waiting outside, the driver says he is for Miss Scarletti.'

'Then I must depart,' said Mina. 'I hope we may meet again, and I wish Mr Henry every success.'

The door was opened for her, and Mina peered out cautiously, but the weather remained mild and the east-west orientation of the narrow street protected her from any dangerously inclement gusts. 'Good morning, Miss,' said the cab driver. 'Am I to take you to Montpelier Road?'

'Not yet. I would like to go to the offices of Phipps and Co solicitors.'

Chapter Thirty

'I felt sure it was only a matter of time before you came to see me again,' said young Mr Phipps, permitting himself one of his rare smiles, as he ushered Mina to the chair that faced his across his desk. Mr Phipps had a newer, less humble office than the one he had occupied the last time Mina consulted him. Still only the most junior Phipps in the firm, he nevertheless merited a fractionally larger carpet than previously and a slightly bigger desk, the better to accommodate the increased amount of work he was expected to do. As he moved up the Phipps ladder towards the top rung, so the workload would grow until he reached the midpoint then it would start to decrease as some of it tumbled from his desk and fell to land on the desks of younger iterations of Phippses.

'I assume this is concerning poor Miss Brendel. All I can say about her is that the unfortunate young lady is the puppet of her mother, who commands when she shall breathe in and when out again.'

'I have visited them a second time, and friends of mine have also, but I have found no evidence that the Brendels are asking for payment for their sittings,' said Mina. 'Have you discovered anything?'

'No, nothing. I simply attended on that occasion to accompany my aunt, who maintains a lively curiosity in such things. But the young lady is an heiress and there are single gentlemen clustered about her like flies around a honey jar. I think that is the real interest.'

'Did *you* find her interesting?' asked Mina, teasingly.

Mr Phipps actually reddened a little, and neatened some papers on his desk, an action that was quite unnecessary. 'I — no. In fact, following my visit, I did receive a little note from Mrs Brendel inviting me to take tea with them. I expect she has heard of my recent admission to the partnership and deems me eligible. But I have declined the invitation due to extreme pressure of work. When I marry, as I hope to do one day, my wife will be a sensible woman, and most definitely not one who has visions.'

'Are you acquainted with Mr Quinley?'

'No, ought I to be?'

'He is not a visitor, but Mr Brendel's solicitor, staying in Brighton as consultant and protector to the wife and daughter.'

'I have not heard of him, but then there are very many solicitors.'

'But the Brendels are not the subject of my call.'

'Oh?'

'I happened to visit Mr Dorry's art gallery in St James' Street earlier today. He claims to have a lifetime of experience in the art world and I have been told he has another gallery in London. There was a picture being offered for sale — a pencil drawing which was described as being in the style of a Mr Turner, a deceased artist whose work is very much admired. The thing is, I happen to know who the artist is, and the picture is not by Mr Turner.'

Mr Phipps gave a deep frown of concern. 'It is not being described as by Turner, I hope?'

'No.'

'Is it signed by the artist?'

'It is unsigned, and labelled as being by an unknown artist.'

'Does Mr Dorry know who the artist is?'

'He does, because it is he who commissions them. But a buyer might imagine that they are early works by Turner.'

'But there is nothing in writing to suggest it?'

'No.'

Mr Phipps plunged into further thought. 'What of the buyers who make enquiries? Are they in any way, even by a hint, being led to believe the picture is by Turner?'

'No, and Mr Dorry says that if openly asked he would reply truthfully. But he is hoping that buyers suspect they have seen something he has missed, in which case they would not ask him for fear of having the price increased, and so miss securing a bargain.'

'I see. And you want to know if this activity is breaking the law?'

'I think that Mr Dorry, who knows his business, is being very careful to avoid something openly fraudulent. He never tells an outright untruth but leaves it to the inclinations of his customers to supply the conclusions he hopes for. I did point out that his card described the picture as being by an unknown artist, which is not true as he knows who the artist is. He tried to persuade me that the expression simply means one who has not made a name for himself. I do not know if that is true or not.'

'Neither do I. He does not invoke the spectre of Mr Turner to bolster his sales?'

'Only in the manner of style,' said Mina, suddenly realising that Mr Phipps had made a humorous reference to her previous activities. 'I believe that the artist is quite innocent of the somewhat dubious way in which his work is being presented.'

'Your concern is for the artist.'

'It is.'

'Perhaps I ought not to ask you if you know the artist.'

'I would be grateful if you did not.'

'I can only supply an opinion on what I know so far, but I feel that if the artist has created the works in good faith, and sold them to a dealer, then he cannot bear responsibility for how they are sold once he has parted with them. If, however, he receives some of the fruits of Mr Dorry's underhand measures, then he may unwittingly be making a profit from duplicity, and might find it hard to convince the authorities that he knew nothing of the scheme. It would be as well if you were to warn him of any potential dangers. In the meantime, I promise I will keep my eyes open for any news of Mr Dorry.'

On her way home Mina called in at Mr Smith's bookshop and reluctantly parted with five shillings for a copy of *The Brighton Hauntings* by Mr Arthur Wallace Hope. Mr Smith did not carry any of the works of Sir David Brewster or Dr Hibbert and suggested that in view of the age of those publications she might try an antiquarian bookseller. She returned home disappointed. Richard had gone out, but she resolved to speak to him on the subject of Mr Dorry as soon as possible, although it was always hard to get anything useful from him on the subject of money. There was a letter from Edward and she opened it hoping for good news.

Dear Mina,

Little has changed here. I visit Mother and Enid almost every day, as they make poor company for each other, but nothing I do is appreciated. The twins continue to thrive, if the noise they make is anything to judge by. Would it be too much trouble for Richard to write a few lines? Mother is actually sending him money, so the least he could do is thank her.

If a memoir such as you describe had been published then a copy would be held by the British Museum Library. One of my authors is often in that library, so I asked him to look for any record of such a volume. He has just reported to me that as far as can be determined, Dr Sperley did not write a memoir, since there is no mention of that author's name in the catalogue.

As you are a great reader with a penchant for history, I should mention that the author to whom I referred is writing an account of notable executions at the Tower of London. I have to confess that I am somewhat concerned about publishing something in such dubious taste, and would welcome your opinion on the matter. To my mind, it is of the same unpleasant ilk as the tales of supernatural entities and horrible disasters that Greville will insist on presenting to the less discerning portion of the public. He assures me, however, that these alarming stories are a useful source of income, so I suppose I must tolerate it. Their author, a Mr Neil, is certainly a person of doubtful mental stability and you should avoid reading his works.

At least the book I have commissioned is English history and there is no getting away from that, even if it is an aspect I would not personally wish to dwell upon. I would far rather publish nobler and more elevated forms of literature, and I hope that may come in future. A medical memoir would be something I might consider, and you must ask Dr Hamid to send it to me when it is complete.

Greville tells me that your stories for children are well received, and I am glad that you have something interesting to occupy you. Mother worries constantly that you are still risking your health by spending time with spirit mediums. I have reassured her that that particular concern is a thing of the past, but I am not sure she listens to me.

Affect'ly,
Edward

Mina, disappointed that there was no memoir written by Dr

Sperley, spent the afternoon composing a new story about a whale, which having made the long journey from the North Pole, unexpectedly appeared cavorting in the sea at Brighton. Even amongst whales, which were naturally large, this one was a veritable monster of its kind, its shining body hung about with ribbons of bright red seaweed, and assiduously groomed by a battalion of fawning eels. The unusual sight naturally created great excitement in the town, and both population and visitors came to the promenade and walked along the pebbled beach in droves to see the spectacle, only to find to their horror that the whale was able to come on shore and cause mayhem. The huge creature of massive girth would rise up to a terrifying height, before allowing its weight to fall, crushing unsuspecting onlookers to death before returning to the sea with a flip of its tail. Boats set to sea to try and conquer it, but they and their crews were eaten at a gulp. The danger was finally averted by the hungry beast swallowing an abandoned torpedo, resulting in an explosion that scattered evil smelling blood-stained debris over half the town. Once the mess had been cleared, however, Brighton was well supplied with whalebone, meat and oil for some months to come.

Mina laid aside her pen and examined the writings of Dr Hamid. The proposed title was *The Indian Medicated Herbal Vapour Bath and Shampoo: Methods and Benefits*. It did not have quite the immediacy of *Attack of the Killer Whale*, but it did undoubtedly describe the subject of the book. The introduction gave some of Dr Hamid's history; his father making his way as a doctor in a foreign land, the tribulations of his sister Eliza, afflicted from childhood with advanced scoliosis, his determination to study medicine with particular attention to conditions affecting the spine, and his struggle to establish a practice in Brighton. The first chapter was an overview of the many conditions that would benefit from the treatments offered by Dr Hamid's practice. That was all he had written so far and there followed notes as to the subjects of the remaining chapters — how the treatments were applied — the value of herbs and spices in medicine — some examples of patients cured or improved. Mina, bearing in mind that his readership was likely to be different to hers, decided to concentrate on faulty spelling, and punctuation and grammar, which were occasionally highly eccentric.

This did lead Mina to think further about Dr Sperley. True, he had never published a memoir, but he might have left notes and diaries, not in a publishable form, which could cast further light on the mystery. Mina returned to the package of newspaper cuttings supplied by George Fernwood. It included a letter to the press from Dr Sperley, on the subject of how great caution was to be used in the employment of arsenic as a vermin killer, as accidents had been known to occur. Was this a clue? Did Dr Sperley believe that the poisoning of Thomas Fernwood had been an accident? If so, why had he not said so at the inquest? Or was he merely doing his duty as a doctor? The letter was signed 'S. Sperley, M. D., Newland House, Lincoln'.

Mina took up her pen.

To: Mrs Sperley
Newland House
Lincoln
Dear Mrs Sperley,
I am writing to you on behalf of the Scarletti Publishing House. We are looking for suitable memoirs written by noted medical practitioners. While we cannot guarantee publication we are interested in seeing anything of

promise. Can you advise us if your late husband kept any notes, perhaps for a memoir he was intending to offer for publication?

I hope very much to hear from you.

Yours faithfully,

M. Scarletti

Montpelier Road

Brighton

Mina enclosed a Scarletti Publishing business card to establish her bona fides, and sealed the letter.

Richard returned in time for dinner but, unusually, with little appetite. 'The sea is such a bore!' he said. 'I had been hoping for a good shipwreck but there has been no such luck.'

'Richard dear, can you enlighten me as to the nature of your arrangement with Mr Dorry? Does he pay you an agreed price for each of your drawings, or do you receive payment only when he sells one to a customer?'

Richard looked mystified. 'Arrangement? I don't know. I draw what he asks for and he says I will be very successful one day. He has made some small advances of funds, but that is all.'

'You have nothing from him in writing?'

'No. Is that usual? I mean, Dorry must know his business. He's done well enough out of it, after all.'

'Do you know if any of your drawings been sold?'

Richard began to look uncomfortable with the questioning. 'He hasn't mentioned it. I think he has sent some to his London gallery. He says the exposure to the public there will advance my career.'

'Well, if something does sell, it would be very interesting to know how much it fetches.'

The only answer Mina received was a shrug and silence, and she knew she would learn no more.

She retired to her room to read Mr Hope's *The Brighton Hauntings*. It was a book written by a true believer, a man who on hearing an unexplained noise thought it to be the sound of a spirit knocking without ever considering a thousand other more natural causes. His book provided a colourful account of the sensational sightings said to have taken place in the Royal Pavilion earlier that year, declaring his absolute belief in them. It was Mina's actions that had exposed the deception, something he appeared to have either forgotten or swept aside as a delusion. He had taken great care, however, not to name her. He knew she was a writer and part of the Scarletti publishing family, and could not impugn her honesty without fear of a legal reprisal. What he had written was, however, far worse. 'There is,' he concluded, 'a person now residing in Brighton who I know is destined to become one of the greatest and most celebrated spirit mediums of our age. For the present those eyes remain firmly closed to the truth, but I am as certain as I see the sun rise every day that they will open, and open soon. When the world is threatened with catastrophe, it is to this individual we will turn to lead us to the light. One day I will stand in that wonderful faerie aura again, and this humble being with a mighty soul will be ready at last to acknowledge the power that lies within.'

To Mina this could only mean one thing. Mr Hope, confident that she would read his words, was sending her a warning. He had not forgotten her. He was still her enemy.

Chapter Thirty-One

That evening, Mina and Miss Clifton were to make their first test of the veracity of Mr Castlehouse. Miss Clifton called at the appointed time, bringing with her as promised, a set of folding slates in a brown paper parcel tied with cord. She pulled back the paper to show that the slates were in a light-coloured wooden frame. 'These are quite unlike the ones Mr Castlehouse uses, where I recall that the wood is darker. And look, I used my needlework scissors to make a little scratch in one corner. So even if by chance he had something similar, we would know this set from any other.'

Mina examined all the surfaces of the slates with great care, and, satisfied that they were clean and smooth, pronounced them ideal for their purpose, re-wrapped them in the paper and tied the cord.

'I have been wondering about how best to introduce them,' said Miss Clifton.

'We should be bold with him from the start — no whispering in corners — the others in the room should all be aware of what we are asking. That will make it harder for him to refuse us. I also think, if it is at all possible, that we should not allow Mr Castlehouse to handle the slates.'

'Would he permit that?'

'We shall see.'

'But it would be a sign in his favour if he did, surely?'

'Only if we saw any result. We must make certain to show them to everyone present so they can satisfy themselves that all the surfaces are perfectly clean. And it should be one of us who dusts them and then ties them up in the cord.'

Miss Clifton nodded emphatically. 'You have thought of everything.'

'Even if he can open a set of slates and write on them by sleight of hand without people noticing I doubt that he will be able to untie them quickly if we make very secure knots. He might want to take them from us, but we have to resist that.'

It was early evening, and there was a fresh bite of winter in the air. Darkness had spread like ink over a cloudless sky that offered no shelter from the wind. The cab waited outside, and the driver with the tartan muffler, knowing that some assistance would be needed, had already descended to hand the ladies into the comparative comfort of the interior.

'There is one small matter that I was wondering about,' said Mina, as they proceeded on their way. 'When I last spoke to Mr Fernwood, it was soon after your return from Lincoln. Am I correct in thinking that neither of you has been there since the family moved away?'

'That is correct,' said Miss Clifton.

'When I asked if you had visited Dr Sperley, Mr Fernwood replied that you would have done, if he had not passed away six months ago, and he spoke very movingly of the doctor's last days. If he had not visited, how could he have known?'

Miss Clifton was unembarrassed by the question. 'George corresponds with a friend in Lincoln whose family was also attended by Dr Sperley and they exchange news.'

'Ah, I see. I recall that Mr Fernwood placed great trust in Dr Sperley and would not hear a word spoken against him, but I know you have another view. Even if Dr Sperley was blameless, do you think he knew anything about your great uncle's death; I mean, something he didn't say at the inquest?'

Miss Clifton needed no time for consideration. 'If he did, I don't know what it might have been. He certainly never confided in me.'

Mr Castlehouse's séance was as well attended as before. The usual pile of slates was on the sideboard, and included a number of double slates that Mina was careful to examine. She was quickly able to establish to her satisfaction that none of them could be mistaken for the set Miss Clifton had brought. There was a new addition to the sideboard, a row of books bound in dark brown leather, which comprised the volumes of a dictionary of the English language, with additional notes on grammar. Rather more attractive was a copy of *The Pickwick Papers*, prettily bound in maroon and stamped with gold. There were also some slips of paper, pencils and envelopes.

Young Mr Conroy was present, as was the timid lady, and Mina inclined her head to both in greeting. The lady was accompanied by a gentleman Mina did not recognise.

Mr Conroy looked reluctant to approach Mina, but after a few moments, decided to do so. 'Good evening,' he said and Mina introduced him to Miss Clifton but giving her companion's name as Miss Clive. 'I see that you too have abandoned the Brendels' salon for what we must hope will be a calmer place,' he commented. 'Did you hear of what occurred there lately?'

'There were rumours of a disturbance.'

'Indeed. I was present at that event, which was highly unpleasant, but at least it served to open my eyes. Mrs Brendel has finally shown herself in her true colours. She may be the wife of a wealthy man but she has the manners of — well — something quite different. I will admit that I entertained great hopes that the daughter was genuine, and for all I know she

253

may be, but now I have seen in her mother what she may become in future. I will not go there again.'

'Miss Scarletti,' whispered the timid lady, making a cautious approach, 'we have not been introduced, but we have encountered each other before. I am Ethel Landwick and this is my brother, Charles.'

'I am delighted to make your better acquaintance, Miss Landwick,' said Mina warmly, 'and pleased to meet you, sir. Allow me to introduce Miss Clive and Mr Conroy.'

'Miss Landwick and I are already acquainted,' said Mr Conroy, and his expression suggested that he thought this circumstance to be no very bad thing.

'I was also at the last séance of Miss Brendel's,' explained Miss Landwick, 'and it is thanks to Mr Conroy that it ended as peaceably as it did. I thought young Mr Tasker was about to lose control and have to be restrained. It is a wonder the police were not called.'

'I am sorry I was not there to witness it,' said Mr Landwick, stiffly. 'Not that I place any value on Miss Brendel's visions, which may have their origins in another kind of spirit altogether. But I am sorry to have missed the opportunity of correcting a man who has no idea how to behave in the company of ladies.'

'We must hope that the chastisement of his mother will be more than sufficient punishment,' said Mina. 'Do you hope for better fortune from Mr Castlehouse?' This was a question for both the Landwicks and Mr Conroy.

Miss Landwick looked unsure and glanced at her brother for guidance, but he only grunted.

'I have been unable to explain what he does by any other means but that he is in touch with the spirits,' said Conroy, 'so yes, I am hopeful.'

'Perhaps you might volunteer when he asks for someone to come forward,' said Miss Landwick. 'Or you, Miss Scarletti.'

Mina smiled. 'Oh, I do have a plan for this evening which I hope will add to the interest of the occasion.'

The gaunt-looking maid entered the room, and in sepulchral tones urged the company to be seated. When everyone was comfortably settled, Mr Castlehouse appeared, as dapper as ever, and smilingly introduced himself. He took a number of the single slates from the sideboard, and scattered them on the table in a casual manner that suggested their precise arrangement was of no importance. 'I would like a lady or gentleman to select from these slates any two that they would like to use today, and examine them carefully to show that they are blank.'

A lady from the front row jumped up at once, and almost ran forward in her eagerness. After careful study, she picked out two slates. At Mr Castlehouse's request these were minutely examined on both sides, washed with a sponge, dried with a cloth, and placed side by side on the table.

'Now then,' said Mr Castlehouse, picking up a small box, 'I have here a number of chalks of different colours. In a moment I will place pieces of six different ones on the slate. If the lady would be so kind as to look at what colours we have, and think, but do not state out loud, three colours in which she would like to receive messages.'

The lady peered at the box of chalks and spent what seemed to Mina to be a wholly unnecessary amount of time making her selection. After her conversation with Nellie, Mina was aware that any choices made by the sitters that were under Mr Castlehouse's control would have no effect on any result. Was there, however, another motive? The lady's attention had been distracted from the slates on the table, and more to the point, the sitters were probably watching her rather than Mr Castlehouse.

'Have you made your choice?'

'Yes, I have!'

Mr Castlehouse held up one long warning finger. 'Do not say what it is just yet. I now take one piece of each colour and place them on the slate, like so. Next, I take up the second slate and use it to cover the first. They now lie in the middle of the table, with the six chalks between them. I will no longer touch them.' He stepped back gesturing with both hands open and arms held wide. 'Now you must put your hand on the slates to ensure that they do not move.'

The lady, a little timorously, since she knew that the slates might be visited by spirits, placed her hand on them.

'And, at last, you can tell us all, which colours did you select?'

'Oh — er — white, and red, and green. I think it was green.'

'Notice,' said Mr Castlehouse to the onlookers, 'that I am standing well away from these slates. I cannot influence anything that might occur.' He took a deep breath, his eyelids fluttering closed. 'I call upon the spirits to announce their presence and write messages for us in the three colours selected. Is there a spirit here?'

There was a silent pause, and then Mr Castlehouse extended one hand, directing the palm towards the slates, making circles before him like the mystic passes of a wizard of old, his head thrown back, his body trembling. A minute or two elapsed, then a sound broke the expectant quiet, the rasp of a chalk scratching on slate, and the lady cried, 'Oh! I can hear it! I can hear it!'

'Are your powers strong tonight?' demanded Mr Castlehouse to the air.

There was the sound of further scratching. Mina tried not to gaze at Mr Castlehouse's theatrical one-handed gesture, but tried to see how his other hand was employed. It appeared to be behind his back.

'What message do you have for us, oh spirit!' he called.

There was a further outbreak of busy scratching followed by three taps.

Mr Castlehouse opened his eyes. 'Now, dear lady, I think the spirit has done all it can for tonight. Please lift the top slate.'

The lady reached forward and did so. There on the slate were three messages, one in each of three colours. There was certainly a red and a white but it was hard to determine in the lamplight whether the third was green or blue.

'Please read out the messages.'

The first message was 'yes', the second was 'the power is strong' and the third was 'those who listen to the spirits will prosper.'

Once the messages had been read, and subjected to much wonderment and admiration, Mr Castlehouse took charge of the slates and chalk, and by means of a courteous bow dismissed the lady back to her place.

Mina took the opportunity afforded by this pause in the proceedings to rise to her feet. 'Mr Castlehouse, if you would be so good?' she called out in a voice that pervaded every corner of the room.

He turned towards her in surprise. 'How might I assist you?'

Mina had untied the cord around the parcel and she now unwrapped the purchased slates. 'I have brought my own set of slates. I assume it would be no more difficult for the spirits to write on these than it would using the ones provided by you?'

'Their ability to write depends on the spiritual power and not on any earthly means,' he said, but there was a wariness behind the geniality.

'That is very good to know. So, you will have no objection to employing these?'

'None whatsoever.' Mr Castlehouse reached out for them but Mina simply smiled.

'If you don't mind, it would be such an interesting thing for me to display them to the company. Please do indulge me.'

A knowing smile told Mina that he was well aware that he was being tested. He inclined his head briefly. 'Nothing could give me greater pleasure.'

Mina turned and faced the assembled company, who were all attention, and opened up the hinged slates to reveal that they were blank. She then took up the duster and passed it over the surfaces of the slates in view of the onlookers. Next, she selected a fragment of chalk from the box, placed it on one of the slates and closed the pair. Finally, she used the cord that had tied the parcel to bind around the slates, securing it with a number of firm knots.

Once again, Mr Castlehouse offered to take the slates from her but at the risk of being impolite, Mina shook her head and placed them on the table herself. He maintained his good humour. 'You take great care, but I am not offended. The spirits will come if they please.'

He picked up the duster. Mina thought he was about to replace it on the sideboard but instead he whirled it deftly around like a miniature cloak and covered the slates with it. 'And now, while we wait, I would be obliged with your assistance on another matter.'

Mina had been making her way back to her seat, but stopped. 'Of course.'

'If you would come and look at the books I have displayed here.'

Mina obliged.

'Take a slip of paper and an envelope. Select any book you please, but not just yet. When you have done so, open the book, choose the number of a page, the line and position of a word. You will have three numbers. Write these numbers on the paper and place it in the envelope and seal it. Take another slip, write down the word and put it in your pocket. So you may be assured that I cannot possibly see what has been written, I will leave the room for a minute or two. Please, while I am absent, no-one must disturb the covered slates or we will have no result from them.' He bowed, and departed.

Mina was half tempted to pick a dictionary, which would lead to the word 'fraud' but did not want to antagonise Mr Castlehouse. He was clearly assuming that she would select the book with the attractive cover and not one of the dingy volumes that flanked it. She pulled out a volume at random, found the word 'Story', recorded the page, line and word number on the sheet, sealed it in an envelope and noted the word on a second slip. As she regained her seat Mr Castlehouse returned. He paused only to direct a sharp glance at the books on the shelf, but Mina had been careful and no clue remained as to which one had been selected.

He then turned and stood a little back from the table, gazing down at the set of covered slates but made no attempt to come near enough to touch them. 'I would like everyone to concentrate on calling the spirits here present to give us a message.' He stretched both his arms forward palms down, and moved his hands in slow circles like a lazy swimmer.

There was a long expectant silence, in which ears were alert for any sound of chalk on slate. Mina stared at the duster on the table and wondered if it had been touched or disturbed in any way while her attention was elsewhere. Had that been the purpose of the exercise? Had Mr Castlehouse somehow managed to put a message on one of the bound slates before leaving the room, while she had been distracted contemplating the books? It seemed impossible, for if he had done so, then the others in the room must have seen him, and no-one had spoken out. Time passed, five, perhaps ten minutes, and Mr Castlehouse, still making mysterious movements of his hands was shaking his head in disappointment and looked to be about to announce the experiment a failure when there was the unmistakable sound of writing. Everyone stared at the cloth on the table. The noise lasted only a minute, and then there were three loud taps.

Mr Castlehouse, looking exhausted, allowed his arms to drop to his sides. Still he made no attempt to touch the slates, but glanced at Mina. 'I would be grateful, since these are your slates if you could come and look inside and confirm that they are the same ones you brought.'

Mina crossed over to the table and lifted the cloth. The slates certainly looked the same, and they were still tied with a cord. Mina untied them, and opened them up, and as she did so, the fragment of chalk dropped to the table. To her astonishment a message was written on one of the inner faces of the slates. She made a quick examination to see if the tell-tale scratch Miss Clifton had made was there, and it was.

'Please read the message,' said Mr Castlehouse.

Mina held up the slates. She was trembling, not so much because of the appearance of the message but its contents, and what it would mean to Miss Clifton and Mr Fernwood.

'I am to blame. I thought only to stop him drinking. J,' she read.

'Does that mean anything to you?' he asked.

'I am not at liberty to say,' replied Mina. She looked at Miss Clifton who, her eyes wide and frightened, had clasped both her hands over her mouth as if unable to trust herself with what words might emerge. Mina returned to her chair with the slates, and showed them wordlessly to Miss Clifton so she could see the scratch mark. Her companion could only nod.

The room was enlivened by an outbreak of whispers, in tones of awe and admiration. Mina caught the word 'evidential', being the highest accolade any medium might desire. Mr Castlehouse had provided what so many devotees of the supernatural had been earnestly seeking — a phenomenon considered tantamount to scientific proof of communication with the deceased.

Mr Castlehouse did nothing to still the conversation. 'I accept that some messages might be of a highly confidential nature, and I will not press you for details. Perhaps you can now supply the envelope you prepared before?'

Mina had almost forgotten it, but it still lay in her pocket, and she passed it to Mr Castlehouse while Miss Clifton stared at the slates on her lap.

Mr Castlehouse called up another sitter who was prepared to place the envelope between two slates and assist in holding them under the table. Mina barely observed what was happening and Miss Clifton was too distracted to watch at all. The result after several minutes was only the words 'We can write no more. Good-night.'

'It appears that the power of the spirits is exhausted tonight,' said Mr Castlehouse. 'We will hear no more from them.'

Miss Clifton carefully closed the slates, without disturbing the message, wrapped them in their paper and bound them in cord. 'I must show this to George,' she said.

'I trust that you are not too distressed?' said Mr Castlehouse, approaching them, as the other sitters dispersed. 'We do not always receive the messages we expect.'

'It was a surprise, to be sure,' said Miss Clifton. 'But not unwelcome.'

'Let me summon you a cab,' he offered.

'That would be very kind, thank you.'

He looked on them both very kindly. 'Do please call again. The spirits are powerful in your presence, and we receive good results. I would not be surprised if you are both mediums.'

'I have been told so before,' said Mina, although she did not add that those persons who had said so were now residing in prison.

Chapter Thirty-Two

The cab driver was instructed to take Mina home then to go on to the railway station with Miss Clifton. Mina hardly knew what to say as her companion sat absorbed in her thoughts, the wrapped slates clasped to her bosom.

'Miss Clifton,' she ventured at last, 'I know you were watching very closely when I was not in a position to do so. Did Mr Castlehouse touch the slates at any time after I tied them?'

'He did not; I can assure you of that. And how could he have untied them and written on them and tied them up again all in plain sight of everyone in the room?'

Mina agreed. There had been a brief moment when the duster had been whirled about, and then again as she had turned her back to return to her seat, but her companion had been a second pair of eyes, and there had simply not been enough time for the deception to be carried out.

'What do you make of the message?'

'J can only be my aunt Jane.'

'But she was confined to her bed, was she not?'

'She was able to walk a little. And the message explains everything; it is an answer we had never thought of. I think Aunt Jane must have given arsenic to my uncle Thomas, not meaning to kill him but with good intentions. It was only to make him a little unwell so he would forswear the brandy. Do you see what this means? It means that no member of the family had murder in his or her heart and George and I may marry with confidence.'

Her eyes were glittering with unshed tears, and Mina decided that this was not the moment to cast any doubts on the result. If the message was a genuine one then it could only mean happiness for the couple. Even if it was a fraud, and a member of the family was indeed a murderer, no doctor could confirm that this constituted a risk to the next generation. The chance might be small or not exist at all. Mr and Mrs George Fernwood would make good parents. That must count for a great deal.

The cab brought Mina to her door and the driver was kind enough to descend and help her down the steps. 'You take care now, Miss, it's mighty cold out,' he said. 'There'll be ice about soon.'

Before long Mina was sitting by the fire with a bowl of hot broth, wondering about what she had just witnessed. Did spirits really write on slates with pieces of chalk? And if they did why did the slates have to be closed shut or held underneath a table? Why did the power not work in the open? She would have thought it easier to move chalk on an uncovered slate than between two close surfaces. It was not as if the spirits had anything to hide. In fact, the only person who had anything he might want to hide was Mr Castlehouse. If he was a conjuror, he had every reason to conceal how the writing was done.

She finished her broth, and went to her desk, taking out a sheet of paper, pen and ink. She needed to write down all she could recall of what had occurred that evening. It was not, she realised, an easy task. In what order had events occurred? Where had Mr Castlehouse been standing? What movements had he made? She did not know the identity of the lady who had selected the two slates for the first sitting, and tried to recall how many slates had been on the table. Several, she thought. The slates had been washed and dried with the duster, and the chalks laid on them before they were placed together. Mina realised that she had simply assumed that it was the same two slates, but what about the others on the table? Could Mr Castlehouse by sleight of hand, have substituted an already written slate for one of the blank ones? It was possible. The messages were innocuous enough. He had, however, successfully predicted the chalk colours that would be chosen. Even that was not too hard. Red, white and blue might be an obvious choice, and it was hard to see whether one of the chalks was blue or green. Even if he had been wrong about one colour, or two, or all three, it was still a convincing demonstration.

Mina had kept a hold of her set of slates right up to the moment they were laid on the table. Miss Clifton was right, they could not have been interfered with in front of so many people in so short a time. Mina looked at her notes and realised that she had concentrated on her own actions, but had omitted one vital fact. When she had been told to make a note of a chosen word from the book, Mr Castlehouse, saying that he did not want to be accused of being able to see what she was writing, had actually left the room, and been absent for some two minutes. Could he, while appearing to place a duster over the slates, have quickly substituted another one and left the room with Mina's slates hidden under his coat? A conjuror could certainly do such a thing. While she was engaged in selecting a book and recording her chosen word and its location, he was untying the cords, opening the slate, writing the message and re-tying the cord. Had he had the opportunity to restore the slates to their place under the duster? Mina could not be so sure of that. Her back had been turned as she went back to her seat and Miss Clifton was sure he had not tampered with anything, but a moment's inattention was all a conjuror needed.

Mere suspicion was not enough, however, and Mina was loath to declare Mr Castlehouse a fraud without proof, especially as the results were so favourable. Interestingly the message not only removed the fear of an inheritable taint, it placed the guilt of the murder on the one member of the family who was deceased, thus ensuring that there could be no further grief to the Fernwoods and Cliftons. This was all very well as it stood, but what the young couple sought was the truth behind Thomas Fernwood's death. The message would only suit their purpose if it was a genuine solution to the mystery. Supposing Mina could show that Mr Castlehouse, imagining that he was providing what was wanted, had invented the message, then all their fears would be restored. Under the circumstances she might be best advised to leave well alone, but there was still her own curiosity to satisfy, even if she then decided not to communicate her doubts to another person.

Mina could deduce that conjuring could have produced the writing, but how had the medium come up with the contents of the message? How likely was it that he had by pure chance devised something that appeared to solve the dilemma of George Fernwood and Mary Clifton? Mina could not believe this. Either the message was genuine and came from a spirit or somehow Mr Castlehouse knew about the Fernwood case. If he did know, then his motive in creating the message was obvious enough — any medium who appeared to have knowledge of something he could not reasonably have known had made a strong claim to being in contact with the spirits. Producing the message in the presence of a person who recognised its import was crucial to this. The impact on the other sitters had been immediate.

Both George Fernwood and Mary Clifton had been adamant that they had told no-one in Brighton of their family tragedy. Was it possible, however, that one or other of them had incautiously let something slip that had led Mr Castlehouse to make further enquiries and discover the true reasons for their visits?

They might, thought Mina, have talked to visitors at other séances, the ones they had attended before consulting her. Miss Clifton, despite her eagerness, had not been incautious in the séances she had attended with Mina, she had always been careful not to supply her real name, and to make only the most general comments. George Fernwood, however, had continued to visit the Brendels, and these were séances at which Mina had not been present. Mr and Mrs Myles, she recalled, had attended both Miss Brendel's and Mr Castlehouse's séances. Mrs Myles was a sad, suffering creature that anyone might have taken pity on and there could have been an exchange of comforting words. Mr Conroy, too, had visited both mediums, and there must be others who Mina did not know about.

The thought struck her that if the Brendels and Mr Castlehouse were in collusion, exchanging information about their clients, then although she had not given her name to Mr Castlehouse he might still know precisely who she was and was acting accordingly.

But there was some distance between a carelessly dropped word and a message that revealed greater knowledge. What other sources of information were available to Mr Castlehouse? Mina's past experience had taught her that mediums cast their nets wider than most people imagined, and gathered news from all available places, sometimes exchanging titbits that could be brought out to astonish sitters. Some had vast collections of material, newspaper cuttings, notes made from gravestones or gossip. Did Mr Castlehouse or Mrs Brendel know people who had visited Lincoln and were familiar with the Fernwood case? Mrs Brendel, Mina reminded herself, was only recently arrived in Brighton, and had previously resided in Wakefield. This was near enough to Lincoln that she might well have seen some northern editions of the newspapers, and therefore know the story behind the Fernwood mystery.

The other possibility, Mina was obliged to remind herself, was that Mr Castlehouse, for all his theatrical methods, was a genuine medium and he really had received a message from the late Jane Fernwood.

Chapter Thirty-Three

Mina was hoping that the library would be able to furnish her with the volumes recommended by Mr Marriott, so when going out for her weekly trip to the baths, she departed rather earlier than usual to make one journey serve for two. On making enquiries about books by Sir David Brewster and Dr Hibbert, however, she was informed that their works of scholarship were not held. She contented herself with a volume entitled *Traditional Ghost Tales of Olde England*, something she would not have borrowed if her mother had been at home. The reading room was well supplied with newspapers and periodicals, and she took the opportunity to examine them in case there was anything more she might learn about Miss Brendel and Mr Castlehouse, but there was not.

She had also hoped she might encounter either Mr Castlehouse or Mrs Brendel there, since the reading room was a useful source of local information that might well be patronised by those purporting to be mediums in order to gather material that they could then reveal at a séance. Miss Eustace and her confederates had used it and they had also attended Dr Hamid's and Brill's Baths, where the ladies and gentlemen's lounges were formidable gossip exchanges. Mina, enjoying the warmth and the quiet of the library, decided to remain as long as she could, in case her two suspects made an appearance, but neither did.

Disappointed, she was about to leave, when a sudden, unusually sharp movement caught her eye. A veiled lady who had entered the reading room had stopped and quickly turned her head aside. She was too short to be Mrs Brendel, too stout to be the daughter, yet there was something in the abrupt way she had turned that suggested she had done so to avoid someone's notice. Could it be Mina she did not wish to meet, or someone else? The lady hurriedly picked up a journal, placed it on a reading stand and bent over it, examining the pages in a manner that suggested keen interest in its contents. To do so, she was obliged to slightly lift her veil.

Mina decided to walk about the room towards the stand where the periodicals were displayed, her path taking her past the intent reader. As she neared, the lady, who seemed to be disturbed in case Mina was coming to speak to her, shot a brief glance in her direction, then, as Mina continued to walk on in the direction of the periodicals, quickly fastened her gaze onto the page before her.

Mina had now glimpsed enough of the face to feel that it looked a little familiar, but there was nothing about the clothing that she recognised. If the lady had not acted as she had Mina might have assumed that there was simply a resemblance to someone she knew, and departed, but her suspicions had been aroused. She opened a journal on the subject of notable buildings of Sussex, and gave the question some thought. The reader was not a maidservant sent on an errand, being better dressed than a servant, and in any case she did not resemble either in face or form the Brendels' or Mr Castlehouse's maid. Mina dared another quick look, and realised that the lady bore a close resemblance to Mrs Myles, who was grey haired and normally to be seen in deepest mourning, but now had brown hair and was wearing a mustard coloured ensemble with a matching bonnet. Ladies did dye their hair, so that was not altogether unusual. They did emerge from their weeds but not so abruptly as this. And if they knew the secret of shedding twenty years in age they would not need to visit public reading rooms.

Mina put down the journal and turned to the lady. 'Mrs Myles? What brings you here?'

'Oh,' said the lady, dropping her veil, and holding a gloved hand in front of her face. 'I think you are in error. That is not my name, but I am often addressed in that way since I bear a remarkable resemblance to another person called Myles. Please excuse me.' She closed the journal and made to return it to its stand.

'I am sorry for my mistake,' said Mina, but as the lady replaced the journal she saw, through the lace of the right glove, a mourning ring of domed onyx, with a single pearl. Mina hurried to her side as fast as she was able. 'There is no mistake. You are Mrs Myles, who attended the séances of Miss Brendel and Mr Castlehouse. We spoke, and I remember you distinctly, although you were not dressed as you are now, which did confuse me initially, or I would have known you at once. And I think you must have been wearing a wig. Come, now, what do you mean by this masquerade?'

'Do not speak so loud!' hissed the lady, who Mina was now quite sure was Mrs Myles.

'I promise to keep my voice down, but only if you agree to explain yourself.'

'Very well,' said Mrs Myles reluctantly, 'but let us go out as people are beginning to stare at us.'

'I have no fear of that, people always stare at me. But we will go only as far as the entrance hall. We may talk there. Do not run away from me. That will have consequences.'

They retired to the entrance hall, and found a location where they would not impede anyone coming and going. Mina, despite her warning, took care to place herself between Mrs Myles and the door. 'Well? What do you have to say?'

Mrs Myles, recovering from her initial discomfiture, drew herself up to her full height, lifted her veil, and squared her shoulders with pride. Her dissimulation had been a good one, since Mina did not think the lady could be much over thirty-five. 'Myles is not our real name, but Mr Myles is my husband and we have been theatrical artists for some years. We provide a service. It is an ancient and honourable profession. Similar to that of mourners. We do that too, but we are particularly in demand by mediums.'

'So — let me understand this — you pretend to be bereaved persons; you attend séances and claim to have received communications from the dead when you have not?'

Mrs Myles seemed perfectly satisfied with that description of her activities. 'That is a part of what we do. We will also ask certain questions when required to. What most people do not appreciate,' she went on, speaking indulgently, as if explaining to a child, 'is that the art of the medium is not something that may be lit or unlit like a lamp. Sometimes it blazes brightly and at other times it does not. But the medium does not know when that will be. Each séance is a journey into the unknown.'

'Do you mean that there might be unbelievers at a séance emitting negative energy which will stifle the medium's powers, or the atmospheric conditions might prevent the spirits from getting through?'

'I am so glad you understand,' said Mrs Myles with some relief, failing to appreciate the satirical nature of Mina's tone. 'And that is why our particular skills are needed. The public, in their ignorance, expect to receive results every time, especially if they have paid. So, in order to satisfy them we attend to make sure that there is some activity at least. It is a comfort to the bereaved.'

Mina did her best to control her annoyance. 'You see nothing dishonest in what you do?'

'No, of course not. We are actors playing on a stage. We like to vary the characterisations; sometimes we are an elderly couple in deep mourning, other times we are younger and searching for a lost child. For much of the year we are in London and then we come to Brighton for the winter. We did especially well last year when so many lives were lost in the sinking of the *Captain*, and the relatives of the drowned men were wanting to speak to them. All the best mediums employ us.'

'I have no doubt of it,' said Mina. 'You are very convincing. If I might be permitted to ask an impertinent question, do you receive a percentage of what they take, or a fee?'

'Oh, that depends on the nature of the event.'

'What of Mrs Brendel, since she does not charge for her séances?'

'We have asked for nothing as yet. We agreed to attend gratis three times as a demonstration and hope for business in future.'

'And Mr Castlehouse?'

She gave a simpering smile. 'Now that would be saying. But the public is not being cheated; they get a good performance for their money. We are actors, after all. If we stepped on stage and said we were Anthony and Cleopatra it would be the same thing.'

'But that is not what the public go to a séance for. They hope to receive the truth.'

Mrs Myles waved away the objection airily. 'Oh, who can tell what the truth is?'

'Do you perform other services for mediums? I mean, do you collect information about sitters and pass it on?'

'We are not specifically engaged to do so, but then we are artistes, not detectives. We do converse with the other sitters, and the mediums ask us afterwards if we have learned anything of interest. This is because the knowledge will assist the spirits in coming through to the right persons.'

Mina could not trust herself to comment on this. 'If you believe there is nothing wrong in what you are doing, why did you try and escape from me just now? Why did you deny who you were?'

'Because your opinions are well known in Brighton. We have been warned about you. I feared that you would spoil the illusion.'

'Then you admit that everything at the Brendels and Mr Castlehouse's is an illusion?'

Mrs Myles hesitated, glanced about to see that no-one was approaching, then stepped closer and spoke more softly. 'Well, to be frank with you, Miss Scarletti, what I said to you just before, about the art of the medium, that is what they would have us believe. But I see now that you are more astute than that. Of course it is all an illusion. I have never been to a séance that was not. But most sensible people know that, don't they?'

'One would hope so. I notice you wear a mourning ring.'

'Ah yes, my grandmother's.'

'That is how I was so certain it was you. So, in all the séances you have ever attended, and I assume it is a considerable number, you have never received a genuine communication?'

'Why no.' She glanced at the ring. 'I had better be more careful of this in future.' She smiled contentedly. 'It has been a pleasure to make your acquaintance, Miss Scarletti. I do hope you will attend the Theatre Royal to see the grand Christmas pantomime, *Goody Two-Shoes and her Queen Anne's Farthing*. We are understudies for King Counterfeit and Fairy Spiteful, and it promises to be excellent.'

Mrs Myles exited stage right, and Mina was left wondering what to do if she should encounter the lady and her husband at a future séance. They were instrumental in promoting deceit but denouncing them would most probably lead to an unpleasant scene, and rebound on Mina who would then be branded as someone who had made distressing accusations against a bereaved couple. Such consummate thespians would have no difficulty in remaining in character and retaining the upper hand.

Chapter Thirty-Four

Mina was pondering this problem on her way to the baths where she once again encountered her new acquaintance, Miss Landwick. The lady's previous companions, who enjoyed their cosy gatherings in the salon where they could descant on the deformities of others, were astounded to see her greet Mina as a friend, and move apart from them to talk to her. There was much whispering behind hands.

'Your companions disapprove of me, I think,' said Mina.

'No matter,' said Miss Landwick. 'I disapprove of them, and was only in their company before to have someone to speak to, but such empty-headed conversation I never knew.'

'I have just had the most remarkable encounter,' said Mina. 'Mrs Myles, fashionably dressed and looking twenty years younger than she had at the séances she attended. I challenged her, and she admitted with no trace of shame, that she and her husband are actors, paid by persons such as Mr Castlehouse to pretend to receive messages from the spirits.'

Miss Landwick was suitably shocked. 'Oh my word, whatever next! So Mr Castlehouse is a fraud?'

'I am sure of it, although mediums will always claim that they only cheat occasionally when the spirits are reluctant or unable to appear, so as not to disappoint sitters who are in need of comfort. It is very hard to prove that they cheat all the time. Your brother seems confident that he could do so, however.'

'Oh, he is,' said Miss Landwick, eagerly. 'From the first moment he ever saw a conjuror, when quite a small child, Charles has wanted to do conjuring tricks and he has amused himself with this interest ever since. He entertains us all after dinner, and really he is marvellously adept, good enough to take to the stage, though he would never do so, of course. When I first went to see Mr Castlehouse I was very impressed by him and told Charles what I had seen, but he pooh-poohed the whole thing and said he could do the same thing perfectly easily without any spirits being involved.'

'I am less mystified about the manner of writing on the slates than the content of the message,' said Mina. 'If your brother could explain that to me, I would be extremely grateful.'

'I will be sure to ask him. In fact, you may ask him yourself, as he is coming here to meet me and you may share our cab.' Miss Landwick paused. 'Miss Scarletti — perhaps you could inform me of something. Mr Conroy — is he by any chance connected with Jordan and Conroy, the garment emporium?'

'He is the younger brother of the Mr Conroy in question.'

'Oh, I see.'

'He has his own business manufacturing military uniforms. A highly successful one, I understand.'

'And he is in mourning — is he a widower?'

'He is. I believe his wife passed away about a year ago.'

Miss Landwick did not comment but absorbed the information.

'And there are four small children.'

Miss Landwick smiled. 'How comforting for him. I am so very fond of children.'

When Miss Landwick and Mina were ready to depart, they boarded the cab hired by the lady's brother and all three proceeded together.

'I would be interested to hear your opinion of Mr Castlehouse's performance,' said Mina to Mr Landwick.

'As I anticipated,' said the gentleman, with a grunt of derision, 'the entire evening was an illusion. The man is no more than a stage conjuror pretending to be a medium. He uses sleight of hand to change a blank slate with one he has written on before. I know about these things because I do a little myself and I know what to look for.'

'But Miss Scarletti, you brought your own slates did you not? How could he trick you?' said Miss Landwick. 'I can see that he might have changed like with like using his own slates, but he didn't have another set like yours. And they were tied up with a cord.'

'I have given that some thought,' said Mina, 'and I believe that when he covered my slates with the duster he quickly substituted a set of his own, just so that it would look as though mine were still there, and then he slipped mine under his coat.'

Mr Landwick nodded. 'I thought at the time that there was some trick with the duster.'

'Then he distracted me by asking me to choose a word from a book, and left the room, taking my slates with him. He said his purpose was to ensure that he could not see what I was writing but I think that while he was out of the room he untied the slates, wrote a message, and re-tied them. When he came back I didn't notice him at first, and he might have done anything behind my back. I think he must have lifted the duster on the pretext that he just wanted to look at the slates, apparently an innocent movement, but he used it to perform more sleight of hand, and substituted my slates for his. Were you watching him? Did he do something of that sort?'

'I was looking very carefully,' said the gentleman, 'in fact I followed him with my eyes as soon as he re-entered the room. I remember thinking that as you had brought your own slates, there would be no result unless he could somehow abstract them and write on them, so I was watching for the moment that might provide the opportunity, even if he could do it too quickly for my eyes to detect the movement. I agree with you thus far, he might have taken the slates, certainly, but when he returned to the room, he did not go near the table at all. I saw him cast a glance at the books on the sideboard, and thought to myself he is trying to see which one you chose. Then we heard the sound of scratching, which I know he must have made himself. Perhaps with something in his pocket, or with his foot. But at no time before you uncovered he slates was he within arm's reach of them. I must confess that my initial thought on seeing the message was that you were in collusion with him, and the slate was a trick slate of some sort.'

'I can understand why you must have thought that, but I can assure you that the slates were of quite the usual kind, and so far from being in collusion with Mr Castlehouse I was trying to test him. If you can offer any suggestions as to how he achieved the trick, I would be very grateful.'

'Well, I might be able to help you, there,' said Landwick. 'I attend exhibitions of conjuring quite often and am acquainted with several of its best practitioners. I will make some enquiries and see what I can discover. I am not of their fraternity, but they approve my interest and admit that I have some ability. I am sure Mr Castlehouse is no mystery to them.'

'I would be extremely grateful to hear from you on that matter,' said Mina, and cards were duly exchanged.

'Perhaps Mr and Mrs Myles helped with the trick,' said Miss Landwick. 'I saw them there, but Miss Scarletti has just told me they are confederates of Mr Castlehouse paid to pretend they receive messages.'

'Outrageous!' said Landwick.

'But the message you received!' exclaimed the lady turning to Mina. 'How extraordinary! What did it mean? I could see that you were very shocked by it.'

'Yes, I was, but I regret I am not at liberty to reveal why.'

'Oh, I promise I will tell no-one, it will be our secret!'

Mr Landwick rolled his eyes.

'I would tell you if I could, and one day if I am permitted, I might. But not today.'

There were two quite separate puzzles engaging Mina's mind. How had Mr Castlehouse written on the marked slate? And how did he know what to write? The answer to the Fernwood mystery, now Mina thought about it, was too simple, too pat. If Jane Fernwood had really wanted to confess to murder from beyond the grave why had she not done so long before and saved her family years of miserable uncertainty? If she had been too ashamed or fearful to confess it, why had she not left a sealed letter of confession to be opened after her death? Mina was not at all convinced that the message was genuine but it was exactly what suited the needs of the young couple. As to how Mr Castlehouse had written on the slate, who knew how he had done so if he had not taken it from the room? Perhaps he had some dexterous ability to abstract the slate, hold it behind his back, untie the knots, write the message with one hand and re-tie it, then replace it when the sitters' attention was distracted elsewhere. Most men could not do so, but a conjuror might be trained in that art. Now that Mina thought about it there had been something unusual about the slate when she had untied it. She had been so eager, in fact far too eager, to untie the cord and look inside, that she had not especially taken note of how it had been tied. If she had had her wits more about her she would have sealed the knots with wax. But now she recalled that although the slates had been tied as before, in the common style of a parcel, the ends of the cord were shorter than she remembered. Either it was a different piece of cord, or more likely the same piece re-tied more loosely, as it might have been if only one hand was employed. Was that the answer?

Mina determined to ask Nellie about this the next time they met. There only remained the more complicated question of the message. It seemed so very remote a chance that Mr Castlehouse had ever resided in Lincoln and was therefore acquainted with the Fernwood tragedy, or even that he knew someone who recalled it. He had been given no clues that Miss Clifton had any connection with the event. Dr Sperley, even if he had written a memoir had never published it.

This speculation, Mina told herself, was idle. Mediums were adept at providing information that their dupes were convinced it was impossible for them to know, but once all was revealed, the trick was seen to be simple enough. The only person who knew the secret was Mr Castlehouse.

Chapter Thirty-Five

Dear Mr Scarletti,

Thank you for your letter. I have been trying to go through my late husband's papers, but it has been something of a trial to me as my old eyes are just not what they were and his handwriting is very hard to read at the best of times. I enclose some notebooks, which appear to be a journal of some sort. If you can make anything of them it would be such a boon to me, as it would relieve me of a difficult task. There may be more, but I cannot lay my hands on them at present.

Yours truly,
Sophia Sperley
Newland House
Lincoln

Enclosed with Mrs Sperley's letter were about two dozen notebooks, all closely written. Mina quickly replied to the sender to confirm that they had been safely received and she would take great care of them. Then she sat down to read.

As she had been warned, the writing was small, and it took a while to acquaint herself with the style so she could make out the words.

Most of the notebooks were appointment diaries covering the period from about 1840 to 1862 when Dr Sperley had retired from practice. Others were a series of observations on patients, and fortunately, these were dated. Mina found a number of entries concerning the Fernwoods and the Cliftons. Mrs Jane Fernwood featured often as the doctor visited her regularly to attend to her back and legs. Privately, however, he thought that the lady preferred to be thought of as an invalid, and was better able to move about than she liked to pretend. He had tried to encourage her to make more of an effort to walk regularly as it would do her good.

The boys, cousins Peter and George, had never required the attention of a doctor, and neither had Mrs Clifton and her daughter. Mrs Clifton was skilled in home remedies and did what was needed for colds and coughs and the scraped knees from boyish games. Ada and Ellen, Thomas Fernwood's granddaughters had received occasional treatment for the usual female complaints. Fernwood himself had been told repeatedly that he drank more than was good for him, and had taken this advice with very ill humour. It had changed his behaviour not one whit.

Sperley had recorded in detail the events of Thomas Fernwood's death; the appalling symptoms, the suspicions of poisoning from the outset, Fernwood's last communication that he had been murdered and knew the culprit, his death before he could divulge the information, the post mortem examination carried out by four doctors, of whom the writer had been one, the many indications that proved beyond any doubt that death was due to arsenic, and the inquest. Mina read it all with great attention, but there was nothing further to be learned.

In 1861 Mrs Jane Fernwood had died peacefully from heart failure with her loving family at her bedside.

The final entry in the last journal was in the smallest writing Mina had ever seen.

Today I was informed by William Fernwood that the family will be removing from Lincoln. I had attended them for more than twenty years and have seen them at their best and worst. I was aware from the very beginning of my acquaintance with them that theirs was a desperately unhappy household, and this was due to a single cause, Thomas

Fernwood, whose bad temper, meanness and ill treatment of his family cast a shadow over the lives of all who shared his home.

Following Thomas Fernwood's death, the darkness that had shrouded the Fernwoods and Cliftons largely dispersed. I say 'largely' because there are some things that are so terrible they can never be undone.

I have no doubt at all, although I cannot prove it, that Thomas Fernwood was murdered by a member of his own family. Of course, I suspect who that individual is, but I must not put a name to that suspicion, as I might be mistaken. Better to stay silent unless I have proof. I have no wish to add to this family's unhappiness.

It is true that every member of the family benefitted by Thomas Fernwood's death. I am not referring only to money, although that is one factor. Mrs Fernwood was undoubtedly a far happier woman for the loss of her tyrannical husband. She was able to stir from her bed of pain, walk about more than she had done before and have some pleasure in life. She enjoyed the companionship of Mrs Clifton, and the two became great friends. I believe that her previous insistence that she was an invalid was largely due to a desire to be ignored by her husband as far as was possible, and in that she was successful. Her son, Mr William Fernwood inherited the bulk of the property, and he and his wife were able to enjoy a more comfortable life free from excessive hours of labour.

The three girls, Ada, Ellen and Mary, were no longer treated as unpaid drudges, and were sent to good schools to complete their education.

As to the boys, I am sorry to say that Thomas Fernwood had been in the habit of using severe corporal punishment on them if they failed to do well at school. Both Peter and George were beaten in a manner that far exceeded what even an advocate of that kind of chastisement would think acceptable. George was much the better scholar and so suffered less, but Peter, who was a little slow for his age, was beaten often and hard, in a manner that caused great distress to Mrs Clifton, who begged Fernwood not to hurt her son. I am convinced that it was only the threat of the *workhouse for Mrs Clifton and her son and daughter that kept them in the house.*

There is only one person who I know for certain did not commit the murder, and that was Mrs Jane Fernwood, not because she did not have a motive, but because she had suffered a fall the day before, and in addition to her painful back and legs she had twisted her ankle which was very swollen and would not bear her weight. She was therefore quite unable to walk unassisted. To go downstairs and get the arsenic and put it in her husband's tea, however much she might have wished to, was beyond her capabilities.

I can say no more. The murderer will be punished one day, if not in this life then the next.

Mina was still wondering what it was that Thomas Fernwood had seen which had so convinced him that he had been deliberately poisoned. If he had noticed someone putting something in his tea and thought it suspicious, then surely he would not have drunk it. Perhaps the poisoner had told him it was sugar being added or it was being stirred simply to cool it, and he had only found out differently when the corrosive savaged his throat and intestines.

Mrs Clifton, Mary's mother, was an obvious suspect since she had made the tea and bought it to him. She, Mina reasoned, would have put the poison in the tea when it was made, and not added it later, at the bedside, unless there was a potential witness in the kitchen or on the stairs. Once again, she studied the inquest report. No-one else had said they were in the kitchen when the Thomas Fernwood's tea was being made, and no-one had seen Mrs Clifton take it up to his bedroom. Mina began to wonder if Fernwood had not, after all, seen anything suspicious, but had simply assumed that it was Mrs Clifton who had poisoned the tea.

If it was not she, then the poison must have been stirred into the tea after it was made. Mrs Clifton had not left the cup unobserved at any time right up to the moment it was placed beside Thomas Fernwood's bed. There was then a clear ten or fifteen minutes for the deed to be done. William Fernwood, as his father's main heir, was an obvious suspect although his wife Margery might have carried out the actual poisoning at his behest.

Did Peter, though only ten, poison his great uncle to avoid more beatings? But would Peter have even known where the arsenic was kept in the house? It was in a kitchen drawer to which he was unlikely to have gone. Also, the inquest evidence suggested that all the children were at the breakfast table at the crucial time.

And yet, Mina thought, memory being what it was, no-one would have been paying attention from moment to moment where everyone in the house actually was. The only record of it was in recollections too fallible to trust. Anyone might have absented themselves from a room for a minute or two, an incident so trivial that the others might not have remembered or even noticed it.

Mina was obliged to remind herself that fascinating as the puzzle was, it was none of her business who had killed Thomas Fernwood, but she needed to consider the question if only to judge how truthful or possible any messages from mediums might be. If Dr Sperley's notes were correct, then Jane Fernwood was innocent, and Mr Castlehouse's message did not apply to the Fernwood case at all, although Miss Clifton was understandably convinced it was.

And now Mina had a terrible dilemma. Should she tell George Fernwood and Miss Clifton what was in Dr Sperley's notes? The message on the slate had taken away their fears and would enable them to marry with a clear conscience. Perhaps, Mina thought, she ought to leave strictly alone.

Chapter Thirty-Six

Dear Mina,

I am returning to Brighton at once as I have some very exciting news, which I can't wait to share with you! I will call on you tomorrow afternoon, at 3 and tell all. Oh, do say you will be at home!

Yours,

Nellie

Mina wondered if Nellie, several months married, was anticipating an addition to her domestic scene, but suspected that news which many women would have met with great happiness was not something which would bring Nellie so much satisfaction. She dispatched a note to say that she would be at home and would be delighted to receive a visit.

'Well!' said Nellie, her face glowing, as she kissed Mina on both cheeks. 'It is the most wonderful thing I have to tell you! I do hope you have a beautiful gown as you will be required to wear it!'

'Dare I ask for what event?' asked Mina, adding cautiously, as they made themselves comfortable before the glow of the parlour fire. 'From the tone of your letter, I had suspected a christening.'

Nellie's eyes opened very wide, then she laughed. 'Oh, no, nothing of that kind, not if I am concerned. That will never be.'

'Never? Does Mr Jordan know that?'

'Not yet.' Nellie placed a hand flat to her waist, which was as trim as it had always been. 'Mina, my dear,' she said confidingly, 'you and I, we are not made to be mothers. I did think, when I was with M. Baptiste, that there was a danger it might happen, but instead, I learned that it never could.' Her voice softened and her face became solemn as she went on. 'Believe me, we two are better off that way, I am sure of it.' A bright smile jumped into life, bringing fresh warmth to her features. 'Well, enough of that. No, the news concerns my dear friend Kitty Betts, the miraculous Princess Kirabampu, who Richard drew so beautifully at my *salon*. Would you believe, she is to be married! And before the year is out!'

Rose brought the tea tray, and cook's attempt at almond biscuits, which were more icing than biscuit and topped with roughly chopped almonds. 'Thank you Rose,' said Mina, kindly, and the maid withdrew.

'Richard has flattered cook into attempting confectionary but she is a little heavy handed at present. Still, we hope for improvement with practice.' Mina poured the tea. 'I didn't know Miss Betts was betrothed.'

'Well, that is what is so surprising,' said Nellie, selecting a biscuit, examining it to see if it was edible, and taking a careful bite. 'When you met her at my house she wasn't. It was all so sudden. And to think it was actually my doing, as she first met her future husband on that very evening. It seems that soon afterwards she was shopping in St James' Street and chanced to meet the gentleman again, and they started to converse. There could not have been more romance in the air if it had been spring blossom time. They agreed to meet again and it was all settled in days. The license has been applied for and they will be married before Christmas.'

'St James' Street?' Mina recalled that this was the location of the art gallery. 'She is not marrying Mr Dorry, is she?'

'Mr Dorry? Oh, goodness me, no, Mr Dorry will never marry unless the law is amended so one can wed a statue. Did you not know? He is in love with a beautiful Adonis, all in marble, and quite nude. No, Kitty is to marry Mr Honeyacre.'

Mina was so astounded she nearly dropped her teacup, and for a moment thought she had actually misheard. The last time she had seen Mr Honeyacre he had assured her in perfect seriousness that his ideal life companion was a respectable lady of culture and good sense, and he was now about to marry a flirtatious contortionist. Once again, she felt thankful that men and marriage were things with which she did not need to concern herself.

'I am to be matron of honour,' Nellie continued, placing the uneaten half of her biscuit on her plate, where Mina felt sure it would remain, 'and tomorrow night there will be a delightful supper to celebrate the betrothal, which you must attend.' Nellie handed Mina an invitation.

Mina felt obliged to mention the recent misunderstanding between herself and Mr Honeyacre and Nellie laughed until tears started in her eyes and then assured Mina that she would see things put right. 'And now I must hurry away as there is so much to do. Kitty is choosing her trousseau and her going away gowns, all from Jordan and Conroy, of course, and I am to advise her. No expense will be spared. The wedding breakfast will be held in the assembly room at the Grand Hotel, and the entertainment will be second to none. Kitty's mother is a Red Indian and will be sawn in half, her father is a Chinese sword-swallower, and her brothers are Greek acrobats. It will be the wedding of the year.'

'I have spoken to Nellie,' said Richard, as he and Mina ate luncheon the following day. 'We met at a coffee room, suitably chaperoned by Miss Kitty Betts and Mr Honeyacre, who has quite forgiven me for being your secret *amour*. The private detective who was watching us from the next table will be able to report that there was no unseemly behaviour. I am given to understand that I am not to attend the little celebratory gathering tonight, as Mr Jordan prefers not to sit across a table from me unless it is very much wider than the Grand Hotel can accommodate. No matter, I can do without his presence, which would quite put me off my food. He has a stare that would curdle milk. He hopes it will curdle my blood but it does no such thing.'

'Poor Richard, I hope you will be at the wedding.'

'Oh yes, Miss Betts wants me for an usher, and has asked me to sketch the event.' He served himself a large helping of trifle, which was mainly composed of custard and leftover almond biscuits. 'Tonight, however, I will take my busy pencil to the theatre, where that shining star of the Brighton stage, Mr Marcus Merridew, will personating all the great heroes of Shakespeare with a dozen changes of costume and twice as many wigs, after which there will be champagne and laughter.' Once luncheon was over, he departed in far better humour than Mina had feared.

For that evening's select gathering Mr Honeyacre had secured a table in a private portion of the restaurant attached to the Grand Hotel. As Mina awaited the cab he had ordered, Rose, who must have received a schedule of instructions from Dr Hamid, loaded her in enough layers of clothing to promote heat rash and escorted her down the front steps.

'Where too, Miss?' asked the cabdriver with the tartan scarf. He had already climbed down and opened the door for his passenger. 'Will it be Mr Castlehouse's again?'

'Not today,' said Mina with a smile. 'Is Mr Castlehouse's a very popular destination?'

'Oh, he is, yes, Miss. I take a great many people there, both ladies and gentlemen. They tell me all about it, too. Very strange it is, and all. Some of them even come straight from the railway station so they have come a long way special to see him. One lady even went there twice in one day.'

Mina, leaning on his arm, was about to step into the cab but she paused. Was this the evidence she had been looking for, that Mr Castlehouse conducted private séances at high prices?

'Two sittings in one day?' she exclaimed. 'How extraordinary. He only advertises one in the newspapers. Are you certain?'

'Well, not for a sitting, as she wasn't there above ten minutes the first time. That was the same lady you travelled with.'

Mina was so astonished by this news it made her shiver. 'Twice in one day? The lady I travelled with went to Mr Castlehouse twice on the same day? Tell me more.'

The driver was a little taken aback by her intensity but did his best to remember. 'Well I took her from the station to Mr Castlehouse's lodgings. She told me to wait for a few minutes, and then she came out again and straight after that I took her to you. Then I took both of you to Mr Castlehouse.'

Mina had been to Mr Castlehouse's twice, both times in the company of Miss Clifton. 'Do you recall what day this was?'

He scratched his head. 'Not rightly, no.'

'Was the lady carrying a parcel?'

He thought hard. 'Yes. Something. Two parcels, I think. Yes, that's right, she had two, and she left one with Mr Castlehouse and then she took the other one to you.'

Mina hardly dared ask the next question. 'Two parcels the same size and shape?'

'Yes.'

'Tied with cord,' said Mina, faintly, though it was less of a question than a statement.

'Both of them, yes, I think so. Are you alright Miss?'

Mina nodded, speechlessly.

'May I help you, Miss?' He offered his arm and assisted her into the cab.

Mina wanted to stay at home. She wanted to sit quietly alone by her own fireside with hot soup and bread and a glass of sherry and think about what she had just learned. Instead she was obliged to go to the shine and bustle of the Grand Hotel, and pretend that all was well.

Miss Betts and Nellie chattered away the evening, and Mr Honeyacre, after attempting to apologise to Mina for his rapid departure at their last meeting without actually saying why it had occurred, sat bemusedly gazing on his vivacious betrothed. If Mina said less than was usual, it was scarcely noticed. She did take the opportunity to ask about the expression 'unknown artist' and Mr Honeyacre replied that in his experience it referred to the fact that no-one knew who had created a work. He could not say why lack of a signature could ever be thought a good thing.

Once home, Mina wrote a letter to Miss Clifton, saying that she would like to speak to her when she was next in Brighton, as she had something of great significance to impart.

Chapter Thirty-Seven

Miss Clifton was able to call on Mina in two days' time, and arrived in tremendous good humour. 'I am so very excited to hear what you have to say! Why could you not have put it in a letter instead of making me wait so?' she teased. 'Have you been to Miss Brendel again? Or Mr Castlehouse? Or is it another medium? But I must tell you, George was so astonished when I showed him the slates. He is almost convinced, now, I am sure of it. We are planning to go to Mr Castlehouse together as soon as possible, and this time I am certain we will receive proof that even George cannot dismiss!'

'Miss Clifton,' said Mina, quietly, 'I am sorry to have to say this to you, but I have discovered that you have deceived me. I have chosen to speak to you alone because I do not as yet know whether you have also deceived Mr Fernwood, or whether the two of you were working together, or if the deception was actually his and you were merely his agent.'

Miss Clifton looked shocked, and as she recovered from her initial surprise, a host of emotions flickered across her face. Mina watched this procession carefully. Since she had been careful not to reveal what she knew, her visitor had been plunged into a state of uncertainty. She could guess what Miss Clifton must be thinking. What, precisely, did Mina know? How much could be denied or safely revealed? 'I am sure I don't know what you mean,' said Miss Clifton at last, with a fragile defiance that sounded doomed from the start not to last.

Mina continued. 'What I am not yet sure of is if you intended to deceive me from the very beginning or turned to the scheme afterwards. Either way, it is clear that I cannot assist you further. I do have some passing interest in your motives, but if you choose to tell me nothing that is your affair. I regret that after today we cannot meet again. You may say whatever you wish to Mr Fernwood. That is your business.'

Miss Clifton looked as if she was about to say more, but remained silent.

Mina reached for the bell to summon Rose. 'If there is no more to discuss, then I bid you good-day.'

'Please!' said Miss Clifton, impulsively. 'I am so sorry, but I believe I have done nothing very wrong. I only wish to be married before I am middle aged. That is every woman's desire — a husband — children.' She paused and blushed suddenly, recalling that this was an ambition to which Mina could not aspire.

Mina stayed her hand. 'And you thought you could achieve that by consulting a medium? Even though at one time you had no belief in them?'

'I had never visited a medium before, I only knew what I had heard and read, but George and I were desperate for an answer, and it seemed the only way. But when we went to our first séances I concluded that as I had originally thought, these people were charlatans intent on making money from unhappy people. The replies they gave us were so general, so vague they could have applied to anyone. The other sitters — I felt so sorry for them, grasping at little hints they thought were meant for them. They wanted to believe, but if I ever had any faith in such a thing, it soon vanished.'

'And yet you went on. In fact, you gave me every impression that you were a devoted believer, whereas Mr Fernwood doubted that any result was possible.'

Miss Clifton chewed her lip and moved her hands convulsively. 'You must understand, Miss Scarletti. When George and I consulted our doctor as to whether it was advisable for us to marry and have a family, he said he thought that the dangers were slight, but he could not reassure us that there were none. I was willing to take the chance. I know I can be a good mother and lead my children along the paths of honesty, but George said he could not accept even a small risk of what terrible things might ensue from the mixing of the same blood. I thought that if there was some answer that would satisfy him we might yet marry, but he said that it was hopeless as the only person who knew the answer was uncle Thomas. George always thought that Dr Sperley had his suspicions, but he had passed away not long before. Then I read in the newspapers about the trial of Miss Eustace and her confederates, and the evidence you gave in that affair, and it gave me the idea of consulting you to see if there was a genuine medium who could help.'

Mina was not placated, and her manner did not waver. 'But it was more than that. Perhaps you did entertain the possibility of finding a genuine medium, but you must have thought it far more probable that you would find another clever and convincing cheat like Miss Eustace. My feeling is that you never became a believer; you began as a sceptic and continued as one, and remain one still. You pretended to believe solely in order to persuade Mr Fernwood to visit mediums. In fact, I will go further; you were never really looking for a genuine medium at all, were you? You were looking for one who was capable of providing evidence that would convince Mr Fernwood, and could be bribed into doing so. Am I correct?'

Miss Clifton began to look afraid.

'You told Mr Castlehouse what to write on the slate, didn't you? You made it up.'

Miss Clifton nodded.

'You bought two identical sets of folding slates, and made the same secret mark on them both, one of which you gave to Mr Castlehouse before the séance.'

'How do you know that?'

'Let it remain a mystery. So, am I correct that Mr Fernwood knows nothing of your deception?'

'You are. But I beg you not to tell him!'

'That is really none of my business. As a matter of curiosity, do you think your solution was the correct one? Your great aunt was an invalid and might not have been able to commit the crime. What if she was unable to stir from her bed?'

'She could walk better than she liked to admit. But I don't mind or care if it is right or not. It is the answer we need in order to live our lives. The past is past, and we can't change it, we must accept that and look to the future. If we dwell forever in the past we will have no future. All I want is to marry George and help him with the shop and have a family. Is that really too much to ask?'

Mina's annoyance with Miss Clifton began to soften. 'No, it is very natural. But I think under the circumstances I have done all I can, and more. I now leave it to you to convince Mr Fernwood that he has nothing to be anxious about, and I wish you both every happiness for the future.'

It was a formal parting of the ways. Once Miss Clifton had left, Mina gave further thought to the question of Thomas Fernwood's death. It was possible that the children did not know about Jane Fernwood's twisted ankle. A visit from Dr Sperley to attend her was a regular event and would not have invited curiosity. Even if Dr Sperley was correct, however, and

Jane Fernwood could not have left her bed to poison her husband's tea, it was, Mina realised, still possible that Miss Clifton had stumbled on the right answer, and her aunt was the guiding intelligence behind the murder. The unhappy Mrs Fernwood had been tended by Mrs Clifton and granddaughters, Ada and Ellen, and her own son and daughter in law must also have visited her. She could have suggested to any one of them the idea of curing Thomas Fernwood's fondness for the bottle with a little medicinal arsenic. His death could still have been due to an accidental overdose, or maybe his drinking had weakened his stomach and made him more likely to die from a dose that would not have killed a healthier man. Whoever had actually added it to the tea had been horrified by the unplanned death, and understandably chosen to remain silent. There was still, to Mina, the puzzle of how Thomas Fernwood had known the identity of his poisoner. It was something she was now sure she would never know.

It was done. Mina had no intention of seeing either Miss Clifton or Mr Fernwood again. Neither did she wish to visit Miss Brendel or Mr Castlehouse. What she needed was an hour at the baths, surrounded by scented vapour and then the delicious ease of perfumed oils being gentled into her skin. The baths were her haven, where no-one could demand she do anything or deliver complaining letters. She could let her thoughts glide through the ether and pick up the story ideas that swam there. She would write a story about a magic herb, whose vapours made bad people good and discontented people happy, that took away pain and selfishness, and anxiety. The more she thought about it the more she saw that such an invention would only bring chaos to the world.

Once her treatment was over, she thought of going to see Dr Hamid to tell him how things had transpired, but on learning that he was busy with a patient, she decided not to wait, and ordered a cab home.

Mina was just descending from the cab when she heard a rapid tapping of footsteps, and was advanced upon at speed by Mrs Brendel who had clearly been lying in wait for her.

'At last!' exclaimed that lady with a face of fury. 'Your maid was very rude to me just now, she absolutely refused to allow me to come in and wait for you!'

'I am very sorry,' said Mina, mystified, wondering how Mrs Brendel had obtained her address. 'That is so unlike Rose to behave in that way. I will be sure to reprimand her.'

'But you cannot escape me now! You will not!' Mrs Brendel waved a determined fist from which a forefinger emerged like the claw of a savage bird. 'I demand to know where my daughter is!'

Mina had been about in invite Mrs Brendel in, but in view of the ferocity of her manner, hesitated. She wasn't at all sure if Richard was at home, and was not happy to deal with this potentially violent situation alone.

'Mrs Brendel,' she said, trying to speak calmly, 'I am very sorry that you are upset, but I am afraid I can't help you. I don't know where your daughter is. I have not seen her since the supper at Mr Honeyacre's. Why do you think I would know?'

Mrs Brendel stamped her foot in annoyance. 'Because she has run away from home, and I know the culprit, it is that horrid Mr Dawson from the music shop who has tempted her to elope with him. He has been sending the most disgusting love notes to my daughter, and I suspect that you were his agent in this.'

'I can assure you, I was not.'

The agitated mother threw up her hands and paced back and forth, her cloak rippling in the wind. Mina wanted to make for her front door but knew that she could not reach it before Mrs Brendel, and did not want the distracted woman forcing her way into the house in that state. 'I was only from home for a short while!' wailed Mrs Brendel. 'Mr Quinley, who watches our affairs, is away on business, and a villain has taken advantage of that and abducted my daughter, my poor innocent girl! She will be ruined!' Mrs Brendel pulled a handkerchief from her pocket and pressed it to her eyes. 'I thought it was safe to go out and leave Athene under Jessie's care, but on my return just now, I found a note to the effect that the maid had been called away as she was needed for some emergency. I am convinced that this was a ruse by Mr Dawson, a forged appeal to lure Jessie from the house and leave Athene alone and unprotected.' She wiped her eyes and gulped, a new burst of fury overtaking her distress. 'I went to see him at Potts Music Emporium and the scoundrel denied everything, but then I made him turn out his pockets in front of the manager, and found a note he was intending to send to Athene making plans for her to run away with him. He is even now being questioned by the police. And I found one other thing — a card with your address on it.' She glared at Mina. 'You must be his confederate.'

'I am not his confederate,' said Mina, beginning to tremble with cold, and pulling her cloak more closely about her. 'When I first paid you a visit Mr Dawson approached me outside your house and expressed his concern for your daughter's health. I suppose I took pity on him and we exchanged cards, but nothing more.'

'Where is Athene?' demanded Mrs Brendel. 'Have you lodged her somewhere?'

'Mrs Brendel, please believe me, I don't know where she is. I did not even know she was from home until you told me just now.'

Mrs Brendel was not a lady who gave up easily. 'Is she in your house?'

Mina knew she could not stay outside much longer or all the good of the vapour bath would be undone, and even reversed. There was only one thing she could do. She mounted the front steps, with Mrs Brendel running after and overtaking her, unlocked the door and pushed it open. 'Come in, Mrs Brendel, do. You may search my house from attic to basement, every room there is. Question the servants if you must, examine my private papers. I give you complete freedom. I promise you will not find your daughter here.'

Mrs Brendel hesitated.

'Well? What are you waiting for? Search to your heart's content. Under the beds, in the wardrobes, everywhere.'

Even Mrs Brendel declined to commit that outrage. She shook her head. 'Very well,' she said reluctantly, 'I accept your assurance. There are other places for me to look. But Dawson is the villain and he will not get away with this!' She shook her fist again, and strode away.

Mina thankfully entered the comparative warmth of her hallway and closed the front door. Moments later Richard opened the door of the front parlour and peered out.

'Has she gone? She was making a dreadful fuss earlier. I had Rose send her away, and tell her no-one was at home. Why did she come here?'

'She thinks I have connived with Mr Dawson to steal away her daughter. As if I would do such a thing!'

'No, of course you would not. But do come into the parlour, and warm yourself by the fire. There is cocoa and sandwiches. And I have some good news for you. You are going to be very pleased with me. I have found out all the secrets of the Brendels!'

Chapter Thirty-Eight

'You never cease to surprise me,' said Mina, hoping that her brother had not done anything foolhardy or indelicate. She removed her cloak, bonnet and muffler, and followed Richard into the parlour where she was astonished to see the Brendels' maid Jessie, sitting at the table. There was the promised jug of cocoa and a plate of sandwiches, and every sign that both Richard and Jessie had been enjoying an early supper. The maid, on seeing Mina, looked highly embarrassed to be there at all, and immediately got to her feet and curtseyed.

'Oh, please, do sit,' said Mina, and poured some cocoa for herself. It was very welcome, and she hoped it might just stave off a nasty chill. Jessie had a half-consumed sandwich on a tea plate before her, but was reluctant to eat above stairs with Mina present, and let it lie there.

'I will tell you everything that has happened,' said Richard, cheerfully, as Jessie remained nervously silent. 'Earlier today, I was sketching Miss Brendel, as I have been doing this last week, and Jessie here was sitting by as chaperone, as was all good and proper, when quite suddenly, the poor young lady came over faint, and had to be revived with her tisane. While this was being done, Jessie quick-mindedly took the opportunity to tell me all her worries and very pleased I am that she did. Jessie, I want you to tell Miss Scarletti what you told me.'

Jessie gave a little cough to clear her throat. 'Yes, well, I've been very worried for quite some while. It's a good place as places go, but there is something strange happening in that house and I don't know how to account for it.'

'Have you been there long?' asked Mina.

'No, only a few months. I was engaged by the landlady, Mrs Fazackerly, as general maid. There were three tenants in it before, and then Mrs Brendel came and took the whole house on a quarterly rent. She is very particular about how things are done, not that there's anything wrong in that. Only, I'm concerned about Miss Brendel, as I can see she is very delicate. She told me once that she had been in good health until her stomach turned bad and she lost her appetite. That was when her visions began. Very peculiar they are, too. She sees all sorts; men, women, children, animals, even carriages. She doesn't like to see them, but she can't make them stop. But her mother; she thought it was all very interesting and ever since then the poor girl has been kept on short commons. Just fed enough to keep body and soul together. If she feels hungry I'm under orders to give her nothing except her tea. It isn't right. The poor thing hasn't had a proper square meal in six months.'

Mina was appalled. 'So you are saying that her mother starves her in the belief that if she feeds her properly the visions will stop?'

'That's what I think, yes.'

'This is monstrous! Someone should send for the girl's father. I'm sure he would have something to say about it. What about Mr Quinley, the solicitor? I thought he was there to look after the welfare of the family on behalf of Mr Brendel. Does he say nothing?'

'No, he's been at the beck and call of Mrs Brendel. But only until recently. He's gone now.'

'Gone? Not for good, surely?'

'Oh, I don't know about that. Last week Mrs Brendel had a letter — from Mr Brendel it was. At least, I think it was from him because it was from Wakefield where he lives. I didn't see what was in it but when she read it there was a big upset, and Mrs Brendel and Mr Quinley had a long talk about it. I had the feeling it was about money. Then Mr Quinley said that he would go straight up to Wakefield and see Mr Brendel and make it all right, because he didn't think it could be mended in a letter. Then he ordered his bag to be packed. He left the same day.'

'And has he made it right?'

'I don't know. I don't think so. He hasn't sent a letter. There's nothing at all come from Wakefield. Mrs Brendel has looked very unhappy ever since.'

Richard helped himself to more cocoa and sandwiches, content to allow Mina to ask the questions.

'You say that you have been worried about Miss Brendel's health. Has her mother been worried? In all the time that they have been in Brighton, has Miss Brendel ever been examined by a doctor?'

'No, there's no doctor come to see her, that I am sure of. I did once mention to Mrs Brendel how thin her daughter was, but her mother just said that gentlemen liked a lady with a trim waist, so that was all to the good. I didn't dare say anything about it again.'

'Scandalous, isn't it,' exclaimed Richard. 'I am sure that the reason the mother would never allow her daughter to be seen by a doctor is because that would reveal her cruel treatment. So I have taken the liberty of summoning Dr Hamid. I sent him a note just before you arrived.'

'You have summoned him?' queried Mina. 'Where to?'

'Why here, of course.' Richard bit into a sandwich.

'But Miss Brendel is not here.'

'Mmm. Yes she is. I gave her some tea and now she is lying down to rest upstairs.'

Mina was astounded. 'Richard! I can scarcely believe what I am hearing! You abducted her?'

'Not at all. She came of her own accord.'

'But her mother doesn't know where she is!'

He laughed. 'I certainly hope not.'

Mina was aghast at the situation, and its potential for hideous embarrassment. 'I have just told Mrs Brendel that her daughter is not here. I invited her in to search the house and prove it to herself.'

'Just as well she did not.'

'She is beside herself with worry!'

Richard shrugged. 'I don't know why. Miss Brendel penned a little note to say that she was safe and happy.'

'Little enough comfort for her mother, I fear. She is determined that her daughter has run away and is being hidden somewhere by Mr Dawson, the young man who wants to marry her. In fact, she has had him arrested, on the strength of some love notes he had intended to deliver. Richard, please tell me you have not been delivering Mr Dawson's love notes for him.'

'I'm not sure I have ever met Mr Dawson, and I know I haven't delivered any notes. Jessie can attest to that.'

Mina looked sharply at Jessie. 'Oh, no, Miss, I've not delivered any notes to Miss Brendel, I promise.'

Richard finished his sandwich. 'Dear me. Poor Mr Dawson. I suppose Miss Brendel had better write another note to say she isn't with him.'

'If such a note would be believed,' said Mina.

'True. But we should try. Shall I see it written? Rose can deliver it. Of course, even if Dawson is exonerated Mrs Brendel might still think her daughter has run away with an unsuitable man.'

'She has,' said Mina drily. She thought quickly. 'Very well, I agree that it would be no bad thing if a doctor was to see her and learn how she has been treated, but immediately that has been done we should return Miss Brendel to her mother who will, we must hope, accept sound advice from Dr Hamid as to how her daughter ought to be looked after.'

'But she doesn't want to go back,' Richard objected.

'I doubt that she will have any choice. She can't stay here. Sooner or later when Mrs Brendel does not find her daughter she will return. How come she does not suspect Mr Richard Henry of being her abductor?'

'Ah,' said Richard, 'now that was where I was very clever. Miss Brendel didn't leave with me. I left the house this afternoon, after the sketch was completed, and then Jessie here made all the arrangements, and later on I sent a cab round and when Mrs Brendel went to do her shopping, they crept out.'

'The only reason I stayed on was to look after Miss Brendel,' said Jessie. 'I've sent a note to Mrs Fazackerly and left one for Mrs Brendel to say I've been called away urgently to look after a sick lady, but to be truthful I don't want to go back. I don't know what to do.'

'We'll think of something!' said Richard, confidently. 'In the meantime, will you stay here to look after Miss Brendel until she is restored to health?'

'I'd like to, yes.'

'There we are!' said Richard. 'That is all arranged.'

The doorbell prevented Mina from further comment and Dr Hamid was admitted.

'I was called to a serious case,' said Dr Hamid, as he came in, looking quickly about him at the occupants of the parlour. 'Please tell me what is wrong.'

'Yes, it is Miss Brendel, who was visiting with her maid, and I am sorry to say arrived in a state of collapse,' Mina explained. 'Jessie, could you show Dr Hamid to where Miss Brendel is resting?'

'Has her mother been sent for?'

'Mrs Brendel was out, but a message has been left for her,' said Richard.

Fortunately, Dr Hamid required no further information and hurried upstairs with Jessie to see the patient.

'What were you thinking of?' demanded Mina when she and Richard were alone.

'The lady's health, of course. What should I have done?'

Mina had nothing to suggest. 'I only hope the matter is settled before Mrs Brendel sends the police here. Thank goodness Mother is away.'

Richard munched on another sandwich, while Mina wondered what to do, and decided that she would take no action until she had consulted Dr Hamid.

He returned shortly. 'You did right to call me. I understand that Miss Brendel has been deliberately kept short of food by her mother. The maid, Jessie, has been very helpful. She assisted Mrs Brendel in the composition of the tisane and has given me a precise list of what it contained. I have been extremely foolish not to notice before what I now perceive. All the herbs used, while essentially harmless, and with some beneficial effects, do have one thing in common. They all suppress the appetite. Mrs Brendel's actions have seriously endangered her daughter's health and may well amount to a criminal offence. I have no alternative but to notify the police of my findings. I shall also write to the father and suggest that as soon as Miss Brendel is strong enough to travel, he comes and takes her home. In the meantime, I have advised that Miss

Brendel should rest, and be given what nourishment she can manage. I will prescribe a tonic, and have written full instructions as to her care and feeding. Would it inconvenience you if she was to remain here for a few days?'

'Not at all,' said Richard. 'She has her maid to attend her.'

'What if Mrs Brendel should discover where her daughter is, and comes to take her back?' asked Mina.

'Say that she is not to be moved on my orders. I take full responsibility. Other than that, I trust you are all well here?' he asked, glancing at Mina particularly.

'Yes, thank you,' said Mina.

'All we need to do,' said Richard, once Dr Hamid had departed, 'is keep Miss Brendel away from her dreadful mother until her father comes.'

'I think that is for the best,' said Mina, 'although I am hoping to resolve this without a great commotion in the street and a paragraph in the *Gazette*.'

'And now, as we have two more mouths to feed, I suggest you order an extra large breakfast for tomorrow morning. Oh, and I will need a little loan. I spent my last money on the cab for Miss Brendel and Jessie. And I am not sure of being paid for my sketch work now.'

Chapter Thirty-Nine

Next morning, Miss Brendel, having enjoyed a restful night, appeared at the breakfast table, looking petulant.

'I am supposed to be dosed with this tonic three times a day!' she exclaimed, peering at the label on a brown glass bottle. 'It tastes very nasty. I prefer my tea.'

'Dr Hamid has left strict orders that you are to have Indian or China tea in the daytime from now on, and camomile at night, but not the green brew your mother gave you,' said Mina. 'I know she meant it for the best, but it was disagreeing with you, and making you unwell.'

'Let me help you to some breakfast,' said Richard, waving a serving spoon over a laden sideboard. 'We have scrambled eggs and bacon, and kidneys, and toast and muffins, and marmalade, and honey, and once you have eaten all those then you can go around to the start and eat it all again.'

'Oh, just a little dry toast, please,' said Miss Brendel. Richard brought the toast rack to the table. She took the smallest piece and nibbled a corner. 'Mother says my digestion is very delicate and I will upset my stomach if I eat too much.'

Richard piled his plate high with food and sat down. 'When was the last time you ate too much?'

She frowned. 'I can't remember.'

'You know, that toast will be too dry to swallow easily unless you put a little scrambled egg on it.'

Miss Brendel paused and looked at the toast, then put it down on her plate and Richard spooned some scrambled egg on top. She picked up her knife and fork, and sawed off a tiny piece, then lifted it to her mouth and chewed thoughtfully.

'Can you tell us about your visions?' he asked. 'How did they start? When did they start?'

'Oh, it was last spring. I ate something that upset my digestion, which is why it has been so poor of late. Fish, I think it was. I didn't eat a morsel of food for a whole week. And that was when the visions came. I started off only seeing Father at first. Mother said it was caused by my worry at his being away, and it wouldn't happen again once he was home. Then one morning, as I opened my eyes, I saw them, standing at the foot of my bed.' She took a larger bite of toast and egg.

'Who were they?'

'I wasn't sure. Just people, ladies and gentlemen, as one sees in the street or the shops. I was frightened at first. I wondered why they were in my bedroom. I called out for Mother, but by the time she came, they had disappeared.' There was a pause and some loud munching as Miss Brendel cleared her plate, then she took a good gulp of tea. 'It was strange, to see them grow paler and paler until they vanished like mist. Mother insisted I had had a dream, but I knew I was awake.' She dabbed her lips with a napkin.

'A little more, perhaps?' Richard suggested. 'The bacon is very good.'

'Oh, I have not eaten bacon for so long. Just one slice. And I think I could manage another piece of toast.'

After breakfast, Miss Brendel, afraid to go out lest she should encounter her mother, returned to her room to hide behind the pages of a book, and Jessie agreed to sit with her.

Soon afterwards, a letter for Mina was delivered in an envelope embellished with the address of Phipps and Co. Mina opened it with trepidation and the contents were far worse than she could have imagined.

Dear Miss Scarletti,

I hope this finds you well.

As we discussed recently, I have been keeping my eyes and ears open for any news of Mr Dorry. I chanced to read in today's Telegraph *that his gallery in London has been suddenly closed down, amidst some controversy, and I have made some further enquiries to discover the circumstances. All I have been able to glean is that it was in connection with a recent exhibition of signed early sketches by J. M. W. Turner. I will let you know at once if I should hear any more.*

I would advise any artist to be very cautious about carrying out work for Mr Dorry.

Yours faithfully,

G. Phipps

Mina went up to Richard's room, to find him stretched out on the bed like the dying hero of a tragic novel.

She sat beside him and stroked his tumbled blond curls. 'Are you well, my dear?'

'Oh,' he groaned, 'as well as a man can be whose life is one of boredom and disappointment and penury.'

'Are you really so poor? Has Mr Dorry not paid you anything more, or were those two guineas the sum total?'

'Yes, that was all so far. And I had to spend most of it on materials in his shop. Art paper is deucedly expensive, you know!' He made an effort and struggled into a sitting position. 'You couldn't lend me a spot of cash? Just until I sell some pictures?'

'No, Richard, I could not. Tell me, how many sketches have you done for Mr Dorry?'

'Oh, about twenty I think. I have five more I am supposed to be taking to him today. Perhaps I shall ask him for something on account.'

'That might be an idea. Richard — I know you told me that you had not signed any of the sketches you did for Mr Dorry. Is that still the case? Has he asked you to put a signature on any of the recent ones? Your name or — another, perhaps? I know they are in the style of Mr Turner. Did you write Mr Turner's name on them?'

'No. He did once ask me if I could copy Mr Turner's hand, just as an exercise, you understand, and he showed me how it was done, and I tried but I couldn't get it right. He was much better at it.'

Richard, with the prospect of money in mind, eventually stirred himself, put his new sketches in a portfolio case and went out.

Mina sat at her writing desk and composed a new idea for a story about an evil sorceress who created a potion that deluded people into believing that blank sheets of paper were valuable works of art, which they bought at high prices. They were so proud of their purchases, that they hired a gallery for an exhibition and invited the press. The sorceress attempted to fool the visitors by serving them with her potion, but one of the pressmen distrusted the strange looking drink. When he argued that the papers were blank, the buyers all saw that they had been duped, and demanded their money back. The sorceress fled with the angry men in hot pursuit, and tried to escape them by taking wing from the edge of a cliff. But the creation of the potion had depleted her powers and she plunged into the sea and drowned.

Richard returned two hours later and came into Mina's room without knocking. He was even more despondent than he had been when he had set out, and was still carrying the sketches. He sat down heavily on the bed. 'Well, here's a thing. I go all the way to St James' Street only to find that Mr Dorry's gallery is closed down. There isn't even a sign to say when it will open again, or where customers are to go in the meantime.'

'Is the shop empty?' asked Mina.

'It could not be emptier if it had been burgled. All the pictures are gone, including mine, and the statue, and the man himself is gone too, and no-one knows where, although it is rumoured that he is on his way to Italy. And his assistant has vanished as if he had been conjured away. It's too bad, Dorry is nothing more than a thief!'

Mina came and sat beside him and gave him a hug.

'So I thought, well, I still have all these pictures to sell, and someone else might want to buy them, so I went to Dickinson's gallery on the Kings Road; you know, where they are exhibiting the new portrait of the Queen. And they have some very good watercolours of fine ladies. I'm not sure I could do anything nearly as good. So I showed the proprietor my drawings and asked him if he would buy them, or display and sell them for me, and do you know, he became quite annoyed. I don't know why. He even said that if I didn't leave at once he would call the police. Now what do you think of that?'

'I think,' said Mina, concluding that Richard had probably had a lucky escape, 'that it is time you gave up doing sketches of the sea and went back to your original plan of illustrating articles for the new journal. At least that way you will meet pretty ladies.'

'True,' said Richard, 'I was getting rather tired of the sea. Do you ever tire of it? I mean, you look at it more than I do.'

'It's never the same twice,' said Mina. Now she thought about it, so many of her stories were inspired by the sea. She loved its mysteries, its power, even its sinister invitation, promising pleasure but concealing a lurking threat of danger. In fine weather, its sounds soothed her, and the constant changes of colour and form refreshed her eyes and mind. How easy it was, she thought, to see dead faces in the water, fingers rising up like ghostly wave tips, all to be swept away in a heartbeat. But Richard could never be refreshed by the sea; his senses demanded something more.

Richard looked through his portfolio of sketches and threw them to the floor disconsolately. 'And now I have to hope that Mother doesn't get to hear about Mr Dorry being such a cheat. But if I don't tell her, she will think I still have a patron and expect me to be doing well. I'm sure Edward will hear of it in any case and have a joke at my expense.'

'Perhaps,' suggested Mina, 'you could make a sketch of Mr Dorry?'

Richard pulled a face. 'That scoundrel! Why would I want to draw him?'

'Because he is a scoundrel. And you need not think to flatter him, make it an honest portrait. If he is the villain we think he is, the newspapers will be clamouring for an image of him. And the police might find it very useful indeed.'

Richard, who had been slumped in misery, suddenly sat up straight. 'Ah, I understand! They will need the likeness to help them find him. And I would be instrumental in his capture!'

'You would.'

He leaped off the bed with renewed energy. 'I'll do it now!'

Dear Edward,

I hope the family is in as good health as is possible in this dreadful weather. You are very kind to take so much care of them, and I am grateful for everything you do.

You may have read in the newspapers that Mr Dorry's London gallery has closed, and as it so happens his Brighton premises has met a similar and sudden fate. It might be best if Mother was protected from this news until such time as Richard's standing improves.

We are all well here.

Fondest love

Mina

With Richard busy, and her story complete, Mina looked in on their unexpected houseguests. Jessie was making herself useful with some mending while Miss Brendel was sitting up in bed with a glass of milk, a plate of biscuits and *Traditional Ghost Tales of Olde England*, all three of which were absorbing her attention. She glanced up at Mina and brushed crumbs from her lips. 'When is luncheon?'

Chapter Forty

Luncheon an hour later was minced beef turnovers with mushrooms, which Miss Brendel attacked with relish, and Mina was pleased to see Richard arriving at the table more cheerful than he had been earlier. 'I have made a portrait of Mr Dorry in which he looks like a large hirsute frog. It is an excellent likeness and I shall take it to the police this afternoon.'

When the plates were empty, which took very little time, Rose cleared them away and brought bottled fruit, sponge cake, and two letters for Mina, one of which was in the printed envelope of Scarletti Publishing. 'A cheque, I hope?' said Richard.

'No,' said Mina. 'A letter, from Mrs Caldecott.'

Dear Miss Scarletti,

Your recent questions concerning the Wakefield mine-owner Mr Brendel piqued my interest, and I have made some further enquiries with acquaintances who are prominent in the best Yorkshire society. The have advised me that Mr Aloysius Brendel is a widower with two sons, and does not, as far as they are aware, have a daughter. He is expected very shortly to announce his betrothal to Miss Araminta Cartwright, eldest daughter of Sir Wilfrid and Lady Margaret Cartwright of Dundersby Hall near Harrogate. The ladies residing in Brighton calling themselves Mrs and Miss Brendel are undoubtedly imposters. While Mr Brendel does not care to move in society, the Cartwrights do. Friends of theirs who knew of the impending announcement are in Brighton for the season, and on learning of the situation, were impelled to advise both the Cartwrights and Mr Brendel, who will be taking appropriate action.

Yours, E. Caldecott (Mrs)

The second letter was from Dr Hamid, and there was an enclosure.

Dear Miss Scarletti,

As you know, I wrote to Mr Brendel, advising him that his daughter was recuperating at your house, and requesting that he should, at his earliest convenience, call to take her home. I have today received a letter from him which astonished me and which I enclose.

I trust that Miss Brendel is recovering her strength, and I will be informed should a second visit be required.

Yours faithfully,
D. Hamid, M.D.

Dear Sir,

I thank you for advising me that a young woman calling herself Athene Brendel is staying at a respectable house in Brighton. It has recently been drawn to my attention that a female who I feel sure from the description is Mrs Martha Jones, a former housekeeper of mine, has been staying in Brighton with her daughter masquerading under the name of Mrs Brendel, and claiming to be my wife.

Earlier this year, I had agreed, in view of Mrs Jones's long and loyal service to my house, to meet some of her expenses, but I certainly did not authorise her to use my name, to which she has no entitlement. This outrageous imposture, which has caused me no little inconvenience, renders that agreement void, and she will receive nothing more from me. Miss Athene is, so I have always been told, Mrs Jones's daughter, but her paternity is something no-one can determine, and I am under no obligation to keep her. I will not, therefore, call to remove her to my home, and she and her mother may do as they please.

Yours faithfully,
Aloysius Brendel
Westgate House, Wakefield

Mina undoubtedly held in her hands the reasons behind the sudden upset in the household at Oriental Place and Mr Quinley's abrupt departure. But the letters could not, she thought, contain the whole story. Would Mr Brendel really have agreed to the generous support of a former housekeeper and her daughter, of whose parentage he could not be certain, a daughter he had brought up and educated so carefully? On that evidence alone, Mr Brendel was in no doubt at all concerning the identity of the young lady's father.

Mina could only guess as to the reasons why Mrs Jones, as she must now be known, had left Mr Brendel's employ, but a strong possibility was that the housekeeper, mother to her employer's natural daughter, to whom he had been very generous, had demanded that Mr Brendel marry her and legitimise Miss Athene, only to be thwarted when the radiant Miss Cartwright, a younger, well-connected rival had appeared. Mr Brendel, wanting to keep peace with all parties, had agreed to support his former housekeeper and her daughter, imagining that she would be content with that arrangement. He had not reckoned with the lady's effrontery which had led her to adopt the name she thought was due to her, an action which must inevitably have threatened his marriage plans. Under the circumstances he had seen no alternative but to withdraw funds and deny any blood connection with the daughter.

As for Mr Quinley, who must have been a confederate of Mrs Jones in her career of deception, he had left Brighton in a hurry with not the slightest intention of returning, and was probably now in Wakefield assuring his client that he knew nothing about her scheme.

'Miss Brendel,' said Mina hesitantly, 'if that is your name...'

Miss Brendel's eyes opened wide. She was devouring a hearty portion of pudding, and hardly paused. 'Of course it is my name.'

'And you are the daughter of mine-owner Aloysius Brendel of Wakefield?'

'Yes, I am.'

'And the lady you lately resided with is your mother?'

'She is. I don't understand; why are you asking me this?'

'And your mother is Mrs Brendel, wife of Mr Brendel?'

There was a long silence.

'I see we have finally reached the point where the lies begin,' said Mina.

'Well,' said Richard, 'my sister is as full of surprises as ever. What do you say, Miss Brendel? Is that your name?'

Miss Brendel looked surly, and curled a defiant lip. 'Yes. It is the name I have always been called by. I admit that Mother and Father are — not exactly married. But it was intended they should be. They are as good as. Mother has kept house for Father for more than twenty years. He has been a widower for a long time, but all he thought of was business. He was too busy to think about marrying again. She did keep reminding him, but...'

'But he would not?' asked Mina. 'Perhaps she pressed him too hard? Or maybe he never meant to?'

'I don't know. Mother tells me very little. But I know things were very friendly between them and then suddenly it all went cold. Perhaps that is why we left Wakefield.'

Mina held up Mrs Caldecott's letter. 'I have just received news that Mr Brendel is on the point of announcing his betrothal to another lady. A Miss Cartwright. Do you know her?'

Miss Brendel affected a look of supreme disdain. 'Yes. She is very plain, and has no figure at all, but her father has money and likes to think of himself as gentry.'

'Mr Brendel has been told by friends of the Cartwrights that your mother has been passing herself off as his wife. This at a time when he is about to become betrothed. Her actions have naturally excited his displeasure.'

Miss Brendel was so startled she put down her spoon. 'Oh dear. That would explain...'

'Yes?'

'Mother received a letter from father a week ago. She wouldn't tell me what was in it, but she and Mr Quinley had a long talk and then Mr Quinley said he would go to see father and smooth things over. He left the same day, and promised that he would write as soon as he got there, but we have heard nothing since. And Mother is very upset because there are bills to be paid, and nothing to pay them with.'

'Mr Brendel was paying your bills in Brighton?'

'Yes, through Mr Quinley. Mother said that if we didn't hear from him soon we would have to go back to Wakefield. But I don't want to go back to Wakefield. I like it here. I'll be twenty-one soon and then I'll be able to live where I please.' She picked up the spoon, and attacked her pudding again.

'Do you have any income of your own?'

'No. Not as such. Father has made a settlement on me. When I am twenty-one I will have a hundred pounds a year.'

'We must hope he does not revoke it,' said Mina, 'or you will be cast adrift in the world. Your mother will be obliged to find employment, and you will have to make what you can playing the piano and holding séances.'

'Oh, I don't get the visions anymore,' said Miss Brendel airily. 'I hated them. I'm glad they have gone.'

'You could always marry Mr Dawson.'

To Mina's surprise, Miss Brendel laughed. 'Oh, I'm not interested in him.'

'Is that so? He thought you liked him.'

She shrugged. 'I don't know why.' She scraped her dish clean with the spoon.

'I doubt that he could afford to keep you, in any case. When is your birthday?'

'In two weeks.' She licked the spoon. 'Do you have any cheese?'

Mina was left wondering how the difficulty could be settled. She could hardly keep her unwanted guest indefinitely. If the worst came to the worst, she decided, Miss Brendel would have to be sent to Wakefield with Jessie, at Mina's expense, in the hope that her father would relent and take her in.

Chapter Forty-One

Once luncheon was over, Richard went to take his sketch of Mr Dorry to the police station, and Miss Brendel explored the kitchen in search of cheese. Jessie had proved to be a useful addition to the household, as she knew a recipe that would improve cook's handling of pastry, and Mina was hoping for fancies that a hungry bird would not have refused.

The doorbell rang, and soon afterwards, Rose appeared at Mina's door. 'There's a Mrs Fazackerly wants to see you. I don't know her. She did ask for you by name.'

Mina remembered that this was the name of the landlady of the house in Oriental Place, and wondered how she had obtained her address and what had brought her to her door. She could only hope that Mrs Fazackerly would not be troublesome. 'Show her into the parlour, and tend to the fire. I will come down.'

Mrs Fazackerly, Mina was pleased to see, did not look as if she was about to make trouble, rather she was deeply concerned. She was a widow in middle life, very neat about her person, her face framed in a black bonnet that only emphasised her anxious pallor.

'Oh, Miss Scarletti,' she gasped, as Mina entered, 'it is so kind of you to see me without warning!'

'Not at all, what may I do for you?'

'I am the landlady of a property in Oriental Place, which I believe you have visited.'

'That is true,' said Mina, 'although I have not done so recently.'

'I should explain. Mrs Brendel, who took the house, has not paid her quarterly rent, which has come due. I called on her again this morning, to ask about the rent, but to my great surprise, I found the house locked up. The maid has been away of late, as she was sent for to deal with a sudden illness, but I thought she would have been back by now. Of course, I have a key, and when I let myself in, I found that no-one was in residence and all of Mrs Brendel's boxes were gone. I had half a mind to sell her piano to pay the debt, but while I was there some men came from Potts Music Emporium and took it away. They said it was only on hire and she had paid the first quarter and not the second. Then the police came, saying they wanted to talk to the tenant as there had been a complaint made, and they had been trying to find her. They asked me where she was, but I knew no more than they did. It was all very upsetting. It is a very superior residence, as you will have seen, and I am used to having respectable tenants. I went home, not knowing what to do, and next thing I received a letter from a solicitor, a Mr Quinley who wrote on Mr Brendel's behalf.'

'Where was he writing from?'

'Wakefield, that is where Mr Brendel lives. He told me that the woman who took the house who calls herself Mrs Brendel is not Mrs Brendel at all but a Mrs Jones. His client had been paying her expenses out of an old friendship, but he had not given her permission to make free with his name. He had just found out what she had done, and as a result there would be no more funds forthcoming. So now I have all the trouble of cleaning the house and finding a new tenant, and I am still owed for the quarter. If Mrs Jones is a married lady then I must find her husband and ask him to pay my rent and expenses. If she is not a married lady then I must seek the money directly from her, but she is nowhere to be found, and neither is her daughter. I searched the house and found some papers, which included names and addresses of visitors, and have been calling on them to discover if they know my former tenant's whereabouts. So far, no-one has been able to help me. This morning I discovered the carrier who took her boxes and was told that she went with them to the railway station. But where she went from there I don't know.'

'It is some days since I last saw the lady and she did not then inform me that she was about to leave her lodgings,' said Mina. 'But if I was to hazard a guess, I would say that she has realised her mistake in angering Mr Brendel, and has gone to Wakefield to plead with him.'

'I don't suppose you know his address?' said Mrs Fazackerly, hopefully.

'As a matter of fact, I do.' Mina went to fetch Mr Brendel's letter and her grateful visitor made a note.

When Mrs Fazackerly had departed, Mina felt obliged to inform Miss Brendel that her mother had vacated the house in Oriental Place and had almost certainly fled Brighton. Miss Brendel might have asked Mina where her mother had gone, but she did not, in fact she seemed not to care.

On the face of it, Mrs Jones's actions since leaving Wakefield had seemed foolhardy, but, thought Mina, the housekeeper, knowing Mr Brendel's habits so very well, had gambled on the fact that he did not take an interest in society and was therefore unlikely to hear of her deception. She had tried to arrange a fashionable wedding for her daughter to afford her the security of wealth and position that Mr Brendel had promised but not provided. Perhaps she hoped that her daughter's advancement would persuade Mr Brendel to relent from his decision not to marry her. Mrs Jones had not, however, reckoned with the aspirations of the Cartwrights, which had proved her undoing.

Mrs Jones, thought Mina, was not a foolish woman. At present, she might seem powerless in the face of Mr Brendel's fortune, but she would use every weapon at her disposal to retrieve the situation. She might plead her old alliance with Mr Brendel, and the future prospects of their daughter. And there was one other path she would surely explore. On the evidence of his letter to Mrs Fazackerly, Mr Quinley was in Wakefield and was still being entrusted with Mr Brendel's affairs. For that to be the case he must have told his client that he had no knowledge of the masquerade. If Mrs Jones was the woman Mina thought she was, she would have kept any documents which would demonstrate that when Mr Quinley had paid her bills he knew full well that he was paying them on behalf of a woman calling herself Mrs Brendel. Her silence on that point could be a winning card.

Chapter Forty-Two

The next day, a small package arrived for Mina from Lincoln. On opening it she found a letter from Mrs Sperley, and an envelope. The envelope was inscribed with one word: 'Fernwood' and it was in Dr Sperley's handwriting.

> *Dear Mrs Scarletti,*
>
> *I have made another search of my late husband's writing desk, and found a great clutter of rubbish. I chanced to find a compartment whose existence I had not even suspected, containing this envelope, and as the name is written clearly I was able to make it out. It refers to a strange medical case that my husband knew of many years ago. I know it troubled him and he would never speak of it to me. Perhaps it might interest you?*
>
> *Yours truly,*
> *Sophia Sperley*
> *Newland House*
> *Lincoln*

Mina stared at the envelope, which had once been sealed, but the gum had dried and cracked and it was possible to open the flap and extract the contents. She hesitated. The name Fernwood might mean that it was intended for someone of that name, but if that had been the case there would have been a Christian name, or at the very least an initial. No, she told herself, Fernwood was not the intended recipient, but the subject matter.

Mina opened the envelope and removed some closely written sheets also in Dr Sperley's hand. The first words struck her with apprehension, so much so that she informed Rose that she did not wish to be disturbed until further notice, retired to her room, and sat at her desk before continuing to read.

It is with a heavy heart that I commit these words to paper. Indeed, it is a secret I would have kept hidden within my breast if it had not been for the fact that it might one day save a life. I have advised Mr Grundy, my solicitor, that should anyone be charged with the murder of my former patient, Thomas Fernwood, who died after being poisoned with arsenic in 1851, this letter should be opened and passed to the police. Its existence and place of concealment is known only to Grundy. I hope that it never sees the light of day! I take upon myself the entire responsibility of keeping this secret. I am an old man, and nothing can be done to me now.

Just two weeks after the death of Thomas Fernwood, with the man barely cold in his grave, I was called to the Fernwood house once more. My first thought was that I would be shown to the bedside of Mrs Jane Fernwood, the only member of the family to be in poor general health. To my surprise, Mrs Fernwood, whose twisted ankle had healed, was up and about and doing well. It pains me to record it, but her health and spirits had greatly improved following the death of her husband, indeed, it is not too much to say that the improvement came as a result of his death. Her only anxiety was the health of her granddaughter, Miss Ada Fernwood, who had been suffering from fits, and was in considerable pain. Despite this, Miss Ada had begged her not to summon me, but such was the young lady's torment that Mrs Fernwood had ignored that entreaty. I was deeply concerned, as Miss Ada had never shown signs of hysteria before, rather she was a quiet and modest person. My greatest fear was that I was about to be confronted with another poison victim.

On examining Miss Fernwood, however, I was soon reassured that she had not been poisoned, and it was at first very hard for me to account for her sudden distressing indisposition until unmistakable signs supervened, and I realised that she was miscarrying a foetus, which I judged to be no more than four months from gestation. The misery of this young lady, who was at the time just fifteen years of age, can only be imagined. Soon afterwards she was seized by a fever that rendered her delirious and for some days her condition hovered between life and death, with little indication as to what the final result might be.

One evening, which she honestly thought to be her last on earth, Miss Fernwood begged to be allowed to tell me all her story, assuring me that she was lucid and knew the difference between truth and imagination. I could not deny her, but I might almost wish that I had, as she told such a tale of horror as one could never think might take place in an apparently respectable home.

Miss Ada revealed that the father of the child she had been carrying was none other than her grandfather Thomas Fernwood, and this was not the first time she had miscarried as a result of his assaults on her person, although on the previous occasion, which I deemed from her account to have been at a far earlier stage, she had managed to conceal her plight from her family. She denounced Thomas Fernwood as a thoroughly evil man, who had ruled his family like a tyrant, controlling them through his unyielding hold on the purse strings. His son and daughter in law loathed him for his drunkenness and foul language. His wife, due to her condition as an invalid, had suffered the least, as he had mainly ignored her, but the boys, his grandson George and nephew Peter, had been beaten savagely, often for no reason, and had learned to avoid him as much as possible. Ada had been subject to his disgusting advances since the age of ten, as had her sister Ellen, and even little Mary had found her great uncle frightening, although she could hardly express why, and had begged not to be left alone with him.

Finally, Miss Ada, with what she believed to be her dying breath, confessed to killing her grandfather in order to save her family from torment. Soon afterwards, her fever broke, and within a day it could be seen that she was on the mend.

When she was well again, I took care to reassure her that in view of her terrible sufferings her secret was safe with me. To my surprise, she only *smiled enigmatically and said that she had nothing with which to reproach herself. It then occurred to me most forcibly that she had not committed the murder after all, she had confessed to it when she believed herself to be dying only to save the real culprit from suspicion, and relieve the family from the stress of not knowing the full story. I am ashamed to say that I was overcome by curiosity, and demanded to know the truth from her. I pointed out that if the wrong person was ever to be charged then her silence could lead to an innocent being condemned. She only said that she would never allow that to happen. I asked if the reason for this was that the culprit was a relative, something that had always been apparent. She was silent but she did not deny it. And then I saw how dreadfully naïve I had been. I had imagined that it was only I to whom Thomas Fernwood had voiced his plea, his insistence that he had been murdered, and attempted to name his murderer. How foolish to have flattered myself in that way! During the early stages of his illness, before the acid had corroded his throat and he was better able to speak, he had been tended to by his granddaughters Ada and Ellen, and sister-in-law Mrs Clifton. Mr William Fernwood had made a visit to the bedside, as had his wife, Margery. Had I really imagined that the dying man had not also attempted to tell at least one of these persons what he knew? And succeeded? Yet all of them had been adamant that they could not cast any light on the mystery. Horrible thought — that at least one member of the family probably knows the identity of the culprit and is prepared to take the secret to the grave.*

The letter was dated just two months after the conclusion of the inquest on Thomas Fernwood.

Mina sat for some time drowned in the horror of this terrible letter. Although she had never met Ada and Ellen, how piercingly she felt for those terrified girls. George Fernwood had almost certainly never been told what his sisters had endured. It had been easy for him to assume that their aversion to marriage was due to the fear of an inherited taint, but now she saw it ran far deeper than that. The lives of the sisters had been rendered sterile and joyless, and they could only achieve some small measure of peace in each other's company. The only good thing she had learned from the letter was that Mary had been spared the ultimate insult.

Mina spent an hour or more wondering what she should do with this devastating information. Would it be right for her to tell Miss Clifton and Mr Fernwood that Dr Sperley had believed that at least one family member held the secret they had been so desperately seeking? Important as it was, Mina hesitated to reveal what she knew. She reminded herself that all she had been asked to do was help them assess whether or not the mediums they visited were genuine. She had not been given any authority to delve into their family affairs, beyond the details they themselves had provided, and they might not thank her for doing so. Through Mr Castlehouse's slate-writing demonstrations they had found an answer to their dilemma. It might not be the right one, but it was one that satisfied them, and brought both consolation and the chance of happiness. Did it really matter whether the solution written on the slate was the right one or not? Why cause them unnecessary distress? Once again, Mina decided that her best course of action was to leave well alone.

Chapter Forty-Three

Two days later, Mina received a note from Miss Landwick.

Dear Miss Scarletti,
Have you see the recent edition of the Sussex Times*?*
My brother is triumphant as he has effected Mr Castlehouse's downfall!
Yours,
E. Landwick.

Mina had not seen the journal in question and sent Rose out to obtain a copy. In between the announcement of a fat stock show and the market preparations for Christmas was a letter.

To the Editor;

I am sorry to say that Brighton has once again taken leave of its senses and been subject to yet another outrageous display of duplicity. For some years past I have been entertaining my family and friends with conjuring and legerdemain, in which I flatter myself I have some small skill. I have learned a great deal from studying the performances of some of the most accomplished stage magicians in the country, and while it is not possible to know all their secrets I am confident that I can tell when an apparently impossible effect is being produced by clever manipulation.

I am therefore in a position to announce to the world that Mr Castlehouse, who claims to invoke the spirits to write on his slates with chalk, is nothing more than a conjuror, who finds he can make a better living from fraud than he can from honest performances. It astonishes me that his method of producing writing on a slate which he holds underneath a table has succeeded in mystifying any observer other than the youngest child. The trick whereby he substitutes a blank slate with one on which he has already written is too well known to be worth describing here. Worse than that, after making some enquiries, I have it on good authority that Mr Castlehouse is none other than the same man who once performed as Angelo, and was the very conjuror who exposed the scandalous frauds of Ellison, who so narrowly escaped prison only last year.

I advise Mr Castlehouse to pack up his chalks and slates and leave Brighton before he suffers a worse fate. If he does he should go in the company of Mr and Mrs Myles who are his puppets.

I take full responsibility for the assertions in this letter and if Mr Castlehouse presumes to sue me he is free to do so, but he will not profit by it, and may only increase his woes. I therefore have no hesitation is signing myself,

Charles Landwick

Mina knew too well that Mr Castlehouse would not pack up his slates and chalks on the basis of that challenge. It took much harder work than a single letter to the press to dislodge devoted adherents from a fraud. Those who needed to believe would still cling to their beliefs, and the next week's papers would be awash with their letters all loading insults onto the head of Mr Landwick, who would be declared either grossly ignorant of the subject or himself a medium without knowing it. Mr Castlehouse would bask in still greater fame, and perhaps come up with novel tricks with which to astonish and enthral his audiences. If he was indeed the magician Angelo than he would have many at the tips of his long agile fingers.

Mina wondered if George Fernwood and Miss Clifton had paid a joint visit to the slate-writer and if so, what messages had they received? More worryingly, did Mr Fernwood read the *Sussex Times*, and if he did, what now remained of any belief that his dilemma had finally been resolved?

Mina had heard nothing from either George Fernwood or Miss Clifton for a while, and expected not to see either of them again, however a brief note arrived from George Fernwood. It was on the same notepaper as his very first letter to her, but the handwriting, although recognisably his, was different in quality. What had previously been a measured copperplate had become unsteady and undisciplined, with little flicks of ink that revealed a slight tremor. The message itself was unexceptional. He wanted to pay Mina a visit to retrieve the package of papers he had left with her. He preferred not to have them consigned to the post but wished to collect them in person. Mina replied to make the appointment.

With Mrs Jones, the housekeeper formerly known as Brendel, now absent from Brighton, there was no reason for her daughter not to dare go out on the town. Athene became so insistent about this, that Richard, who was beginning to find her demands tiresome, nevertheless agreed to take her and Jessie out for a ride in a carriage, something to which Miss Brendel agreed, making the condition that their excursion should include a visit to a cake shop and the purchase of cheese. Mina was naturally expected to pay for this, but she thought it worth the expenditure it if only to have some peace in which to write. She wanted to complete her latest story before Mr Fernwood's visit that afternoon.

She was busy at her desk anticipating a nice brew of hot coffee, when an unexpected visitor was announced, Mr Ernest Dawson. She went downstairs and found him shivering by the parlour fire. 'Please don't be anxious, I am well,' he said, 'but even the walk here did not warm me.'

Mina sent Rose to fetch the coffee. 'I understand that Mrs Brendel caused you some embarrassment recently. But you need not fear her any more as she is no longer in Brighton.'

He looked relieved. 'That is the best news I have had in an age. Did you know she dared to come storming into Potts, making a terrible commotion, disturbing all the customers, and accusing me of abducting her daughter? The manager ordered her to leave and when she would not, he was obliged to call the police. In the event we were both taken to the station. Of course, I had no idea where Miss Brendel was, and when it was proved that I had actually been at work at the time she left the house, the police soon saw that there was no truth in the accusation, and let me go. But I came very near to losing my position.'

'Mrs Brendel came here afterwards. She actually accosted me in the street and accused me of being your confederate.'

'Did she? How extraordinary! The woman is quite deranged.'

'She told me that you had been searched and my card was found in your pocket, together with a love note you intended to deliver to Miss Brendel. Is that true?'

Dawson looked guilty. The coffee arrived and was poured and he warmed his hands on the cup. 'That is true, yes. But why shouldn't I? It was all perfectly proper.'

'Mrs Brendel claimed that you had been planning an elopement. Was that the subject of your love note?'

'I — well —' He gulped the coffee, gratefully, 'I admit it was a plan that had crossed my mind, but there was nothing of that sort in the note, well, not precisely, only a sincere declaration of affection, and the hope that we might be married one day.'

'Who passed the notes for you?'

There was a moment of reluctance, and then a shrug. 'Oh, I suppose there is no harm in telling you, now, but you must promise not to say anything. It was a young fellow by the name of Tasker. I knew him because he bought sheet music, and I had seen him being almost pulled into the house in Oriental Place by his mother. He told me he didn't want to go there, as his mother was going to make him marry Miss Brendel and he didn't want to. So I said I could help him, if he helped me. If he could deliver notes to Miss Brendel when he visited, then I would be able to marry her and he wouldn't have to. He seemed very happy to do it.'

'I see. Well, he will not be visiting Miss Brendel again. But how might I assist you? I assume that is the reason you have called?'

'Yes, if you would be so kind. The thing is — my manager told me that if I wanted to keep my employment I must not go near Oriental Place again, and I have tried really hard to comply, but this morning I just couldn't help it, so I went there again, and the house was empty. It has a letting sign outside. A neighbour told me that the Brendels had gone away but no-one knew where. You have just told me that Mrs Brendel has left Brighton. But what of Athene? Is she still here or is she with her mother? Do you know where she is?'

Mina hesitated, since Miss Brendel was still a few days shy of her twenty-first birthday. 'At this moment I am afraid that I cannot say with any precision where either of them might be. The one thing I do know is that Mr Quinley has returned to Wakefield.'

Dawson looked downcast at this evaporation of his hopes. 'I suppose it is pointless for me to write to him. If I only knew that the dear girl was safe and well!'

Mina took pity on him. 'All I can say on that point is that the last time I set eyes on Miss Brendel she did look very much better than previously. Her appetite has returned, and she also informed me that she no longer has the visions.'

'Where did you —' Dawson stopped, with a shocked expression. 'No visions?'

'Yes. It seems that they were produced by something she ate which disagreed with her. Fish, I think it was.'

'Fish,' said Dawson, blankly as if the concept was new to him.

'Yes. I think that as long as she is careful not to eat fish or at least to make sure of its absolute freshness, she may be assured of not being troubled with the visions in future.'

Dawson continued to look dumbfounded. 'That is — quite — extraordinary.'

Mina sensed that this was a piece of news he was less than happy to hear, and she should test him further.

'The other thing I should mention, and that may be partly to blame for Mrs Brendel's distracted state when you last encountered her, is that she is not actually Mrs Brendel.'

'I beg your pardon?' said Dawson, incredulously.

'Yes. She is actually a Mrs Martha Jones, Mr Brendel's former housekeeper, and has no real call upon him at all.'

'But that can't be so!' Dawson protested. 'He paid her bills! I have seen them myself!'

'I suspect that he did so out of old affection and duty to Miss Athene, who I believe may well be his daughter, but that, I am sorry to say, no longer concerns him, as he was very annoyed when he discovered that his housekeeper was pretending to be his wife, especially as he was courting another lady. As a result, he has ceased to support them.'

Dawson took a little while to come to terms with this information. He was still clutching the coffee cup, but put it down, the drink unfinished. 'I am — somewhat confused by all this. You say that Miss Brendel is Mr Brendel's natural daughter, not lawful?'

'Yes. But she has been well brought up and given every advantage.'

'I thought —' he paused. 'I was told that she was his only daughter and I assumed his only child, since no brothers were mentioned.'

'Oh no. He has two sons by his late wife.'

Mr Dawson looked undeniably dismayed. 'That explains a great deal. The quarterly hire for the piano has not been paid, and the instrument has been returned to the shop. I had imagined it was due to some delay on Mr Brendel's part, but now you say he is no longer paying her bills.'

'So it appears. And he has chosen no longer to acknowledge Miss Brendel as his daughter, which must be very painful for her. But I do have some good news for you.'

'You do?' said Dawson, hopefully.

Mina favoured him with a smile of pure delight. 'I do. You will be pleased to know that Miss Brendel — as she still continues to call herself — will be twenty-one very soon, and will be able to follow the dictates of her heart.'

Mr Dawson was now looking distinctly alarmed. 'Oh. That is — I am sure that will be a wonderful thing for her.'

'If I should chance to encounter her again, is there any message you would like me to give her?'

'I — thank you, I will give that some thought and let you know.' He rose to his feet.

'I can always pass a note to you at the music shop.'

'Indeed. I must take my leave of you now. Thank you for all your assistance and advice.' Mr Dawson departed with rather more haste than Mina thought strictly necessary. It was as if he had arrived in the hope of finding Miss Brendel, and left in fear that he might do so.

Chapter Forty-Four

When George Fernwood arrived, the parcel of papers was wrapped ready for him to collect and a nice pot of hot fresh tea was ordered. He was not, Mina saw at once, the same man he had been on his first visit. Then he had seemed worried, anxious, and uncomfortable. He was now in pain.

Mina poured the tea. 'Mr Fernwood, forgive me for mentioning it but you do not look at all well. Is there something I can obtain for you? Or I could summon a doctor. You only have to say the word.'

He clutched the parcel with an expression of sheer misery. 'Thank you. I am in bodily health, and need no medicine, but you are right, I am suffering.'

'Perhaps a small glass of brandy?'

He shook his head. 'No. No! I shall never touch that wretched drink again. It was the curse of our family. It would have to be forced down my throat. It would choke me.' He took a large handkerchief from his pocket. 'I'm sorry, I think I might have a chill after all.' He wiped his eyes, and eventually gave up all pretence and sobbed, noisily.

Mina could do nothing but wait until he was recovered.

He blew his nose. 'My apologies for this unseemly and embarrassing display. What you must think of me!'

'I do not judge you. I only wish I could help.'

'There is one thing you can advise me about. The last séance you attended of that villain Castlehouse. Tell me your impressions. Did you think he was a fraud then?'

'I suspected it, but I had no proof. My difficulty was that the result made Miss Clifton so very happy, I did not have the heart to express a contrary opinion without being sure of my ground. I could see that the performance might have been one of a conjuror, but I was quite unable to explain the content of the message.'

'Yet, you later accused Mary of deceit. And in that, as I now know to my cost, you were quite right. She has confessed it to me.'

'I did so as a result of information I received subsequent to the visit. Miss Clifton had obtained duplicate slates, given them to Mr Castlehouse and told him what to write on them. Sleight of hand did the rest. She explained her motives to me, which were the natural ones of achieving contentment. What should I have done? Written to you and destroyed your chances of happiness? I reckoned without Mr Landwick, however. I asked him to report his conclusions to me, but instead he could not resist announcing them to the world.'

'Yes, Mr Landwick,' said Fernwood, miserably. 'You see, after the séance, Mary showed me the slates, and said that neither she nor you could explain the message by any other means except that it was a communication from my grandmother. As you say, she was happy, she said that it was all the reassurance we needed. I wasn't so certain, so she persuaded me to go and see Mr Castlehouse. We went together. We took our slates with us. At the séance we received a message from my grandmother begging our forgiveness and wishing us happiness. And so — I allowed myself to be convinced. It was the easy way, I suppose.

'We went home and told Aunt Dorothy and my cousin Peter that we intended to announce our engagement, and marry in the spring. I also explained the reasons for our initial hesitation and gave them the good news that the concerns about our family tragedy could now be laid to rest. We showed them the slates as proof. Now that I look back on it, Aunt Dorothy reacted very strangely, almost as if she was not pleased at all, and I think she had to work hard to conceal her real thoughts.

'I wrote to my parents, and to my sisters, Ada and Ellen to tell them our happy news. We agreed on a wedding day. Mary began to plan her trousseau. And then,' he groaned like a man whose heart was being twisted savagely in his chest, 'Mr Landwick wrote his horrible letter to the *Sussex Times*. I had to show it to Mary, of course. She tried her best to defend Mr Castlehouse, saying that he was really a medium, but I knew something was wrong. In fact, I think I knew it before, when I saw the expression on my aunt's face, and I had been denying it to myself ever since. So I told Mary that I would go and see Mr Castlehouse and make him tell me the truth, even if we came to blows. Mary begged me not to, and at last she was forced to admit how she had practised on all of us. Until that moment I had no idea that she could even contemplate dishonesty.'

'You told me, at our very first meeting in fact, that Miss Clifton was at one time even more sceptical of mediums than you.'

'That is true, yes.'

'Yet she came to me that day as a believer. I know people can go from doubt to belief when they see something that convinces them, especially if it meets what they wish to believe, so I didn't question it at the time. But now I see that I should have done. I only had to assume that Miss Clifton had never changed her beliefs about mediums, but simply appeared to do so, and the real purpose of her actions became clear. She was not searching for the truth, whatever that might be. She was looking for a medium who was a convincing fraud whom she could bribe into providing the answer she needed in order to put an end to the doubts over your grandfather's death. But she did it from the best of intentions. She did it for the future happiness of you both.'

Fernwood shook his head. 'And look what it has brought.'

'What will you do?' asked Mina.

'Do?' He threw up his hands in despair. 'I can do nothing. There will be no wedding, not now or ever. Mary has packed a box and left. I don't know where she has gone, and even if I did, I shan't go after her.'

'That seems very extreme. What did you say to her? I know it was a disturbing thing to do, but considering her motives, could you not have forgiven her?'

Fernwood looked on the verge of another flood of tears. 'Mary did not leave because of anything I said. It was to avoid what she knew must follow once matters were being spoken of openly again. The day after she left Ada and Ellen and my parents all came to see us. We sat down as a family and talked about what had happened in Lincoln for the first time in many years. Peter and I spoke of the whippings we had been subjected to, but it was only then — only then that we learned that for the girls, my grandfather had a worse fate, something I cannot name. Then Aunt Dorothy tried to take the blame for Grandfather's death on herself, saying that she had put the arsenic in the tea, and she had done it to save the girls, but Ada put her hand so lightly on her arm and soothed her and said she knew it wasn't she. She knew that my aunt had lied at the inquest when she said she had taken the tea up to my grandfather that morning. Ada knew who had really killed Grandfather, really carried up the teacup, really added that fatal pinch of arsenic and stirred it well in. Ada had seen who came down the stairs carrying the empty cup and laughing at what she had done. Perhaps Grandfather heard that laugh also, too

343

late, after he had drunk the tea, and realised that he had been poisoned.' New tears streaked George Fernwood's face. 'She was only eight years old.'

It took a moment for Mina to understand whom he meant. 'Mary?'

He gulped and nodded.

'Perhaps she didn't know what she did,' said Mina. 'She would have been too young to understand. Perhaps, as in the message she devised, there was no intention to murder.'

'Oh, she knew,' said Fernwood bitterly, 'yes, she knew. Even so young she knew the difference between alive and dead. Ada told me that Mary used to sprinkle arsenic on the bread and butter and put it down for the mice. That old house, it was a nest of vermin. We used to find the little bodies twitching in agony. Ada said that Mary used to like watching them die, and as she watched, she laughed. "They won't bother us again" she used to say. That's almost what she said when she came downstairs bringing Grandfather's teacup. "He won't bother us again".' Fernwood wiped his face. 'My grandfather knew it was Mary. He didn't see her put the poison in the cup but he heard her laugh after he had drunk from it. He knew. And he told Ada and Ellen what he knew, but they said nothing to anyone.'

There was a long silence of contemplation. 'Do you mean to accuse her?' asked Mina.

'No. Even if we could find her, it would be pointless. I cannot imagine Ada or Ellen or my aunt giving evidence against her. No court could convict her. No, I must go home and stand in my shop and run my business, and make the best of things.'

'Might I ask you one more question?'

'Yes?'

'When you heard of Dr Sperley's death, was that just before or after you and Miss Clifton decided you wished to marry?'

He pondered this for a while. 'I think — yes I am sure. It was just before. I recall Mary saying how sad it was that we would not be able to give him the happy news.' He paled. 'Of course. Sperley must have suspected something. I wonder if he ever spoke to her, or gave away perhaps by a look or a gesture that he knew the truth. So it wasn't until after his death that she felt truly safe.'

He was about to leave when the door opened and Miss Brendel peered in. The cold wind had stung her cheeks so they glowed red, and her eyelashes were damp with mist.

George Fernwood started in amazement. He saw before him a new Miss Brendel, no longer a fading flower on a stem that looked ready to break, but a young beauty in full bloom, with hair that shone and skin like that of a chubby child advertising good health.

'I thought I heard a familiar voice,' she said, brightly. 'Mr Wood, is it?'

'Ah, yes.' He scrambled to his feet and stared at her. 'Miss Brendel. If you don't mind my saying so, you are looking remarkably well.'

She smiled. 'I thank you. It seems that my malady was all down to eating some bad fish, and I am now quite cured!'

'I am glad to hear it. Wholesome food is so important to health. If you are ever in Haywards Heath, you must call in at my business, Fernwood Grocery, where purity and cleanliness are held in the highest regard.' He handed her his card.

She studied it with approval. 'Do you sell cheese?'

Chapter Forty-Five

Dear Mina,

I am not sure if I will be able to come and see you over the festive season, as there is just too much to do in London, most of it trying to keep Mother and Enid from the madhouse.

I see Richard has covered himself in glory once again. Very well, I promise not to mention Mr Dorry's downfall to Mother, and see what fiction Richard can dream up to conceal the truth from her. He did send me a portrait of the renowned antiquarian Mr Honeyacre together with his betrothed, Miss Kitty Betts. It is a good picture, but I am not sure whether this should go in the society column or be classed as humour.

He has also sent me a great many sketches of the sea, which are not at all interesting. Please tell him to stop.

Affect'ly,
Edward

The missing Mr Elmer Dorry got as far as Marseilles before he found that a man of his impressive waistcoatage could not go unnoticed forever, especially if his portrait was in all the leading newspapers and he was accompanied by a life-sized marble statue of a nude Adonis. He was arrested on charges of fraud and forgery that had arisen in six different countries. The only thing remaining to be decided was where he was to stand trial.

Dear Mina,

Did you know that one of Richard's drawings has been published in the Telegraph? *My darling boy has been so very clever! I actually had a letter from him explaining everything, and as he writes so rarely I will treasure it* especially. *All this time he has been working in secret for the authorities helping them catch the most dreadful criminal. I hope he did not take any risks, and am so greatly relieved to hear that the police now have their man. What a cruel place the world is, and how fortunate to have clever people like my son to put things right! Who would have thought he could turn detective? But it is a dangerous profession and he should not go on with it.*

Richard's success has brought me a little ease. The twins are over the worst with their teeth, and the house is more peaceful now, which is a mercy, as I don't think my poor head could have stood any more.

Enid is a trial, but at least her bilious attacks have ceased, and she complains less than she did, which means only about every ten minutes instead of every five. I can't imagine who she takes after, she can be so difficult at times.

Edward is no further forward in discovering the fate of Mr Inskip, and we have all but given him up as lost. He has complained so bitterly about Richard borrowing his warm coat and hat that I have bought him new ones.

Your sorely tried,
Mama

As the season of merriment and goodwill approached, and Great Britain breathed a sigh of relief at the recovery of the Prince of Wales from typhoid, it appeared that romance was all around.

Young Mr Conroy finally shed his mourning and invited Miss Landwick to accompany him to a concert at the Dome.

George Fernwood continued to visit Brighton, where he made every possible excuse to call upon Miss Brendel. Whether it was the result of the pleadings of her mother or Mr Quinley was unknown, but Mr Brendel relented from his determination not to support his daughter further, and she did receive her annuity on her twenty first birthday. Soon afterwards she left Brighton to take up a post on the cheese counter at Fernwood's Grocery store, sharing a lodging with Mrs Clifton. A month later Mr Fernwood and Miss Brendel announced their engagement. The event met with the approval of the bride-to-be's mother, who had in the meantime exacted her full revenge on Mr Quinley by marrying him.

Mr and Mrs Myles were not seen in Brighton again, although a Mr and Mrs Morton who bore a strong resemblance to that couple, presented a season of dramatic and tender dialogues from the classical repertoire at the best Brighton hotels, with afternoon tea and biscuits.

Mr Castlehouse continued to practice slate-writing, although he was not as popular as he had once been, as Brightonians in search of something more appropriate to the season turned to other entertainments. Declining business obliged him to leave Brighton. Almost immediately, Angelo the magician made a re-appearance in London, thrilling audiences in the best theatres, where he created brilliant illusions. The best part of his performance, as everyone agreed, was causing his new lady wife to disappear from a locked cabinet and reappear in a sack, to the wonderment of all. Mrs Angelo, dressed in a spangled costume that revealed shapely limbs, bore it very well, though there was a hint in her expression that this was far beneath her dignity and not at all the life she had imagined for herself. One of Mr Angelo's most mystifying tricks involved making writing appear on sealed slates. These were first given an expert cleaning by his wife, who showed by the energy in her shoulder and the dexterity of her action that she was no stranger to scouring surfaces.

Shortly before Christmas, Mr Honeyacre and Kitty Betts were married in a grand and unusually spectacular occasion, and the happy groom bundled his blushing bride into a carriage and swept her away to his manor house, which had finally been restored to its old fashioned glory.

Mina had half expected to spend Christmas alone, as Richard was wondering whether to return to London and Edward's hospitality, but so it was not to prove so. On the day after the Honeyacre wedding their mother arrived in Brighton, leaving Enid and the twins in the care of a stern and capable nurse. She was overjoyed to see Richard and listened with maternal pride to his tales of how he had caught a master criminal. Thereafter she declared herself too exhausted to plan the family celebrations and left it to Mina to make all the arrangements.

Dear Mina,

Much as I would like to come to Brighton for Christmas, I fear it will not be possible this year. I am to dine with the Hoopers who have been heroically patient about the time I have spent with Enid and Mother. Mr Greville has also been very kind allowing me to deal with our family upheavals but now I must buckle down and catch up with my work.

Please tell Richard he may keep my best caped coat and tweed travelling cap. If he is to go about pretending to be a detective he should at least be dressed warmly for it.

I was just about to close this letter to you when I unexpectedly received two communications concerning Mr Inskip. They are not from him but from his client in Carpathia, the first dated October and the second only two weeks ago. The weather has been too poor to allow any post to either reach or leave that dreadful region until now. It appears that Mr Inskip was preparing to depart for home when he was suddenly taken very ill. He has spent the last few weeks in a state of delirium, but has been well cared for in the nobleman's castle, where some holy sisters skilled in medicine have tended him, and they are hopeful of his eventual recovery.

Enid has begged me to reply at once reassuring Mr Inskip that he is not to even think of stirring until he is entirely well. There is no danger of that since I am told that he is not yet strong enough to travel home, and may well remain where he is for some months. I have not mentioned this to Enid, but I am told that when she next sees him, he may not be quite the man he was.

Affect'ly,
Edward

A NOTE TO THE READER

Dear Reader,

Thank you for taking the time to read this third adventure of the indomitable Mina Scarletti. I hope you had as much fun reading it as I did writing it and will want to see what she and her family and friends do next! I love exploring the stranger and more colourful areas of Victorian life and beliefs, and for this book I researched the techniques and careers of the slate-writing mediums, and read studies of people who reported seeing spectres of the living as well as the dead. For more details of the actual persons and places mentioned in the book, see my Historical Note below.

Reviews are so important to authors, and if you enjoyed the novel I would be grateful if you could spare a few minutes to post a review on **Amazon** and **Goodreads**. I love hearing from readers, and you can stay up to date with all my news via **my website: http://lindastratmann.com/**

HISTORICAL NOTES

The books for which Mina searched unsuccessfully in the library and bookshop were:

Letters on Natural Magic, addressed to Sir Walter Scott, by Sir David Brewster, (London, John Murray, 1832).

Sketches of the philosophy of apparitions; or, an attempt to trace such illusions to their physical causes, by Samuel Hibbert, (Edinburgh, Oliver & Boyd, 1825) Both these books may be viewed for free on the splendid website www.archive.org.

Sir David Brewster (1781-1868) was a noted scientist and author, especially renowned for his contributions to optics.

Samuel Hibbert, MD, FRSE (1782-1848) was a geologist and antiquarian.

Christoph Friedrich Nicolai (1733-1811) was a German author, editor and bookseller, who wrote about his experience of spectral illusions in 1799.

The originator of slate-writing séances was American medium Henry Slade, (1836-1905) who is thought to have devised them around 1860. He was later copied by other mediums. He visited Britain in 1876, was exposed as a fraud, and prosecuted for obtaining money under false pretences. Found guilty, the verdict was later reversed on appeal and he left the country. Slate-writing soon fell out of fashion. All its proponents have been shown to be frauds.

Pennyroyal (*mentha pulegium*) was once used as a culinary and medicinal herb, but is now known to be toxic. In the nineteenth century it was sometimes used to try and procure an abortion and occasionally proved fatal.

Widow Welch's Pills, first manufactured in 1787, were a popular remedy for all female disorders including what the advertisements described as 'obstructions in the Female System.'

Potts and Co was a prominent dealer in musical instruments at 167 North Street, Brighton.

Brighton sauce was a popular relish for meat.

On Tuesday 7 November 1871 a 39-year-old Scottish wine merchant Athole Peter Hay was found dying in his apartments in Oriental Place Brighton, having cut his throat. A surgeon was called but by the time he arrived the man had died. Hay had been badly injured in a railway accident in April 1866 in which he had suffered a concussion. Since then he had been troubled with weakness, depression and partial paralysis, and the delusion that he was guilty of a crime for which he felt great remorse. (Reported in the *Hastings and St Leonards Observer* 11 and 18 November 1871)

The story of Mrs Brendel is partly inspired by a Mrs Henrietta Bradshaw, a fraudster who took a house in Oriental Place Brighton and ran up considerable debts. See the *Brighton Gazette* 3 November 1870.

In November 1871 the panorama of 'Paris in its grandeur and

in flames', including many scenes connected with the late war was exhibiting at the concert hall West Street, Brighton, and was so popular it prolonged its stay to Saturday 19.

The annual bazaar for the children's hospital was held at the Dome in November 1871, and attracted over 8,500 people.

The County Hospital ball, recognised as the official start of the Brighton fashionable season, was held on 22 November 1871. Dancing commenced shortly after 10pm to the band of the nineteenth hussars, and carriages did not depart until the early hours of the morning.

Lowes Cato Dickinson was a portrait painter who with his brothers established the business of Dickinson Brothers in Brighton and London. In 1871 Dickinson's gallery at 107 King's Road Brighton was exhibiting a new portrait of the queen in her robes and jewels of state, while in the adjoining gallery there were watercolour portraits of ladies of the British aristocracy.

John (later Sir John) Cordy Burrows was elected Mayor of Brighton for the third time in November 1871.

The Times of 21 October 1871 reported on a recent German expedition to the North Pole. Dispatches confirmed the discovery of an ice-free North Pole sea, swarming with whales.

The 1871 Christmas pantomime at Brighton Theatre Royal was *Goody Two-Shoes and her Queen Anne's Farthing*. Leading characters were King Counterfeit and Fairy Spiteful. Mr and Mrs Myles were not called upon to perform.

In 1824 J.M.W. Turner painted the chain pier from the sea, with the Pavilion in the distance. He rotated the Pavilion by about 90 degrees in order to show the whole of the east front. http://brightonmuseums.org.uk/discover/2016/04/15/stormy-weather-turners-sublime-vision-of-brighton-in-1824/

In September 1870 *HMS Captain* capsized with the loss of nearly 500 lives.

Sapere Books is an exciting new publisher of brilliant fiction and popular history.

To find out more about our latest releases and our monthly bargain books visit our website:
saperebooks.com

Made in the USA
San Bernardino, CA
04 January 2019